...ave fallen for the Cornish Girls

T0120500

The Cornish Girls series:

Betty Walker lives in Cornwall with her large family, where she enjoys gardening and coastal walks. She loves discovering curious historical facts, and devotes much time to investigating her family tree. She also writes bestselling contemporary thrillers as Jane Holland.

Victory for the Cornish Girls is the sixth novel in Betty Walker's heart-warming series.

BETTY WALKER

Victory for the Cornish Girls

Published by AVON
A division of HarperCollins*Publishers*
1 London Bridge Street
London SE1 9GF

www.harpercollins.co.uk

HarperCollins*Publishers*
Macken House, 39/40 Mayor Street Upper
Dublin 1
D01 C9W8

A Paperback Original 2023
1
First published in Great Britain by HarperCollinsPublishers 2024

ISBN: 978-0-00-861584-0

Typeset in Minion pro by Palimpsest Book Production Limited,
Falkirk, Stirlingshire

Printed and bound in UK by CPI Group (UK) Ltd, Croydon CR0 4YY

For my readers, with heartfelt thanks – I couldn't do any of this without you!
Betty x

CHAPTER ONE

London, April 1944

It was dusk and the dome of St Paul's Cathedral gleamed ahead of her in the dying rays of the sun, its famous outline protected against incendiary bombs by patrolling fire wardens. Hands thrust into her coat pockets, face hidden beneath the brim of her hat, Alice limped uphill towards the old cathedral. Buildings to either side of the street had been reduced to rubble during the worst of the Blitz, only a few left standing, the lucky survivors of the German bombing campaign. There wasn't much traffic as the blackout hour approached, and her heels clacked on the pavement in the silence, heart-poundingly loud. To her right the vast black-silver ribbon of the River Thames rolled silently under glowering skies. A barge was mooring up somewhere below her; she could hear the boatmen's cries as they began to unload their freight.

Somewhere on a street corner ahead, in the shadow of the cathedral dome, a young man should be waiting, as arranged.

Rain was imminent, dark clouds obscuring the sunset. Alice glanced up at the sky impatiently, having forgotten her brolly again. She suspected it was still leaning in the umbrella stand at headquarters where she'd left it to dry after the torrential downpour that morning. But her hat, sloping forward at the rakish angle that was all the style in the movies these days, would keep her hair dry at least.

As she walked, she was constantly looking about, scanning the gloomy street for the young man she was supposed to be meeting, but also for anyone who might be watching *her*. It was worrying to imagine herself being the target of enemy observation. But it was all part of the job. And her training was almost complete. Tonight's mission could make the difference between another few months of 'dry runs' and poring over manuals at HQ, and being sent into the field.

If she wanted to pass the course, Jim had told her it needed to go well tonight. No foul-ups.

Last time, she and Barbara had watched completely the wrong targets and been sent back to their boarding house in disgrace after five hours' wasted effort. Barbara had since left to join another war department and Alice was the only female left on the course, so had been paired with Jim instead.

It had begun to spit with rain by the time she reached the agreed rendezvous point. Shivering, she shrank back against the wall and dragged the lapels of her raincoat closer. Where on earth was Jim?

At last, she caught sight of a shambolic figure lurking in the shadows opposite, a few doors up.

Trying to appear nonchalant, she crossed the road and stopped in the shelter of a doorway, pretending to tie her shoelace.

'Hello,' she whispered.

At twenty-two, Jim was older than Alice by three years, and had been training for six months already. But he'd always treated her like an equal, ever since her first day at London headquarters. Brought up in the East End, not far from her own birthplace of Dagenham, Jim shared not only her accent but her quirky sense of humour. They had bonded early on. 'Bunch of stuck-up toffs,' Jim had murmured in her ear during a lengthy training session in her first week where everyone else had seemed intimidatingly posh. 'Fancy a dance later? I know a few clubs that ain't been bombed to smithereens.'

Alice, who found most boys a mystery, had been charmed by his quick wit and direct approach, and readily agreed to go dancing with him.

Jim had never been anything less than a gentleman. But one thing had soon led to another, and after a few dances and fumbled late-night kisses, she'd realised with a shock that she had fallen in love with him.

Her, Alice Fisher, in love with a boy!

It was strictly *verboten* for trainees on the espionage course to date, even though it happened all the time. So they'd kept things quiet, neither wanting to risk trouble and possible expulsion from the course. But the truth was, things between them had escalated, and last week she and Jim had become secretly engaged.

'We'll marry after the war,' he'd promised her at the time, 'when all this malarkey is over. And why shouldn't we? I love you and you love me.' Alice, swept up in the giddy excitement of her first love affair, had agreed. Though not without misgivings.

She was still only nineteen years old, after all, and everyone she loved was back in Cornwall and had never so much as met Jim Price. Plus, she didn't like keeping secrets from her beloved sister Lily and her aunt Violet, and she could have sorely used her gran's advice right now.

Was she too young to be considering marriage? A whirlwind romance was all very well, but what about when her feet finally hit the ground again?

Everyone was saying the war could be over soon, and she wasn't sure if she was ready to abandon her independent lifestyle and settle down as a housewife before she was even twenty. Part of her also wondered what her dad would say. Though since Ernest Fisher was officially dead – while in truth behind enemy lines, working undercover for British intelligence as a native German speaker – there seemed little point pondering that question.

Besides, she was in love . . . How could anyone even *try* to think straight while feeling like this?

What she felt for Jim was the most dizzying thing she'd ever experienced, her heart pumping furiously whenever he was around, her head in a permanent flat spin. Some days, it was a wonder she could manage to button her coat straight, let alone make serious, grown-up decisions about her future, for goodness' sake.

'You're late,' Jim muttered, not looking at her.

Still pretending to fiddle with her shoelaces, Alice glanced up at him, flustered by his tone. They had grown so close, sometimes she forgot that Jim was her superior, having been requisitioned from serving in the army to train for special missions behind enemy lines. He was right too, which didn't help. She was late, but only because she couldn't walk as fast as usual.

'Sorry,' she whispered, feeling awkward.

Jim expelled a long breath, saying, 'Oh, never mind. You're 'ere now, ain't yer?' He shot her one of his dazzling smiles, and she felt her crushed spirits lift, his reprimand quickly forgotten. 'Besides, them geezers 'ave been up in that room for bleedin' hours tonight. I've been so bored, it's a wonder I'm still awake.' He paused. ''Ow's the ankle, love?'

'Not too bad, thanks.' Alice had sprained her ankle a week back, tumbling down a steep flight of steps while learning how to chase a suspect, and had been put on light duties, so had not left headquarters all that time. Jim, meanwhile, had been going out on missions and training exercises as usual. 'Miss me, did yer?'

Straightening, she gave him a shy smile. The thought

filled her with pleasure. She had never had a boy pine for her and it felt rather nice.

But Jim didn't laugh, stiffening instead. 'Hang on, the light's gone out up there. Something's happening. I think they're on the move at last.' There was excitement in his voice. ''Ere, we two shouldn't be seen together. If you carry on up the hill—'

He stopped abruptly and cursed under his breath.

Glancing over her shoulder, Alice saw the door to the narrow building had already opened, a thin electric light spilling out onto the pavement. The light was hurriedly snapped off, to comply with blackout regulations, but not before she'd seen several burly, coated and hatted figures silhouetted in the doorway.

As she tried to melt into the shadows as they'd been trained to do on these occasions, Jim turned to her. 'No time for that,' he hissed. 'Quick . . . Kiss me!'

His hands grabbed her shoulders and suddenly Alice was being kissed ruthlessly.

It was hardly the first passionate kiss they'd shared. They might only have been courting for six weeks now but Jim wasn't backward at coming forward, as her gran might have said. Yet she felt shaken all the same, perhaps because of how public this place was. Before, their kisses had always taken place more privately, usually after a late-night visit to some London club, embracing discreetly in the shadows on their way home or on her doorstep as they said goodnight . . .

Blimey, she thought, her head spinning as his lips

worked against hers. Jim certainly knew his spy craft. Now when those men coming out of the building spotted them, they'd likely assume they were just a courting couple in a doorway. Not spies trained to watch them.

At least she hoped so. Otherwise, they were in serious trouble.

Gently, Jim released her.

'It's all right, they've gone.' Studying her face, he brushed a finger under her chin, saying deeply, 'You okay?'

'Um, of course,' she stammered, hot-cheeked.

He smiled as though he understood, and bent to kiss her again. This time it was only a fleeting contact though. 'We need to get going,' he said softly, 'or we'll lose them.'

'Right.' But as they began walking uphill in the direction the men had taken, Alice stumbled more than once, thrown off-balance by what had just happened.

Jim glanced back, frowning in quick concern. 'What's up? Your ankle hurting again?'

'No, I'm fine,' she insisted more firmly, hurrying to catch up with him. 'Where are they going, do you think?' she asked, not wanting him to dwell on her reaction.

But her flustered response to his kiss was a reminder of why team-mates were not supposed to get too close. Feeling like this made it hard to stay focused on the mission. It wasn't the first time she'd wondered if they were making a big mistake, secretly being a couple while working together. But unless she left the unit, which she didn't want to do, there wasn't much they could do about it.

'That's the big question. If this is an enemy spy ring, as HQ suspects, maybe they're paying a visit to the head honcho tonight.' As he turned to take her hand, a grin illuminated Jim's lean face under the brim of his working man's cloth cap. 'Blimey, can you imagine old Carstairs' face if we was to give 'em a leader for this treasonous lot? The major wouldn't be able to believe his eyes.' He gave her a wink. 'C'mon, better hurry before they give us the slip.'

After a tip-off some weeks ago, they'd started watching a man who worked at the Ministry of Defence in some minor role. The target's frequent visits to disused offices near St Paul's had set a suspicious pattern, and when a second and then third person of interest had also been spotted going in and out of the same building, a team had been set up to keep an eye on the location. Their supervisor, Major Carstairs, was convinced this cell of enemy sympathisers could lead them to higher-up figures, perhaps even traitors working in positions where they could influence military strategies. Alice knew that if they could expose any big names by following this gang, her career in British Intelligence would be assured. The mere thought of her dad hearing about such a success filled her with pride and enthusiasm.

Until tonight, the men had always come and gone singly. Never in a group like this. It was exciting to think they might be reaching the end of the chase. Though it was dangerous too, she knew, and wished the rest of the team could be here to back them up. Especially with her ankle still giving her the odd twinge.

'Jim, do you really believe these three blokes could lead us to someone high up in a spy ring?' Alice whispered. 'I mean, this could be a wild goose chase.'

'True.' He squeezed her hand reassuringly. 'But it's worth finding out, ain't it? We just 'ave to be careful not to get spotted.'

She and Jim followed the men at a discreet distance. The three kept muttering amongst themselves but it was impossible to hear what was being said. Finally, about half a mile from St Paul's, they turned down a narrow, cobbled passageway and disappeared from view.

'Damn.' Pushing back the brim of his cloth cap, Jim peered into the yawning mouth of the passageway. 'I don't like the look of this place.'

'What should we do, then?' she whispered.

'There's no *we* about it.' Turning to her, he pulled her close and met her gaze earnestly. '*You* are going back to headquarters. Tell Major Carstairs I'll need two or three more men to back me up.' Night had fallen and his face was in shadow, but she could hear the strain in his voice. 'Meanwhile, I'll go in after this lot and keep tabs on 'em until reinforcements arrive.'

She couldn't believe her ears. Was he trying to get rid of her?

'Is that so?' Alice glared at him, hands on her hips, a gesture learned from many times watching her aunt Violet remonstrate with her husband Joe. 'Not a bloomin' chance, Jim Price. If you're going down that alley after them, I'm coming with you.'

'Sorry, love. Too dangerous.'

'Oh, too dangerous for me, is it?' Her chest heaved with indignation. 'Exactly 'ow safe is it for *you*, then?'

He blinked, frowning. 'I didn't say it were bleedin' safe, did I? Thing is, love . . .' Jim hesitated, running one finger under his shirt collar as though it was too tight.

She opened her eyes wide, waiting. 'Go on, I'm listening. Why can't I go with you?'

'Well, for starters, you're a girl, and it ain't right to put you in danger . . .' Catching her furious expression, he took a deep gulp of breath and blurted out, 'I couldn't bear to lose you – that's the truth.'

Her heart softened at the anguish in his eyes. 'Oh, Jim.'

'Besides, you know the rule about female operatives,' he added, rather spoiling the effect. 'I can't risk your neck, not with men likely to turn violent.' She began to argue but Jim shook his head. His bright gaze pleaded with hers. 'There ain't no time to argue, love. I'll lose the blighters if I don't head off now.'

'You're right,' she muttered stubbornly, 'we don't have time to argue.' And Alice darted down the unlit passageway ahead of him.

With a horrified gasp, Jim made a grab for her but missed in the darkness. 'Alice, no!'

'If *you* can risk your neck, so can I,' she hissed over her shoulder. 'I'm doing this for king and country, not the sake of my bloomin' health.'

Further in, the enclosed passage between buildings narrowed to single file and bent away to the left. The three men were waiting for them around the blind corner. Too late, she realised her mistake and stopped dead with a muttered curse. Jim, following fast, bumped into her from behind.

'Alice, get behind me,' he said desperately but she stood rooted to the spot, not wanting him to risk his life for her.

The targets must have spotted them on their tail and decided to lay a trap, precisely at the point where the alley was too narrow for them to walk abreast. Only they'd probably been expecting to see Jim in front.

'That's far enough, friend,' a large, broad-chested figure said from the darkness, his deep voice echoing against brickwork. 'If you know what's good for you and the girl, you'll turn around and go back the way you came.'

'Why's that, then?' Jim snarled over Alice's shoulder.

'Keep going, and you'll find out,' one of the other men threw back at him, pushing forward, hand outstretched.

'Look out,' Jim exclaimed, 'he's got a gun.' Dragging Alice back against the damp brick wall, he lunged forward in her place. As he did so, there was a loud crack, and Alice flinched as the deafening sound reverberated in the cramped, enclosed space.

Jim grunted and fell back.

The man turned his revolver on her, its barrel glinting. Alice froze.

'Not the girl, you fool!' the first man told him gruffly, thumping his companion's arm as he fired.

But the gun still spoke in the darkness.

11

Alice felt a sharp burn just below her shoulder, and sagged against the wall, knees giving way as she collapsed onto the cobbles.

Then the men were running away, their booted feet thudding . . .

Minutes passed while she fought back pain and dizziness, trying hard not to pass out. Her own rasping breath was loud in her ears. Somewhere in the distance, she caught a voice calling down the passageway and then hurrying footsteps. Someone must have heard the shots from the street, she guessed, and come to see what had happened.

'Oh Lord,' a male voice said. Posh, well-modulated. She was vaguely aware of someone standing over her. 'Hang on, there's a police box on the corner. I'll get help.'

Then he too was gone.

She was lying alone on the damp ground. With a grimace, she pulled herself together. They had been trained for this, hadn't they?

Ascertain the condition of any wounded first. Only then go for help.

Jim . . .

Everything seemed so dark, the light at the mouth of the passageway a dim mist. Slowly, she began to crawl across dirty cobbles towards Jim, who was lying a few feet away. She winced at the searing throb in her right shoulder, unable to put much weight on that arm. Broken glass and dirt bit into her bare palms but she ignored the agonising pain. All that could wait.

Ascertain the condition of any wounded first.

Jim was sprawled on his back. His chest was heaving, but there was blood everywhere, a sticky dark-red mess spreading on his chest, a trickle from his mouth.

'Jim,' she croaked, cupping his cheek.

He blinked up at her, but there was only a gurgle in his throat as he mouthed her name.

Somewhere far off, she heard a shrill whistle. A single note, repeated urgently. A policeman calling for assistance, her brain told her.

'Hang on, Jim, help's comin' . . .' She held his hand and felt his fingers tighten about hers, squeezing. His eyes sought hers through the gloom, straining to convey a message. 'Try to breathe, love. That's it.'

She forced herself to smile, though she felt more like screaming. *I ain't a nurse or a doctor. I can't do nothing for him. If only I knew what to do*, she kept thinking desperately. But she didn't know. She'd never bothered to learn all those clever nursing skills her sister Lily had in spadefuls.

Only then go for help.

She couldn't leave him. There was no time. Besides, she was wounded too, wasn't she? The pain in her shoulder was growing steadily worse. How far down the street would she get before fainting?

All she could do for Jim was reassure him, keep him company, stare into his eyes, grip his hand as tightly as though they were tumbling off a cliff together . . .

'A . . . Alice,' he mouthed again, a horrid wet sound.

'I love you,' she whispered.

* * *

Sometime later, she heard heavy footsteps come running, and then a portly man in uniform bent over her. It was a policeman. 'Miss? Are you hurt?'

He had a torch, its thin beam of light picking out Jim's face first, and then her own averted profile. He stooped to examine her shoulder. Gently, but even so, she cried out in pain.

'Don't you worry, Miss. There's an ambulance on its way.' He turned to study Jim's fallen body again. There was pity in his face. 'Then you can tell us what happened.'

'It's too late for an ambulance,' she said dully, still holding Jim's hand, still looking into eyes that could no longer see her. 'He's gone.'

'Yes, I see that.' Lowering the torch beam to bloodstained cobbles, the policeman crouched beside her. 'The ambulance is for you, Miss. We'll come back for . . . for him later.'

The ambulance is for you.

The sleeve of her jacket was sticky with blood, she realised belatedly, glancing down at it in surprise. That much blood wouldn't wash out. She'd have to throw the whole jacket out. But what did it matter? Nothing was important anymore.

'I don't need no ambulance. I'll be fine, d'you hear?' When he began to argue, Alice shook her head, gripping Jim's hand more tightly. She would never let go. *Never.* 'You leave me alone, Copper,' she told him fiercely. 'I'm stayin' right here.'

But the policeman was having none of it. And he was

14

stronger than her. 'Come on, Miss,' he said, lifting her away from Jim's motionless body. 'You're in shock and you need help.'

In shock, Alice repeated in her head, blinking down at Jim. Of course she was in shock. His cloth cap had fallen off, his bare head tousled. He looked so young in the glinting torchlight . . . Even younger than her. Barely a man, in fact.

It was horrible. But everything would be sorted once she woke up from this bad dream. She had clearly dreamt the whole bloomin' thing. None of this could really be happening.

Except it was.

And it was all her fault.

'Jim,' she cried, sobbing brokenly as the policeman carried her away towards that distant halo of misty light. 'Jim . . .'

CHAPTER TWO

Bude, North Cornwall, May 1944

'Morning, Miss,' the boy loading the butcher's barrow said with a wink, tapping his cap. 'Lovely weather for it.'

Imogen, not lowering herself to respond to such a cheeky fellow, shot the boy a fleeting smile and continued on past the butcher's shop, head held high.

He was right, though. It was a beautiful morning. The skies above the seaside resort of Bude in North Cornwall were a deep, cheerful blue, though the striped shop awnings were snapping noisily in the breeze and Imogen even had to raise one hand to the brim of her hat on the corner to prevent it from flying off.

On such a glorious day, in such a gorgeous spot, miles from anywhere important, if one didn't know better, one might be forgiven for thinking all was right with the world.

But one would be wrong.

The truth was, the war with Germany had been dragging on for ever. Britain and her allies had broken no significant ground against the enemy in recent weeks, and although everyone was holding their breath in anticipation of some imminent change for the better, there was no reason to hope that the war was finally going to shift their way. Indeed, everything still hung in the balance. Nobody could afford to be complacent. Not even with May sunshine sparkling on the Atlantic Ocean and the prospect of a perfect summer beckoning holidaymakers – if there were any left in Britain – for a few days on the Cornish coast.

Mr Parsons, the librarian, nodded respectfully on his way past, saying, 'Good morning, Miss Crombie. How are you? And your sister, Mrs Miller? I hope she's well.'

Imogen stopped, smiling automatically. 'We're all very well, thank you. In fact, I've just been posting a letter for Florence to her husband. I hope it will find him. He's with the US Rangers and their location seems to be top-secret.'

'Isn't everything these days?'

'You're right, of course. So dreary.' She paused, looking past him at a sturdily built woman heading into a teashop further down the hill. 'And how are you? And your son?' She hesitated. 'Simon, isn't it?'

'We heard from him last week,' Mr Parsons assured her. 'He's nearly finished his basic training and was boasting of how well he's getting on with all the other young chaps.' He tried for a smile but failed miserably. 'It's clear he's missing his mum though, poor lad.'

'I'm sure he'll settle in soon,' she said soothingly.

After being reassured that Mr Parsons was also well, as was his wife, Imogen said a quick goodbye and crossed the road. Nothing had changed. The sun still shone down on a windy Bude. Yet suddenly the morning seemed less bright and cheerful.

Simon.

That name had thrown her back into a more turbulent past. Though it wasn't the librarian's son she was thinking of, but quite a different Simon.

She'd still been a girl, living with her parents in Exeter, when she'd tumbled head-over-heels in love with a muscular, fair-haired god called Simon. He and his quieter-spoken twin had been regulars at the church club her devout parents had dragged her to most Sunday mornings.

As they'd grown up together, she'd hung on Simon's every word, fascinated by his good looks and lean physique, and the way he'd played practical jokes on their friends and flouted rules with apparent impunity, rarely punished for misdemeanours that would have earned her and her older sister Florence the strap. An impressive athlete who ran for the county, popular with teachers and other children alike, she guessed Simon's pranks had been seen as boyish high jinks, so had gone unpunished.

Simon had never given her more than a few amused glances though, not interested in a girl three years his junior.

As the years had passed, Imogen had begun to wonder

if she'd been more envious of his male confidence and freedoms than 'in love' with the lad. Yet there was still a little ache in her heart whenever she thought of Simon, which was more often than she cared to admit, even to herself.

The morning train into Bude had arrived on time. She'd heard the familiar whistle as she left her sister's boarding house on Downs View Road, and muttered, 'Drat!' under her breath, still buttoning her jacket against the sharp sea breeze. But it wouldn't have been a good idea to draw attention to herself by rushing, so she had walked into town in her usual leisurely way, stopping at the post office to post Florence's letter to Miles. She had promised to do so before the afternoon postal collection and she did not wish to disappoint her sister, knowing that Staff Sergeant Miles Miller would reply the same day he received the letter, as always.

The love between them was truly humbling, especially given the awful possibility that they might never see each other again.

'Any day now' was what everyone was saying about Britain's liberation of France, and the US Rangers who had been stationed in Bude all winter, though had now moved on to a secret location further east, would almost certainly be among the first to cross the Channel. But given Germany's defensive positions along the French coast, only too aware of the combined forces gathering opposite, the Allies' planned invasion was considered by some to be a suicide mission . . .

Imogen didn't know how her newly-wed sister could bear to think about the future, and guessed that Florence probably coped by never doing so. She herself had also given up thinking of the future. It seemed better than endlessly worrying about things she couldn't affect or control.

Though she did worry, deep down. There was no point denying it. And she wished that she could be more candid with her family. Her father knew what she did, as she'd felt forced to admit it early on after being caught in an embarrassing situation. But her mother thought she had emotional issues, while Florence had once believed her utterly amoral. Nowadays, since Imogen had come to live with her in Bude, her sister was more friendly, especially after Imogen had explained about her war work.

Her heart beating fast, Imogen paused to check her reflection in a shop window. Her hat was slightly askew, so she adjusted it, smoothing out the soft brown rolls of her hair at the same time, glad to see that her scarlet lipstick was still flawless. She had chosen a demure navy-blue skirt and jacket for this meeting, coupled with a businesslike white blouse, and was wearing a charity lapel pin sold to support veterans. She looked efficient and professional, no sign of nerves in the face staring steadily back at her.

'You'll do, my girl,' she told her reflection before moving on, back ramrod-straight, handbag in the crook of her elbow.

Reaching the new teashop, she peered cautiously

through the window before heading inside. There was only one woman seated alone, and she was sporting the same lapel pin that had been sent to Imogen through the post for easier identification.

With a polite smile that hid the uneasiness churning inside, Imogen strolled towards the corner table and stuck out her hand. 'Hello, you must be Mrs Elliott,' she said to the woman who had risen at her entrance. 'Lovely to meet you at last.' They shook hands, each studying the other with interest. 'I'm sorry if I've kept you waiting. I had to post a letter on my way here.' Seating herself opposite, she removed her hat and set it beside her handbag at her feet. 'How was your train journey? Not too uncomfortable, I hope.'

She had hoped to sound composed, but could hear the nerves in her high, breathy voice. Though that was hardly surprising. Mrs Elliott was her new regional supervisor. Her letters so far had suggested a strict and inflexible mind, and not one that suffered fools gladly. It was only natural that Imogen should feel some trepidation at a face-to-face meeting and she'd been worrying why it was necessary.

Did Mrs Elliott have some complaint to make? Or did she intend to push Imogen into more challenging work that she didn't feel able to handle yet?

'It was surprisingly pleasant,' the other woman was saying, raising a hand to summon the waitress. 'I never used to take the train before the war. But what with petrol rationing . . . Car journeys are simply impossible now, aren't they? Over long distances, at least.'

Mrs Elliott had a well-modulated voice, better suited to a BBC radio presenter than to the sort of customers who commonly frequented teashops in Bude. She was dressed in a deeply unflattering high-necked dress that made her ample chest look like a shelf, her hair steel-grey and cut short, no doubt for convenience.

'But it was important to come,' she continued, lacing her fingertips together on the tabletop. 'In fact, I've been visiting many of the Cornish towns on my list. Bude is one of the last.' She hesitated. 'I hope you don't think I've been neglecting you?'

Thrown by this unexpected question, Imogen blinked. 'Of course not. I'm still new to this work. But eager to learn. I was delighted when you asked to meet me.' She smiled to cover her lie. Though it was more of a fib, really. She *had* been delighted, though only at the suggestion in Mrs Elliott's letter that her work was making a difference to the war effort. 'Shall we order tea?'

A waitress was approaching the table, order pad in hand. She took their order for tea and scones, and disappeared back into the kitchen.

Mrs Elliott glanced about. The teashop was not crowded, but the hubbub of conversation was loud enough to drown out their own quiet exchanges, in case of curious listeners. Discreetly, she drew a folded paper from her pocket and passed it to Imogen. 'Your new instructions.'

Imogen began to open the paper but stopped when Mrs Elliott coughed and shook her head. 'Sorry,' she muttered, and slid the piece of paper, still folded, into her handbag.

The waitress was coming back with a heavily laden tea tray.

'The weather has been good this past week, don't you think?' Mrs Elliott asked.

'Oh yes, quite. Almost Mediterranean.' Imogen waited in silence while a teapot, cups and saucers, a pot of hot water and a sugar bowl were placed on the table. She smiled at the waitress, thanking her. Once the woman had disappeared again, she fixed a bright smile to her lips. 'Shall I be Mother?'

Mrs Elliott pushed her cup and saucer forward. 'Please.'

Once the tea had been poured, Imogen asked quietly, 'Are you able to tell me anything about this new task I've been given, Mrs Elliott?'

'Indeed.' Before she could say more, two scones arrived, pre-split and smeared thinly with butter, no doubt to permit their rations to go further, and the woman helped herself with an enthusiastic air. 'Mmm. Such a luxury. Of course, scones aren't the same as they were before the war. Not with rationing so tight.'

'No.'

'Though still tasty.'

'Exactly.'

Mrs Elliott bit into her scone. 'So,' she said indistinctly between mouthfuls, 'I've been following your progress with interest. Your tip about the old lady almost certainly saved lives.'

'Doreen?'

'Yes, an excellent pick-up. You suspected her as soon as you came to Bude, is that right?'

Imogen nodded, checking that nobody was listening. But cakes had arrived at the nearest adjacent table, so it seemed safe to say quietly, 'I noticed she was forever snooping around the US Rangers and listening to their conversations. Even after dark,' she added, 'which was suspicious in itself for a lady of her age.'

'You were right to be suspicious. We later discovered she'd been passing information about Cornish airfields and troop movements to the enemy since early in the war.'

Imogen was shocked. 'But why? Forgive me, but . . . I don't understand how anyone could betray their country like that.'

Mrs Elliott finished her scone, hunting regretfully for crumbs on her empty plate. 'Her son lives in Berlin with his German wife and children. It seems he'd told Doreen her grandchildren were in danger of being arrested and tortured by the Gestapo . . . unless she could provide him with useful intelligence against the Allies.' Mrs Elliott shook her head. 'Instead, his mother will likely now hang for treason.'

'Poor, gullible woman.' Imogen felt awful.

'Don't waste your pity, Miss Crombie. Her German daughter-in-law is personal secretary to one of Herr Hitler's foremost political advisers. Every report Doreen made, however insignificant, was going straight to enemy headquarters.'

'But how was she getting the information out?'

'One of our own people in Bude had been helping her. Name of Gladly. Head of a local enemy sympathisers' group, hiding in plain sight.' There was disgust in Mrs Elliott's face. 'He was arrested too, the filthy traitor, and soon gave up another of his fellow conspirators in the region. So your information has helped uncover a spy ring here in Cornwall.' She nodded with satisfaction at Imogen's shocked expression. 'You've a good nose for a lie, Miss Crombie. Which is why I'm here in person. To thank and congratulate you for making such a brilliant contribution to the war effort, and to impress on you how vital it is that we discover who the others are.'

Imogen was confused. 'What others?'

'We suspect there must be at least five in Mr Gladly's spy ring. Yet we've only caught three.' Mrs Elliott sipped at her tea, studying Imogen over the rim of her cup. 'The powers-that-be want you to find the other two.'

'Me?' Imogen squeaked, and heads turned.

'Hush.' Hurriedly, Mrs Elliott began to talk loudly about the weather again, and for a few minutes their conversation revolved around that innocuous topic. Only once the hum of conversation in the teashop had risen again did she whisper across the table, 'We can't spare anyone else. All other operatives are focused on the big push now.'

Imogen blinked, not understanding at first. Then whispered back, 'France?'

The other woman nodded slowly, checking the teapot with the back of her hand and then adding more warm water from the steel jug. 'France,' she agreed. 'So it's up to you and me. Well, you. I'm busy with a situation in Truro. But I'll keep in touch. All the information you need for your new job is on that slip of paper I gave you.'

'Oh.'

'It's a vicar,' the other woman whispered, leaning forward.

Imogen was shocked. 'A *vicar*?'

'Oh, we get all sorts these days. It's disgraceful who will turn traitor. Though it's only a rumour at this stage. Your task is to befriend your target, watch him discreetly and see what you can discover. But stay safe. No endangering yourself, understand? If any further action is required, we'll alert the proper authorities.'

'Of course.' She knew the rules.

'Now,' Mrs Elliott went on, rummaging in her own handbag, 'I have aniseed balls in here somewhere. Ah, here we are. I do love a sweety with my tea, don't you?' And with a covert glance at the waitress, she offered Imogen the paper bag of aniseed balls, adding with an embarrassed smile, 'Thank goodness they're on ration, otherwise life would be hell. I have such a sweet tooth.'

While they finished their tea, they spoke of her previous assignments, including the two brief reports she'd made while still living at home with her parents in Exeter. She had been recruited to the unit soon after leaving school, one of her teachers having also worked for them and spotting that Imogen was good at that sort of thing and could also be trusted to keep quiet about it.

'Being watchful,' had been her recruiter's description of the work. Nothing more. Watching and waiting was basically what she did for the war effort. Plus keeping a journal for longer surveillance tasks.

Each town had a unit like theirs, operating in secret, simply being watchful and aware. Anyone behaving suspiciously – as her sister's neighbour Doreen had done, hanging about and eavesdropping on the American troops' conversations – became a person of interest to the unit, and would be watched in small teams, as often as deemed necessary. Once potential wrongdoing had been established, such persons would be reported to the area supervisor for further action, either round-the-clock observation and in-depth note-taking, or arrest by the authorities.

Her sister had been shocked when she learned the truth about her activities in Bude. But at least Imogen no longer had to keep things secret from Florence.

'Did you have something to do with Doreen being arrested?' Florence had asked Imogen quietly, just before her wedding to Miles, and she had been forced to explain, in faltering tones, about her 'secret' work.

Thankfully, Florence had been strangely proud rather than upset, hugging her and saying, 'I knew it!'

Imogen could only hope nobody else suspected her.

It had been uncomfortable, these past couple of years, unable to admit what she was up to. Those around her had tended to misinterpret her behaviour as wild and wilful, irresponsible, even downright reckless. Though being misunderstood or misjudged was the nature of the job. She'd learned early on that was part of the price one paid for serving one's country.

But to befriend a vicar, of all people, simply in order to watch, follow and inform on him . . . That would be a severe test of her resolution.

She'd only ever looked forward to church as a girl so she could see Simon, and once he'd moved away had rapidly found excuses to avoid going. All the same, she knew that an active, thriving church could knit a community together and that a vicar should be the one man you could absolutely trust in a fix. She might not be sure how she felt about God, or even convinced there *was* a God, especially given all the suffering of this war. Yet it still didn't fit easily with her to be spying on a man of the cloth.

But that was mere superstition talking, she told herself with a little shake. Surely she had learned by now that *nobody* was above suspicion? Not even a vicar.

On leaving the teashop together, the two women did not shake hands, in case anyone happened to be watching, but parted without a word.

Imogen pretended to be gazing into a shop display while watching covertly as Mrs Elliott headed back downhill towards Bude train station. It had been necessary to meet in public, since it would have been too conspicuous for Mrs Elliott to come to the boarding house on Downs View Road, but the teashop was new and far enough out of the town centre to be relatively quiet. And if anyone had spotted them, Imogen had prepared a cover story to explain their meeting.

With a quick glance at her watch, she hurried through town to the curving bay of golden sand at Summerleaze.

There, she found her sister Florence sitting in the May sunshine with her young son Billy. The little boy was rather inexpertly digging a hole to fill his bucket with sand, but stopped to wave enthusiastically on spotting 'Aunty Migen'. At his high-pitched cry, Florence looked up from the letter she'd been reading and smiled.

'There you are at last, Immi,' she said, and reached for the wicket picnic basket she'd been packing that morning when Imogen left the house. 'We're both starving. How did your meeting go?'

She was itching to read more about her new mission. *A vicar* . . . How appalling if the rumour should turn out to be true.

But she wanted to study the information in private at the boarding house, not out here on the beach. Now the Americans had left Bude, Florence had allocated her a room of her own, for which Immi was hugely thankful. She loved her sister dearly but sleeping in the same room with both Florence and little Billy for the past few months had not been easy. Especially once, when she'd been pretending to be attracted to a young American soldier with reported odd sympathies, and her sister had caught them together in their shared bedroom . . .

Luckily, the young man had been innocent. But it had been an awkward moment. Though at least Florence's appearance had allowed Imogen to avoid taking things further with him. A flirtation was one thing when trying to slip under a male traitor's guard, but that young man had clearly intended other activities than mere kisses.

'Brilliantly,' Imogen said, removing her heels to cross the warm sands and squeezing onto the tartan blanket beside Florence.

She wasn't much of a beachgoer. But since revealing her secret to her sister, she had begun to enjoy spending more time with her. Previously, they hadn't got on well, since Florence had always assumed her antics were down to bad behaviour. Now she knew the truth about Imogen's war work, things were much easier between the two sisters.

'So, you got a letter?' Imogen smiled when her sister blushed. 'Is that from Staff Sergeant Miller, by any chance?'

Last year, the whole town of Bude had been taken over unexpectedly by the US Rangers, who had come to winter on the north Cornwall coast while they trained up and down the cliffs and along the beaches. Almost every home with spare rooms in the town had been commandeered in order to accommodate so many American troops. Florence, who had been widowed early in the war, had just closed her boarding house on Downs View Road for the season. But when a handsome US Ranger turned up on her doorstep, making arrangements for the troops to be billeted on the town, Florence had reluctantly opened Ocean View Boarding House again, and helped him organise the mass accommodation of Rangers around the town.

Out of mourning, yet still pining for her late husband, Florence had not warmed to Staff Sergeant Miller at first. In fact, sparks had flown between them, according to Florence's fond recollection of that time. But Imogen, arriving in Bude to find her sister's boarding house overrun with Americans, had not missed the chemistry between Florence and Miles. She had not been surprised, in fact, when the two announced that they were getting engaged.

Miles, aware that his unit would be leaving Bude soon for an undisclosed location, had suggested they marry before he left. To Imogen's surprise, Florence had agreed. The couple had been married earlier that year, shortly before Miles left Cornwall, along with the bulk of the American troops.

Imogen didn't disapprove of her sister's choice. How could she? But she was afraid for Florence, who had already lost Percy, her first husband, to the war. Now Miles was likely to be involved in the imminent Allied liberation of France that everybody had been whispering about for months, sure that the government was finally about to make a move. What if he never came back? Could Florence cope with another blow to the heart?

'Of course. Who else would be writing to me but my own husband?' Florence unfolded her letter again, beaming. 'It's so wonderful to hear from him and to know he's still stationed here in Britain, even if he can't tell me precisely where.' Then her smile faltered. 'Though Miles says – and I'm reading between the lines, because you know they're forbidden to give anything away about locations or troop movements – he seems to be saying something big is about to happen.'

'You think the Allies are about to begin the liberation of France?' Imogen asked in a cautious whisper, glancing about in case of observers. But there was nobody except Billy within earshot.

'Maybe, I don't know.' Florence put a hand to her mouth. 'I know an invasion of France has to happen. It's the only way we can make a difference in this awful war. But what hope can there be for all those brave men, facing so many German guns? They say the Normandy beaches have been heavily mined too. Oh, Immi, what if . . .' Her voice died away as she stared at nothing, perhaps reliving the horror of her first husband's death.

'Don't think about it,' Imogen urged her, touching her sister's arm. 'Focus on what you've got. We're safe here in Cornwall. You're a married woman again. And you have Billy.'

'Yes, I have Billy.' Florence found her smile again, glancing quickly at her young son. 'You're right, of course. We have plenty to celebrate, don't we?' But she hugged the letter to her chest, her eyes still misty. 'I only pray Miles will come back to me safe.'

CHAPTER THREE

Stratton Hospital, near Bude, North Cornwall, May 1944

Pearl came to a halt, staring at the handsome young man lying in the end bed of the half-empty Men's Ward at Stratton Hospital, which was situated less than two miles from the centre of Bude, a brisk but delightful walk on such a lovely spring day. Sunlight poured through the window behind his bed, forming a misty halo about his head. The mere sight of him left her ecstatic, all her doubts flying out of her head. Terry was her fiancé, she reminded herself, and he loved her. Why else would he have proposed?

Yet her nerves had been in a jitter since leaving the boarding house on her way to visit him, almost afraid to speak to him after what had happened last time. Their unexpected row at her previous visit had left her sadly nervous and unsure of herself, even biting her perfectly manicured nails, a habit she could ill afford, given that her appearance was how she earned her living. Or had been, until recently.

Still, she had eventually worked up the nerve to speak to Terry again. Not only had she tramped all the way here from the oceanside boarding house in Bude where she was staying, but she had spent good money on this swell bunch of flowers besides. Money she could ill afford now she was out of work.

But now that she saw him again . . .

Her heart flooded with love and she sighed softly, remembering all the good times they'd had and sure that he'd soon be back to his old self. Of course he was crochety at the moment, suffering as he did, poor darling.

His head was turned away on the pillows, and he appeared to be asleep. But she felt her heart lift, studying the name on the chalkboard above the bed.

Private Terence Gardiner.

She hoped to share that surname with him before long. She breathed in the delicate scent of the Cornish flowers in her hand, smiling as she rehearsed her soon-to-be new name in her head.

Mrs Terence Gardiner.

Ah now, that sounded mighty good after twenty-eight years as Miss Pearl Cratchett, a name she had swiftly changed on becoming an entertainer, using the flashier name Pearl Diamond on stage instead. Her identity papers were in the name of 'Cratchett' though, an embarrassing legacy from her father, a dull man, set in his ways, who disapproved of show business.

Terence had turned his head, spotting her. He did not smile, but no doubt he was still in agonies from his accident.

'Why, hello there, Terry,' she gushed, hurrying forward with her fragrant bunch of flowers. She laid them gently on his bedcovers and leant forward to kiss him on the lips. 'How are you, sweetie?'

He said nothing and almost seemed to shrink away at her kiss, which upset her again. Her heart ached with the fear she might have hurt him inadvertently.

She pulled up a chair to sit beside his bed, careful to speak in a low voice in case his head was still paining him. 'You look better today, honey. Has the doctor been to see you yet?'

'Later,' Terence mumbled, with a glance at the ward clock. 'After lunch, the nurse said.'

He shifted to sit up, and she instantly jumped to help, adjusting his pillows so he would be more comfortable.

Poor soul, she thought affectionately, pausing to smooth down his white bedcovers before taking her seat again. Bad enough that he'd missed his unit's departure from Bude earlier that year after falling from Maer Cliff during last-minute rock-climbing practice, but he might never be able to rejoin the Rangers after the doctors had discovered a hairline fracture in his spine. The injury wasn't severe enough to keep him in a wheelchair for the rest of his life, apparently, but he was unlikely ever to be fit enough to serve in the Rangers again.

That crushing disappointment had left Terence pale and

silent at first, but he'd soon rallied, and she felt sure her frequent visits must be what was cheering him up. But like most young men, he was naturally unwilling to open his heart to a woman. Especially a woman of her age, she thought, aware of a secret nagging doubt that was proving harder to dispel with every visit to the hospital.

Was she too old for him?

But no, that was ridiculous. Terry had never mentioned it as a problem and the age difference between them was only seven years. Then again, that might feel like a lifetime to a twenty-one-year-old soldier. It never mattered when the woman was younger, she'd noticed. Yet when it was the man . . .

When they'd kissed for the first time at the Christmas dance, he'd whispered in her ear, 'I love you.'

Hearing these three magic words, she'd looked into his earnest smiling face and felt almost overwhelmed by a tidal wave of happiness. And yes, she'd been grateful and mighty relieved too. She'd had her fair share of male admirers in the past, yet they'd never gone beyond a crude desire to take her to bed, approaches she had always slapped down with disdain. Certainly no other man had ever declared his love for her before, perhaps put off by her profession as a dancer and singer. With any other man, maybe she would have held back . . . Yet the gentle attentions and naivety of this youthful soldier had made her tumble rapidly into love with him too, touched by his undoubted bravery in risking his life for freedom and democracy.

Weeks later, lying together on the windswept dunes of the beach under cover of darkness, she'd protested at how far he wanted to go, and Terence had assured her they would be married once the war was over. Or perhaps as early as that summer if he could get permission from his commanding officer. The next day, standing outside a shop in town, she had pointed out a pretty ring in the window display, and he'd marched into the shop and bought it for her, there and then.

Since his accident though, Terence had not repeated those three little words, nor joined in when she spoke of her plans for their wedding.

Was it possible he had changed his mind about marrying her? Or worse, had lied simply to get his way with her?

Pearl shivered, pushing those doubts aside and trying not to be so negative. Her fiancé was unhappy about his accident – that was all. Small wonder, poor boy, trapped in a hospital bed in Cornwall while all his friends had moved to a top-secret location further east, training for an imminent invasion of German-held territories across the Channel. Or so everyone was whispering these days.

There was a letter open on his nightstand, the single sheet covered in small, dense scrawl. 'Had some mail from your Ranger buddies?' she asked, leaning forward to take his hand. He gave her a fleeting smile, which she took for a yes. 'Who wrote you? Private Benson?'

Private Benson was one of her favourites among his friends, a lively lad always ready with a joke or a risky anecdote. She'd told Bill Benson more than once that he could make a performer himself, having the looks as well as the ability to turn a comic line. Though a stage career wasn't for everyone, as she knew. It could be lonely up there, facing the lights, waiting for applause or laughter, and feeling empty without them.

'Yeah, Benson wrote me,' he agreed, but she could tell he was unhappy. His gaze kept sliding away whenever she looked at him.

She felt another momentary doubt. Terence had always been such a gentleman with her. Not merely charming and smooth-mannered, but the kindest, most polite man she'd ever known. Lately though, he had become almost cold, and she couldn't understand what she'd done wrong. Unless he'd received bad news from his friend.

'What is it?' Pearl urged him. 'You can tell me anything, honey. We're going to be married, remember?'

Now she was sure he was upset with her, for he stiffened at those words and withdrew his hand.

'Please, Terry,' she whispered, glancing about at the few other occupied beds in the ward. But they were all older men, reading newspapers or sleeping, none of them paying any attention to her and Terence. 'You're making me worried.'

'I got something to tell you,' he muttered, the words almost surly. He was staring down at the white coverlet, not looking at her.

Alarm flashed through her. 'Is it about your injury?' When he shook his head, she bit her lip. 'Benson, then?

Has he been hurt? Not been put on another charge, I hope?' His friend was the kind of soldier who was always getting into trouble.

'It's nothing to do with Benson.' There was a flush of dark red along his cheeks as he glanced up, meeting her eyes at last. 'Thing is, Pearl, you're a swell gal. I couldn't have wished for better company while I've been out here in Cornwall. But we can't be married.'

'Can't . . . Can't be married?' she repeated in a daze, her heart starting to thud violently. 'But you gave me a ring.'

He shrugged, saying nothing more.

She thought for a moment. 'Honey,' she said hesitantly, 'if it's because you don't want me marrying a man in your condition, don't waste your breath. You won't be in that bed for ever.'

'It's no use,' he burst out, shocking her. 'I can't marry you because I'm *already* married.'

She gaped at him, frozen. 'W-Wwhat?'

'I got married a few weeks before I left the States,' he explained wretchedly. 'Emmy was in the family way, so our parents made us get hitched. I swear I don't love her . . . It was just a one-time thing.' He nodded to the side cabinet, where the letter he'd been reading still lay. 'That's who the mail was from. Emmy, to say she's had the baby. A little boy. Six pounds, three ounces.'

Pearl put a hand to her mouth, shaking her head and fighting back tears. What he was telling her sounded fantastical. It couldn't be true. Could it?

'I'd put the whole thing out of my mind until that letter came from Emmy. But I'm a daddy now, and I got to stop messing about with other girls.' Terence looked at her guiltily, though with an edge of accusation too. 'Still, you never asked me.'

'Never asked what?' she choked.

'If I was already spoken for.'

Her stomach churned at his words. 'Wait . . . You're saying this is *my* fault?' She couldn't believe what she was hearing.

'Maybe, yeah. You never thought twice on the beach that night, did you? Too quick to kiss a man before asking anything about him . . . That's what Benson used to say about you. That you were just an entertainer, one of the Donut Dollies. He said I should forget about Emmy and let you . . . entertain me.' He raised his chin, glaring at her now. 'Except he didn't use the word "entertain".'

'Dear Lord . . .' Scraping back the chair, Pearl dashed from the ward, feeling sick, a hand clapped over her mouth.

It was some hours before she finally trudged back to her lodgings on Downs View Road. She knew she looked a mess, her make-up ruined, her hair windswept and tangled after a long walk along the high cliffs. But at least she hadn't thrown herself off into the plunging surf below, a terrible act she'd contemplated briefly as she stared out across the Atlantic Ocean towards America and home . . .

Her landlady Mrs Miller, in dark green utility dungarees,

was sweeping the hallway and glanced round at the sound of the front door opening.

'Hello,' Mrs Miller said cheerily, and put her broom aside. Then frowned. 'You all right, dearie? You don't look well.'

The British had a wonderful talent for understatement, Pearl thought, but she forced a shaky smile to her lips.

'There, there.' The landlady gathered her in for a hug, and Pearl felt comforted by the embrace, despite barely knowing this woman. 'Had a row with your fiancé – is that it?'

'We're not getting married anymore,' Pearl admitted, but then promptly embarrassed herself by bursting into tears.

Mrs Miller drew back to stare at her. 'Oh, you poor dear . . .' She hustled Pearl through to the guests' lounge, an arm about her waist. 'Sit down here while I fetch a nice hot pot of tea. That'll soon set you right.' Bundled up in an armchair, Pearl sat sniffing into her handkerchief and gazing out at the tossed blue waves of the Atlantic, her thoughts whirling in despair, until the landlady came back with the tea tray. 'I brought biscuits too. The nice ones. And the sugar bowl as well. Yes, I know we're all meant to have given up sweet tea, but hang the rationing.' Mrs Miller poured a cup of tea, stirred a little sugar into it, and handed it to Pearl. 'Now, love, drink up and tell me all about it.'

Pearl balanced her cup and saucer on the arm of the sofa, dabbed at her damp eyes and resolutely pushed her handkerchief up her sleeve. To be honest, she would have preferred a strong cup of coffee. But she didn't want to hurt this lady's feelings by saying so. The Brits did love their tea, even if it tasted like dishwater to her. 'Thank you, Mrs Miller, you're a darling.'

'Call me Florence, please. And have some biscuits.' Mrs Miller passed across a plate. 'Go on, dig in. I've been saving them for a special occasion. But this is more important.'

Between nibbles on a ginger biscuit and gulps of watery tea, Pearl explained what had happened at the hospital that morning. Florence exclaimed at intervals, her kind eyes suddenly wrathful, and kept shaking her head.

At the end, she took Pearl's hand and squeezed it. 'Men can be such beasts. What a wicked thing to do . . . Not just to you but to his wife too. I daresay she'll never know what he's been up to overseas.' Florence munched absentmindedly on a biscuit. 'Poor lamb, stuck at home with a new baby to care for, and her husband so far away.' At Pearl's renewed sobbing, she broke off hurriedly. 'And he's left you in the lurch too. Still, no real harm done, eh?'

Pearl, having retrieved her handkerchief to soak up fresh tears, didn't dare tell her how far things had gone between her and Terence. What an idiot she'd been. But he'd seemed so charming at first, she could still scarcely believe it . . .

'I've been such a fool,' she moaned.

'None of that, my girl. It's not your fault Private

Gardiner turned out to be such an untrustworthy young man. I only hope he's thoroughly ashamed of himself now the truth has come out.' Florence stood up as the front door opened again, her brow lightening as she called out, 'Is that you at last, Immi?'

Imogen was the landlady's younger sister, and the reason why Pearl was living with them at Ocean View Boarding House. She and Imogen had met at the now fateful Christmas dance where she'd kissed Terence for the first time. Imogen was a lively young woman a few years younger than her, with sparkling eyes and a sharp, amusing wit. Unlike most of the other women in Bude, she also hadn't looked down her nose at Pearl for being an entertainer. The two had hit it off at once, and since then had continued to meet up for coffee and the occasional lunch.

When the troops had left Bude for an undisclosed location further east, and Pearl had been offered the opportunity to travel with them, as part of the overseas entertainment troupe, she'd declined. A stupid decision, in hindsight, but she'd been planning to marry Terence once he'd recovered from his accident and then travel home to the States as his wife. But once the Rangers had left town, her free accommodation as part of the US entourage had no longer been available to her, and she'd faced homelessness.

To her relief, Imogen had offered her a half-board room in her sister's boarding house on Downs View Road, and at a price she could afford. Though not for long. Pearl had a few savings set by from her work, but that money wouldn't last for ever. She'd been hoping to marry Terence that summer, of course, and so had not regarded her lack of a job as an issue. But now she would need to look for work. Or perhaps follow the entertainment troupe to wherever they'd been billeted in the East of England, for she had not been made privy to that top-secret information before everyone left.

Perhaps she could go home to Chicago instead. Her parents had never approved of her job as an entertainer anyway. Perhaps Poppa could get her a job in his cousin's diner. Right now she'd be happy to wait tables or wash dishes – it didn't matter. After two years of travelling about with the entertainment troupe, being wolf-whistled and stared at on a stage by hundreds of women-starved troops, it would be nice to melt into the background for a while and pretend none of this had ever happened . . .

Pearl blew her nose, trying to stop crying.

At least she had made a few friends in Bude since the Rangers left. Imogen, for example, and a cheerful young woman called Penny who also lived at the boarding house on Downs View Road and worked at the hospital. Though she feared she would always be somehow 'alien' to her friends in Cornwall, being an American.

Imogen hurried in with a basket of shopping over her arm, clearly surprised to find them in the guests' lounge at that time of day. But once Florence had explained the situation, her shocked gaze flew to Pearl's face. 'Oh my goodness, how absolutely dreadful. What a rat he must be. I'm so sorry, Pearl. But don't you worry . . . We'll soon take your mind off him, won't we, Florence?'

'Will we?' Florence blinked, and then hurriedly nodded. 'Oh yes, of course we will. Cake is what you need. And maybe a night at the pictures with Imogen. That always cheers me up when I'm down.' Her mouth curved abruptly into a smile. 'How silly of me. I quite forgot. A letter came for you this morning, Pearl, after you'd gone out.' She reached into her dungaree pocket and pulled out an airmail envelope, postmarked from the States. 'This should cheer you up. A letter from home, isn't it?'

Her heart thudding, Pearl took it, saying mechanically, 'Yes, thank you. That looks like my mother's handwriting. I'd better go and read it at once.'

Florence nodded approvingly. 'Good idea. And it's sausages for tea. With lashings of hot gravy. You enjoy your letter and take your time coming down for your meal. You and Penny are our only lodgers at the moment, though we are expecting a few new guests tomorrow. One young lady just visiting for a few days, and a widower who's coming to stay as a permanent resident with two children in tow.' She laughed at Pearl's astonished stare. 'I know, yet more children in the house! But their father assures me they're very well behaved. So let's hope for the best, shall we?'

Putting on her best smile, Pearl agreed with this wholeheartedly, though she doubted it could be true. Florence's young son Billy had an astonishing capacity for making noise. It gave her a headache whenever he

45

sat banging his toy drum or zoomed enthusiastically about the dining room with his arms wide, pretending to be a Spitfire.

How much noise would *two more children* make?

Having thanked both sisters for their kindness, she hurried upstairs to read her letter.

It was indeed from her mother in Chicago, to whom Pearl had written only two weeks before to insist she would be marrying Terence soon, regardless of her disapproval. Her parents had written earlier that spring to warn her against making hasty decisions and to indicate their disapproval if she dared to marry a penniless young soldier in a foreign country, especially one who was seriously wounded and might never be able to work once he returned to the States.

She unfolded the letter with shaking hands, biting her lip as she scanned its short, unfriendly lines. Now she had upset her parents too, and for no good reason.

Dear Pearl,

I hope this letter finds you well. But Poppa and I can't pretend not to be hurt by your last letter. It wasn't what we expected to receive from our only daughter, who we've always supported as best we could. It may not be our business to say who you can marry and where. But it is our business as parents to warn you not to rush into marriage without your nearest and dearest there to advise you, nor even to meet this young man, who sounds – according to Poppa – like he might not be the best match for you. But you know your own mind, it seems. And maybe there's more to this hasty engagement than meets the eye. So all we can do is wish you happy.

Momma x

P.S. I'm not saying you won't be welcome here once you're wed. But you might want to leave it a year or two before coming home. To let your father calm down.

Curling up in a tearful ball on her bed, Pearl groaned and hid her face in her hands, those stinging final words in her mother's letter running through her head, refusing to be silenced.

But you might want to leave it a year or two before coming home.

Dragging off her 'engagement' ring with a wounded cry, she threw it across the room. She wouldn't be going home to Chicago with a husband on her arm. But she'd offended her parents so badly she wouldn't even be welcome turning up on their doorstep still unmarried, as she'd half planned to do after leaving the hospital this morning.

Whatever in the world was she going to do now?

CHAPTER FOUR

Bude, North Cornwall, June 1944

As the train pulled into Bude in a white cloud of steam, Alice hurried to pack away her paperback and smooth the wrinkles out of her skirt caused by sitting all the way from London to Cornwall. She settled her hat on her head and smiled faintly at the lady opposite who for hours had been regaling the whole carriage with tales of the grandchildren she was coming to visit. She was feeling nervous though. This was hardly the triumphant return she'd envisaged when she left Cornwall for the big smoke a little over three months ago. Especially given that she was nursing an arm in a sling. Under different circumstances, she might have worn that sling with pride. But given that her own headstrong behaviour had killed the man she loved . . .

Swallowing, Alice gathered her meagre possessions and

disembarked along with the others, peering through steam to see if anyone had come to meet her. Though why would they?

To her surprise, a large hand reached out from the steam to take her suitcase. 'I'll carry that,' a deep familiar voice said, and Sidney's face swam out of the thinning white cloud. His rare smile brought tears brimming in her eyes. 'Welcome back to Bude, Alice.'

It was her old instructor.

'Oh, Sidney.' She struggled not to weep, aware that they were in public. 'You're a sight for sore eyes, all right. How . . . How are you?'

'Better than you, by the look of things.' The words stung, reminding Alice of her failure. But he shot her a reassuring grin. 'Don't worry, I've had worse.'

'You have?' she asked dubiously.

'Bullet here.' Sidney tapped his elbow. 'And here.' He pointed at his side. 'Got shot in the leg in the first show, back in 1918. Can't have been much older than you at the time. Bloody German sniper . . . Shattered my left femur.' Sidney nodded at her shocked expression, for her instructors had never once spoken of their past during basic training. 'I was stuck in bed for months. Missed the end of the war. But I survived and got over it.'

She thought of Jim and her eyes misted over again. He hadn't *survived*. He would never *get over it*. And that was all her fault.

Sidney must have seen her tears, for he gave her a bracing nudge. Thankfully, in her good arm. 'Come on, young scallywag,' he said heartily, seizing another of her bags. 'Let's get you back to headquarters. I've arranged for Mrs Miller – Mrs Pritchard, as was – to put you up at Ocean View Boarding House again. For a few days at least, while you decide what to do.' His small eyes peered at her. 'Unless you've already chosen?'

Back in London, after leaving hospital, a stark choice had been laid before her. Return to Bude and join a small team of locals working together to spot and infiltrate cells of enemy sympathisers, while continuing to hone her skills under her old instructors. Or go 'home' to Porthcurno, the tiny Cornish seaside village where her family had settled after being evacuated from Dagenham, for a few months of rest and recuperation.

Aunt Violet had written to her in hospital, distraught at the news that she'd been hurt but delighted to welcome her back to the farm above Porthcurno. Her husband Joe was a good-natured Cornishman who'd been discharged from the navy after part of his leg had been amputated, but who ran his cliff-top farm with the help of three Land Girls. She missed them all madly and wanted nothing more than to be back in her old attic room at the farm, and to talk to her sister Lily and play with her new nephew.

But she'd been so determined to make a go of her training as a spy, and to only return home once she'd achieved something and the war was won . . .

How could she go home now, wounded and with nothing to show for her efforts but a failed mission and a dead team member?

'No,' she admitted huskily. 'I still haven't decided what to do. But I've only been given a week to decide. So I'd better hurry up.'

'Sounds about right. Those in the corridors of power at Westminster do enjoy moving us little folk about like pawns on a chessboard.' Sidney gave a resigned shrug. 'But whatever you decide, Alice, if you need help, remember you only have to ask. Everyone back at headquarters has heard what you did in London and we're proud of you.' He had spoken gruffly but his words touched her heart nonetheless. 'I hope you know that, girl.'

Overwhelmed by emotion and unable to speak, Alice made a tearful, incoherent noise of assent and followed him along the platform, clutching her handbag and wishing her old instructor wouldn't keep treating her like a hero returning from war. Put to the test in London, she'd forgotten all her training, made a mess of things, and got someone killed. By rights, she ought to be shunned. Not welcomed home with all this fuss.

They left the station together, mingling discreetly with the shambolic crowd of visitors ambling towards the centre of Bude and the beaches, the women in broad-brimmed sunhats, holding picnic baskets and their kids by the hand, the men carrying deckchairs, already with shirtsleeves rolled up and ties loosened, no doubt intent on spending a summer's afternoon on these lovely Cornish sands, despite the war, despite the general lack of money, despite everything . . .

It felt strange to be back in Bude again. It had still been winter, the early days of February, when she'd left here, under grey skies and with even greyer seas. She had headed back to Porthcurno first to see her gran married to Arnold Newton, the white-haired old shopkeeper in the village, and then boarded a train from Penzance to London, travelling east for the first time in years.

She had expected to stay in London for at least a year, completing her training. In the end, she'd barely lasted three months.

Sidney had been supportive in his reply when Alice had written from the hospital to let him know she'd been ordered to report back to his training unit in Bude, and giving him the likely date of her train. But she was sure he and the team must have been disappointed in her.

A young man in uniform, hands in his pockets, whistling as he passed, caught her eye and gave her a cocky smile. She half-smiled in return, and then choked, abruptly reminded of how Jim had looked at her like that once . . .

'Your arm hurting you?' Sidney asked, sounding concerned.

Thrusting away the bad memories. Alice forced a brave smile to her lips. 'Lord, no,' she told him airily. 'I'm just glad to be back. But ain't this sunny weather bloomin' glorious? It always seems to be pouring down in London – you noticed that?' She knew that Sidney had spent time in the capital, for he'd told her so himself in the past.

He grinned, raising his gaze to the warm blue skies. It

was in fact a perfect June day. 'I have to admit, the weather down here has been beautiful these past few weeks. And let's hope for even better times ahead.' He slowed his pace as his gaze met hers. There was a significant pause. 'You know what everyone's saying, of course?'

Rapidly, he glanced up and down the narrow, hilly street as though to make sure nobody was listening to their conversation. But they'd been walking slowly enough to have fallen behind the crowd of holidaymakers they'd followed out of Bude station, so it seemed unlikely anyone would overhear them.

'The big push, you know,' he murmured, but left the rest unspoken, trained to be cautious in public, regardless.

She knew what he was talking about. The liberation of Northern France, which must surely be mere days away, though nobody dared speak of it openly. But there was a hum of excitement in the air, and every day for the past few weeks had seen Londoners glued to the wireless at news time and scanning the newspapers on street newsstands with half-anxious, half-hopeful expressions. 'Any day now,' people kept whispering. Yet the days came and went with no news.

'I don't know more than you,' she admitted. 'All I can say is London's buzzing with it. People say, *tomorrow*. Or the next day, maybe. But nobody knows for sure.'

He nodded, ushering her down the alley that led to the ramshackle printers' workshop they used as 'cover' for headquarters. She had spent months there last year, training with a small team, making friends – yes, and almost a few enemies too – among the other raw recruits. It was bittersweet to walk through the printers' workshop and see the usual mess of half-printed sheets on the floor, smell the ink and hear the clack of a printing press being operated in one of the side rooms. They did indeed print posters and government pamphlets there for the war effort, and organise their distribution to Bude townsfolk and the surrounding areas. But the place had a deeper purpose, in a secret room hidden deep under a corrugated iron shelter in the backyard, where the would-be spies had their training sessions and debriefs after 'missions'.

As they went down the steps into the underground room, Alice let her breath out in a rush, seeing a familiar figure there at the chalkboard.

'Mr Rawlings!' she exclaimed.

'Welcome back, Alice,' Rawlings said, smiling broadly as he came forward, hand outstretched. 'It's good to see you again.'

Within minutes she was seated between them with a steaming mug of tea, telling the two instructors everything that had happened to her since she'd left for London. Everything she was allowed to tell them, that was, for much of her specialist training had been 'hush-hush' as the bigwigs had termed it, and she barely said a word about Jim, of course, for much of that story was personal. Except that she and Jim had been working as partners on the night he'd been shot and killed by enemy sympathisers.

'I was so sorry to hear about that. Poor lad,' Rawlings

said as she finished her lengthy account, shaking his head. 'Did they ever catch the wicked blighters who shot him?'

She nodded, swallowing. 'I told my team as much as I could from the hospital and they ran 'em to ground a few days later.'

'Those traitors deserve to hang,' Sidney said darkly.

'And probably will,' Rawlings agreed, his face sombre. 'Not only for treason but cold-blooded murder.' He saw her shudder and added more gently, 'They nearly did for you too, Alice. Another inch the other way and we'd have been talking about you in the past tense. Think of that.'

'It's hard to think of anything else sometimes,' she muttered.

Sidney studied her averted face and then took away her empty mug, his smile sympathetic. 'So, what now?'

'That's up to you, I guess.' Alice looked around at the classroom she remembered so well. 'I was told to offer you my services for training new recruits, if needed. Or there's a group I could join here in Bude, looking out for enemy sympathisers.'

'What do you want to do?' Rawlings asked.

Frowning, Alice knitted her fingers together in her lap, ignoring the twinge in her hurt shoulder. 'I don't know,' she said frankly.

'What about your family in Porthcurno?'

'I could go to them for a while,' she agreed reluctantly. 'But my wound's on the mend and . . . I still want to be useful.'

'You didn't fail in London,' Rawlings said astutely, no

doubt reading the embarrassment on her face. 'These things happen in times of war. People get killed. Good people.' He paused. 'And we have to deal with that as best we can and keep going.'

'I know,' she whispered.

He withdrew an envelope and handed it to her. 'This is from George Cotterill at Eastern House. You know him, I believe?'

Alice blinked, staring at the envelope that bore George's distinctive handwriting. 'Mr Cotterill? Yes, indeed . . . He's a family friend.'

'This is an invitation for you to join his communications team at Eastern House in Porthcurno, if you feel up to it. You'd be going back to basics, learning about code-breaking and deciphering messages. But it's vital work, perhaps more than ever now.' Rawlings passed her the envelope, and she took it uncertainly. 'We'd be proud and glad to have you join us here in Bude, Alice Fisher. Or you can return to your family in Porthcurno while you recuperate and *still* make a difference to the war effort. It's up to you.'

'Blimey.' Alice clutched the envelope without opening it. There were tears in her eyes again. 'Sidney, Mr Rawlings . . . I don't know what to say.'

That was such a generous offer from George Cotterill, and one she hadn't been expecting. Indeed, it was hard not to imagine that her silver-tongued aunt had persuaded her friend Hazel, George's wife, to get Alice a place at Eastern House, so much closer to home. Still, she knew they rarely if ever took on female cipher clerks at

Porthcurno, which made it an even more exciting possibility and one she was sure she didn't deserve.

'No need to say anything yet.' Sidney rose, grinning. 'Let's get you settled back at Ocean View Boarding House first, shall we? I asked Mrs Miller to prepare dinner for you tonight. You can think about your options over the next few days, and then come back to let us know.'

Ocean View Boarding House lay at the far end of Downs View Road, with – as the name suggested – a glorious view of the Atlantic. The tall, attractive buildings with balconies and large front windows housed families as well as holidaymakers, and during the war some had gradually taken in foreign refugees and evacuees from London. Last year they had been home to the US Rangers, smart uniformed Americans soldiers who had swooped on the small seaside town in their hundreds, taking up every spare room in Bude and crowding noisily into venues for hot meals, social occasions and training sessions. Alice herself had shared her boarding house with about a dozen Rangers, all cheerful young men, who had taught her to dance to big-band music and slipped her cigarettes and mugs of homemade gin which tasted more like paint stripper.

She had not been the only female staying there, of course. There had been the widowed landlady, Mrs Florence Pritchard, now Mrs Miller, and Florence's vivacious younger sister, Imogen. Plus her own dear friend, Penny Brown.

Penny was a Land Girl who had come to Bude with her from Joe's farm, not just to keep Alice company in her grand adventure, but to seek a new life for herself too. And she'd found it. Penny had got a job at a shop in town where she'd soon met a young fisherman, John Pascoe, and the two were now engaged to be married. Penny had ambitions beyond marriage though; she'd left her shop job and taken on work at the local hospital instead. According to her frequent letters, she had swiftly risen to become receptionist there.

The boarding house door opened and her friend stood there, mouth curving into a broad smile. 'Penny!' Alice exclaimed. 'Oh, 'ow I've missed you.'

The two hugged, though gingerly, Penny careful not to knock Alice's hurt arm. Penny looked somehow older, even though they'd only been apart a few months. She was wearing her hair differently, no longer the casual style of her youth, but cut neatly with soft rolls over her forehead and framing her face. Her tidy, professional appearance was further enhanced by a brown linen skirt suit paired with a severe white blouse with wide lapels.

She was also wearing make-up, Alice realised with a start. A typical Land Girl, Penny had always refused to use face powder or lipstick except for special occasions, preferring a 'natural' look. And that choice had done her no harm in landing her a handsome young fisherman. But it seemed she had changed her ways since Alice's departure . . .

Seeing her staring, Penny blushed. 'I know, I probably

look like my mother,' she admitted with an awkward laugh. 'But the hospital likes their office staff to look smart.'

'Well, you certainly fit the bill.' Alice chuckled, and then turned to thank Sidney who had carried in her bags. 'You're a diamond, thanks. I'll come round tomorrow to talk about the job offer, all right?'

'We'll be busy tomorrow,' Sidney told her mysteriously. 'And the day after. So take your time, Alice. Understood?'

'Whatever you say, boss.' With a wink, she shook hands with him, and once he'd gone, closed the front door and smiled with relief at her friend. 'Oh, Penny . . . I've so much to tell you.'

'So it would seem.' Penny commented, her brows raised. 'Job offer?' she echoed curiously.

Quickly, Alice explained what Mr Rawlings had told her. 'Though I haven't read George's letter yet. So it might all be a misunderstanding.'

Penny was beaming though. 'What a brilliant opportunity for you. You'll be able to live at the farm and walk down to Eastern House every morning.'

'If I decide to go,' Alice pointed out.

'But why wouldn't you want to go home?'

'What will Aunty Violet and Uncle Joe think of me coming home so soon after leaving? I hate people knowing how badly I've failed.'

'Don't be such a goose,' Penny exclaimed. 'You're hardly a failure.'

Before Alice could explain any further, the door at the

end of the hall opened and Florence bustled out in a wide-skirted blue dress with her fair hair tidied away in a net. 'Come here, my poor love. Got yourself shot, didn't you? I was so shocked when I got Mr Rawlings's note.' After a gentle hug, the landlady studied her with kind eyes. 'It's good to see you back in Bude, Alice. I've given you your old room, and dinner will be ready at six as usual.'

'Thank you, Mrs Pritchard,' Alice said, laughing, and then corrected herself, 'Sorry, Mrs Miller.'

Florence had fallen head-over-heels in love with one of her own boarders, a US Ranger, Staff Sergeant Miller, and married him before the Rangers left Bude. It had been a whirlwind romance that had taken all of them by surprise. Penny had told an envious Alice all about the wedding service in a letter, about the guard of honour outside the chapel and Florence's lovely dress . . .

'I wish I could 'ave been here for your wedding day and wished you both well,' she added apologetically. 'But I sent a card.'

'And we received it, thank you.' Florence gave her a smile, but Alice thought she looked rather strained. Which was only natural, given that she had spent only a few days with her new husband before he'd been required to join the rest of the Rangers heading for their next top-secret location. 'Now, let me help you up with your bags.'

'I've got them, Flo,' Penny said, bundling the bags under her arm and starting up the stairs. 'You don't want to leave Billy alone too long.'

'Oh, he's with Imogen, bless her.' Florence glanced at Alice, no doubt noting her raised brows. 'My sister helps out with Billy far more these days. She's a changed woman.' She paused. 'Though Billy's in a bit of a lather today. Got out of bed the wrong side, I daresay.'

Right on cue, a high-pitched wail could be heard from the back of the house, and Florence blenched, hurrying away. 'We'll take extra care of you while you're here, Alice,' she called over her shoulder. 'And at least you won't be sharing the bathroom with a dozen American soldiers. Though we do have one American staying with us . . . Well, you'll see!'

With that, she disappeared back into the dining room.

'There's still an American here?' Alice turned to Penny in confusion.

'A woman called Pearl. She was one of the Donut Dollies, and an entertainer too, but chose to stay on in Bude when the Rangers left. She doesn't always eat dinner here but I expect you'll meet her soon enough.'

Alice nodded, though she still didn't quite understand. The Donut Dollies were a small group of women who travelled with the troops to hand out doughnuts and other sweet goodies, as the name suggested, but who also acted as good listeners to any homesick men, quite informally. Some of them were entertainers too, singing and dancing to keep the soldiers' spirits up as they prepared for war. So why would a Donut Dolly not simply follow the Rangers to their next destination? It seemed odd to her.

'Come on,' Penny said cheerfully, picking up her cases and leading the way upstairs. 'I'm glad it's mealtime soon. I'm famished!'

At last, Alice was installed in her old room, her bags on the bed ready for unpacking, and Penny had hurried away to wash and change before supper. She stood a moment looking out across the backyard and sunny rooftops of Bude, and then opened the letter George Cotterill had sent her.

It was indeed an invitation to the secret communications facility housed in the cliffs behind Eastern House in Porthcurno.

Last time she had worked there as a cleaner, alongside her mother and sister, mopping out the underground tunnels while important-looking men in suits and ties listened to enemy messages via a range of top-secret machines.

Now she was being asked by the government to undertake specialised training in codes and ciphers and help her country in its hour of need, no doubt because young men everywhere were still being drafted into military service and the unit at Eastern House was running out of recruits with the right skills.

Alice studied the letter a moment, then returned to the last few lines, curiously numb inside.

If you're interested, come and see me at Eastern House as soon as possible. I'd be glad to show you around the facility. I expect you remember most of it from your days working here. But we've made a few changes since your time.

I'm around most days, so just turn up whenever you feel healed enough for work again. We badly need people of your calibre. So I hope you'll say yes.

With my best wishes,

George Cotterill

Her aunt would have called such a letter 'flattering' and urged her to accept the invitation. In fact, after reading this letter, Aunt Violet would probably have marched Alice down there on the spot and made her say yes to George's face.

But things weren't so simple.

Standing in her old room in Bude, it seemed to Alice that she had come full circle, ending up right back where she'd started, and hadn't gained a thing through all those weeks of special training in London. Though she'd lost plenty. Her confidence, for starters. And her dear sweet Jim.

One of those was never coming back.

As she stooped to unpack her bags, Alice wondered if she would ever again be the confident young woman who'd left here with such hope in her heart. But would returning to Porthcurno and her Uncle Joe's farm hold the answers to that question? Or would she merely make a fool of herself by once again biting off more than she could chew?

Yet Alice already knew, even as she deliberated over those questions as though there was still doubt in her mind, what she was going to do. She would head back home to the quiet fields of Porthcurno and accept George Cotterill's mysterious invitation to visit him at Eastern House. Because she was Alice Fisher and she had never shied away from a challenge in her life.

Besides, codes and ciphers . . .

The idea of wrestling with complex mental puzzles excited her in a way that spy craft had never done. She'd always wanted to do her dad proud, to be a chip off the old block, bold and brave in the face of physical danger. But it was time she followed her own path through this war, and right now, it was a path that led to Porthcurno and Eastern House, back where it had all started . . .

CHAPTER FIVE

The bells were ringing for Sunday service as Imogen strolled up the leafy pathway to the church, glancing from side to side at gravestones, marking the final resting places of Bude residents going back generations. She had never enjoyed churchyards and church itself even less, though her parents had made both her and Florence attend every Sunday in their youth. Her parents were not particularly devout, of course. Indeed, she wasn't even sure her mother believed in God, though nobody would ever have discussed such a thing in their very conservative household. But church was where they met their neighbours after the service and exchanged gossip, and it would have been considered odd not to go. One of the great joys of finally leaving home had been choosing to lie in bed on a Sunday morning and listen to the distant ringing of bells without having to get up, dress smartly and make her way to the nearest church.

Now she was being forced to go through the old rigmarole. But for the sake of her country rather than to placate her traditionally minded parents.

Not that she had always been so unenthusiastic about attending church. Once, she had been very keen on all things ecclesiastical. Her heart sank and her cheeks flushed as she remembered those embarrassing days . . . All because of Simon, of course. His father had been the local churchwarden near where they'd been living in Exeter, a stern man with twin sons. Naturally, Simon and his brother – whose name she couldn't recall – had gone to church with their father every Sunday. And since Imogen, having reached a certain age, had found Simon's sandy good looks and broad chest irresistible, she had gone too, often wearing skirts so tight that her mother had despaired.

Imogen had been determined to pursue her new-found obsession, regardless of what people might say. For Simon had been three years older than her and therefore wonderfully exotic. Plus, he'd been spirited and exciting, and so handsome, she had barely been able to take her eyes off him. But Simon had barely looked twice at her, preferring to court Rosie Drayfield, a pretty young woman nearer his own age, and in the end, she had given up in despair. Then the family had moved away from Exeter, and the last she'd heard of him, Simon and Rosie had been engaged to be married.

Not long after, the country had begun to edge towards war, and fear of what lay ahead had taken over her thoughts.

'What's wrong with Imogen these days?' one of her mother's friends had queried, laughing, when young Imogen had uncharacteristically refused an invitation to a local dance.

But her mother had not laughed, for she'd understood. There was a war coming, and many of her friends would soon be signing up to fight, and might never come home. Imogen had been terrified that Simon would join them, along with all the other patriotic young men that they knew. And she had been right to fear for their safety, for many had never come back, and still the war raged on abroad, like a monster always just out of view, inexorably devouring the best and bravest of their generation . . .

'Good morning,' a cheery voice hailed her from the cool interior of the church porch, and she stopped, startled. 'Welcome to St Swithin's. I don't believe we've met.'

She stared at the young man past the wide brim of her hat, her heart thumping wildly. He was wearing a dog collar that proclaimed him to be the vicar. But that wasn't what had caught her attention. No, it was his voice and familiar accent that had stopped Imogen in her tracks, and the sandy fringe falling carelessly over his forehead, and a cluster of freckles about a generous, smiling mouth.

Good Lord, she thought, fighting a temptation to turn and run. She ought to have recognised the surname. But he was the last person she had expected to see here . . .

Thankfully, he mistook her shock and confusion for shyness. 'Newcomer to the parish? No need to worry, I'm fairly new myself. Only arrived in Bude a few months back and still finding my feet, to be honest.' A large male hand was thrust in her direction. 'I'm Reverend Linden. How do you do?'

Stepping closer, she took his hand and tilted her head so he could see her face properly. 'Simon?' she said huskily, meeting his eyes.

His blue gaze widened and fixed on her face. '*Imogen*?' But he shook his head before she could reply. 'Not Simon,' he corrected her, his brows tugging together in a pained way that she remembered with sudden, awful clarity. 'I'm Richard. His twin.'

'Of course. I'm so sorry.' Her smile was feigned, automatic. 'You look so alike. Exactly alike, in fact. As one would expect with twins.' She was rattling on to hide her emotions. With an embarrassed laugh, she released his hand at last, though this meeting was far from humorous. 'It's good to see you again, Richard. It must be four or five years since we last met. How have you been?'

Richard. That had indeed been the name of Simon's twin brother. The name she hadn't been able to remember. And he was the new vicar here? The man she had been sent to investigate?

Reverend Linden.

What an idiot she'd been not to recognise the surname on the information sheet. Though she could hardly have guessed it would be someone she'd once known. This was a long way from where they had grown up together in

Exeter, after all. And there had to be plenty of Lindens in the country.

'I'm very well, thank you, but the thing is . . .' Richard hesitated, still frowning, but before he could finish whatever he'd been planning to say, another man, tall and lanky, in drab ecclesiastical robes, appeared in the church doorway.

'We're ready to start, Reverend,' he said with an apologetic glance at Imogen. 'Excuse me, Miss. Sorry to interrupt.'

'Not at all,' she said politely.

Richard cleared his throat and nodded. 'Thank you, Andrew, I'll be right there.' The man disappeared with a nod, and he turned back to her. 'This is certainly a surprise. It's good to see you too, Imogen. But perhaps we could speak privately after the service, if you have time? The vicarage is only a few minutes' walk.' His eyes searched her face in a strange manner. 'There's something I need to tell you. Something . . . important.'

'Of course.' Imogen followed him into the church, sinking into one of the back pews with a grateful smile as though glad to be out of the heat and folding her hands in her lap.

To any onlookers, she would seem calm and unperturbed. At least, she hoped so. But inside, her senses were clamouring.

For an instant there in the church porch, she'd looked into Richard's light blue eyes and thought his twin, Simon, was smiling back at her. And her heart had leapt with irrepressible emotion, her nerves jangling madly, breath constricted.

She couldn't focus on the hymn they stood to sing, though she sang along with everyone else, her head whirling with confused thoughts. Bad enough that Simon was a married man now and not someone she could legitimately yearn for, but hadn't she moved past such childish attachments yet? Since her war work had begun, shrouded in secrecy, she had found it useful to act young and impulsive when trying to conceal her true motives. But inside she'd been sure of her maturity, convinced that she was long past her crush on Simon Linden. Wrongly, as it turned out.

Just as her breathing had begun to settle, Richard opened his sermon with a prayer for their Allied servicemen, and she was once more jerked into the past. His face was achingly familiar, his voice exactly how she imagined Simon's must sound now, warm and mellow, reaching out to her across the quiet space of the church . . .

As she listened though, she was surprised not only by how passionate he was in his beliefs but how deeply his sermon resonated with her.

In particular, she enjoyed his simple, common-sense advice on how to cope with the constant strain of being at war: turning to neighbours for help with everyday tasks, how to support a friend through a bereavement, and even a recipe he'd heard on the radio for easy beef brisket.

'But don't forget to cook the meat slowly, ladies,' he added with a twinkle in his eye, 'so it's nice and tender.'

After the service had finished, Imogen stood apart, pretending to study the lichened gravestones while covertly watching Richard as he waited at the church door to shake hands with his parishioners.

Was it really possible that Simon's brother was an enemy sympathiser? Someone must suspect him of being a traitor, or at least of harbouring such tendencies, otherwise she would not have been assigned to watch him. To her eyes, he showed no obvious signs of underhand behaviour. Indeed, he seemed equally friendly to everyone, speaking to every member of his flock as they left, even the elderly ladies who loved to stop and chat about the weather or nothing in particular.

But it was often hard to spot traitors in their everyday worlds, for they had learned or been taught to disguise their true selves, rather as she had done on first becoming 'watchful'.

The softly spoken Reverend Linden might appear perfectly ordinary on the surface. A typical young English vicar, in fact. But in private he might be keeping records on what he saw or heard about the town, perhaps even from those gossipy old ladies, afterwards relaying such information to those who wished to undermine the Allies. Even innocuous comments about a poor selection of meat in the butcher's shop, or the stringiness of their sausages, might provide useful insights for the enemy on how tighter rationing was adversely affecting the morale of British citizens, resulting in yet more bombing of supply ships and further loss of life.

There was a fresh-dug grave under the old wych elm. Imogen studied the gravestone inscription from a respectful distance, tears pricking at her eyes as she recognised his name, a local boy who had lost his life after volunteering to fight. She'd read about his death in the local news sheet and knew his family vaguely from around Bude.

'Poor boy,' Richard said, close at hand, his voice sombre. 'I officiated at his funeral last week.'

Imogen turned, surprised that he had managed to creep up on her unheard. She was usually quite good at being aware of her surroundings. But she'd been lost in her thoughts just then, remembering the old days . . .

'Shall we go?' He indicated the path out of the churchyard.

'How long have you been a member of the clergy?' she asked, falling in beside him as they walked towards the nearby vicarage. 'Forgive me, seeing you here was such a surprise, and you do seem young to be a vicar.'

'I'll be twenty-seven soon,' he murmured defensively.

'Of course.' She paused. 'I remember you being keen on church as a boy. But I didn't realise you were . . .' Her voice tailed off, hunting for the best words.

'One of the God squad?' He grinned at her embarrassed expression.

'So serious about religion,' she corrected him, adding hurriedly, 'No disrespect intended.'

'None taken. Though my father would tell you I only joined the church to avoid having to enlist,' he told her, his tone careless. But she wasn't fooled, recalling how unpleasant his father had been, a bully to his twin sons when they were growing up. 'I started training for ordination soon after I'd finished my theology degree, just before war broke out. I suppose the timing looked bad to him.'

'But how dreadful of him to say such a thing!' she exclaimed, scandalised. 'To his own son too. Besides, the army has chaplains. You could still enlist.'

'Quite,' he agreed, 'and I may try again soon.'

Imogen frowned. '*Again*?'

'My eyesight didn't pass muster, I'm afraid.' He withdrew a pair of thick-lensed spectacles from his pocket and put them on, his face instantly transformed to that of a thoughtful young cleric. 'They turned me down when I first applied, can you believe it? It's not as though chaplains are required to shoot straight, is it? But I've been told the recruiting office is getting desperate, so I might be in with a shout if I reapply.'

Remembering her mission, that she'd been assigned to monitor his attitudes and behaviour, she asked carefully, 'And will you? Enlist, I mean.'

He hesitated long enough for her to become suspicious. Or was he simply unwilling to fight for his country and trying to conceal it?

'Probably, yes,' he said reluctantly. 'The thing is, my mother hasn't been well recently, and with one son already headed for action, I thought—'

'I'm sorry, what did you say?' Imogen stopped dead, staring at him in dismay as she realised what his words meant.

A spasm of fear passed through her.

'Simon,' he explained, also stopping. His brows rose at her expression. 'Didn't you know? My brother was drafted last year and has just finished his basic training. So it's likely he'll be involved in the liberation of Europe in the not-too-distant future. Not that anyone knows anything for sure. It's all rumours and whispers, isn't it? But he'll be fighting at some point, and our mother is terrified, not to mention Simon's wife.' He paused. 'He and Rosie had a little boy, did you hear? Geoffrey. He'll be two years old in August.'

Everything inside her felt numb. So it was true. Simon had indeed married Rosie and now they had a child. How could she have been so stupid to think he would one day regret not courting her? Now he might die in the war and she would never see him again . . .

The vicarage was just ahead, a plain Cornish house but with a pretty cottage garden, bright with summer flowers. As they continued walking, Richard gave a gusty sigh. 'Truth be told, I'm terrified for Simon as well,' he admitted. 'But it has to be done, hasn't it? Fighting Germany, I mean. For the greater good.'

'For the greater good, yes,' she repeated automatically, her heart thundering.

He removed his glasses, peering at her closely. 'I say, Imogen, are you all right? You're looking peaky.' His face changed and he put a hand on her arm. 'I'm sorry if it shocked you, hearing about Simon like that. But everyone's joined up now, haven't they? Apart from men like me, of course, and the protected professions. I assumed you'd know he must be on his way to the front.'

'Yes, of course.'

But inwardly she was screaming. She had vaguely guessed that his brother, like most healthy young men in their mid-twenties, must have been drafted by now. But many had been training on home ground for months, not actually fighting, while those who weren't due to be shipped off to foreign climes had been left hanging about in British army camps instead, waiting for Churchill's big push against occupied Europe. The grim reality of the situation struck her now. Her handsome Simon, rifle in hand, would soon be headed for the front line . . .

Please don't let him die, she found herself praying fervently. *Please, if there is a God, don't let Simon die.*

CHAPTER SIX

Pearl had just grown accustomed to the extraordinary peace and quiet of life at Ocean View Boarding House in Bude when new boarders arrived and everything changed. One was a lively young woman called Alice Fisher, a friend of Penny's who she'd been told would only be staying a few days. But the other lodger was apparently a widower in his early forties with two young children who planned to make the boarding house his home for the foreseeable future, Mrs Miller had said. For a few days, she'd kept mostly to her room, but had heard the kids chattering and thumping up and down stairs, especially at mealtimes. She'd been avoiding taking an evening meal at the boarding house in order to save money, as she was still living off her meagre savings and hadn't yet found new work. But she knew she couldn't keep skipping meals for ever.

Early on the very same morning when Pearl had finally

plucked up courage to write back to her parents in the States and explain with sinking embarrassment exactly why she would no longer be getting married, she hurried down to take the letter to the General Post Office and stopped dead on the staircase, faced with a whole bundle of strangers in the hallway.

Heads turned, many pairs of eyes swivelling her way.

Continuing more slowly, Pearl finished buttoning up her cardigan against the stiff breeze that always seemed to accompany even the brightest sunshine on the Cornish coast, and forced a bright smile for them all.

Her 'entertainer's' smile.

'Why, good morning, everybody,' she said cheerfully, and paused to shake hands with the serious young blonde at the foot of the stairs. 'You must be Miss Fisher.'

'Alice, please,' the young woman insisted in a strong East End accent, her blue eyes steady on her face. Her handshake felt weak, but Pearl spotted her arm sling and recalled something about her having been 'wounded'. Had she been wounded in action? If so, she must be fearfully brave.

'And you must be Mr . . .' She tailed off as she turned to greet the man, unable to recall the name she'd heard from the landlady last week.

He was broad-chested, with short spiky dark hair threaded with a few silvery strands, wearing a smart suit and tie, and a brown felt trilby. As the landlady had said, he looked to be in his early forties, so maybe a little over ten years older than her. He struck her at once as being what her pop would call a 'character'. Not that she was basing that on anything other than the way he held himself and the jaunty tilt of his hat.

'Frederick Tyson,' he said, also in a London accent, though it was not as pronounced as Alice's. He shook her hand in a friendly manner. 'Though Freddy is good too.'

'Pleased to meet you, Freddy.' She nodded, beaming as she crouched slightly to say hello to his children. One was a girl with shoulder-length chestnut hair and a defiant expression, and the other was a younger boy with short dark hair like his father's and a nervous look in his eyes. 'And these two cuties must be your kids?'

'This is my daughter Clara, who's eleven,' Freddy Tyson said, putting his hands on the girl's shoulders. 'And her brother there is Toby. He's seven years old.'

'Oh, my cousin's name is Toby,' Pearl said at once, shifting to shake the boy's hand.

'You talk funny,' he said in a disparaging way.

'Toby, don't be rude,' his father said sternly.

'No, it's perfectly fine,' Pearl insisted, though her heart was aching again, for the mere mention of her cousin had reminded her of Chicago and her furious parents and the letter burning a hole in her handbag. 'You're not wrong, Toby. I talk funny because I'm from America, a country thousands of miles away. I hope you've heard of it.'

'Of course I've heard of it,' the young boy told her, his chin in the air, adding, 'Anyway, I thought it was the *United States of America*.'

'That is indeed its full name. The good ol' US of A.'

She straightened in surprise, seeing Penny pulling on her jacket behind Alice Fisher. 'Hello, Penny,' she said with genuine pleasure, 'I didn't see you there. Are you all off on an outing together?'

She had been out for a drink with Penny several times since moving into the boarding house, when her slender pay packet allowed. She found Penny a pleasure to spend time with, for she was both sweet-natured and plain-spoken. The young woman's conversation was mostly limited to her work – which was at the hospital – and her fiancé John, who was a local fisherman. But Pearl enjoyed a good chat about bosses and boyfriends as much as the next girl, and since she and Penny also shared a love of food, they had quickly bonded.

As an American living abroad and no longer travelling with the US troops she'd come over with, Pearl had not yet been able to arrange a ration book for herself. So money for food was tight. Penny had already invited Pearl to join her and her fiancé at his parents' cottage one evening for a 'slap-up' meal, which might include the special Cornish delicacy of 'stargazy pie' – whatever that was. But it sounded tasty.

'Nothing so exciting,' Penny admitted with a sigh, reaching for her hat. 'I'm going to work at the hospital.'

'And I'm walking these two rascals to school,' Mr Tyson said, hurriedly ushering his two kids out the front door. 'Then I'll be heading to the hospital myself.'

Pearl looked him up and down, surprised. 'The hospital? You look healthy as a horse, Mr Tyson.'

'Freddy,' he reminded her with a grin, closing the door behind her and Alice as they followed him out. 'I'm not ill. I work there, same as Penny.'

'He's a doctor,' Penny whispered confidentially as the man waved a hand at them and then strode confidently after his children.

'Oh my goodness. So he's *Dr* Tyson, not simply Mister?' Pearl was impressed. 'But what's he doing here? That accent . . . He's from London, isn't he?' She frowned, linking arms with Penny as they headed down the road towards the town centre, Alice walking quietly on her other side. 'I would have thought he'd have been snatched up by one of the big hospitals by now, given how desperate everyone is for trained medics.'

'It's a tragic story.' Penny lowered her voice, though Dr Tyson and his kids were surely too far away to hear. 'I heard he'd just qualified as a surgeon when war broke out. His wife was a nurse, working alongside him in a makeshift hospital in London.' Her sympathetic gaze met Pearl's. 'One night, at the height of the Blitz, they were both on shift when the building was bombed. His wife died and Dr Tyson's foot was badly injured. He has to wear a special boot now, he told me, otherwise he wouldn't be able to walk properly.'

'How dreadful, I would never have guessed.' Though he did walk with a bad limp, she realised, watching him turn the corner ahead. 'But those dear little lambs, losing their mother too . . . He's able to work though?'

'Oh yes. They say he's invaluable in the operating

theatre, not just as a surgeon but supervising the less experienced doctors too.'

Alice, who had been listening intently, asked, 'If he's such a bloomin' good surgeon, what's he doing down here in Cornwall? A bigwig like that . . . It don't seem right. Not when all the big hospitals are in London.'

'That's where it gets a bit horrid,' Penny admitted, lowering her voice. 'Apparently, he tried to go back to work in another London hospital after the bombing, but he couldn't even get through the doors.'

'Eh?' Alice's brows tugged together.

'He was so afraid of it happening again, he couldn't bring himself to pass the threshold,' Penny whispered, though the doctor was so far ahead, he couldn't possibly have overheard them. 'So he came down here to join his children. There's been so little bombing in this part of Cornwall, I suppose he feels safer here.' Penny pulled a face. 'Poor man. They say he still has the odd funny turn at the hospital if anything reminds him of the night it happened . . . That he's neither good to God nor men when he hears a plane go over, for instance.'

'Blimey . . . I've heard of that kind of thing.' Alice was staring out over lush green downs that ran alongside the road towards the sea, a strange look on her face. 'It's the trauma. Anything can bring it back. Noises, smells . . .'

Penny nodded. 'Anyway, while he was trying to get better, he came down here to be with his children. They'd been evacuated to Cornwall early in the war, you see, and were living on a farm down the coast. He heard they needed doctors here in Bude, so volunteered to take up a position locally and moved the kids here too. On the hospital grapevine they say he's got pots of money and is on the lookout for a nice home of his own, so I doubt he'll be staying at Ocean View for long.'

'Goodness, that *is* a sad story.' Pearl shivered, sorry for the hard-working doctor who had lost his wife. 'But Cornwall is a good place to heal,' she added, thinking back to how she had fallen in love with the stunning countryside and quiet leafy lanes soon after arriving here with the troops. 'I hope he can find some peace here at last.'

Penny said goodbye to Alice as they reached the attractive white façade of the General Post Office telephone exchange, which stood at the top of Belle Vue. 'I'll see you later, Alice,' she called out as the young blonde strode away in a purposeful fashion.

'Where's she going?' Pearl was surprised.

'Alice has business in town this morning,' Penny said mysteriously, shooting her a brisk smile. 'Well, here we are. Are you making an international call?'

She had dropped into the telephone exchange a few times to make international calls to her mother, to keep in touch with news from Chicago. 'Not today,' she admitted. 'I'm posting a letter to my folks back home.'

She had originally intended to speak to her parents on the telephone but had changed her mind at the last minute, scared of bursting into tears in such a public place if her mother or father spoke to her sharply or, worse, refused to speak to her at all.

Penny gave her a sympathetic look. She had spotted Pearl's unhappiness about the letter from her parents a few days ago, and after a little prompting, Pearl had poured her heart out to the other girl.

'It can't have been an easy letter to write,' she said quietly, and gave Pearl a quick hug. 'Good luck. I'd better get to work before I'm late.'

'Of course. Catch you later,' Pearl said airily, trying to appear unconcerned as she passed through the door, fishing in her handbag for the dreaded letter to her parents back home.

She had tried her best to strike the right note in her letter, but it had not been easy to stay calm and polite. She had hoped her parents would support her in her choice of future partner. And yes, perhaps they had been right to warn her against hurrying into marriage without proper consultation, since Terence had turned out to be a bad gamble. But to say she'd never be welcome home again . . .

Such cold disapproval had left her feeling depressed and unloved. But she had ended her own letter in a friendly spirit, hoping her parents would eventually change their minds. On reading that letter, they would know she wasn't getting hitched after all. Surely then they'd relent?

Having posted her letter to the States, Pearl strolled down Belle Vue in the direction of the hospital, her knee-length summer frock fluttering, one hand to her hat to prevent it blowing off. The Brits, she'd soon discovered, were forever complaining about their weather, and even when the sun finally came out, they would fuss and moan that it was 'too hot'. Personally, she rather enjoyed this unsettled coastal weather, for it reminded her of home. Though the breezes of North Cornwall could never compare to the cruel winds that tore through Chicago's narrow streets. It wasn't nicknamed 'the windy city' for nothing.

Terence would not be pleased by her visit. Nor did she want to see his face again. But she had to give him back the ring.

She had foolishly assumed it was an engagement ring, flashing it excitedly to all the other entertainers. Now she realised Terence had never actually asked her to marry him. It had been implied – that was all. The ring had merely been a gift to keep her happy, not a promise of marriage. If he hadn't landed in the hospital, in due course Private Gardiner would have gone off to the front with his fellow Rangers and never contacted her again.

It had all been a game to him; Pearl saw that now. But to her it had been deadly serious. She had imagined herself in love for the first time, and with a younger man too. Now she was horrified by how easily she'd allowed herself to be taken in. All he'd wanted was female company while he was away from home and his wife.

It was a lowering thought.

Next time, if there was a next time, she would be far more careful over who she let into her heart . . .

But when she reached the hospital, she found someone

new lying in Bed Ten on the men's ward. An old man, head bent, struggling with a crossword.

She faltered, peering up and down the ward. Most of the beds were still standing empty. Where on earth was Terence? Had he been moved to another ward?

'Can I help you?' A nurse was standing behind her.

Startled, she whirled, eyes wide. 'Pardon me, but I . . . I'm here to visit Mr Gardiner. He's usually in Bed Ten. Has he been moved?'

'Terry? Oh, he's a darling. I've seen you visiting him before, haven't I?' The nurse gave her a sympathetic look. 'Didn't he tell you? What a naughty boy . . . You've missed him by minutes.'

'Pardon me?'

'He was discharged this morning. In fact, the ambulance just left for the airfield at Jacobstow. Since he was out of danger, the US Army are flying him to one of their own bases to finish his recovery there.' She studied Pearl with a curious smile. 'That accent . . . You're a Yank too, aren't you?'

'Y-yes,' she stammered before fleeing the ward in confusion. 'I'm sorry to have troubled you.'

Feeling lost and lonely, Pearl only managed a few steps away from the hospital before stopping abruptly.

What was she supposed to do now?

Taking Terence's ring out of her pocket, she studied it hopelessly. If only she could have given it back to him, it would have felt like an end to this horrible business. Instead, she was stuck with both his ring and the memory of her foolishness.

She couldn't even post the ring back to his folks in the States. Terence had never told her whereabouts he lived. In fact, he had told her very little about himself. She'd thought her fiancé shy. Or perhaps she'd feared to look too deeply at his motives, already twenty-eight, ecstatic at having finally found a man who thought highly enough of her to offer marriage.

Her, Miss Pearl Diamond, a good-time gal with a smile for every soldier. A Donut Dolly, entertainer to the troops . . .

Her vision blurred and Pearl bowed her head, weeping softly. What a dupe she'd been. Now she wouldn't even have the satisfaction of throwing his ring back in his face.

'Hello,' a man said behind her. 'Miss Diamond, isn't it?' When she straightened, scrubbing at wet cheeks, he frowned and produced a large white handkerchief. 'Please, take it.'

'I've got my own,' she mumbled, and withdrew her own daintier hanky from her handbag, dabbing at her face in embarrassment. 'But thanks.'

A quick sideways glance confirmed her suspicions. It was Dr Tyson, her fellow boarder at Ocean View. He was no longer wearing his hat and jacket, but looked very smart and professional in a white doctor's coat.

'Forgive me if I'm interfering,' Dr Tyson said. 'But you seem very upset. Is there anything I can do?'

'That's very kind of you,' she said, hurriedly putting away the ring. 'But no, I don't imagine so.'

More sobs shook her, despite her resolve to be more stoical.

Dr Tyson steered her towards a nearby bench outside the hospital entrance. 'There, there, sit down and have a good cry . . . Let it all out.'

Pearl sank onto the bench, weeping, and gulped when he sat down beside her. She had hoped he would soon dash off about his medical business once she'd given him the cold shoulder, not sit next to her in the shade of this tall, leafy beech tree. Instead, far from seeming annoyed by this interruption to his working day, the doctor sat back and crossed his legs, waiting calmly.

'Now, Miss Diamond, once you're ready, why don't you tell me all about it?'

Pearl dabbed at her eyes, feeling uncomfortable. She was a private person at heart and she barely knew this man. 'Is this a professional consultation, Doctor?' she demanded.

'Hardly,' he said in his deep, confident way. 'I'm simply stopping to spend time with a fellow traveller, that's all.'

'A . . . A *what*?' She glanced up in surprise, meeting the doctor's eyes, and found them a warm smiling hazel, flecked with green. It was hard not to look away once their gazes had locked.

'A fellow traveller on life's journey. Sometimes the road forks unexpectedly and we need a little help to get our bearings again. Don't you agree?'

He had lost his wife tragically, she recalled with a start. That was what Penny had told them on the walk into town. His hospital in London had been bombed. *His foot* . . . She tried to prevent herself from looking down at his heavy boots, but couldn't quite manage it.

Frederick Tyson chuckled again and held up his left boot. She hadn't noticed the thick boot in the dim hallway of the boarding house, but she saw now that it was clearly built up higher than the right one. 'Yes, I lost part of this foot in a hospital bombing.' His smile faded. 'And my dear wife Angela at the same time. It was a terrible blow and I doubt I shall ever get over it. But life isn't always fair, is it? We survivors can only grieve and acknowledge our losses before moving on.'

We survivors. He seemed to be including her in that grouping, wrongly. She was hardly a *survivor*. She had not been hurt or bombed or lost someone beloved. Not yet, at any rate.

He caught her confusion and added gently, 'These tears didn't come out of the blue. I thought you already looked unhappy when we met this morning. As though life had dealt you a blow too.'

She stared, shocked at how quickly he had read her after one brief meeting.

'But however severe this blow might feel,' he went on calmly, 'it hasn't destroyed you. You're not dead. You have a pulse, and I'm willing to bet it's a strong one.' He brushed her hand, and his touch sent a shock through her. 'In my book, that makes you a survivor, Miss Diamond.'

'Pearl. That's my real Christian name.' She folded her handkerchief, pushing it back into her handbag. 'Diamond is only my stage name.'

'And I'm Freddy, remember?'

'Freddy,' she repeated shyly, nodding.

A smile lit up his face. Yet still he waited, eyebrows raised. 'Now we've got that sorted, what's made you so miserable? Tell me to mind my own business if you prefer. I won't be offended. But telling your troubles to a doctor is akin to confessing to a priest, you know. You can say whatever you like and I won't breathe a word to another living soul. Or judge you for whatever has happened, if that's what you're worried about.' He paused. 'A problem shared is a problem halved, they say.'

Looking into his kindly, understanding eyes, Pearl instinctively trusted him. And sure enough, she soon found herself pouring out the whole humiliating truth about Terence and his glib, self-serving lies and half-truths. She expected the doctor to exclaim in disapproval and walk away, especially when she admitted to having spent more time alone with the young man than was entirely respectable, even in these wartime 'anything goes' days.

Instead of condemning her naivety, however, Freddy merely nodded and listened to her sorry tale, his expression impassive.

'In other words,' he said eventually, 'you trusted the wrong person and he betrayed you. That's a deep wound. Deeper even than this, perhaps.' He glanced down at his built-up boot, his face sombre. 'But here's the thing, Pearl . . . That experience will have taught you something important.'

'Yes,' she agreed bitterly, 'I've learned not to take people at face value. Not to be so trusting. To never get taken for a ride again.'

His smile was crooked. 'That wasn't what I meant. You were in love with this young man?'

Pearl felt heat creep into her cheeks at this highly personal question. 'Yeah, I guess so. More fool me.'

'You can't be a fool where love's concerned. When you love someone . . . that's special. That's you opening your heart to another human being. Even if that person doesn't deserve it and never loves you back, you can't be hurt by that experience. Not deep down in here.' He tapped his chest. 'You learned something about the nature of love by trusting that young man. Now you need to keep that inside you and let the rest go.'

She didn't really understand what he was saying, but felt the truth of it somehow. It touched her heart. 'Thank you,' she said huskily and sat a little straighter.

'You're welcome, Pearl.' Freddy stood up. 'Now I'd better get back to work before they send out a search party for me. It was nice speaking to you.' And with that, the doctor smiled and walked away.

CHAPTER SEVEN

'You're quite right to go back to the farm, Alice,' Penny assured her as they stood waiting for the train on the busy platform at Bude. 'Besides, the work you've got lined up there sounds frightfully exciting.' She glanced about first to check nobody else was listening. 'Breaking enemy codes?' she whispered. 'If I'd been offered such an opportunity, I'd have gone in a heartbeat.'

'Hush,' Alice warned her, wishing she hadn't told her friend about George's letter. Penny could be trusted – she knew that. But discussing such things in public still made her anxious. 'Loose lips sink ships, remember?'

'Sorry,' Penny said guiltily.

John, Penny's fiancé, who'd also come to see Alice off on the train, had clearly overheard this exchange, despite their whispers. 'I hope you don't mean that, my lovely,' the fisherman murmured in his drawling Cornish accent, slipping an arm about his fiancée's shoulders to soften his words. He had a charming smile and used it to good effect, adding, 'I might have something to say about that, if you were to up and leave me before we're even wed.'

'Don't be a goose, John,' Penny told him with an affectionate smile and seized Alice's hands. 'You will come back to Bude though, won't you? You're to be my bridesmaid, remember? You made me a promise, Alice Fisher,' she said mock-sternly, 'and I intend to hold you to it.'

'Ouch, that hurts,' Alice mumbled.

'Sorry.' Hurriedly, Penny released her. 'I'd forgotten about your arm.'

'Of course I'll come back for your wedding. When is it again?'

Penny's brows soared as she repeated the details. 'I expect you could stay at John's cottage the night before.'

'No room. Most of our blessed family will be pitching up to this wedding.' John grimaced at Alice apologetically. 'Hope you understand.'

'I'm sure the boarding house will have room for me. Or I can kip on someone's sofa.' The train was chugging into the station with a cheery whistle, its large red engine wreathed in clouds of white steam. Her heart thumped wildly as she hugged Penny one more time, and John too, and then gathered her bags, beginning to panic. 'Well, goodbye. Let's hope I ain't forgotten nothing, eh?'

Once it was safe to board, Penny and John helped her into the carriage with her bags, and there was yet more hugging on the steps.

'I don't know why I'm crying,' Penny moaned. 'Not when we'll see each other again so soon.'

'I don't know why either.' But Alice was also wiping her eyes.

She hated goodbyes, and had refused to allow Florence and Imogen to walk with her to the station. Penny and John, however, could not be put off so easily. But then, she and Penny had been friends for ever so long. When Penny had met John in Bude and the two had become engaged, Alice had been thrilled for her. It was all rather romantic, she thought, her eyes misty as she waved at the couple through the carriage window, almost falling over when the train jerked into motion at last.

Ignoring the curious looks of her fellow passengers, Alice sat down and rummaged through the bag Florence had given her on the doorstep. Paste sandwiches, an underripe apple, and five ginger snaps wrapped in brown paper. Crunching on a ginger snap as the train began to gather speed, she peered out at glorious Cornish countryside through thinning steam. Woods and lush meadows flashed past, and once a herd of cows toiling up a steep field in a long line. She tried to relax and enjoy the scenic journey, but her mind was crowded with nervous thoughts and fears.

Had she made the right decision to go back to Porthcurno?

Well, it was too late now, she told herself prosaically. She was on the train. But she couldn't help wondering where her father was, at least, and if he knew what had happened to her in London. Not knowing was part of the war though. She would have to be patient.

As promised, Uncle Joe and Aunty Violet were waiting for her at Penzance railway station. Uncle Joe, a man of few words, said nothing but held her tight, which brought a lump to her throat. Aunt Violet also hugged her, which was tricky, due to her large bump.

'Blimey,' Alice said without thinking, gazing in awe at her aunt's protruding belly swathed in floral fabric, 'you're enormous!'

'Lord bless you.' Violet laughed, thankfully not offended by this candid remark. But then, she'd had years to get used to her youngest niece's abrupt manners, Alice thought unhappily, wishing she could curb her tongue like others did and say the right thing for once. 'The baby's due soon, ain't it?'

'Though not yet,' Joe chipped in nervously.

'Not for another few weeks at least.' Violet pursed her lips. 'Joe was moaning all the way here, worrying I might have the bloomin' thing in the car.'

'It happens,' Joe muttered to Alice as he carried her bags to the van. 'I knew a lady once who gave birth on a hay wagon.'

'Oh hush,' his fond wife told him.

On the drive back to Porthcurno, all three squeezed onto the bench seat in the front of the van. Violet kept up a steady stream of chatter, mostly village gossip. But

Alice didn't mind not chiming in except to exclaim, 'You don't say?' occasionally when necessary. She'd already told them everything – or as much as she was allowed to divulge under the Official Secrets Act, at any rate – in her recent letter home. So there wasn't much to add.

Besides, it was soothing to listen to her aunt nattering on while Joe diced impassively with death through single-track Cornish lanes.

Back at the farm, her sister Lily was waiting in the kitchen, having just arrived off the bus from St Ives with her husband Tristan. But what drew Alice's eye first was the red-cheeked, ginger-headed cherub in Lily's arms, who gurgled and constantly waved his tiny fists like a prize fighter hunting for an opponent.

'Is this Baby Morris?' When Lily nodded with maternal pride, Alice bent to peer at him. 'Blimey, poor little scrap . . . He's as ginger as a tom cat. And look at them ears!' she gasped. 'Why, they're as big as the handles on Gran's old Toby jug.'

Everybody laughed at this, except Tristan, who complained there was nothing wrong with his son's ears and, anyway, generously sized ears were a 'family trait'. Which made everybody turn to stare at *his* ears and laugh even harder, until Alice felt tears prick at her eyes. But they were tears of joy.

Lily, handing the baby to his father, hugged her tightest of all. Her sister's flaxen hair ticked her nose, and all the squeezing gave Alice a momentary twinge of pain, but she didn't mind. It was worth it to be reunited with her family at long last. In fact, she hadn't realised how much she'd missed them until now.

Lily studied her sling with a frown. 'Got yourself shot, I hear. That was silly.'

'Painful, too,' Alice agreed, grinning. 'Though getting shot makes you popular. While I was in hospital, I got double rations of cake every day.'

'That's because of how brave you were, taking a bullet for your country,' Tristan said. Handing his baby to Aunty Violet like a parcel, her brother-in-law stepped forward for his own hug, mercifully gentle. 'Good to see you again, Alice. Lily was beside herself when she heard you'd been shot. It was all I could do to stop her dashing off to London on the next train to fetch you home herself. But that would have meant leaving me with the baby . . . and that's never wise.' She guessed that was meant as a joke, though the Cornishman didn't smile, looking at her sombrely. 'You lost a friend that night, I believe.'

'Yes,' Alice admitted, her voice hoarse, and dropped her gaze, staring down at the cracked tiles of the farmhouse kitchen floor instead.

Jim, she was thinking, that beloved name right there on the tip of her tongue. Yet she couldn't bring herself to say it out loud. Not even here, surrounded by her nearest and dearest, her own flesh and blood. It would hurt too much, she realised in shock, beating back a wave of sorrow. It was as though she'd been suppressing those emotions, desperate not to *feel*, but now she was home, his name was like a gaping hole in her chest. Another gunshot wound, only this time to the heart . . .

'I'm sorry for your loss,' Tristan told her.

Somehow, Alice managed a smile for him. Her brother-in-law had curly ginger hair like his baby – though rather more of it – and an irrepressible toothy grin. Still, he was quieter these days, compared to when she'd first met him and his sister Demelza in Penzance, where they'd been living on their dad's sheep farm.

Tristan had gone away to do his basic training and come back to Cornwall with severe burns. Looking at him now, strong and vital, his shirtsleeves rolled up, his handsome face freckled by the sun, a stranger could never guess at the debilitating scars that Alice knew must lie beneath his clothes.

Unable to serve in the army, Tristan worked for the Fire Service in St Ives, a seaside town on the west coast of Cornwall where he and Lily lived in a pretty cottage. He seemed to be a wonderful husband to her sister, and by the way he'd been cuddling the baby, a good father too. Though no doubt Lily, an experienced midwife, had taught him how to handle a baby as soon as Morris had been born.

Gran bustled into the kitchen, wearing her apron, carrying a tray of empty jars ready for jam-making, and gave a shriek on seeing her.

'Come to your old gran, pet,' she exclaimed huskily, and once again Alice found herself bundled into warm arms and held tight. 'Gawd, you're skinny as a rake. Didn't

97

they feed you in London? Sit down and I'll cut you some fresh-baked bread. And a slice or two of cold meat to go with it. Yes, you may well look amazed. We've cold meat in the house. And none of your chewy mutton either, thank you very much.' Her gran winked. 'Ox tongue, no less. I've still one jar of pickled eggs left in the pantry too. Bloomin' delicious!'

Within minutes, Alice was tucking into a generous sandwich of ox tongue with pickled eggs, a steaming cup of tea in front of her, and all the family gathered around to watch this miracle that was Alice-come-home-wounded.

'Now you're back in Porthcurno, what are your plans?' Tristan asked.

'Leave the girl alone – she's only been home five minutes.' A gnarled hand dropped onto Alice's shoulder and she felt a reassuring squeeze from her gran. 'Plenty of time to make plans once she's settled back in, eh?'

'I've had an offer from Mr Cotterill,' Alice said bluntly.

'Oh gawd, not again,' her aunt muttered, sinking into the seat opposite. No doubt she was recalling the last time their old boss George Cotterill had turned up at the farm with an 'offer' for Alice. That had been at the end of last summer, and the letter he'd been carrying had taken her away from home and family to the spy craft training unit in Bude. And look where that had landed her, Alice thought bitterly. 'All right, spill the beans, love . . . What kind of offer?'

'A job,' Alice said, shifting uncomfortably under her aunt's scrutiny.

'From George Cotterill?' Gran came round to stare at her too, arms folded over a generous bosom. 'Not another blessed cleaning job, I hope? Because he knows where he can stick his—'

'Gran!' Violet exclaimed, looking scandalised.

Gran rolled her eyes. 'All right, keep your hair on. I was only goin' to say mop.'

'What kind of job, Alice?' Lily prompted her gently.

Alice blew out her cheeks, feeling outnumbered. 'I won't be mopping the floor this time, Gran. So you can stop frettin'. Mr Cotterill thinks I might do well as a cipher clerk.'

'What's one of them?' Gran had wrinkled up her nose.

'Well, it's . . . It's top secret,' Alice mumbled.

'As I understand it,' Tristan said slowly, 'a cipher clerk is someone who writes down and deciphers coded messages. Including messages from the enemy, I'd guess.'

'Blimey!' Gran stared. 'Ain't that a bit above your pay grade, love? I mean, we all know you're a bloomin' smarty-pants. Sharp enough to cut yourself, to be honest. But what do you know about enemy codes and whatnot?' She looked troubled. 'Only fancy if you was to get one of them messages writ down wrong? You might send all our soldiers off in the wrong direction. It don't bear thinking about.'

Alice tried to stay patient. 'Mr Cotterill says I'll be given training.'

'Sounds like an excellent idea,' Joe said solidly, who hadn't spoken before. He reached across the table to shake

Alice's hand. 'Congratulations. I daresay Mr Cotterill knows his business better than any of us. You'll do a bang-up job, Alice.'

There was a short silence as everyone digested that.

Violet stood up and began clearing Alice's cup and plate. 'Joe's right, Mum,' she told her mother firmly. 'George knows what he's doing.' She gave a sudden gurgle of amusement, shaking her head. 'I remember once, we got sent to mop out the tunnels behind Eastern House, and saw all them posh machines for top-secret messages. Do you remember that day, Lily? We couldn't make head nor tail of all them buttons and dials, could we? Like a wireless set, only for people with ten bloomin' arms.' She pursed her lips. 'George would never let our Alice loose on all that expensive equipment without proper training, would he?'

'Oh well,' Gran muttered.

A strange humming came to Alice's ears, the walls of the old farmhouse vibrating . . .

'What on earth . . . ?' Dubiously, Joe looked heavenward, as though he could see through the ceiling. Then he limped towards the back door and went outside.

Lily had gone pale. She clutched her baby son to her chest, her gaze shooting to her husband. 'Oh, Tris. You don't think . . . ?'

'Engine note's wrong. Those are our planes, not the Germans.'

With a start, Alice realised what they'd heard. A fleet of British bombers were flying overhead through the quiet

Cornish countryside. Excited to see them, she jumped up and, with the others, hurried out into the farmyard to stare up into the blue summer sky. Startled, the hens scattered underfoot, and one of Joe's working dogs barked, earning a stern look from its master.

'Gawd, will you look at that?' Gran murmured behind her.

'It is quite a sight,' Tristan agreed softly.

Lily came to stand beside Alice, her baby son cradled against one shoulder, and reached for her hand. 'You all right, sis?'

'Don't you worry about me, Lil.' Alice felt her heart begin to beat more quickly as they both stared skywards. 'I'll survive.' She caught the brief glimpse of a face in one of the cockpits as the vast planes banked right. 'Them boys are bloomin' brave though, don't you think?'

Their vast metal wings glinted in the afternoon sun, taking up the whole sky, or so it seemed to her. They were flying very low, though admittedly Joe's farm was high up on the cliffs above Porthcurno. She watched in surprise, but supposed that low flying must be part of their training.

'Lancaster bombers,' Joe remarked, staring wistfully after them as the planes swung out across the sea in formation. 'Aren't they magnificent? Lucky lads . . . What an honour it must be to pilot them.' With a shake of his head, he gave a low whistle as the last plane vanished into sun haze further down the coast, no doubt heading for an eastern airbase closer to London. He banged his stick against the rough ground of the farmyard, frustration in his face. 'I swear, if I hadn't lost my leg . . .'

'You've done your bit, Joe,' Violet reminded him, and he slipped an arm about her waist, drawing his wife close.

'I suppose so,' he agreed grudgingly. 'All the same, it's at moments like this when I wish—'

'You're not alone in that thought,' Tristan interrupted tersely, and the two men exchanged a speaking glance. 'The invasion of Europe must be near. I feel it in my bones.'

Joe nodded his agreement, still staring narrow-eyed down the coast, though the Lancaster bombers were long since lost to sight.

Both men had enlisted and come home seriously wounded, unable to return to active duty. But Violet was right, Alice thought, watching them with sympathy. They had done their bit for king and country. Nobody could ask for more of a sacrifice than they had already made. Besides, there was plenty to do here in Cornwall for ordinary civilians, and not just men who couldn't go to war. Women had been pulling their weight across Britain, and it was time for *her* to do her bit again too.

When she'd been sent to London, she had hoped to work for British Intelligence eventually and be sent undercover behind enemy lines like her brave dad. Only she'd been wounded in the line of duty, like Joe and Tristan, and that dream was over for her. She could still continue the fight against Germany though, just in a different capacity.

It would not be easy. She still woke sweating and afraid some nights, remembering the flash of a gun in a dark alley. Back in London, holding Jim's hand and watching the light go from his eyes, his blood on her hands, she had thought it was all over for her. That she would be too scared to face active service again and should go home instead, shamefaced and with her tail between her legs. But seeing those marvellous bombers pass overhead, perhaps on their way to attack enemy gun emplacements on the French coast, she knew she couldn't still stand idly by while others did their duty for Britain. Not while she still had breath in her body and a skill she could use to protect Britain.

'Anyway,' she said, to nobody in particular, 'I'm going to say yes to George. I'm going to accept his offer and start my training at Eastern House. Even if I do make a few mistakes and send our submarines to the bloomin' North Pole by accident or translate all them German messages into gobbledygook.'

Her sister had been listening, at least.

Lily squeezed her hand. 'That's my girl,' she told her fondly, her eyes misty. 'You'll be brilliant, Alice. You always are.'

On the morning of the sixth of June, Alice woke early for some reason, as light was only just creeping over her windowsill. After getting dressed, she slipped out of the back door and wandered down the lane towards the quiet village of Porthcurno. The white edifice of Eastern

House, a stately country house draped in camouflage, stood silent in the softly spreading dawn light. Its grounds were protected by barbed wire and guard posts, occupied by soldiers in tents and makeshift barracks, while communications personnel toiled night and day in tunnels hidden behind the house, tunnels dug deep into the cliffs long before Alice and her family had even arrived in Cornwall, deciphering and sending top-secret encrypted messages. Indeed, the only reason she knew the secrets of Eastern House was because of her early days there as a cleaner, when she had signed the Official Secrets Act like everyone else, swearing to protect her country by keeping that dangerous knowledge to herself.

The villagers knew it was a government installation, of course. With all the soldiers constantly coming and going, what else could it be? But few knew exactly what went on behind its barbed-wire fences.

The Germans also knew of its existence. Thankfully though, they had not managed to pinpoint its exact location so far. They had tried bombing various spots along the coast, but had always missed Porthcurno itself. One terrible night in the summer of 1941, they had come closest to hitting it, but had bombed Joe's farm by accident instead, and his mother had been killed.

For a long time, Joe had blamed Violet for his mother's death, a whisper having gone around Porthcurno that she was secretly in league with the enemy. A ridiculous lie, but it had persisted because of Alice's German father whom everybody had presumed dead.

Ernest Fisher might have been working undercover behind enemy lines, but in Dagenham, where they'd lived before the war, many had presumed Alice's dad to be a spy for the other side. One day an unpleasant young man from Dagenham had pitched up at Porthcurno as a soldier and started spreading rumours about them. So when Joe's farm was bombed, fingers had pointed accusingly in the family's direction. Thankfully, all that nonsense had been resolved, and Joe and Violet had eventually married.

As she watched, a lanky, dark-haired figure emerged from the back of Eastern House, where the secret tunnels were located, and strolled onto the brief patch of lawn while smoking a cigarette.

Alice stilled, sure she recognised him even at that distance. It looked like Patrick. Her old team-mate from the Bude unit. They'd trained in spy craft alongside each other until an incident had seen Patrick sent away to specialise in codes and ciphers, while Alice had been dispatched to London to join the team there. She'd forgotten that he'd ended up at Eastern House.

Odd that he was there so early though. The code clerks must have been working through the night on something special, she guessed.

'Alice?' Startled, she turned to see Joan at the top of the lane. The Land Girl's voice was high and breathless, as though she'd run all the way from the farm. 'Come, quick!'

Alarmed by her tone, Alice toiled back up the steep track as quickly as she could. 'What is it?' She wondered if Aunty Vi had finally gone into labour.

'Your aunt's been looking all over for you. You'd better come in and listen to the news. There's a special war report due any minute . . . They just announced it on the wireless.' There were tears in Joan's eyes. 'Oh, Alice, I think something big has happened.'

CHAPTER EIGHT

Bude, North Cornwall, June 6th, 1944

Imogen bent her head, listening intently to the man on the wireless. In the sunny dining room at Ocean View Boarding House, the breakfast table stood empty, plates and bowls abandoned. Everyone was gathered around the radio instead, nursing cups of tea and listening to the well-modulated tones of the BBC radio newsreader as he informed the nation that a successful assault had been mounted on the beaches of Normandy early that June morning.

It had been a little after eight o'clock, while the guests had been eating breakfast, that the first announcement had come. Paratroopers had landed in northern France, though details had been scant at that stage.

The breakfast room had fallen silent at that news, their lively chatter dying away. Knives and forks had remained poised as they all stared at each other, astonished.

'Good grief,' Penny had muttered.

'What is it, Daddy?' Clara had asked from the next table, her eyes wide, looking about in surprise.

'Hush, sweetheart,' Mr Tyson had said, giving her hand a reassuring pat. 'We're listening to the news.'

The Bakelite radio set had originally sat in the back snug, rather smart against the dark wood panelling in that room. But her sister Florence had carried it through into the dining room a few weeks ago, concerned they might miss some important development in the war effort. Now the wireless was on almost non-stop during the day.

'I like having the wireless on,' Flo had said after Dr Tyson complained about the constant noise, for the BBC broadcast music as well as news and other shows, such as the regular cookery slot that helped householders manage to produce tasty meals on bare rations. 'You never know what's going to happen, do you? It's best to keep up to date.'

Imogen had noticed her sister was far more worried these days about how the war was going, studying the daily newspaper with close attention and often hurrying home from the shops simply to catch the latest bulletin from the front. Florence was afraid for her new husband, of course. Which was only natural, given that she'd lost her first husband, her darling Percy, in the early years of the war.

Staff Sergeant Miller was stationed somewhere with the US Rangers, probably Kent, and it was common knowledge that the Americans were preparing to launch an attack on France alongside other Allied troops. Why else would the Rangers have been training all winter in their quiet seaside town, scaling rugged Cornish cliffs and fighting mock-battles on the beaches, except in readiness for the liberation of France?

They had all been hanging on so long, Imogen had almost given up hope of hearing good news about the war.

But it seemed something major had happened at last . . .

The grown-ups had gathered about the wireless, leaving the children to finish eating, the need for them to head off to school quite forgotten as the newsreader went on with his announcement.

The BBC were giving little away of what might lie ahead for the Allies – the enemy must be listening too, after all – but the news report fired them all with the same burning spirit of excited patriotism, nonetheless. Germany's star had been in the ascendancy far too long, a powerful, well-equipped empire, holding all the advantages, terrorising innocent people and subjecting a broad swathe of countries to ruthless military domination. Now their own small island nation was bravely fighting back, along with her allies around the world, and the next few days might decide the outcome of the war.

But if they'd expected to hear exactly what was happening far away across the English Channel, they were disappointed. Following that short, electrifying announcement, the BBC began to play stirring music.

'I'm late for work,' Penny said in a shaky voice, glancing at Florence. 'I only hope that . . .' But she didn't seem able to finish that thought, leaving without another word, but with an apologetic look.

Florence was too agitated to have even noticed Penny's departure. She was combing her fingers through her fair hair in a nervous manner, her chest heaving, her gaze wide and fixed on nothing.

'Still hungry,' her young son Billy remarked, eyeing the leftover crumbs on his plate.

'Sorry, darling? Oh, you . . . you want more bread and jam, is that it?' Perhaps hoping to distract herself, Florence hurried out to fetch another thin slice of bread smeared with butter, and dabbed half a spoonful of jam over it on her return. She also brought back a jug of hot water to freshen the teapot, which had gone cold while they were listening to the wireless.

'The children must go to school and I'm late for work,' Dr Tyson said at last, getting reluctantly to his feet. 'Won't do for the nurses to go in while the doctors stay idly home.'

At that moment, another special bulletin was announced.

Imogen, pouring more tea for herself and Florence, glanced over her shoulder at the clock on the mantel. It was half past nine.

Dr Tyson sat down again, his expression tense.

'D-Day has come,' the BBC newsreader John Snagge told them with undisguised excitement, and Imogen's heart leapt at those momentous words.

D-Day.

'Oh goodness!' Florence's hand crept to her mouth and her skin was now as pale as wax.

D-Day was the code that had been bandied about as being the day when the Allied forces would finally attempt an invasion of France. People had been talking about this planned invasion for weeks, even months. Even the BBC had been mentioning it more frequently in recent days, causing a buzz of anticipation among the British public. Warnings had recently been broadcast to any French citizens living close to the northern coast, telling them what to do in the event of an invasion, which had excited everyone, as it suggested that Allied troops were finally ready to cross the Channel. Yet so many days had passed without fresh information, Imogen had long since stopped expecting to hear anything new.

The newsreader went on in the same level tone, calmly explaining how British forces along with the help of Allied forces, including the Americans, under the leadership of General Eisenhower, had mounted an assault on the beaches of northern France early that morning.

The newsreader continued to outline how Allied naval and air forces had begun landing troops on the coast of France. As more details gradually emerged, it was soon clear that the fightback against Hitler was indeed underway at last. If they were ever to turn the tide on Germany and win the war, Imogen thought, today must be the beginning of that arduous process . . .

Florence gave a sudden sob and dashed from the room, hiding her face behind her hand.

Perplexed, Billy stopped chewing his bread and stared. 'Wass matter, Mummy?' he called after her in his high-pitched voice.

Quickly, Imogen turned off the wireless, fearful there might be some mention of casualties. That was the last thing any of them needed to hear. Not today, at any rate. Today was a time for them to *hope*.

With a determined smile, she scooped up her nephew and gave him a cuddle. 'I think Mummy was going to sneeze – that's all,' she fibbed, not wanting him to be upset. 'Don't worry, Billy. I'm sure she'll be back soon.'

'Mummy sneezin'?' Billy beamed with relief at this explanation. 'Aitchoo!' He pretended to sneeze too. 'Aitchoo!'

'Bless you,' Dr Tyson told the little boy, but his own smile looked forced. 'Remind me, Imogen . . . Your sister's husband is with the US Rangers, isn't he?' When Imogen nodded stiffly, he sighed. 'I'm sorry to hear that.'

His young son Toby tugged impatiently at his hand. 'Can we go now, Dad? The vicar's visiting the school today to teach us about chess and I don't want to miss the start of his lesson. Apparently, he's a chess whizz.'

'Also, we'll be punished for being late,' his daughter Clara pointed out, looking worried.

The doctor was contrite at once. 'Of course. We'll leave straightaway. Though I'm sure the teachers will understand you being late, today of all days.' Dr Tyson turned to

Pearl, who'd been sitting still and silent since the first announcement had been made. 'Forgive me, but are you feeling all right, Miss Diamond?' His eyes were full of concern.

'Sure,' Pearl said softly, and got to her feet, gathering up their teacups and saucers. The platinum blonde had spoken calmly but her face was pale, her eyes shining with unshed tears. 'Thank you for asking, Dr Tyson. This is a difficult time for everyone, isn't it? It's the waiting that I can't handle. I'm afraid we may have lost many brave souls today. All those guns on the French coast . . .'

Her voice faltered on those words and she hurried after Florence, carrying breakfast things into the kitchen even though it wasn't her place to clear the table. She was a paying guest, after all. But perhaps having something to do would help her cope, Imogen thought, looking sympathetically after the American.

Following his children to the door, the doctor glanced back at Imogen. 'A difficult time indeed. I know you'll be wanting to comfort your sister today but could you check that Pearl is all right too?' He paused. 'The thing is, I expect the US Rangers Second Battalion will have been heavily involved in this invasion force, and she knows many of them by name. Some of those young men fighting on the beaches of France may even be good friends of hers.' He sounded regretful, his expression grim.

'Of course I'll check on her too,' Imogen assured him, surprised by how solicitous he was being towards the American, whom he barely knew. Though no doubt being kind was part of his job as a doctor. 'You'd better go to work. I expect the hospitals will be very busy soon.' That sounded rather more sinister than she'd intended, Imogen realised, grimacing at her own insensitivity. 'Sorry.'

She'd heard from Penny that beds at the hospital had been standing empty for some weeks now, as non-urgent patients were being sent home wherever possible, leaving room for more serious casualties to be tended. Cornwall was far west of the Channel ports, yet it was widely believed that casualties from the invasion force would be sent to hospitals all around Britain, due to the very high numbers of injured personnel expected to be shipped home once the assault had begun. Which was a daunting thought.

'No, you're quite right.' Dr Tyson pulled on his jacket with a frown. 'Poor blighters. Well, let's see what the rest of the day brings . . .'

Feeling duty-bound to check on the other two women, Imogen popped her head around the kitchen door to find her sister and Pearl deep in conversation over the washing-up, and decided to leave them to it. They were probably better able to commiserate with each other than she could, after all, and she could always talk to Florence later, while they were preparing dinner together.

Heading out into the hall, she found Dr Tyson ushering his children out of the front door while the two kids squabbled, hitting each other with their school bags. He didn't seem to be paying much attention to them, still

114

frowning, his expression distracted. No doubt the doctor had more serious matters on his mind after this morning's broadcasts and was itching to reach the hospital.

A thought occurred to her. *The vicar* was teaching them about chess today, the boy had said. He must mean Richard, surely?

It was too good an opportunity to miss.

Imogen dashed forward with a smile before they could leave. 'Dr Tyson, why not let me walk the children to school for you today?'

He looked taken aback. 'That's very kind, but I couldn't possibly—'

'Honestly, it's no trouble. I'm going that way myself.'

It was only a little white lie, she told herself, and for a good cause. After all, it was her mission to keep tabs on the new vicar. Which would mean going to church more frequently than before as well as attending any local events where he might turn up and talk to other Bude residents. A necessary part of her task, even if tiresome.

She wasn't particularly religious but she knew the church had become even more vital to this little seaside community since war had broken out. Especially now, for with so many women working towards the war effort, days off school had become a trial for those also needing to keep children occupied outside school times. She could even volunteer to help out with the children's church club. That would give her a plausible excuse to watch the vicar without arousing his suspicions.

'In that case, thank you.' Dr Tyson followed his daughter

out to the garden gate. 'Miss Crombie will be walking you to school today,' he explained, and stooped to warn his young son, 'Best behaviour, yes? No running ahead.'

'We don't need a grown-up to take us to the school,' his daughter insisted, shooting Imogen a resentful glance. 'It's not far and we know the way.' Despite being only eleven, she was clearly a very independent young lady. The doctor had his hands full there, Imogen thought with secret amusement.

'I'm sorry if I offended you, Clara. I was rather hoping to speak to the vicar about helping out with the church club, as I don't know the lady who organises it.' Imogen gave the girl an encouraging smile. 'You go on Saturday mornings, don't you?'

'You want to meet the lady who runs the church club? Her name's Mrs Priestley,' the boy chimed in, his face brightening. He took her hand as Dr Tyson opened the garden gate to let them out onto the street. 'She's not a bad sort,' he added in a conspiratorial tone. 'But she does have funny teeth that stick out like this.' And the boy drew back his lips to make his front teeth more prominent.

'Oh dear, poor lady,' Imogen said, trying not to giggle.

'Toby!' His father exclaimed. 'What did I tell you about being on your best behaviour? It's rude to talk about other people behind their backs, young rascal, as well you know.' Catching Imogen's eye, the doctor burst out laughing. 'I'd better go before these two embarrass me any further. If you're sure you can cope with them?'

'I'll be fine,' she assured him, and grinned at her new

companions. 'You'd better lead the way, then. Since you two are the experts.'

Her luck was in. As they approached the school gates along with a few other latecomers – it was clear that quite a few children had stayed home that morning to listen to the special news bulletins – she caught sight of Richard chatting amiably with a heavy-set gentleman in an elderly tweed jacket with leather-patched elbows, his hair Brylcreemed to a high shine. One of the teachers, she rather suspected.

Letting the children run through their respective school entrances – one for Girls, the other marked Boys – Imogen hurried forward with a smile and outstretched hand.

'Reverend Linden,' she exclaimed, pretending to be surprised. 'How lovely to see you again. I've just walked my friend's children to school . . . Isn't it wonderful news about the Allied forces? Perhaps the end of the war is in sight at last.' She also shook the bemused other man's hand. 'Hello, I'm Miss Crombie.'

'Hello,' the man said gruffly. 'Mr Featherbright, Science Master.'

'So pleased to meet you.' She turned back to Richard, still beaming. 'I'm so glad to have bumped into you again. I meant to ask you about volunteering.'

'I'm sorry?' Richard looked blank.

'For the church club. You must need volunteers, especially with the summer holidays coming up soon.'

'Oh . . . Yes, of course. We always need volunteers.' He blinked, and she got the impression he was thinking fast. 'That's awfully kind of you. Perhaps I could ask you to come along on Saturday morning? I'll introduce you to Mrs Priestley who runs the club for me. It's held in the hall near the church.'

'Of course,' she agreed, but injected a pleading note into her voice, 'though it's only Tuesday today and there was something else I needed to talk to you about. Perhaps we could meet up before then?'

She glanced at the leather briefcase he was carrying, which no doubt contained his chess equipment and guides to technique, and then at the school buildings. 'Are you here in your official capacity today? How delightful. I do approve of the church taking a lively interest in education.' She paused. 'Do you need a helper? I could tag along . . . Carry your bag, perhaps?'

This lame excuse simply to keep an eye on him had sounded better in her head. Heat entered her cheeks in the short silence that followed. The two men looked at her in astonishment, as well they might. But to her relief Richard was already nodding.

'That's most kind of you, Imogen, thank you.' He gave the perplexed teacher a reassuring smile. 'Miss Crombie and I know each other. We went to the same school for a while.'

'I see.' Mr Featherbright scratched his head. 'Well, in that case, I'd better show you both inside. We assembled our most promising chess players in the hall some time ago, but things have got off to a slow start this morning. All the excitement of this news of an invasion, as you say, Miss Crombie.'

'Quite,' Richard agreed, suddenly sombre. 'I could barely tear myself away from the wireless. May God preserve those brave souls.'

Heart thumping at her own audacity, Imogen tagged along behind as the two men entered the school. They were shown into an assembly hall where a group of children sat cross-legged in front of a long table where three chessboards had been set out as though for demonstration purposes, all the pieces lined up neatly on the correct squares. Among the younger children, Imogen spotted Dr Tyson's son, Toby, a look of eager anticipation on his face.

Richard put down his briefcase to shake hands with the two teachers who had been waiting with the children, apologising profusely for the delay.

While the teacher was addressing the children, Richard turned to her, saying in a conspiratorial whisper, 'To be honest, I'm thankful you're here, Imogen. I'm not as good with children as I ought to be. It's part of a vicar's job to be on easy terms with everyone, young or old, rich or poor. But, to be frank, children terrify me, especially in large groups like this. They're always so loud and ask such impertinent questions . . . At church club last week, one of them even asked whether I wear my dog collar in bed.' He flushed, clearly horrified. 'I'm awfully sorry. Please forget what I just said.'

'And do you?' she asked.

His embarrassed gaze swivelled back to her face. 'Do I what?'

'Wear your dog collar in bed.'

'Goodness me.' Looking baffled, Richard peered at her and then gave a low chuckle. 'Oh, I get it. You're trying to distract me, aren't you? So that I won't be so nervous...' He fiddled with the dog collar in question, the white clerical band at his neck that denoted his calling as a vicar. 'Excellent job, Imogen, I must say. I'm definitely, um, *distracted*.'

His name was being called, she realised, but he hadn't noticed.

'Reverend Linden,' she hissed. 'That's you.'

'Hmm?' He was still staring at her, his air vague. Perhaps he needed his spectacles just to find his way around, she thought, suppressing an urge to laugh.

'Reverend Linden,' the teacher repeated in a booming voice, and signalled him to step forward before continuing, 'Children, I'm pleased to introduce our new vicar. I've been told he's an expert chess player and will soon have you all opening your games in a winning manner.'

'Not... Not an expert, exactly,' Richard muttered under his breath, but turned to face his audience with a benevolent smile that transformed his face. 'Good morning, children.'

'Good morning, Reverend Linden,' a dozen young voices chorused, gazing up at him in wide-eyed expectation.

'It's g-good to see so many of you here today,' he stammered, clasping his hands nervously before him, 'keen to learn more about this great game. I've been told you all know the basics, but put your hand up if you've ever actually *won* a game of chess?' With a gulp, he cleared his throat as many hands shot up. 'Ah, most of you? That's excellent. Yes, indeed.'

As he struggled on through his introduction, Imogen was surprised by how hard he was working to appear friendly and put the children at their ease, given he'd just privately admitted to finding them difficult to handle in a group. Some men might have come across as brusque and unapproachable in such an uncomfortable situation. But he was a vicar, as he'd said. It was his duty to make everyone feel welcome and part of the community. All the same, she found herself impressed by Richard's determination to push past his apparent nerves and do a good job.

At last, he moved to the first chessboard on the table, frowning down at the pieces. 'Erm, let's start with a few opening moves, shall we? Now, let me see . . .'

Well, Imogen thought, handing over his briefcase when requested and smiling secretly to herself as he ummed and ahhed his way through the next hour, if Richard *was* an enemy sympathiser, he was unlikely to be a terribly effective one.

Not unless he was also the world's finest actor.

CHAPTER NINE

As that eventful morning wore on, Pearl sat drinking coffee with the landlady – who was drinking tea, of course – as they listened to the wireless in the dining room, hoping for further bulletins about the ongoing assault on the Normandy coast. But there was precious little information after that first startling announcement that the Allied Forces' 'big push' against occupied Europe had begun. It seemed to Pearl that the newsreaders were merely repeating the same report in their well-to-do British voices, with occasional tweaks or interesting comments from military spokesmen. Nonetheless, it gave both women relief to keep listening, trying to decide how the 'invasion' was going, while struggling not to imagine what was happening on that heavily fortified coastline so far away . . .

'I'm sure they'll be fine,' Florence insisted for the umpteenth time, stirring the dregs in the bottom of the teapot as though this would make her next cupful look more appetising. 'They're all so well trained.'

'Sure,' Pearl murmured, not believing a word of it.

She sipped her weak coffee, her attention only half on the wireless, currently playing big-band music, her head somewhere in northern France, where all those young men she'd travelled alongside for months, entertained and sung for, danced and laughed with, might even now be dying in a hail of machine-gun bullets or being bombed to bits as they assaulted gun emplacements. Her whole being flinched from the thought. Yet there was no point pretending they would all come back. Even the most headstrong and bravest of the Rangers she'd met on army bases and the road had known that was an impossibility. This past year, American boys had grown used to prefacing their future dreams and plans with: 'If I get home,' or 'If we make it through this war,' while pushing aside the reality that faced them. Because what else could they do?

'War is hell,' she added bitterly, without meaning to. 'Hell for our men, hell for us.'

'Yes,' Florence agreed with a broken sob.

'But we didn't have a choice, did we?' Pearl's heart squeezed in pain at how much Florence was suffering. Gently, she reached out to touch her hand, giving it a reassuring pat. 'Not with that Adolf Hitler acting like a schoolyard bully, only with guns and tanks instead of sticks and stones. Someone had to make a stand and stop him.' She finished her coffee with a grimace. It tasted nothing like the strong black brew she was used to back home. But it was better than endless cups of tea. 'All we can do is pray for our boys and hope for the best.'

'Yes.' The landlady blew her nose and looked away.

Florence's son Billy, who looked about five years old, was sitting at the dining room table with them, colouring in a picture with wax crayons, apparently not listening either to their conversation or the wireless. But he glanced up at the heavy drone of planes overhead. 'Wassat?'

Florence dashed to the window but returned slowly. 'Only our planes, dearest,' she told her son, and ruffled his hair. 'You keep drawing – there's a good boy. Meanwhile, it's washday, so I should get on and sort out some laundry. All those brave soldiers may be storming the beaches of Normandy, but sheets and towels still need to be washed. Life must go on.' Again, she stifled a sob, gulping hard. 'For some of us, at any rate.'

'Need a hand?' Pearl asked, getting to her feet.

'Goodness, no.' Florence looked horrified. 'You're a guest here, Pearl.' She forced a smile to her lips. 'Besides, my son will help me, since Imogen's gone out. Won't you, Billy?'

Billy glanced from his mother to his crayoning, clearly less keen on laundry than drawing, but nodded obediently. 'Washday,' he chanted.

'Let me rinse these cups for you, at least,' Pearl insisted, and cleared the table, carrying their tea and coffee tray back to the kitchen as Florence hurried upstairs to fetch down the laundry basket.

Later, setting out rinsed cups and saucers on the draining board, Pearl heard the familiar drone of airplanes overhead again and glanced out through the net curtains, catching sunlight glinting on a wing.

'Them air force boys sure are busy today,' she murmured to herself, wondering how many were bound for the Channel, summoned to provide further air cover for the Allied invasion force. Or to bring back wounded, perhaps.

As she grabbed a tea towel and began drying the cups and saucers, her mind drifted from the horrible thought of casualties being flown back to Britain to the possibility of them arriving at the cottage hospital in Stratton where Dr Tyson worked. And then to the doctor himself, though she had not purposely intended to think about him. Nor did she know why her mind had drifted to Freddy Tyson, because he certainly wasn't her 'type'. He was nothing like Terence Gardiner, for instance. She tended to find men in the armed forces more interesting than other men, perhaps because of their smart uniforms or because they were so brave. It might be superficial to enjoy the company of men in uniforms, but there was something about a soldier . . .

Besides, Freddy was a fair bit older than her, and she preferred younger men. He was also broad-built, with short dark hair that stuck up in places, giving him an odd, rough appearance. His looks weren't those of a typical doctor – that was for sure. In her experience, medical experts in hospitals were well-dressed, distinguished-looking gentlemen with aloof manners and what the British would call a 'plummy' accent. Freddy had a strong London accent and a casual way of speaking. But he'd known just how to comfort her outside the hospital the other day, without being awkward or preachy about the situation, and he was clearly skilled at putting people at their ease.

After finishing her task, she went upstairs to fetch her handbag, and then put on her coat and hat before heading out into town. Everyone she passed in the street looked either shell-shocked or excited, which was hardly surprising, given the news from the front. The Allies were finally pushing back against the enemy in German-occupied Europe and nobody was quite sure what the next few days would bring. As for Pearl, she herself hardly knew what she was doing or where she was going, but at least her feet seemed to know, as they steered her automatically out of town towards the small village of Stratton and the cottage hospital . . .

There was an odd hush at the hospital, nobody in sight in the lobby, the corridors empty. Pearl hovered in the entrance lobby, feeling awkward and uncertain. For a moment, she considered backing out and heading home again. It wasn't too late to change her mind . . .

But from her seat behind the receptionist's desk, Penny spotted her and pushed aside the paperwork she'd been frowning over. 'Hello,' she said in her usual friendly manner. 'What can I do for you, Pearl?' Her voice sharpened in concern. 'Don't tell me you've gone and hurt yourself?'

'I don't really know why I came here, to be honest.' Pearl felt bashful. 'But I think, after the news this morning, I should probably offer my services as a hospital volunteer. It's quiet now but you'll need extra help soon, I daresay.'

'Oh, rather! All hands on deck, as John would say,' Penny agreed. Her smile faded, though, as she indicated the paperwork she had been studying. 'We've just received advance notification of fresh supplies on their way to us. We only have a handful of patients on the wards, yet we're being allocated hundreds of rolls of crêpe bandages, vats of silicon powder for dusting wounds, and all these needles for stitching . . .' She looked pale, her eyes wide. 'I won't lie. I'm worried about what's ahead.'

'It gives me the heebie-jeebies too. But I wanna do my bit.' With a determined smile, Pearl took off her hat and glanced about the deserted hospital lobby. 'Please, put me to work. I don't have any medical training. But give me a mop and bucket, and I'll have this place sparkling in no time.'

'That's the problem,' the other girl exclaimed. 'Everything's been cleaned and prepared three times over. And the wards are mostly empty, so there's nothing much to do. Though we've been warned to expect a first wave of casualties soon.' Her voice dropped conspiratorially. 'Maybe the day after tomorrow. I've been told that once our side has managed to capture the Normandy beaches, the most seriously wounded will be treated in field hospitals on the French side or shipped straight back to Dover. We'll only get the less urgent cases here in Cornwall, plus the long-term wounded.'

Pearl digested that information. 'So I should come back in a day or so?'

'That sounds about right,' Penny agreed, handing her a fawn-coloured form. 'Fill that out and bring it with you next time. That way you'll get paid. It's not much but it should cover your bed and board at Ocean View.' Pearl gave her an embarrassed smile. 'None of my business. But I couldn't help overhearing you talking to Florence the other day about your money situation.'

'I've applied for a temporary residency permit,' Pearl told her, 'but it takes a while to come through.'

'Meanwhile, you don't have a ration book, yes. That must be hard. Especially now that Terry's gone home.' Her voice tailed off as Pearl's eyes filled with tears. Penny bit her lip, coming round the desk to hug her. 'I'm so sorry. What a crashing idiot I am. I swear, I'll never mention his name again.' Her chest heaved in indignation. 'Though I must say, John and I both agree he deserves a good boot up the . . . Well, I said I wouldn't mention him again, and I won't.' She let out an exasperated breath. 'I'm just glad I got one of the good ones.'

She was talking about her own fiancé, John. Pearl had met him a few times since moving to Ocean View, where he was a frequent visitor, and she thoroughly approved her friend's choice of future husband. In fact, she couldn't imagine a nicer beau for Penny to marry.

'You sure won the jackpot with John.' Pearl smiled. 'Where is he, by the way?'

'He went out fishing on the *Mary Jane* a week ago.

Though I've heard all boats are being ordered back to shore after this morning's news. The coastguard aren't taking any chances.'

'In case of retaliation by the enemy, you mean?' Pearl gave her friend a return hug. 'Oh, honey, he'll come back safe to you, sure as eggs is eggs.' Though inwardly she too dreaded what might happen to any British fishing vessels spotted by enemy planes or submarines now the invasion had begun in earnest. 'Your John's got true grit.'

'He better had come back safe.' Penny gulped, drying her eyes with the back of her hand. 'We're due to be wed soon. The church is booked and my parents are coming to stay at Ocean View. So heaven help him if John gets himself killed before our wedding day; that's all I can say.'

Pearl had to chuckle at her fierce expression. But before she could say anything, she spotted Dr Tyson heading their way. At first glance, she didn't recognise him, for he looked aloof and professional in his white doctor's coat, a stethoscope hung about his neck. But his intent stare gave him away.

However much authority that white coat gave him, underneath he was still Freddy, the friendly, easy-going man who had comforted her after Terence had broken her heart. Confused by this thought, Pearl found herself backing away, even bristling . . .

This man had the oddest effect on her. She'd always been good at reading people. But Freddy Tyson was a mystery to her. She wasn't sure she should trust someone whose motives she couldn't pin down. Yet here she was, volunteering for work in the one place where she knew she would have the chance to see him every day, as well as every evening at the boarding house. That couldn't be a coincidence. Oh, the workings of her mind were quite unfathomable sometimes . . .

'Miss Diamond,' Freddy said, frowning as though displeased to see her. 'I trust you haven't had an accident? Or feel unwell?'

'Pearl has come to volunteer as a hospital orderly,' Penny explained briefly, collecting up her paperwork. 'Sorry to dash off, but I have to take these up to the office for the hospital supervisor to sign. See you both at dinner?'

Left alone with the doctor, Pearl studied the notices on the wall rather than looking at him directly. As an entertainer, she was accustomed to speaking to all kinds of people and very rarely felt nervous in social situations. Yet something about Dr Tyson had her tongue-tied and stammering as she replaced her hat and said hurriedly, 'I . . . I should probably head off too. You must be busy, Doc.'

'Not yet,' Freddy said with a crooked smile, and inclined his head. 'Would you mind coming with me? If you have a minute, I'd like to show you something.'

Reluctantly, she followed him down a bewildering succession of corridors and through a side door into a small circular garden with climbing roses and a wooden bench.

'Shall we sit?' he suggested, and she sat down meekly

enough, for she had walked a long way that morning and her feet ached in her black heels, which were eye-catching and glamorous, but more suited for performing on stage than trekking several miles across town in full sunshine.

Dr Tyson sat beside her on the bench, settling back with a smile. 'Pretty, isn't it?' he said softly, watching her. 'I stumbled across this rose garden the first day I arrived at the hospital. It's a good place to come when things are going wrong in there,' he added, indicating the hospital walls behind them with a jerk of his head, 'if only to clear my head for a few minutes and breathe fresh air instead of disinfectant.' He paused. 'I thought you might appreciate it too.'

'Yeah, it's swell,' she agreed, though she wasn't feeling very relaxed. It was hard to focus on anything but his face when they were sitting so close together. But when a bird came to perch on the wall, pouring out sweet notes as it sang, Pearl gave a delighted sigh, closing her eyes to listen. 'Oh, how lovely.'

They sat without speaking for a while, then the doctor cleared his throat.

'Forgive me for being personal,' he said, 'but I couldn't help noticing how upset you were during that special news bulletin earlier.' When she said nothing, he murmured, 'I believe the US Rangers formed part of the Allied invasion force who crossed the Channel this morning. Is that right?'

Mutely, she nodded, not trusting herself to speak

without dissolving into tears. She wasn't the sort of gal who could readily cry in front of other people. Besides, she didn't want this man to think she lacked gumption.

'I'm sorry,' he went on in his calm, professional way. 'It's been a difficult day for all of us. But far worse, I imagine, for those with loved ones and friends on the front line, and no way of knowing how they're faring.' He took her hand in his, and she did not protest. It was only a friendly, comforting gesture, after all. 'I perfectly understand you wanting to help in any way you can. It's a human instinct and I salute you for it. But any Tom, Dick or Harry can do the work of a hospital orderly. Are you sure your particular skills won't be wasted here?'

She looked him in the eye, not bothering to hide her anguish this time. 'I need to do *something*, Doc,' she whispered, 'or I'll go plum crazy.'

'Of course, and I wouldn't dream of trying to stop you.' He was still holding her hand. 'But maybe we can find some more appropriate work for you.'

Pearl was confused. 'Appropriate how? I'm not trained as a nurse,' she told him, adding hurriedly, 'though I'm willing to learn, if someone can be spared to show me the ropes.'

Dr Tyson laughed, finally releasing her hand. 'I was thinking more of your skills as a singer and dancer, Pearl.'

'Excuse me?'

'The hospital is likely to be overrun with wounded servicemen soon, shipped back from France. Morale may be low, especially if things haven't gone well today. So they're going to need cheering up. In fact, we all will. How better to keep our spirits up than by putting on a show, right here in the hospital? Something for the wounded to look forward to, not to mention the staff.' He paused. 'What do you think?'

Her mind was reeling as she realised what he was suggesting. It was a wonderful idea, but she could instantly see the flaws in his plan. 'I want to help but I'd have to plan out my own routine and I . . . I've never done that before. In the troupe, a trained choreographer would always give us the dance moves for each performance.'

'I have faith in your abilities.'

Pearl smiled, though she didn't share his calm air of confidence. She had never planned her own routine before, and had always sung and danced with others, so had no experience of performing solo. Could she even manage to hold an audience's attention on her own for more than five minutes? A show was usually at least an hour long . . .

'That's mighty kind of you,' she said shyly, 'but it's not the only hiccup. Without music, I'm not sure how it could work. When me and the other gals were entertaining the Rangers, you see, we always had a big band to back us up. And a microphone too.' She chewed on her lip, considering the problem. 'At the very least, I'd need a pianist.'

'Leave the music to me,' he said smoothly. 'Those problems aside, will you do it?'

He had a persuasive way about him she thought. There

didn't seem much to say except 'Sure thing, Doc,' though she was still concerned about the details. 'I'm happy to help the war effort in any way I can. If that means singing and dancing for wounded soldiers, I'm game.'

'I knew I could count on you.' There was approval in his smiling eyes as he got to his feet. 'Look, I'll let you know more once our first patients begin to arrive. Meanwhile, try not to fret about the invasion. I know it's the hardest thing in the world, but there's nothing we can do except wait . . . and hope for the best.'

As Pearl made her way back to Bude, the sunshine seemed a little warmer than it had been before, the world somehow brighter. The salt breeze off the Atlantic Ocean that snatched at her dress was suddenly refreshing rather than bracing.

She stopped for a delicious ice cream wafer on her way home, trying to cheer herself up, the news of the invasion still weighing heavily on her mind. All the same, she no longer felt as cold and alone as she had done only a few days ago.

She might have said goodbye to all the handsome Rangers and the other entertainers in her troupe, and her family might have turned their backs on her in disgust, but at least she'd made new friends here. There were people in Bude she could turn to when things looked bleak, and that was going to make all the difference.

CHAPTER TEN

Two days after the excitement of D-Day, Alice combed her hair, put on a smart tweed skirt and blouse she'd bought in London, and strode down the hill from Joe's farm into the village of Porthcurno. At the barbed-wire fence by the guard post, she showed her identity papers and waited to be escorted up to Eastern House. Trudging up the steep path to the big white house, she glanced about herself in a covert fashion. The place seemed essentially unchanged. Yet everything felt very different compared to two years ago when she, Violet and Lily had worked there as cleaners alongside Hazel, now Mrs George Cotterill.

She recalled Porthcurno as a quiet, idyllic spot on the Cornish coast, boasting a beautiful stretch of white-blond sands that lay only a few hundred feet from Eastern House, reached via a shady track through a copse of softly rustling trees.

The beach and woods were still as lovely as ever, of course. But there was an air of urgency to the site these days, soldiers marching about at the double, orders being shouted, and a siren going off somewhere in the distance, its alarm muted. Given the momentous world events of the past two days though, that was hardly surprising. 'The cat's among the pigeons now, and no mistake,' Joe had muttered as they stood about the wireless on D-Day, listening avidly to the news bulletins and Special War Reports as they flooded in during the day, unable to believe their ears. 'Now we'll see some changes.'

Win or lose, the Allies had made their big push into Europe at last. Now everyone back home could only hope for the best while preparing for the worst. Which in Gran's case meant endless wailing and weeping into hankies over the lives being lost on the beaches of northern France, and for Aunty Violet entailed collecting ingredients for a fresh batch of cakes and biscuits to donate to the hospital in Penzance, 'for when the wounded arrive, poor souls.'

Solemn-faced, Tristan had whisked Lily and Baby Morris back to St Ives, for all firemen and other auxiliary volunteers would be called on for extra duties now, in case of enemy strikes, and his job was coordinating the rotas.

Alice and Lily had hugged tightly in the farmyard, knowing it might be a long time before they saw each other again. 'Take care of yourself, little sis,' Lily had whispered in her ear, and Alice had felt a tear slide down her cheek, choked up and nodding. She had hoped they would have more time together. But it seemed the war had other ideas . . .

George Cotterill himself came out to shake her hand at Eastern House, greeting her with genuine enthusiasm. 'It's good to see you again, Alice, even if you're looking the worse for wear,' he said, nodding to her sling. 'So you got my letter . . . I hope you've come to offer us your services and not turn me down?'

'I won't turn you down, Mr Cotterill.' Alice gave him a wan smile. 'It's this or work on the land up at Joe's farm,' she said jokingly, though they both knew that wasn't true. She could have been teaching new recruits in Bude, passing on everything she'd learned in London. But the pull of home was strong since Jim's death, and this felt like the right choice. The only choice, in fact. Still working for the government but staying close to her roots.

Perhaps it was cowardice, she thought. The fear of being shot again, maybe killed next time. Or perhaps it was common sense, knowing her own limitations. Either way, she had chosen Eastern House, and didn't want to let the side down by making a mess of things again.

'Come on,' George said, 'let me introduce you to the men you'll be training with.'

George Cotterill led her around the back of Eastern House and through the checkpoint into the secret tunnels dug deep into the cliffs.

They passed several new checkpoints to get there, which showed how important security had become on this top-secret base. Inside the tunnels, everything looked –

and smelled – much as she recalled. She wrinkled her nose, remembering the soda crystals they'd used in their buckets of foaming hot water, and the slopping of the wet mop over concrete floors. Though the listening station had more personnel today than she remembered, many of them hooked up to complicated machines in the monitoring room, headsets on and pencils in hand, clearly intent on whatever messages they were intercepting.

'This way.'

They threaded through more narrow tunnels to a side room where a group of men sat with heads bowed over strips of paper, scribbling with pencils and arguing with each other. The room fell silent as she followed George inside, and the men all looked round, surprised. Two of them even stood up, chair legs scraping noisily, and Alice blushed, realising they'd only got to their feet because of her. As though she was a proper lady, for goodness' sake . . .

'Blow me,' one of the younger men said with a sly grin, leaning back in his chair to study her. 'George has got a girl in tow. How extraordinary!'

'Behave yourself, Jenkins,' one of the older men told him sharply, and the young man fell silent. 'Pay no attention to him, Miss,' he said, shooting her an apologetic smile. 'His father spared the rod and spoiled the child. As we have daily proof, unfortunately.'

She surveyed the room, quickly sizing up the men there and storing away their details for later analysis, as she had been taught. They were all dressed in a similar fashion to George, with tweed jackets and white shirts and dark ties, and several of them had cigarettes on the go, the room thick with smoke. Public school boys, all of 'em, she thought, her heart sinking. She'd have her work cut out trying to fit in with this toffee-nosed bunch.

With a quelling glare at the young man who'd spoken so disrespectfully, George introduced her to the group, and then went around the room, giving her their names in return. Surnames only, she noted. Tomlinson, Jenkins, Blenkinsop, Crowley, Smith, and Hurst. Some of the men smiled back at her as their names were called, though Jenkins, whose fair hair was slicked back from his forehead and who had a narrow face with a pointed chin, merely sneered.

The man who had greeted her as 'Miss' was Hurst. He was in his late fifties, silver-haired and distinguished-looking, and he held a large pipe in his hand, though it was unlit. She got the impression he was their group leader, as the others had seemed to defer to him when he spoke.

'So this is our new recruit,' Hurst said to George, frowning slightly. 'You didn't say it was a girl.'

Young woman, Alice thought rebelliously. But she didn't correct him. There was no point putting their backs up from day one. Besides, there'd be plenty of time for her to put their backs up later, if her past record was anything to go by.

George took out his own pipe and fiddled with it, though also not lighting it. 'Thing is, Hurst, I'd like you to give her a chance. She's young but she's rather good. And she took a hit for us, up in London. Got a wing down and needs a desk job for a spell. I thought you would be the best person to bring her on. She's already had some cipher training, so not a complete novice. And I'll vouch for her good behaviour.'

Hurst did not look convinced, though his eyes had narrowed at the mention of her London escapades. He glanced enquiringly at her sling. 'Looks like she's had an accident.' His gaze lifted to Alice's face, hard and probing. 'How did that happen, if you don't mind my asking?'

Everyone was looking at her. Alice felt her cheeks flood with heat. How to explain such a horrid night's work? She opened her mouth, hunting for the right words, but her tongue was too thick and woollen to manage a single one of them.

To her relief, George jumped in to rescue her. 'Miss Fisher was shot, pursuing enquiries. The other agent she was with that night died. A bad show all round. There were three of them and she was lucky to get out alive.' George sounded furious on her behalf. 'They caught them in the end. I hope they hang.'

'Good God.' Hurst cleared his throat. 'Well, in that case . . .' He gestured her forward, indicating an empty seat at the far end of the table. 'We'd better see what you're made of, Miss Fisher.' He rubbed his chin, glancing at George. 'I'll give her a trial period. Two weeks to prove herself. How's that?'

George looked relieved. 'Thanks, Tom, I appreciate it,'

he murmured, and the two men shook hands. 'She'll do you proud, I'm sure.'

Alice could only hope George was right as she shuffled past the others to sit down. Because otherwise this could prove an embarrassing fortnight for both of them.

'Took a b-b-bullet for your country, did you?' The young man to her left grinned as she took her place at the end of the table. He looked to be about her own age. Blenkinsop, she thought, recalling his name. He had red hair and a smattering of freckles, and seemed to be struggling with an awkward stammer. 'Jolly g-g-good show, I must say. None of us have been that close to the action. Sounds awfully exciting. You must tell me all about it later, over tea and b-biscuits.'

Tea and biscuits?

Alice's spirits lifted. So they would actually feed her? Food had always been a little sparse at headquarters in London. Perhaps here in Porthcurno they were more generous with the rations. But before she could respond, the door to the room flew open and a dark-haired young man dashed in, breathless and clutching a notebook.

'Dreadfully sorry for being so late, Hurst. I overslept again and none of the chaps thought to wake me.' As the others laughed, he glared around the table, and then his eye fell on Alice. His cheeks flushed and he blurted out, 'Good Lord . . . Alice? Is that really you?'

Everyone in the room stared from her to the young man, and then back again. Though cringing with embarrassment, Alice somehow managed to say, 'Hello,

Patrick. How you doin'?' It was the first time she'd spoken. Out of the corner of her eye, she saw Hurst bristle again, no doubt at her common East London accent. But there wasn't much she could do about the way she spoke, so this posh lot would just have to like it or lump it. 'Still forgettin' to set your bloomin' alarm clock, I see.'

A general rumble of male laughter greeted this remark. Patrick, red-faced, stuttered something and then stood at a loss, Alice having taken the last seat at the table.

'Grab yourself a chair from next door,' Hurst told him impatiently. 'We've no time to lose. Since our boys landed at Normandy, the wires have been buzzing with hundreds of new communiqués between enemy units, and they've been changing their codes more frequently too. The deciphering machines aren't up to speed yet. So, it's up to our lot to crack them.' He handed out bundles of flimsy sheets typed up with coded messages. 'Study these and let me know what you think.'

Alice stared down at the typed sheet in front of her, her head spinning. With strings of nonsensical words and numbers, it all looked like gobbledygook to her. Blimey, she'd been thrown in at the deep end, and no mistake. Mr Cotterill had told her to expect training. But this was serious top-secret work. Lives were at stake here.

Glancing up at Patrick as he dragged a chair into the room for himself, she saw the ferocious scowl on his face and decided not to admit she was all at sea. She was new there, and the only female. She didn't want to stand out by being the only one without a clue what she was doing.

Besides, maybe she did have a clue. She'd undertaken a short course in codes and ciphers in London, and as she studied the lines of code again, something curious caught her eye. Was a pattern emerging there?

After a few minutes of silent study, Hurst cursed under his breath and thumped the table with his fist, making Alice jump. She stifled her exclamation of surprise though, keen to fit in with all these clever blokes.

'Come on, people,' he barked. 'Every minute counts in this game. Let me hear what you have. Thoughts, ideas, suggestions?'

Nobody said anything.

Alice gulped, her heart pounding away like a steam hammer. It was now or never, she told herself. Maybe she was about to get everything wrong and look like a prize idiot. But she wouldn't know unless she spoke up. Besides, she owed it to brave people like her dad to have a proper go at this code malarkey. If a suggestion of hers could save British and Allied lives – maybe even her own dad's life – it was worth falling on her face a few times to get it right, wasn't it?

She stuck her hand in the air. 'Erm, sir, I might 'ave an idea,' she began tentatively, and was amazed when the whole roomful of men looked towards her, listening with interest instead of telling her to shut up and go home.

'That's an excellent suggestion,' Hurst said after she'd finished explaining the pattern she'd spotted, his smile approving. 'Let's take a closer look at Alice's solution, shall we?' Turning to the blackboard with a piece of chalk, he began sketching out her suggested code key while the others watched.

Goodness me, she thought, not quite able to believe they were taking *her* seriously, of all people. *Alice Fisher, my girl, maybe you do have a brain under that mop of fair hair, after all . . .*

After their session had broken up for lunch, Alice wandered out of the tunnels and into bright sunlight. Blinking and disorientated, she found her feet following a familiar path around the front of Eastern House and along the track that led eventually to the soft white sands of Porthcurno Beach. She felt dazed after the long hours spent poring over papers, pencil in hand, her vision blurring until the letters and numbers she was looking at made no sense at all. But she knew they had achieved something important in that time, all of them together, battling mentally to crack the enemy's new codes. It might be exhausting and horridly frustrating at times, especially when you realised your grand idea wouldn't work and you'd spent the last hour following a false lead. But it was all worthwhile and she was glad she'd said yes to the opportunity.

As she approached the final gatepost before the beach, where a soldier on guard stood smoking, a rifle slung over his back, his cap pushed back from a sweaty forehead, she heard a shout behind her and turned, surprised.

It was Patrick, hurrying after her down the shady track. 'Hang on a tick, Alice,' he called out breathlessly. 'I want a word.'

A little taken aback, she waited. They had not spoken much in the code room. But she'd noticed him glancing at her covertly from time to time, just as she had been studying him. Patrick had changed since their Bude days at the training unit. He was no longer so pimply, for a start. Maybe Porthcurno's fresh country air had done wonders for his spotty complexion. Though he looked older too, she thought. Still lanky but his chest had filled out, it seemed to her. And his gait was no longer so gangly and awkward. The boy was becoming a man, in fact.

Reaching her, Patrick wiped his brow. 'I say, you're a hard one to catch up to. Those long legs, I suppose . . .'

Unsure if that was a compliment, Alice merely said, 'I'm on my way to the beach. Is it still mined?'

'Porthcurno beach? Sorry, haven't been there in yonks. But I expect so, yes. Now we're pushing back the Germans, they may try the same on us, and Cornwall must look like a soft target. So we're watching the coastline round here like billy-oh in case the enemy try landing their blasted boats here while we're busy further east.' Patrick paused, thrusting out a hand with a grimace. 'Look, I owe you an apology. Shake on it?'

Astonished, she peered at his outstretched hand. 'What are you sorry about?'

'I misjudged you in Bude. Thought you were a bit of a joker. Only it turns out you were probably the smartest of us all. Plus, I messed up that day in the woods.' He gave a wry shrug. 'I expect that's why they booted me out of the training course.'

He was talking about when the two of them had been sent on a training mission to follow an unnamed American. Except the man had turned out to be testing *them* on standing up to interrogation. She and Patrick had been taken prisoner, tied up in a hut in the woods at Bude, and questioned for hours. Not the most fun she'd ever had, and Patrick had been a bit wet, to be honest. But at the time it had seemed very real. No doubt he'd feared they were both about to be shot. After that, she'd been sent to London for further spy craft training while Patrick had been told to report here.

'I'd hardly call it booting you out. More like a promotion.' She recalled seeing him with a notebook written in code and wondering what he was up to, only later learning that codes and ciphers were his speciality. 'Not many people get sent to Eastern House.'

'You did,' he pointed out frankly.

'Oh well, that's different.' Alice was oddly self-conscious. 'Anyway, it's probably just a . . . *an administrative error*,' she added, imitating Hurst's posh accent.

Patrick threw back his head and laughed. 'I'd forgotten your sense of humour. All right, yes, let's call it an administrative error. But that goes for both of us. All the same, we've landed here now and we'll have to do our best with it. Agreed?' They shook hands. His look was complimentary. 'You certainly did a good job back there in the code room.'

Blushing, Alice muttered, 'Oh, shut up. We're all in the same boat.'

'No argument there. You and I . . . We've both suffered in this war, haven't we?' Patrick gave her a speaking glance, and she recalled with a twinge of conscience that he was an orphan, and thought she was one too, not knowing that her dad was still alive.

She looked away, suddenly uncomfortable. She didn't like the idea of lying to him. Which was strange, as she'd kept her dad's secret this past year without any qualms.

'Shall we take a quick look at this beach, then?' Patrick glanced at his watch. 'Lunch is in ten. So you won't have time for a paddle. And even if you did, you'd probably get blown up,' he added with a grin, pointing out the large red sign warning of mines ahead. 'But you can certainly look.'

Together, they walked briskly down the track towards the beach. As predicted, the foreshore was fortified with barbed-wire fences, another lone guard on duty, seated lazily on a rock in full sunshine, who jumped to his feet at the sight of them.

Alice stood at the barbed-wire barricade and stared out across the rippling blue waves of the sea. The white sands were just as beautiful as she remembered, the sun blazing down in a perfectly blue sky. In peacetime, she would have taken off her shoes and stockings to sink her bare toes into its pristine sands, then padded down to the shallows to let frothy ribbons of surf wet her feet. Even with barbed wire and all those ugly anti-landing-craft structures littering the beach, it was hard to believe that somewhere across the sea, hundreds of miles away in northern France, men were fighting and losing their lives. It was all such a waste.

But Patrick was right. If the Allies hadn't crossed the Channel a few days ago and taken the fight to Hitler, sooner or later the enemy would have been landing here instead, murdering and imprisoning British citizens. She shuddered in horror. But that nightmare might yet happen if they couldn't break the enemy's codes . . .

'We're going to win this war,' she said fiercely, more to herself than to him.

Beside her, Patrick stirred. 'We better had,' he agreed and clapped her on the back. She didn't usually like being touched, but this friendly gesture sent a burst of exhilaration through her. It felt just like old times, the two of them on the same team again. 'You feeling peckish yet? Let's head back for lunch.'

'Peckish? Are you kiddin' me?' Alice exclaimed, 'I could eat a bleedin' 'orse!' and they both laughed.

On getting back to Eastern House though, they were met in the doorway by George Cotterill, who held up a hand to stop them going any further, grinning as he told her, 'Alice, you'd best take the rest of the day off. Your aunt's gone into labour and you're needed up at the farm.'

CHAPTER ELEVEN

Imogen's back hurt and she was trying not to sneeze. She had spent the last hour helping her sister strip and remake all the guest beds, her arms full of musty-smelling linen that was making her nose twitch, when someone knocked at the front door of the boarding house. 'Oh blow!' Heading out onto the landing, she glanced uncertainly at Florence, who was bent over a stack of clean linen, sorting out fresh sheets and bolster covers for each room. 'Do you want to answer the door or should I?'

'You'd better go, Immi,' Florence muttered, straightening with a flushed face. 'I need to finish this before lunch. Here, just drop those on the floor. I'll deal with them.'

Only too happy to release her bundle of dirty washing, Imogen tidied her hair and hurried downstairs to answer the door. She and Flo had been toiling over the housework all morning, making the most of Billy having been dropped at his little friend Emily's house for the day, her mum Charlotte having offered to have him in return for Florence having looked after Emily last week.

On the doorstep, she found Richard, his lean face sombre, hands clasped behind his back, his dog collar decidedly wonky. Taken aback, she stared, not quite sure how to react to this unexpected visit. She was supposed to be keeping tabs on the vicar, not the other way around, wasn't she?

She was aware of a secret pleasure though, not needing to pretend to be pleased to see him. 'Hello,' she said shyly, and hoped she didn't look too dishevelled from her housework. 'This is a surprise. How are you, Reverend?'

'Richard,' he muttered, not meeting her eyes.

'Richard,' she repeated, smiling.

From upstairs, her sister called down, 'Who is it, Immi?'

'It's the vicar,' she replied.

She had already explained to her sister how she'd recognised the vicar at their local church. What she hadn't mentioned was that she had been asked to watch him. Flo knew she was working with the Bude intelligence group, thankfully, but that didn't mean Imogen was permitted to share all her information with her sister.

'Richard Linden from Exeter,' she added. 'Do you remember him and his brother Simon?'

There was a short silence, then Flo appeared on the stairs. 'Richard,' she said with a welcoming smile, taking off her apron as she descended. 'How very good to see

150

you again.' They shook hands. 'So you're a vicar now and ministering to our parish. Isn't this a small world?'

'Florence, how do you do?' He was polite but his smile struck Imogen as forced. 'Though that should be Mrs . . . Mrs . . . Forgive me, I've forgotten your married name.'

'Mrs Miller,' Florence said kindly and stood aside. 'Please, Vicar . . . I mean, Richard. Do come inside. I'll make us some tea.'

'Thank you,' he said, though his voice seemed to choke on the words.

Florence glanced at Imogen, frowning.

'Let's sit down, shall we?' Perplexed, Imogen led their guest through to the sunny front lounge while Florence bustled away to put the kettle on.

But Richard didn't sit. He stood instead, his back stiff, hands clasped behind his back again, staring out across the sandy rolling downs that lay between the boarding houses and the ocean.

'Is something wrong, Richard?' Imogen asked, and felt a twinge of fear as she wondered if he had discovered her secret: that she had been set to watch his movements . . . Yet how could he possibly know?

'I . . . I have bad news, I'm afraid,' he said heavily, pausing before adding, 'Please, you must tell me if my coming here is inappropriate, and I will leave at once. I would not offend you for the world. But you and your sister are the only acquaintances I know in Bude from back home. So when I heard . . .' Again, he choked, and bent his head, not finishing what he had been going to say.

'Heard what?'

He turned then, and she saw tears in his eyes, his mouth quivering. That was when the fear dug in, striking deep. Only she was no longer afraid for herself, but for him. Coming on the heels of her pleasure at seeing him on the doorstep, it was a strange realisation. And a dangerous one. Had she begun to see Richard as a friend again? As more than a friend, indeed?

She thought she'd known better than that. This was a job, after all. Befriend them, follow them, stay close . . . But keep a cool head and remember that any 'friendship' should only ever be an act. Otherwise they risked losing perspective and falling into the same trap as the enemy sympathisers they were tailing.

Yet she couldn't help what she felt, could she? Especially when it was all tangled up with the past. Some emotions were beyond control.

'Richard?' She gulped, her heart beginning to thump. 'What . . . What is it?'

He came towards her and took her hands in his. 'You must be brave,' he muttered. 'Because I know how close you were to Simon once. How much he meant to you when we were younger.'

'Please, Richard . . .' She sucked in a breath, staring at him. 'Don't tell me this is about Simon. Say it isn't.'

She had loved his twin brother once. Still loved him, in her heart of hearts. Simon was the one who had got away. They would have been so perfect together.

'I'm so sorry,' he whispered.

'No.'

'I received a telegram this morning from my parents,' he told her. 'Simon was killed on D-Day. There were no other details.' The words were stark. 'All I know is that my brother died serving his country and his wife is now a widow.'

She moaned, pulling her hands from his. 'Oh no, no.'

The door opened and Florence stood there, tea tray in her hands, an odd look on her face as she took in the scene. 'Immi? What on earth is it?'

'It's Simon,' she said between numb lips. 'He . . . He went across with the troops on D-Day and . . . Oh, Florrie, he's gone. He's dead.'

She couldn't bear to hold back her tears any longer and ran from the room, ignoring her sister's quick instinctive protest. It was a Saturday morning and the doctor's children were still in the house. His young daughter was coming downstairs, a book in her hand. Imogen had intended to lock herself in her room and cry her heart out. But she couldn't face the girl's questions if she pushed past her on the stairs. So she wrenched open the front door and dashed outside instead, barely suppressing her anguished sobs as she did so.

Halfway to the gate, she stopped and stood blindly in the sunlight, head bowed, tears coursing down her cheeks, wanting to escape the terrible blow that life had dealt her but knowing it was impossible. Wherever she went, there was no way to escape reality. Simon would still be dead and she would still feel lost and bereft.

'Imogen . . .' Richard's deep voice brought her round. She shook her head, pushing him away with a wordless protest, but he ignored her, pulling her into his arms anyway.

Her face buried in his dark clerical shirt, she shook with sobs, unable to control her grief. She needed to weep on somebody's shoulder, so it might as well be his. Besides, who else could she weep with? She had lost someone she cared for deeply, but he had lost his brother. Not merely that, but his twin. She could not begin to imagine how that must feel.

'I can't believe it. Simon can't be g-gone.'

'I couldn't believe it either when I first heard. But it's true.'

'If only he hadn't obeyed his orders when the draft came. He could have said no.' Though she knew Simon would never have declared himself a conscientious objector. Not even to save his life. He hadn't been a bloodthirsty man, any more than his brother was, but he had always believed in doing his duty.

'Impossible.' His voice was husky. 'Simon died for a good cause. The best, in fact. He died for his king and country, and we must honour that sacrifice.'

'Hang sacrifice!' she burst out, though she knew he was right. But why Simon? Why him of all people? He had been so young and strong, so handsome and full of life. It seemed impossible that he would never again draw breath. 'Poor Rosie,' she added feelingly. 'And their little boy too.'

'Yes, they must be distraught. I shall write with my condolences at once.'

'This bloody awful war,' she swore, not caring what he thought or who might hear her. 'When will it ever end?'

Richard said nothing. Perhaps he was shocked by her bad language. Or perhaps he was silently agreeing. She didn't know and she didn't care. All she could see was Simon's face in her mind's eye. And when she lifted her head and stared at him, he might as well have been Simon, standing there before her.

Twin brothers. Two peas in a pod, as her mother used to say about them. And it hurt to look at this handsome man and know the other one, his double, was gone forever.

'How can *you* bear it?' she whispered. 'He was your twin.'

'I don't think I can bear it.' Richard released her at last, taking a step back. He ran a hand over damp eyes. 'But I have to, don't you see? I have responsibilities here. This parish. My church. It helps to steady you, Imogen, thinking of others at times like this. Stops you turning in on yourself.' Digging his hands into his trouser pockets, he swallowed hard, as though forcing the grief away. 'Is . . . Is there someone here you can think of instead of Simon? Some duty you need to perform? It might help with the pain.'

Imogen sucked in a breath, considering that question seriously. Yes, she had a duty to perform. But it involved *him*.

Could Richard be a traitor to his country? The country that his brother had just died for? That guilt would surely darken his grief and make him more reckless, more likely to betray himself.

He was right. Focusing on the cold demands of duty and responsibility could help her crest these waves of grief rather than drown in them. Her 'duty' lay in being able to read this man's soul and any secrets he might be harbouring. So that was what she must do, even if what she found led Richard to the noose, and left his parents childless and in agony.

That was the nature of her work, and for Simon's sake, she must do it. As he had done his duty for his country.

'You're a good man, Richard,' she said slowly. 'Yes, I do have duties that might take my mind off this horror, if only for a few hours. But perhaps we could meet for a drink one evening, and talk about the old days.' She met his eyes. 'Talk about Simon.'

Richard drew a deep breath, a frown in his eyes. But he didn't decline the offer. 'That sounds like a good idea. Would it bring you comfort to talk about him?'

'Yes,' she lied, everything inside twisting in agony.

'Then I will gladly meet you for a drink. To help ease your grief at his passing. It's what Simon would have wanted, I'm sure.' Richard looked past her at Florence, who had appeared in the doorway to the boarding house, twisting her hands unhappily. 'I felt it was important to bring you the news in person, but I have deeply upset your sister, as you see. So I should go away.'

'Oh, Richard.' Florence came forward to embrace him. 'I'm so sorry for your loss,' she said, a catch in her voice. 'Poor Simon. He was such a force of nature. You and your parents will miss him terribly. I shall write them a card of condolence.'

'Thank you, yes, he was a wonderful brother . . .' His voice failed, and Richard turned abruptly away, saying over his shoulder, 'You're both very kind. But I must go. I have a sermon to prepare for tomorrow and letters to write. Goodbye, Mrs Miller.' At the garden gate, he glanced back, his blue gaze tormented. He was so good-looking, so brutally like Simon at that moment, it took her breath away. 'Goodbye, Imogen.'

After Richard had gone, Florence held her tight. 'How are you feeling, love? I know you and Simon were close once upon a time.' Her sister peered into her face, frowning. 'I thought that was all over a long time ago, though.'

'It was . . . for him.' Imogen pulled a hanky from her sleeve and dabbed at her eyes, wishing she could stop crying. 'There's no point denying it. I was still holding a torch for him. I just didn't realise how deeply I felt until just now . . .' She couldn't go on and bowed her head instead.

Florence sighed. 'It's the worst possible news. Richard must feel like his world's fallen apart. I know it's no consolation, but there'll be many more families in the same position. I saw in the newspapers today . . . Well,

I won't repeat it. But we lost a lot of good men in those first few days, across the Channel.' There were tears in her eyes too. 'Let's hope it's all worth it. That we can beat Hitler and his thugs. But I'm afraid this is just the beginning.' She stopped and gasped, checking her wristwatch. 'Oh Lord, I promised to collect Billy before lunch. Charlotte has to take Emily to the nurse. Her eczema is flaring up. I'll have to dash. Will you be all right, Immi?'

'Of course I will. You go, get Billy.' Imogen managed a watery smile. 'I'll sort out that laundry for you, shall I?'

Once Florence had gone to fetch Billy home, Imogen trudged upstairs to collect the dirty sheets she'd left in a heap, bundled them up in her arms and carried them down for washing. Outside in the backyard, the doctor's two children were playing. Though shrieking would have been a better word for it. But it wasn't a straightforward argument, she discovered, on bustling out into the yard with the laundry tub. 'Hey, you two, what are you making all that noise for?'

Neither of them paid any attention to her. The boy had found a knobbly stick that Florence sometimes used for walking over the cliffs and was pretending it was a Tommy gun. Aiming it at next door's cat, who was sitting in the middle of the yard, ears flattened on the back of its head, he was shouting, 'Rat tat tat tat!' and shaking the heavy stick about as though shooting the cat. 'Rat tat tat tat!'

'Stop it, you horrid boy!' his sister was shrieking. 'You're scaring the poor little thing, can't you see that?' Before Imogen could intervene, Clara had dashed forward and scooped up the black cat, holding it close in her arms. 'There, there. Pay no attention to that nasty boy.'

But the cat, struggling in the girl's arms, hissed and struck out with its claws. Shocked, the girl dropped the cat and sucked on her finger, while the cat dashed across the yard, leapt the fence into next door's garden and disappeared. 'Ow, that hurt!'

'Should have let me shoot it, then,' the boy told her scathingly.

His sister gave him a narrow-eyed look. 'It scratched me because you scared it with your stupid game. You can't shoot people with a stick.'

'I can,' the boy insisted and turned the stick towards her. 'Rat tat tat!'

'Oh, shut up! This is all your fault.' Clara began to cry, her chest heaving. 'Look, Imogen . . . It's ripped my finger to shreds.' She glared at her brother through her tears. 'I'm t-t-telling Daddy when he gets home from the hospital.'

Pushing aside her own grief, Imogen forced a smile to her lips and put an arm about the girl's thin shoulders. 'Oh dear. Better let me see those scratches. Goodness, they do look painful. Let's get you inside and clean them up. I'm sure Florence must have some plasters.'

While the boy graduated to shooting seagulls with his knobbly stick, Imogen led his sister indoors to have her wounds tended. Clara sat at the kitchen table until the deep-gouged, bleeding scratches had been thoroughly washed and disinfected. Then Imogen crouched beside her, applying a plaster to the worst areas to keep the skin clean.

'I'm afraid next door's cat isn't terribly friendly,' she told the girl. 'They call him Napoleon. I'm not sure why, because he isn't a *French* cat,' she said with a chuckle, trying to distract Clara from her ordeal, 'but he certainly has an overinflated sense of his own importance.' Imogen put away the plasters. 'And he hates being picked up.'

'I found that out the hard way,' Clara admitted, studying her plastered fingers. 'Though it was my brother's fault. I don't blame the cat at all. It was probably *terrified*.'

'If you like cats, there's a pretty ginger three doors down. She's very nice and doesn't mind being petted.'

'The orange cat with the white patch on her forehead?' the girl asked, perking up. When Imogen nodded, she smiled, showing a gap in her front teeth. 'Oh, I've seen that one. She's a beauty, all right.' Shyly, she thanked Imogen and slipped back outside to remonstrate with her brother again, showing him her plasters as proof of his perfidy.

Imogen stood washing her hands at the sink with carbolic soap and water, watching the two siblings squabble in the backyard. She smiled, reminded of herself and Florence as children, though the age gap between them was much greater, so they had rarely squabbled in the same way as these quarrelsome two.

Richard had been right. Focusing on the young girl instead of herself, tending to those nasty cat scratches and trying to cheer her up, had momentarily eased her own grief over Simon's death. Though even that realisation brought a rush of fresh tears to her eyes and she gulped, hurrying upstairs before Florence could come home and catch her crying again.

In her bedroom, she knelt to pull out her suitcase from under the bed, hunting for a little scrapbook she'd kept when she was younger. Inside were various mementos that she liked to look at sometimes, including an old photograph of her and some friends when they were younger, including Simon and Richard.

With a trembling finger, she traced the twins' faces, and realised that she'd only ever known which boy was which because Simon had been the one holding her hand.

'I'll never see you again, my darling boy,' she whispered.

Simon smiled back at her out of the pre-war photograph, youthful and good-looking and entirely unconcerned by a future he knew nothing about. He and Richard had both loved poetry and often discussed it. That day, the two brothers had been talking about the poet Rudyard Kipling, as she recalled, arguing over the importance of his popular poem, 'If'.

If you can meet with triumph and disaster
And treat those two imposters just the same

Pressing the photograph to her chest, Imogen lay down on her bed, closed her eyes with a howl of distress, and let the tears come flooding again.

CHAPTER TWELVE

Pearl patted her hair, studying herself in the mirror in the ladies' WC at the hospital, then hastily refreshed her scarlet lipstick. Perhaps it was overdoing things to doll herself up before meeting a doctor. But she preferred to make a good impression every time than risk making a poor one just once. 'You never know what might happen when you leave the house,' her momma used to say when Pearl was growing up, urging her to dress smartly and keep her hair nice. 'Always put your best foot forward, honey.'

It was a lesson she'd taken to heart, and one that had gotten her such a wonderful position with the US Rangers, travelling the world and entertaining the troops. It had brought some unwanted attention too, usually from those men who mistook good grooming for easy ways. Freddy was not that kind of man, thank goodness. He seemed to see through the glossy outer wrappings to the real

Pearl beneath, admiring her for more than just her looks. At least, she hoped so. He had certainly not tried it on with her yet. Though she had been mistaken about Terry, hadn't she?

She pouted at herself in the mirror to be sure her lipstick wasn't patchy. Then checked over each shoulder in turn, lifting one leg at a time to make sure her seams were straight.

'Not too bad,' she told herself before heading out of the hospital WC in search of the doctor.

Freddy had asked her to meet him in the hospital lobby. Sure enough he was there ahead of time, impressive in his white coat.

'Doctor?' Pearl smiled as Freddy looked up from the clipboard he'd been studying. 'I'm not late, am I?'

'Right on time,' he said reassuringly and nodded for her to follow him. 'This way, Miss Diamond.'

She hurried after him on absurdly high heels, wondering if it was the hair, the dress or the shoes that had made his eyes widen on seeing her. All three, perhaps. The doctor hadn't said a word about her appearance though, so maybe she'd only imagined his reaction.

Dr Tyson led her down a maze of corridors and into a large room filled with crates and boxes. Some of the crates stood open, their wooden lids leaning against them, sawdust and straw packaging spilt over the floor. From a brief glance inside the nearest crate, she realised these were the medical supplies Penny had been telling her about, and a cold shiver ran through her.

'We've several dozen patients bound for the hospital, apparently,' Freddy told her, correctly assessing her expression. 'In fact, they're due to arrive on this evening's train.'

'Poor souls.'

'Oh, we'll take good care of them here, never fear.' He dragged some of the crates to one side to let her pass. 'Through here . . . What do you think?'

Beyond the crates was a small space with a microphone stand and a piano, of all things. The piano looked ancient, its frame scratched, the stool seat sunken in, but when she tapped a few keys it sounded sweet and true.

She blinked, looking round at him in surprise. 'I don't understand. Is this for me?'

He was watching her closely. 'It's somewhere out of the way for you to practise your routines. The nearest ward is on the other side of the building. So I doubt anyone will hear you singing.' He frowned when she didn't reply. 'Not a good enough microphone? Or is it the acoustics that you don't like? The room is a little echoey, I suppose.'

'No, it's absolutely fine and dandy, thank you. But who's going to play the piano? I can manage a few tunes myself,' she added, tapping another note on the piano keyboard, 'but I ain't nothing special, as we say back home. I'm gonna need a trained pianist to accompany me.'

'And I told you to leave that to me.'

'Okay.'

He sounded confident about that, so she fiddled with the microphone stand instead, trying to imagine how it would feel to perform in front of wounded servicemen instead of hundreds of young men all fired up and ready for action. A very different audience, she suspected.

'So have you found someone yet who can play?'

'I have indeed.' Freddy thrust his hands into the deep pockets of his white doctor's coat. 'You're looking at him.'

'Pardon me?'

'I'll be the one accompanying you on the piano.'

Shocked by this, Pearl goggled at him. 'Are you serious, Doc? No offence but I need a proper musician. Some of these tunes I'm planning to sing . . . Well, they're pretty darn complicated.'

Freddy hesitated, then heaved a sigh. 'I see . . . You need proof first that I'm not going to fluff it. Of course you do.' His steady gaze met hers. 'But I can assure you this dodgy foot of mine can work the pedals as well as any other man's.'

'Oh, Lord, I didn't mean—' Scarlet with embarrassment, Pearl put a hand to her mouth and shook her head.

'Please, no need to apologise. Time for a demonstration, perhaps.' Yanking out the piano stool, Freddy sank onto it, linked and flexed his fingers, cracked his knuckles – glancing ironically over his shoulder at her as he did so – and then began to play.

To her amazement, she heard the familiar notes of a popular song, performed with such aplomb and pinpoint accuracy that she could have been listening to a star turn back home. She soon found her toes tapping and her hips swaying to the catchy tune.

As he finished, he spun on the stool to face her, asking quizzically, 'Was that professional enough for you, Miss Diamond?'

'Oh my goodness. What did I just hear?'

He laughed.

'Honestly, where did you learn to play like that?' she demanded, leaning on the piano, mesmerised by this talented man. 'Not in medical school, that's for darn certain.'

'No, though I agree it would add a certain cachet to studying medicine if we added Musical Accomplishment to the approved curriculum,' he said with a self-conscious grin. 'Fact is, my mother taught me. She was a gifted musician. Still is, though she doesn't play much these days. But before she married my father, she often played before audiences. Piano and flute were her favourite instruments. But once she started a family . . .'

'I get it.' Pearl understood at once. 'I've lost count of the girlfriends I never saw again after their wedding day. Some of them amazing singers too. I'm sure it happens to us all in the end. But walking away from a life as an entertainer . . . It's not the same as giving up a job in the typing pool – you know what I'm saying?'

'You tell me,' he said.

She shrugged. 'When you love performing, being up there on the stage with all the lights dazzling in your eyes, and the applause . . . Well, it hurts to give that up and settle down to a life of cooking and cleaning and raising children.' She pulled a face. 'However handsome the man.'

'Yet you were planning to give it all up to marry what's-his-name.'

Struck by the truth of that, Pearl blushed. 'You got me there, Doc. I must have been crazy. But I really thought Terence was the one.'

'I see. *The One.*' Gravely, he played the opening notes of the wedding march and she bit back an incredulous laugh, not sure whether she was outraged or amused.

'Don't make fun of ladies,' she chided him. 'It ain't nice.'

'You're right. My apologies.' The doctor stood up, closing the piano lid. 'Be honest, will this room do for rehearsals?'

'Of course.'

'Thank goodness. Because it was this or a broom cupboard.' He laughed at her expression. 'Listen, we'll need to coordinate. I'm likely to be rushed off my feet for the foreseeable future, once the first wave of casualties arrive from the front.' He checked his watch. 'Not long now. The train's due in around six. We've laid on ambulances and vans to ferry them up here from the station.'

Her spirits fell at that unhappy thought. 'It sounds like you'll be too busy to play piano for me.'

'Impossible! Never mind, we'll work something out.' Freddy was smiling as they left the room, but his smile faded at the sound of a plane in the distance. He stopped and seemed to shrink back against the wall. 'What . . . What's that?'

'Just a friendly.' She meant one of their British planes, since the German bombers had a distinctive note.

'You . . . You're sure?' His chest was heaving and there was perspiration on his forehead.

Pearl hesitated, surprised by his reaction. 'I'm no expert but I reckon so, yes.' Worried for him, she tilted her head to listen again, then told him, 'Listen to that engine note. It's definitely not a German plane. Besides, those damn Nazis haven't been near us for over a week. Not since D-Day, in fact. They'll be too busy defending the French coast to bother sending their bombers all the way up here, I reckon.'

The drone of the plane had passed overhead and was now receding in the distance. The doctor straightened and let out a long breath. 'Yes, of course, you're right. Now the invasion of Europe has begun, the Germans will be falling back on their occupied territories.' He passed a hand over his damp forehead. 'What an idiot I am . . . God, you must think me such a coward.'

Compassion flooded her, hearing the strain in his voice. Bad enough that this poor man had lost his wife and been seriously injured in a bomb blast. But now to be reliving that agony every time he heard a plane pass overhead . . .

'No, I won't allow you to say that.' Shaking her head, Pearl touched his arm gently. He had comforted her after that heart-rending business with Terence. Now it was her turn to make him feel better. 'What you went through in London . . .' She bit her lip at his embarrassed expression. 'I'm sorry, and I hope you don't mind me talking about it. Of course hearing a plane must give you the heebie-jeebies. It gives me the willies every time, I can tell you, and I've nothing like your excuse. So no more blaming yourself for what's perfectly natural, do you hear?'

Freddy gave a short laugh. 'Yes, Nurse Pearl,' he muttered.

'Are you making fun of me?'

The doctor grimaced, dashing a hand through his wayward hair. He really did seem to have been knocked off-balance by that plane going over. 'Lord, no . . . Well, maybe a little. But only because I want to make fun of myself, frankly. Getting worked up over something so trivial.' Up ahead, a nurse was coming towards them, pushing a man in a wheelchair. Freddy cleared his throat, changing the subject. 'Ah, one of my patients. His surgery is scheduled for tomorrow. I'd better speak to him.'

He turned to shake her hand, his manner abruptly formal. 'Thank you for coming today, Miss Diamond, and for agreeing to put on a show for the lads once we've a full house. Maybe we can discuss rehearsal times at dinner tonight, if that's all right?'

'I'd like that,' she agreed shyly.

When she finally got back to the boarding house, feet aching in the impossibly high heels she'd so foolishly chosen to wear, she found Penny rustling up the stairs with a dress wrapped in crepe paper. 'Need a hand with that, honey?' she asked, seeing her struggling with the tight turn at the top.

'Oh, could you? That's so kind.' Penny let her take one

end of the dress, which was surprisingly heavy, with white lace frills and embroidered satin peeping out of the paper. 'You're a life-saver. Here, just on my bed will be fine.'

Together, they laid the dress carefully on Penny's bed.

'Phew!' Penny stepped back, flushed and dabbing at her face with a hanky. 'It's so hot today. And that weighs a ton!'

Curious, Pearl bent to examine the exposed frills without touching them. 'But it sure looks scrumptious. Is it . . . your wedding dress?'

The other girl beamed. 'Yes, and not any old wedding dress, but my future mother-in-law's.'

'Pardon me?'

'John's mother was married in this very same gown, over thirty years ago. Her own mum helped make it too. Only imagine that! A proper family wedding dress. She's kept it stored in her attic all this time. When she first showed it to me, I asked straight out, bold as brass, may I wear that on my wedding day? And she said yes. She was delighted, in fact.' Penny sank down on the bed beside the gown, brushing the foamy white lace with her fingertips, an awed expression on her face. 'It's not only about saving money. We're preserving a tradition. And it'll be lucky too.' She smiled happily, chanting, '*Something old, something new, something borrowed, something blue.*'

'It sure is lucky.' Though Pearl couldn't help recalling how she too had planned her wedding to Terence, flicking through endless women's magazines for trousseau and wedding breakfast ideas, wondering whether she should travel to Exeter to buy a ready-made wedding dress where the shops were more sophisticated, or drain her meagre savings by having a local dressmaker create something to her own design . . .

Pearl's smile faltered and her chin wobbled. But she managed to add softly, 'Congratulations. You'll look lovely in it.'

'Only so long as I don't eat until after the wedding day,' Penny told her ruefully, beginning to remove the crepe paper. 'Right now, it's a bit on the tight side. Truth is, we need to let the side seams out. But there's not much to play with.' When she glanced around, she must have caught the sheen of tears in Pearl's eyes because she jumped up at once, gasping, 'Oh, how thoughtless of me. You and Terry were planning to marry, weren't you? And then it turned out he already had a wife, great horrid liar that he was.' She pulled a face. 'I'm so sorry, Pearl. Me and my big mouth again.'

'No, honestly, it's fine. More fool me for trusting a man I barely knew.' They hugged, and Pearl took a deep breath before going on, 'You know what, honey? John's a thousand times a better man than Terence will *ever* be. You two deserve to be happy.' She managed a bigger smile. 'Hey, how about I help you let those seams out?'

'No need. Ma Pascoe already said she'll do it if we get nearer the date and I still can't fit.' Penny sighed. 'I'm to watch what I eat, she says. It's only an inch or so I need to lose.' Putting her hands on her hips, she pushed inwards with a grimace. 'Easier said than done, though. I do love my food.'

'I'll help you watch what goes on your plate,' Pearl promised, for as an entertainer she knew only too well how it felt to be constantly watching your figure.

'I've already lost tons of weight though,' Penny insisted, and dragged a dingy sweater out of a bottom drawer. 'Look at this baggy old thing. I used to fill this out, can you believe it? When I worked as a Land Girl, I had to eat hearty meals to keep my strength up, especially in the winters when it was bitterly cold and we were up before dawn, tramping across frozen fields.' She paused, a slight flush in her cheeks. 'The other girls used to call me "Pickles" on the farm at Porthcurno. Because I was always eating.'

'That wasn't very kind of them.' Pearl disapproved strongly of mean nicknames and other such bullying. 'We girls ought to stick together.'

Penny grinned. 'I'm glad I've met you, Pearl. You're a breath of fresh air.'

Laughing, Pearl helped her hang the heavy dress on the back of the bedroom door. 'Well, I am from the "Windy City", so that makes sense.' At the other girl's puzzled stare, she explained, 'That's what we call Chicago . . . You need to hang on to your hat down our streets if you don't want it blown off.'

As she was leaving Penny's room, she almost bumped into Imogen, who was looking harassed as she headed for the bathroom, unwrapping a fresh packet of soap for the dish.

'Oh, Pearl,' Imogen said breathlessly, spotting Penny as well, 'and you too, Pen . . . Flo says to come down early for supper tonight. She's making a special announcement. Don't ask me what, because I haven't a clue.' Her gaze snagged on Pearl's dress and widened. 'My, that's a posh frock. And goodness, those heels!'

Pearl felt awkward. 'I've been asked to put on a Christmas show at the hospital. I was just trying everything on to check the fit.' She didn't mention having worn the dress and heels into town, fearing their laughter. Indeed, she herself wasn't sure why she had chosen to wear such a glamorous outfit simply to meet Dr Tyson. He wasn't her type, after all, and was over ten years her senior besides. 'I'll get changed and be down soon.'

And giving them both a cheery smile, she dashed off to change, wondering what on earth this 'special announcement' was all about.

CHAPTER THIRTEEN

The makeshift camp that had been based around Eastern House ever since Alice had first arrived in Porthcurno back in 1941 was finally being packed up, temporary huts dismantled, tents taken down and packed into trucks, the majority of the soldiers heading out in a long convoy of troop transports, leaving only a dozen or so behind to guard the complex. 'We're off to France, apparently,' one of the men told Alice eagerly when she stopped to enquire what was going on. 'Orders just in. Can't wait . . . Been stuck here long enough in the bleedin' back of beyond.' He grinned, patting his rifle. 'We're all looking forward to giving Jerry what for, I can tell you!'

Making her way into Eastern House, she met George Cotterill in the hallway. He was in a hurry as always, reading a piece of paper as he walked, but on spotting her he stopped to ask, 'Ah, Alice . . . How are things with your aunt? I hear congratulations are in order for her and Joe. A little girl, wasn't it?'

Alice nodded. 'Sarah Jane.'

'Healthy, I hope?'

'Well, most nights she makes enough bloomin' noise to wake the dead. So if that's normal, I'd say yes.'

He grinned. 'And how about you? Settling in with the team, are you?'

Alice hesitated. 'Not too bad.' She didn't consider it worth the bother of complaining, but some of the men were clearly unhappy to have a woman in the room. Especially one who could 'barely speak the King's English,' as one of them had muttered on her first day.

Never slow on the uptake though, George read her expression accurately. 'Like that, is it? I suppose things were always going to be rocky, given the circumstances.'

'Me being a female, you mean?'

'Some people take a while to adapt to the changing times, that's all. I hope Hurst isn't giving you grief.'

'No, sir,' Alice said promptly. 'Mr Hurst's as good as gold.'

She blinked, having surprised herself with that unexpected 'sir', for she couldn't recall calling him anything but plain old George before – or 'Mr Cotterill' whenever her Aunty Vi was within earshot. But he was her boss now, and she was no longer a girl who could get away with ignoring the rules, but a young woman trying to make a good impression.

Besides, she had got used to addressing her superiors

as 'sir' during her training in London. Why should she go back to her old ways just because she was living back at home in Porthcurno?

His mouth quirked and he raised an eyebrow. That 'sir' had not been lost on him either. 'Well, *Miss Fisher*,' he told her with amused emphasis, 'let me know if you run into difficulties. I look after my people here, and if anyone treats you badly, I want you to tell me immediately.'

'Will do, sir.' Alice gave him a self-conscious grin. 'It's good to be back.'

'The work's not too hard for you?'

Alice considered that. 'I get in a pickle sometimes,' she admitted, 'but I'm learnin' fast.'

'Threw you in at the deep end, didn't I?' George made a face. 'Sorry, needs must and all that. But I'm glad to have you on board, Alice. We're running out of trainees. As soon as they're good enough, they keep getting drafted to work in London or even the front line.' He put a hand on her shoulder, peering into her face. 'But you'll stay, won't you?'

'Course I will,' she assured him with perfect honesty, horrified by the mere idea of going back to the city. Too many bad memories, she thought grimly. 'Cross my heart and swear to die.'

After grabbing herself a cup of tea from the canteen, Alice showed her special pass to the guard at the mouth of the secret tunnels, made her way through the noisy operations area to the code room, and found the team already assembled at the table. 'Sorry, sir,' she muttered to Hurst, blushing as the others turned to glare at her. She was often last to arrive these days. Even Patrick was there before her today and also looked up as she hurried in, his expression unreadable. She wondered if he was annoyed that she'd held up the start of the meeting. Most of the team lived at Eastern House or in the village itself though, while she had to walk down from the hilltop farm every day.

Feeling more confident after her chat with George Cotterill, Alice took her usual seat and slurped down some lukewarm tea before opening her notebook, ready to work.

'Now we're all here,' Hurst said pointedly, 'I'd like us to study today's conundrum.' He pointed to the chalkboard, where several lines of code had been written up, ready for interpretation. 'The enemy must have guessed we cracked their last change of code. So we're back to square one, I'm afraid. But we did it before, so we can do it again.' He tapped the board with his pointer. 'Right, who wants to go first? Patrick?'

With an apprehensive look on his face, Patrick stared at the chalkboard for a moment and then made a few tentative suggestions, which Alice thought pretty good. Probably what she would have said herself, in fact. As Hurst nodded and began to discuss his ideas, she risked a glance at Patrick and gave him an encouraging smile. His eyes widened, meeting hers, and he looked down at his own notebook, reddening.

'Alice? Do you agree with Patrick's solution?' Hurst

demanded, perhaps having spotted their exchange of looks, and she straightened hurriedly, groping for an answer as everyone glanced her way.

Blimey! Had she just smiled at Patrick as though there was something between them? Whatever had she been thinking? She'd rarely even smiled at her darling Jim like that. Their relationship had been quite dark and intense though, little time for anything light-hearted in those short weeks between their first kiss and the night Jim had died . . .

Now Patrick would think she was 'interested' in him. And nothing could be further from the truth, she told herself firmly.

Her ears still ringing from the clatter of machines clicking and whirring inside the tunnels, Alice began trudging back uphill to the farm after her afternoon shift had finished. It was still sunny and the sky was a delightful soft blue, with the sound of the sea lapping against rocks in the distance. The arduous, brain-taxing work of decoding messages slipped away and she had just felt her thoughts move back towards Patrick when she glanced up and saw Joan hurrying downhill towards her, presumably headed for the village. She was wearing the green jersey and mustard-coloured breeches that made up the Land Girls' uniform, her boots caked in dried mud.

''Ello, Joan, where are you off to in such a rush, then?' Glancing at the parcel she was carrying, wrapped in brown paper and tied with string, Alice rolled her eyes. So much for observational skills. 'Poppin' to the village shop to post that, are you?'

'Hello, Alice.' Joan was wearing a hat over soft brown curls, but even under its generous brim, Alice could see the older girl was looking upset, unshed tears brimming in her eyes. 'Yes, your grandmother suggested I should take it down to Arnie's before the shop closes. It's urgent that it goes off in the first post tomorrow, you see.'

Alice frowned. 'Why, what's the urgency?'

'I finished the bedsocks I've been knitting and I'm sending them off to my brother, Graham.'

Bedsocks didn't sound terribly urgent, especially in summer, but Alice gave her an encouraging nod. 'Oh yes?'

'I was saving the socks for his Christmas present,' Joan continued, sounding breathless, 'but I'm so worried they might send him to the front, I have to get them in the post straightaway. In case I never . . . Just in case he . . .' A tear ran down her cheek as her voice died away.

Alice felt awkward, not knowing Joan very well. But she had enough sense to give the Land Girl a reassuring hug. 'I'm sure it won't come to that, love. Your brother's only just finished his training, ain't he? They won't send him overseas so soon.'

'I don't know. You hear such things . . . Anyway, if he does get sent to France or goodness knows where, I want him to have the socks. I know the weather's hot at the moment but he might still need them.' Joan paused, biting her lip. 'Do you think I'm being stupid?'

'Blimey, course not! He's your brother and you're lookin' out for him. That's what sisters do, ain't it?' Alice walked back to the village shop with her, which she'd just passed. 'I never 'ad a brother,' she confided, 'but if I had, I'd have knitted him a pair o' socks too. Yes, and posted them off as soon as I heard he might be off to the front. Anyway, I'm sure he'll appreciate them.'

Arnold Newton was leaning in his shop doorway, watching them approach. Technically, he was her grandpa now, having married Gran earlier that year. To her, he was still Arnie who ran the village shop, though he did live up at the farm with Gran these days, since she'd stoutly refused to live in that 'scruffy set-up' above the shop, as she'd put it. By which Alice presumed she meant it was untidy and in need of a good clear-out.

The shopkeeper straightened up as they approached, smoothed down his unkempt white hair, and nodded to the parcel in Joan's hands.

'I'll take that for you, Joan,' he said in his thick Cornish accent, reaching for it before she'd even said a word. 'Postie should come by first thing Monday morning to collect the outgoing post. Then it'll be on its way, never you fear.' Arnie coughed, turning his head away, and then apologised. That nagging cough of his was getting no better, Alice thought. 'I'll see you girls later, up at the farm. Hope your gran's cooking up something tasty for our supper.'

'I'm sure she will be,' Alice assured him, adding shyly, 'Grandpa.'

'Don't you Grandpa me,' he exclaimed with a laugh before dissolving back into coughs. 'Plain Arnie will do nicely, thank you.'

After Joan had paid the postage, the two young women walked back up the hill together. Alice felt she ought to make conversation, so asked about her brother, curious to know his name and age, since Joan had only ever mentioned him in passing before.

'Graham's two years younger than me, so he's only twenty. I can't believe he could be going off to war any day now. He's still so young. Not much older than a boy.' Joan threw her an agonised look. 'Sorry, I'm rambling, aren't I?'

'Not at all,' Alice said politely. 'Graham . . . You don't meet many Grahams these days.'

'He hates his name, thinks it's daft. But it was our grandfather's name and I rather like it. It sounds so solid and dependable. Don't you think?'

Alice thought Graham rather a dull name. But Jim had not been the most exciting name in the world either, and yet she had fallen head-over-heels in love with him. A vision of Jim dying in her arms rose unexpectedly to snatch away her breath and tighten her chest with sorrow. For a moment she couldn't say anything, struggling against a strong desire to cry . . .

Joan must have spotted her tormented expression, for she glanced at her curiously. 'Alice? You all right?'

'Oh, yes. I was just thinking . . . Your brother sounds *very* dependable. And you done an excellent job on them bedsocks too.' She swallowed, pushing away her wretched memories with an effort. 'Me, I can't knit for toffee. That is, I try me best. But everything turns out either too bloomin' small or too baggy.'

'But knitting is so easy. I'll help you, if you like.'

'Easy for you, mebbe. Gran must've shown me a thousand times how to knit but it's never took. I don't 'ave a knitting brain. Chess, yes. Knitting, no.' She hesitated. 'Thanks for the offer though, love.'

Joan's brows had tugged together. 'You're a funny girl, Alice,' she said after a moment's reflection. 'But I quite like you. You're different – that's what it is. And it would be a boring world if we were all the same.'

Laughing reluctantly, Alice had to agree with that philosophy. 'That's the nicest way anyone's ever found to say I'm *strange*. I'll be sure to remember that.' She snapped off a grass stalk in the overgrown verge as the hill steepened, and sucked on the tough, sappy end. Thoughts of Jim began to drift sadly back into her head, and she tried to distract herself by changing the subject. 'Erm, 'ow are you getting on with Caro and Selina, then?' she asked, referring to the other Land Girls Joan worked with.

'Fine. Why do you ask?' Joan had stooped to tie up a flapping bootlace, her voice muffled.

'Oh, no particular reason. I was just wonderin' . . .'

Alice reddened at her fib.

Penny, who'd been a Land Girl on Joe's farm before moving to Bude with her, had been bullied by the other two Land Girls after they'd fallen out over a boy. So it wasn't quite a fib. She hoped Joan was not being bullied too. She seemed such a pleasant, soft-spoken girl, and Alice couldn't see her standing up to the other two, especially not Selina with her plummy accent and judgemental ways.

But there was no point dragging up ancient history. Not if Joan was happy where she was.

When they reached the farmhouse, Alice was surprised to hear music drifting out of the open back door. 'What on earth?' she muttered, waiting for Joan to unlace her dirty boots before going inside, aware that Aunty Violet would screech if any of the Land Girls traipsed mud across her clean kitchen floor. At first, she thought it must be the wireless, though the radio was in the snug, far out of earshot. Then she realised it was a fiddle.

'That's a violin.' Joan's face brightened. 'I love music. Don't you?'

Before going to Bude, Alice would have said no and thought nothing more about it. She'd always been obsessed by books and stories, not music. But while she was living in Bude alongside the American troops stationed there, she'd got used to them playing big-band music on the gramophone. Alice grinned, recalling how Corporal Jones had whirled her around the room more than once, and she and Penny had laughed and drunk moonshine and danced long into the evening. But those American troops would be fighting in France, those who had survived D-Day, she thought sadly, and she'd left Bude for good.

Now, the only time she heard music was when Aunty Vi and Joe sat listening to the wireless after dinner.

She admitted, 'I don't mind a snappy dance tune,' and headed into the kitchen, curious to see what was going on.

Incredibly, it was none other than Joe Postbridge himself, standing in the middle of the kitchen, flushed and self-conscious, sawing away with his bow on an ancient-looking fiddle and making a surprisingly sweet sound with it.

Not only that, but the kitchen had been hung with home-made bunting, coloured triangles of card and paper stuck to a length of string and draped around the rafters of the low farmhouse ceiling. On the large pine table stood a cake, a little lopsided but tasty-looking, with yellow icing and a frilly yellow ribbon around its base. Alice could smell something delicious in the oven, while several pans were simmering on the stove top. There were also two large plates on the table, covered with white tea cloths. Sandwiches? Or perhaps pork pies . . .

Alice hadn't eaten a pork pie in ages. Her mouth began to water, but it was hard to focus on the food with Joe scraping that fiddle for all he was worth.

Gran was standing in front of Joe, her back to the door, shifting her feet about as though itching for a dance, her full, old-fashioned skirt swaying back and forth. She'd done her hair up in an elaborate bun for a change too, instead of her usual hairnet or headscarf.

'Oh, thank gawd, you're back at last, Alice,' her gran

exclaimed, turning to grab her hand. There was a faint dusting of powder on her face, and she was wearing bright red lipstick and her best Sunday blouse, the cream one with the red buttons. 'Come and dance with me, gel. You know I don't like to dance on me own. But now you're here, we can have a proper shindig. Come on, shake a leg!'

Alice let her grandmother drag her forward, though she was too stunned to dance. 'I don't understand, Gran.' She was mystified. 'Why are we having a party? And why is Uncle Joe playing the fiddle?'

Joan was looking amazed too, staring bolt-eyed over her shoulder as she washed her hands at the sink, another of Aunty Violet's iron-clad rules whenever the Land Girls entered the house. Cleanliness was definitely next to godliness in *her* book.

'Now don't keep on with all them questions, love! Just move your feet. Like this, see? Mmm, mmm, mmm.' Humming along to the tune, Gran began to shuffle about as she danced, raising her skirt with one hand to show off her footwork. 'Faster, Joe, for goodness' sake,' she told her son-in-law impatiently. 'It's a celebration, not a bloomin' funeral.'

Aunty Violet bustled in at that moment, carrying two heavy earthenware jugs that Alice knew to be full of home-made wine. She thumped them onto the table, looking flustered. 'Mum, where's that sloe gin Arnie laid by last autumn? I don't care if it's not ready to drink yet, I'll take me chances.' Catching sight of Alice, she stopped and gasped. 'And where the blazes have you been, young lady? I needed you earlier to make the sarnies.'

'I was with Joan. She wanted to post a parcel.'

'You took your time. Where was she posting it from? Timbuctoo?'

'It's hot out, so we walked slowly, that's all. Sorry if I'm late. But I don't get it.' Alice wrinkled her brow. 'What's going on, Aunty Vi? What's with all this food?'

'There is a lot of it.' Violet sighed, glancing at the table with its cake and cloth-covered plates of food. 'But with the kids too, and the Land Girls . . . Well, we've almost a full house.'

Gran had stolen half a sandwich from under one of the cloths and was munching on it. 'Alice,' she said indistinctly, her mouth full, 'didn't you hear the news on the wireless?'

'News?' Alice glanced at Joan, who shrugged.

'Gawd bless yer both.' Her gran gave a husky laugh as she finished her contraband. 'The Allies have done it. We've got Jerry on the run, love.'

Joe faltered in his bowing, frowning. 'Now, Sheila, you know we lost a lot of good men to knock out those guns at Arromanches and Pointe du Hoc. And there's plenty more to do. Let's not forget that.'

'I haven't forgotten.' Gran pulled a face. 'Joe doesn't think we should celebrate just yet. He says there's a long time to go in this war.'

'And so there is,' Joe muttered.

Alice couldn't help feeling her uncle was probably right,

especially as he was the only one in the farmhouse who'd seen any action, and had paid the price for it, coming home from the war minus a leg.

'But what I say is,' Gran went on huskily, 'we've been tightening our belts and thinking of Britain for bloomin' years now, and this is the first bit of good news we've had. Yes, some of them brave boys died, and that's awful. To tell the truth, I can't bear to think of it. Their poor mums and dads . . .' Tears sprang readily to Gran's eyes and she sniffed, wiping them away with a shaky hand. 'But I still say, we should *celebrate* what they've achieved, what they laid down their lives for. And I know we're not going to stop there. We're going to keep pushing them bloody Germans back, all the way to their own bloomin' country. But *today* . . . Today we need to celebrate.'

'Agreed,' Aunty Violet said firmly, uncorking one of the jugs of home-made wine and taking a deep sniff that had her reeling back. 'I'll have squash, ta.'

'Just a few hours of cake and sarnies and *dancing*, and yes, something strong to drink. I'll go fetch that sloe gin, Vi. I put it down in the cellar to keep cool.' She squeezed Alice's hand, peering into her face. 'You do understand, don't you, love? We can't go on being miserable month after month, year after year, and not have a good knees-up when we hear how well our boys are doing over there.'

'Course I understand, Gran,' Alice told her, a tear in her own eye. 'You fetch the gin and when you get back, I'll have a dance with you.'

'Smashin'!' Gran exclaimed, grinning. ''Ere, Joe, can

you play an Irish reel? I do love 'em.' As he struck up a fast tune, she hurried out, calling over her shoulder, 'This reminds me of when I was a girl and I met Vi's dad. Ooh, he was a lovely dancer. Like Fred Astaire, he was. La-la-la . . .' And she went singing all the way down the cellar steps.

Alice and Joan grinned at each other, stifling their giggles.

Old Arnie himself strolled in just as they were whipping the cloths off the sandwiches, regaling Joe with how his home brew had almost killed the vicar once. 'Reverend Clewson,' he explained in his slow voice, 'likes a good tipple. But after downing a pint of my best brew on the Saturday night, he couldn't get out of bed Sunday morning to give his sermon.'

The three evacuee kids came running in from the barn soon after, picking straw from their hair and whooping with excitement at the prospect of a party. 'Can we play musical chairs, Uncle Joe?' Timothy shouted as Joe fiddled impressively away, though he wasn't really their uncle.

'No, let's *dance* instead,' Eustace insisted, and seized his brother, the two of them whirling giddily about the kitchen.

'Oi, watch my best china, you noisy so-and-sos!' Violet cried, trying to grab hold of them.

'Does this mean we'll be going home soon?' Janice asked, looking uncertain. The three kids had lost both their parents in the war but an aunt had been tracked down who'd agreed to take them once the order came for them to be sent back to their home in Barking, east of London.

Janice was old enough to live by herself, and even stay in Cornwall if she wanted, but it was clear she preferred to remain with her brothers if possible.

Aunty Violet stopped chasing the boys. 'I don't think that day's far off, love,' she admitted breathlessly. 'But don't let's count our chickens before they're hatched, eh? We ain't beaten 'em yet.'

The two boys ran about laughing and clucking and pretending to flap imaginary wings, while Janice shook her head at their antics.

'Won't you miss Cornwall, Janice?' Alice couldn't help wondering what it would feel like to go back to Dagenham, to the street where they'd lived before the war. Gran had only been renting the café she and Violet had run together, but still owned her house there, assuming it hadn't been reduced to rubble by now.

'Yes,' Janice admitted shyly. 'And you and your family,' she added. 'Though I 'ope we'll all keep in touch.'

'I'm sure we will,' Alice assured her.

And after them came the two Land Girls, Caroline and Selina, who'd been chatting as they fed the chickens. They and Joan sat down at the table together, tucking into the sandwiches with gusto, while Gran and Arnie danced a jig and Violet stood with her arm about Alice's shoulders.

Breaking off from her dancing, Gran unstoppered the sloe gin and poured generous measures for herself and Arnie. 'Cheers, love,' she said with a wink as she passed the glass to her husband, who had sunk into a chair, panting from his exertions. 'This'll blow away the cobwebs.'

'Raise your glasses, everyone,' Violet said when the music stopped. 'Let's drink to our side winning this war.'

'No, Vi, that's unlucky,' Joe began, but she shook her head.

'It's not unlucky. Because, for the first time ever, it feels like we're going to *win*.' Violet raised her glass of squash. 'To our brave, brave lads out there tonight, fighting the Nazis,' she said with a trembling voice. 'May they all come home safe and victorious.'

Solemnly, they echoed her and drank deep.

'Blimey, that gin's strong.' Gran gasped and wiped her eye.

CHAPTER FOURTEEN

At supper, Imogen carried through the last bowl of greens and sat down next to her sister, who promptly got to her feet and said to her, 'Immi, could I have a private word before we eat?'

She gazed up at Florence in surprise, having assumed that she would make her 'special announcement' – whatever it was – quickly so they could all get on with eating dinner. Frankly, she was starving and could see the same hungry dismay on the faces of the two young children opposite. Luckily for Billy, her little nephew had eaten early this evening and gone up to bed already. But she recognised the determined look on her sister's face, so merely shrugged and followed her back out to the kitchen.

'All right, what is it?' Imogen asked wearily, leaning against the closed door and folding her arms.

Florence took a deep breath, turning to face her, her

smart white cooking apron tied tightly around her waist. Rather more tightly than usual, Imogen realised. It looked quite uncomfortable, in fact. Both around her waist and her chest. It was almost as though her apron had shrunk in the wash. Or perhaps as though Florence had started to put on weight . . .

Imogen realised what her sister was about to tell her before the words were even said. 'Oh Lord, you're having a baby,' she blurted out.

Florence's eyes widened and she bit her lip, but said simply, 'Yes.' There was a high flush in her cheeks, but a glow about her too that Imogen should have noticed before, except she'd been so engrossed in her mission to watch Richard and her grief over Simon's loss. 'Is it that obvious?'

'Funnily enough, no.'

Imogen felt like a bad sister for not having even noticed such physical changes. Or having noticed but not put two and two together until now. As a child, their parents had often complained she was the 'bad' daughter, vain and self-centred compared to Florence's dutiful behaviour. It was a lowering thought to realise she hadn't changed much since those days. But it wasn't too late to improve herself and make amends.

'Though now that I look at you properly, you're definitely filling out.' Not wanting to make her sister feel self-conscious about her weight gain, she added quickly, 'Congratulations!'

'Thank you.' Florence untied her apron, its absence

making her rounded belly far more obvious. Though Imogen realised that her odd dress choices recently – wearing old tent-like garments and even dungarees at times, with old shirts hung over the top – had been intended to hide her growing bump. And she had succeeded spectacularly, for Imogen had paid little attention to her sister's shape. Now though, she decided she must be the least observant person in the world, because Flo's rounded belly seemed so astonishingly prominent.

'I was going to tell everyone at supper tonight,' her sister went on, 'but I realised how rude that would have been. Not to have told you first, I mean.'

'I wouldn't have been offended,' Imogen insisted stoutly, yet felt a twinge of doubt. Maybe she would have felt a bit put out if Florence had treated her just like all the other guests, rather than one of the family. 'Though I'm glad you changed your mind,' she finished lamely.

'You don't mind?'

Imogen's brows drew together. 'Mind what?'

'Me having another baby.'

'Good grief, of course not. Why on earth would I mind?'

'I may not be able to pull my weight soon, and that means you'll be needed to take on some of the jobs I usually do.'

'Of course, whatever you need me to do, just ask,' Imogen told her, though again she felt torn. Spending more time in the boarding house might interfere with her vital task of monitoring Richard. But her sister's health was more important.

'Thanks, that's a weight off my mind,' Florence admitted with a grateful smile. 'Luckily, I didn't suffer as much morning sickness this time around, so I was able to cope in the early months.' Florence half-smiled. 'Charlotte says that means it's a girl,' she added shyly, 'and she's probably right, because I was so sick with Billy it was ridiculous. Some days I could barely get out of bed.'

'You told *Charlotte*?' Imogen exclaimed, and then instantly wished the words unsaid. Charlotte was Florence's best friend in Bude, and an experienced mother too. Of course she would have told her first.

'Yes,' Florence admitted slowly, grimacing. 'Though I only told her because I . . . I wasn't sure it would take, and I needed someone to talk to about it. I fell pregnant once before, you see, the year after Billy was born, but . . .' Her voice tailed off and she blenched, looking away.

Her sister had lost a baby when she was married to Percy? 'Oh, Florrie . . . I had no idea. How awful. I'm so sorry.' Imogen felt like a petulant brat again, complaining about nothing, and rushed to embrace her sister. 'And you don't have anything to apologise for. Charlotte was the right person to confide in. I know nothing about babies.'

'Good,' Florence said emphatically, releasing her with a smile. 'Frankly, I'd be worried if you did.'

Imogen laughed. 'You mean, as an innocent *spinster of this parish*?' she said, referring to the common term for an unmarried woman when calling marriage banns in church.

'Something like that.'

They looked at each, both smiling shyly, and then Imogen hugged her again.

'Honestly, congratulations, sis,' she said in her ear, and stepped back. 'When's the baby due? Do you know yet?'

'October sometime. Or so the doctor thinks.'

'Dr Tyson?'

'Goodness, no!' Florence grinned. 'He's a hospital doctor, not a GP. No, I went to see Dr Crowther when I first suspected, and he confirmed it. He looked after me when I was expecting Billy, so that was nice. Also, at my second visit, the doctor said Baby seems healthy and is growing well, and I won't need to see him again until the end of the summer.' She linked hands over her tummy, a happy flush in her face. 'I have my first appointment with the midwife next month, which is rather exciting.'

'Have you written to tell Miles?'

Florence nodded, but her face became troubled. 'I waited a good long time first, just to be sure, but he . . . he hasn't replied yet.'

'I'm sure Miles will write back soon,' Imogen said smoothly, though her heart jumped at the realisation that he hadn't been in touch. He was usually so attentive to her sister. 'There's a war on. And he'll be deep into France now. Army post on the move is always so complicated, isn't it?'

Neither of them pursued that topic, Imogen pushing

away a sick sense of dread with an effort. Miles would have been involved in that first wave on D-Day, mounting a deadly assault at Pointe du Hoc along with the other US Rangers he'd trained alongside here in Bude. It would be futile to ignore the news reports that they'd suffered heavy losses on that first day, the numbers of dead only climbing in the days that followed as the Allied Forces overran enemy gun emplacements and liberated French towns under occupation. And while the absence of an official telegram – which widows would generally receive when their husbands died in action – must be taken as a reassuring sign, Imogen could imagine how chaotic things would be in northern France since the invasion started. It wouldn't be surprising if not all those who had fallen or gone missing could immediately be identified and their families contacted. Her brother-in-law could be dead right now, in fact. He could have been dead for days and none of them would know it.

'Yes, of course . . . Poor Miles. He must be *very* busy,' Florence whispered, but her smile failed miserably. Before Imogen could hug her again though, her sister held up a determined hand. 'No, I'm fine,' she insisted, dragging back her shoulders. 'And we should get back in there before our dinner gets cold.' She gave a mock shudder. 'Nothing less appetising than cold greens.'

Knowing how much her sister valued her steely independence, having relied on it so consistently following Percy's death, Imogen nodded and let her go. But her heart ached for her older sister, who had suffered in love so much. To lose one husband to war was dreadful enough. But to lose her second husband in the same way, and with a new baby on the way . . .

She pushed that horrid thought away.

Once the boarders had each devoured their two sausages in gravy, served with boiled greens and a small dollop of mash, and were thirstily sipping cups of tea – or barley water in the children's case – Florence leant over to click off the wireless and, once the music had faded away, tapped the side of her teacup with a spoon.

'I have an announcement to make,' Florence said, rather grandly, and everyone fell silent, waiting to hear what she had to say.

Dr Tyson put down his cup and raised his eyebrows, glancing from her to Imogen in curious expectation.

'I'm having a baby,' she explained without further preamble, and Penny jumped up with a shriek of delight to hug her. Florence swayed, laughing as everyone around the table cheered and applauded. 'Thank you,' she told them with a bashful smile, 'that's very kind of you. I thought you should know because . . . Well, I've decided to take more of a back seat in running the boarding house, in case I do myself a mischief. And Imogen has kindly volunteered to take up the slack. But I want to assure you that things should go along as usual, at least until the baby's born. Only if anyone needs help moving anything heavy, for instance—'

'Then they can ask me,' Dr Tyson said firmly, and raised his teacup to her. 'Congratulations, Mrs Miller. And don't forget, I'm a doctor. Not a specialist in maternity care, but all the same . . . if you ever need advice, I'm right here.'

'Thank you,' Florence told him, blushing.

'Daddy, what's a *mischief*?' Toby whispered audibly, and everyone laughed.

There was a Special Service announcement posted on the church board for the following Sunday. 'To pray for all those who recently lost their lives in France,' the sign read.

Imogen wore a pale lemon frock with a matching hat for the service, but borrowed a pair of shoes from Florence with a flat, sensible heel. 'Richard has asked me to lunch at the vicarage,' she admitted, 'and to go for a walk with him after we've eaten.' She saw from her sister's expression that Florence imagined she and Richard must be courting, and wished she could tell her the real reason why she was spending so much time with the vicar these days. But although Florence knew she had a minor role in keeping Bude safe from enemy agents, it wouldn't be appropriate for her to cast aspersions on a man's character before she could be certain if he were guilty or not. So she merely added, 'He's grieving, and I think he just wants to talk about Simon with someone who knew him.'

'Of course, what could be more natural? Poor Richard. He must be finding it very difficult, mourning his twin while so far away from home and family.' Florence, who was washing up the breakfast plates, turned to give her a sympathetic smile. 'Will they be holding a memorial service for Simon back in Exeter?'

'I believe so.' Imogen nodded, checking her lipstick in her compact mirror. It was hard to keep her voice steady, emotion constantly threatening to engulf her. 'Richard is planning to attend and spend some time with his parents afterwards, assuming the archdeacon permits his absence for a week or two. Though I don't believe they've set a date yet.'

'Will you go?'

'Me?' Imogen was horrified. She ought never to have admitted her stupid, unrequited love for the vicar's brother. But she'd been caught at a vulnerable moment and blurted it all out . . . 'I had feelings for Simon, yes, but that was a long time ago. The truth is, I barely knew him,' she said stiffly.

Florence looked at her searchingly, then returned to the washing-up. 'If you say so.'

Blushing, Imogen closed her compact with a snap and dropped it into her handbag. 'Anyway, I'd better go or I'll be late for church.'

'Becoming quite pious these days, aren't you?' Florence murmured, setting another dripping plate on the draining board.

Without bothering to respond to that, Imogen swanned haughtily out of the kitchen, though rather spoilt the effect by stopping in the doorway to ask, 'There wasn't anything you needed me to do today, was there?'

'Half a dozen chores at least,' her sister said, but at

Imogen's gasp, grinned and shook her head. 'No, you take your time with Richard. It sounds like he needs you more than I do at the moment. Besides, Sundays are always quiet. I may need a hand tomorrow though. It's laundry day again. More than a hand, truth be told. All that bending and stretching to strip and remake the beds is playing havoc with my back.'

Relieved, Imogen promised faithfully to help with the bed linen next day, and hurried away to church. It was a short, brisk walk to the church, and the weather had turned lovely again, after a few days of clouds and summer drizzle. Discreetly, she shuffled into church behind a few other latecomers and sat in one of the back pews again. Between hymns and prayers, her gaze roved around the stained-glass windows and ornate pillars, resting occasionally on Richard's face as he spoke so earnestly from the pulpit.

Goodness, but he truly had matured into an attractive man. Eye-catching, even. And there was no doubt how deeply he felt about the war and the sacrifices they were all having to make. Sincerity and passion rang behind every word, tinged with grief as he touched briefly on his own brother's death . . .

Recently, she had begun to hope that Richard must be innocent of deliberately betraying his country. He seemed such a kind, thoughtful man. But it was possible he might have been led astray by others here, perhaps in the false belief that siding with Hitler's party would bring a speedier end to the war. Some political factions had suggested that surrender would save lives. For herself, she felt fighting on was the only way forward. Better that than allow her dear country to be invaded and occupied by such a cruel, merciless enemy.

She glanced covertly about the congregation. She was beginning to recognise the regular churchgoers, and while most of them seemed ordinary enough, she knew that even 'ordinary' people could be tempted to betray their country out of fear or to 'save' a loved one.

At the end of the service, they all shook hands and shuffled outside into the sunshine, quietly discussing those they knew who had been killed, both in this action and earlier in the war. Tentatively, Imogen shared her memories of Simon with a group comprising the church warden, two elderly sisters and a young family. But she looked around in surprise when Richard joined them unexpectedly, shaking hands as he accepted their condolences.

'Thank you, yes,' he told the church warden, smiling sadly, 'it's been a shock for the family. A very difficult time.'

'We're both so sorry for your loss, vicar,' one of the elderly ladies said, holding his hand fractionally longer than the others. 'You said there's to be a memorial service for your brother in Exeter? Such a lovely idea. We'll miss you, of course. But you must go. And do please thank your parents for his sacrifice.'

Richard's face tightened, but he nodded, still smiling.

As the others moved on, he turned to Imogen, lowering

his voice so they wouldn't be overheard. 'I'm glad you were able to come today. When you weren't there for the start of service, I was worried.'

'Sorry, I overslept again,' Imogen admitted, pushing aside the strange rush of emotion that looking into his face gave her. She was thinking of Simon again – that was all. His loss continued to affect her terribly, she realised, tears pricking at her eyes. 'I always held everyone up when leaving for church as a girl. My parents were forever complaining about it. I'm not terribly godly, I'm afraid.'

'Why doesn't that surprise me?' Richard gave a reluctant laugh. 'Though, to be fair, I'm not much good at getting up early myself.' He pulled a face, turning to close the church door now everyone else had gone. 'To be honest, Morning Prayer has always been a bit of a trial.'

'It's always best to be honest.'

'Quite.' He straightened his black cassock and glanced up at the sky. 'The weather's turned rather glorious, hasn't it? Lunch first, then a walk, I believe we agreed? It's very kind of you to indulge me. Especially since you know I'm only going to be wittering on about Simon the whole time.'

'I don't mind talking about Simon,' she said softly, walking with him towards the vicarage. 'You must miss him awfully.'

'I do.' He looked away across the churchyard and for a moment said nothing more. Then she saw him swallow. 'And you?'

Imogen bent her head, hoping he couldn't see her expression below the wide brim of her hat. Was he trying to find out how badly she was hurting? Even she didn't know that.

'There'll never be another Simon,' she said huskily, but the words cost her dearly. She kept wondering what his last moments had been like, whether he had died in pain or instantly, and if he had lingered, whether he had thought of her . . . 'I wasn't worthy of him,' she burst out, raising her chin, and saw him stare. 'Your brother was too good for me. He was a . . . a hero.'

'He certainly was,' Richard agreed.

After a light cold meat salad followed by a bowl of stewed prunes in semolina, a comforting dish that took Imogen back to her childhood, they walked out along the cliffs and past the sunny harbour to climb the narrow, grassy track that led up to Compass Point. A brisk wind kept gusting and snatching at her hat and frock, and the crash and tumbles of waves on the rocky shore were audible from a distance, for the tide was fully in. High on the cliffs, overlooking a bay of blue, white-flecked water, stood the coastguard's storm tower, a Victorian-built octagonal structure known to locals as 'the Pepperpot'. It was situated rather too close to the cliff edge for Imogen's liking, but Richard insisted on them walking all around this unique tower before wandering over the springy turf beyond, to gaze down at the ocean.

There was nothing between them and the cliff edge at

that point, and Imogen hung back, her heart in her mouth as strong currents dashed themselves against the cliff base below them, sending foam high into the air.

'Come on, don't be a coward,' he urged her, holding out his hand. 'I come up here all the time, to think and sometimes take a few sketches of the sea. When the weather's not quite so squally, that is. Here, look over the edge . . . It's quite a sight!'

'I'm fine where I am, thank you.'

Richard grinned and shook his head at her, but she remained where she was, holding on to her hat with grim determination.

'I said, no thank you.'

'Don't be silly.' Again, he held out his hand. The wind blew his sandy hair about and tugged at his dog collar. 'It's perfectly safe and the view is amazing.'

'I'll take your word for it,' she said tartly.

'Oh well.' Richard hesitated, an odd, haunted look in his eyes as he glanced back towards the sea. 'Will you wait while I take a look, then? Would you mind?'

She almost said yes, then had the strangest feeling he shouldn't be allowed too close to the cliff edge himself. Not after his sermon today, the deep grief he had spoken of and how hard it was to cope with such strong feelings . . .

'I would mind, actually,' she said flatly, and saw frustration in his face. 'I'd like to walk back now.' Her dress flapped against her legs and she grimaced. 'This frock wasn't a good choice for walking. Though I didn't know how windy it would be up here.'

A shadow had passed over his face when she refused, but he came back towards her without protest. 'Of course. It's a lovely frock, by the way,' he said, casting it a smiling glance, 'but wildly impractical for rambling about rural Cornwall. Let me walk you back to the boarding house before you get blown away.'

Politely, he linked his arm with hers as they started down the rough track towards the harbour. 'You know, Simon would have adored Bude. The cliffs and the old harbour, and as for that storm tower . . .' He nodded back at the domed structure. 'He loved visiting funny little buildings like that, poking around in them, wallowing in history . . .' He stumbled and seemed to choke before blurting out, 'God help me, I don't know what I'm going to do without him.'

'Oh, well . . . You're going to do exactly what he would have done if the boot had been on the other foot,' she told him, though she was burning with grief, her vision blurry with tears. Not just with sorrow over Simon's death but with guilt too, gnawing at her horribly. His grief was real. Yet she was here under false pretences, watching him covertly. It felt wrong, even if it was her duty. 'You're going to k-keep calm and carry on. Like the rest of us.'

She only hoped she could take her own advice.

CHAPTER FIFTEEN

Pearl woke with a start. It was pitch-black in her poky little bedroom at the back of the boarding house. Though that was hardly surprising, given how tightly she'd covered the window with the blackout curtain before going to bed. In the same instant, she realised what had woken her and her heart began to thud with sickening fear. The air-raid siren was going off in the town, its piercing wail too horribly familiar.

Sitting bolt upright, she slipped her bare feet into slippers and lurched forward, fumbling for her dressing gown on the back of the door.

On the shadowy landing, she found Dr Tyson, also in slippers and dressing gown, shepherding his kids towards the stairs. The two children were stumbling and yawning, blankets draped around their shoulders, a library book clutched in the girl's hand. The boy was complaining.

'Hush, Toby. You know the drill, so let's have no more

nonsense.' Freddy's voice was strained, showing his concern at the sound of planes in the distance. Nonetheless he remained calm, no doubt not wanting to alarm his children. Scooping up the boy, Freddy helped his daughter down the stairs. 'Besides, next door's cellar is a huge improvement on those draughty tube stations we had to sleep in while we were still in London. Do you remember those days, Clara?' he asked the girl, clearly trying to distract her. 'Some nights, we were packed in like sardines.'

Clara said nothing, looking pale and frightened.

'I'm tired,' the boy whined.

'You'll soon get back to sleep once you're settled.'

Pearl followed them out of the back door and towards the basement in the next-door building, where most of the street sheltered during night-time air raids.

As they trailed after the others down rickety steps into that dusty, dimly lit space beneath the neighbour's house, Pearl took Clara's hand and gave it a reassuring squeeze. 'Don't worry, honey, we'll be safe down here.'

Clara gave her a wan smile. 'My friend Bobby says bombs can still kill you underground, if one lands right on top of the shelter.'

There was enough truth to that claim to make Pearl uncomfortable. But she could hardly agree, could she? She was trying to ease the girl's fears, not confirm them.

'Well,' she said awkwardly, 'I'm not sure about that. And I don't think they drop many bombs along this coast. We've barely seen an enemy plane over Bude since

D-Day. So it's probably another false alarm. At the worst, it'll be a few Jerries passing overhead on their way somewhere else.'

'Quite right, Miss Diamond,' the doctor agreed with what struck Pearl as forced cheerfulness, setting the boy on his feet. 'Now, Clara, be a brave girl and look after your brother for me during the air raid. Can you do that?'

'But I want to stay with you this time, Dad,' the boy pleaded.

'Sorry, son, but you should try to get some sleep. You've school in the morning.' The doctor pointed to the mattress strewn with blankets and cushions where several other local kids were already camped out, whispering and giggling. 'Us grown-ups have to sit on the chairs. Sometimes even the floor. So you two have got a good deal with that mattress.'

'But Dad—'

'Oh, come on, Toby, and stop fussing, would you?' Rolling her eyes, Clara dragged her brother away to the children's area of the shelter.

Pearl watched them go with a sinking heart, hoping to goodness she was right about it being a false alarm.

'Take your own advice and don't worry,' Freddy said in her ear, as though accurately reading her expression. 'And thank you for helping to calm her down. She'll be fine now. Give Clara a job to do and she soon forgets her fears.' As he dusted off a couple of wooden seats for them with the hem of his dressing gown, she caught a glimpse of his smart, blue-striped pyjamas. 'I just wish I could do the same,' he muttered, with a thin smile that suggested he was more nervous than he sounded.

They sat together against the wall, watching the kids get settled while more elderly neighbours shuffled slowly down the stairs, looking for friends to sit with during the air raid. One man had bought a pack of cards with him and found a foursome to play with, betting with matchsticks. One of the mothers went over to the children and began telling them a bedtime story, which quietened them down.

Pearl drew her dressing gown closer. It was damp in the cellar and she began to wish she wasn't wearing her best negligée, her plain cotton nightdress being in the wash. Not only was it cool against her skin but the fancy lace neckline was peeping over the lapels of her dressing gown. At first, she couldn't work out why such a thing should embarrass her. Then she realised it was because she was sitting next to the doctor.

You fancy him, she told herself sternly.

But of course she did. He was a good-looking professional man and in his prime. While she was lonely and far from home. Her own foolishness made her blush. Hadn't she learned any lessons after falling for Terence and his dreadful lies? Not that the doctor was a liar. But she needed to stop looking to men to make her feel better about this terrible war. Struck by a wave of homesickness, she bit her lip, wishing she could simply travel home to the States and try to forget what had happened. But it was impossible. Travel was very difficult with the war on, and ships crossing the Atlantic had been destroyed before now.

Besides, her family didn't want her back home. The last letter from her parents had made that clear. So where would she go?

'Pearl? Are you feeling all right?' Freddy must have noticed her bent head and tight-lipped silence. 'Honestly, you were right before. We… we probably are safe down here.'

But even as he spoke, the cellar walls shook with an explosion, and he sucked in his breath, staring upwards, his expression tense. And he wasn't alone, a collective gasp running through the two dozen people sheltering there. One woman shrieked and some of the children began crying. Though not Clara, Pearl noticed. Freddy's daughter was holding her brother's hand silently, but with a look of frowning consternation. Brave girl, she thought.

'That sounded bad,' Pearl said, hands clasped tight in her lap, back very straight, refusing to allow herself to react in case she started to cry.

'Yes.' Freddy's jaw was clenched hard. After a moment, he added with an obvious effort, 'But it was probably a fair distance away.'

'Of course.' Pearl gave him a fleeting smile.

Abruptly, he jumped to his feet, making her stare. 'Don't worry,' he said jerkily, 'I'll just be a few minutes.' Taking a deep breath, he went over to the young woman who'd cried out, crouching down to reassure her. She turned a tear-stained face towards him but was soon much calmer, nodding at whatever he was saying.

Pearl watched him in surprise. It was clear the explosion had unsettled him too. But no doubt the doctor found it easier to deal with his own fears when there were others around who needed help and reassurance.

She bit her lip, pushing away a terrible, unexpected memory from childhood. She and a friend had been walking down the street when a car had come careering towards them, being pursued by two police vehicles with their sirens wailing. In the chaos, gunshots had rung out on the busy Chicago street. People had screamed and ducked behind lampposts or under benches, whatever they could find for shelter.

Pearl had dropped to the ground beside her friend, covering her face. Once all the cars had skidded past and around the next corner, she had sat up, gasping in shock.

Only her friend hadn't stirred, lying beside her in a pool of blood. A man had run up and tried to help them. But Shirley had been hit by a stray bullet and was dead before the ambulance even arrived. Now, the sound of sirens had a tendency to bring back the shock and horror of that day, even though she'd long ago learned to shut herself off from such awful memories. . .

'Pearl?'

Looking up, dazed, she realised she had been grinding her teeth so hard, her jaw hurt. It was Florence, the landlady, one hand on her rounded belly, the other held out to her.

'You look awful,' Florence said. 'Shall I sit with you? Billy's sleeping on Imogen's lap, so he won't miss me.' She sat down without waiting for Pearl to say anything, which was just as well, for she was struggling to find the breath to speak. Her arm came around Pearl's shoulder and she bent her gently forward. 'What you need to do is take some good, deep breaths. That's it, nice and slow. There's no hurry.'

Pearl closed her eyes and concentrated on filling her lungs, holding the air there for a count of ten, and then releasing it slowly.

'How is she?'

Now it was Freddy's voice. Her toes curled up with embarrassment and she felt like a fraud. There was genuinely *nothing* wrong with her. Not like that young woman who'd shrieked and wept at the boom of the explosion. All she needed was a moment to collect her thoughts . . .

'She's having trouble breathing,' Florence said softly.

'Yes, I see.' He knelt before her, and she sensed rather than saw him peering into her face. 'Pearl? It's Freddy . . . Dr Tyson.' Did he think she couldn't recognise his voice? He loosened one of her hands from its death grip on the other and chafed the skin. Maybe she was getting cold, despite the heavy dressing gown. But that was hardly to be marvelled at, given the damp state of the cellar. 'Can you hear me?'

Good grief, Pearl thought dizzily, what a question to ask. It was her chest that was tight and refusing to work properly. Not her ears.

'Uh-huh,' she muttered.

Seconds later, another explosion rocked the building, louder and more violent this time. Dust fell from the ceiling and the young woman who had shrieked before gave a moan. Pearl felt something brush her hair and opened her eyes in shock to see a fine grey powder drifting through the air and liberally dusting her slippers.

'Goodness me, that . . . that was close.' Florence, seated beside her, turned to stare at her son across the crowded cellar. But Billy was still asleep, thumb in mouth, cradled on his aunt's lap. Imogen, however, was very much awake, looking wide-eyed back at her sister.

Pearl peered at Freddy. His hand was squeezing hers so tightly now, it was almost uncomfortable, though he wasn't looking at her. Instead, his head was tilted as though he could see the night sky with its wheeling enemy bombers through the ceiling.

Seated beside Imogen, Penny had been flicking through a women's magazine as they waited for the air raid to finish, but laid it aside at this second blast, her face ashen. She whispered something to Imogen who shook her head. Pearl was glad she was not alone down here in this ugly, confined little space under the floorboards. It didn't help that she kept remembering what the doctor's daughter had said about shelters and a direct hit from a bomb . . . She didn't want to be buried alive under rubble. Or killed by falling masonry. For her last breaths to be stifled by dust and debris in her lungs.

Her vision blurred.

'You're all right, Pearl,' she heard Freddy say, his voice muffled as though speaking from a long distance away. Her fingers felt so stiff and cold in his, she couldn't seem to relax them. 'Breathe deep for me. No, don't keep snatching at the air. Here, like this.' The doctor sucked in a deep breath and held it, his broad chest inflated, eyes wide as he nodded at her encouragingly. Then he expelled the breath with a noisy whoosh. 'Can you do that?'

With an effort, she copied what he'd done. Then repeated it several times, her breath shuddering.

'Brilliant,' Freddy told her. 'You're doing well.' He'd loosened his grip on her hands, his fingers rubbing more gently over her cold skin. 'You'll be better in no time. I expect it was just shock . . . We're all a little shaken, to be honest.' He gave a short laugh, and she could see the strain in his face now. 'Bombs in Bude? Whatever next?'

'Oh, we've been bombed here,' Florence informed him. 'Before your time,' she added when his head swivelled sharply her way. 'Earlier in the war. The boarding house had a few near misses, in fact. But I'm sure we'll be fine this time. Listen, the explosions have stopped. I expect the planes have moved on down the coast.'

'Doctor,' someone called from the other side of the room, where a small child was crying. 'Can you take a look at my son?'

'I'll be right there.' Freddy took another deep breath, as though readying himself for a difficult task, and finally released her hands. 'Try to get some sleep, Pearl.' He stood, raising his voice as though to reassure the others around them too. 'I imagine the air raid will be over soon and we can all go back to our beds.'

'If we have any beds to go back to,' an elderly man called out in a thick Cornish accent, banging his stick emphatically on the floor.

'Old Trelissick's right,' another man agreed. 'That last bomb was damn close. Could have taken out one of the houses on this street.'

'Aye,' the elderly man muttered, nodding.

'Oh, thank God it wasn't ours,' cried the neighbour whose cellar they were sheltering in, and crossed herself.

'Don't be a fool, Robbie,' someone else said, sounding impatient. 'It would have been much louder if it had landed on any of the buildings in the street. No, that was away in town. At least a quarter of a mile.'

Others had gathered around to discuss the likely area that had been bombed, but Pearl noticed how Freddy didn't join in but slipped off without a word to examine the crying child.

'I wonder what they were targeting.'

'The beach, maybe. The gun emplacement up on Maer Cliff.'

'Don't be daft,' someone said scathingly. 'They took them big guns down when the Americans left. Took 'em up to Cleave Camp in the back of a truck to protect the airfield there.'

'Oh, well, I didn't know that.'

As the locals argued, Florence kept rubbing Pearl's back. 'You look better,' she said, and gave her a friendly nudge. 'I was worried for a minute there. You'd gone rather a funny colour.'

'I'm sorry. I don't know what came over me.'

'No need to apologise,' the landlady assured her, getting up. 'Look, why don't you sit with me and Immi? The chairs over there have padded seats, you know. Far more comfortable than these wooden ones, I can tell you.' She chuckled. 'I need a wider seat these days, I'm afraid.'

But the all-clear was already sounding, its distinctive falling note lightening the mood. Everyone stopped talking and began to shuffle out of the shelter, no doubt hoping to return to their beds for a few hours' shut-eye before the start of a new day. Parents were stooping to collect their sleeping children from the mattress area, and now she saw Freddy talking to Toby and Clara, who were both yawning and rubbing their eyes.

Pearl tried to leave without them noticing her, blushing as she recalled how much of a fuss she'd made over the explosions.

But they caught up with her as she emerged into cool night air and stood a moment, sniffing the unpleasant sulphurous smell that told of explosions nearby and wondering what had been blown up. She could only hope nobody had perished or been injured that night, taken unawares . . .

'Walk back to the house with us, Miss Diamond?' Clara asked from behind her, interrupting her thoughts.

Smiling, Pearl took the young girl's hand, though she

felt sure it was Freddy who had suggested she ask. 'Of course.'

She didn't meet his gaze and was thankful for the cover of darkness as they slipped back into the house in the wake of Florence, Imogen and Billy, soon followed by Penny, who looked anxious.

'I'm sure it wasn't the hospital that was hit,' Freddy reassured Penny as they all trailed upstairs. 'It's too far away. Those explosions were closer. More likely in the town centre.'

'I was thinking of John,' Penny muttered, looking even unhappier now, 'my fiancé. He lives in town, just by the river.'

'I'll walk with you into town at first light, if you like,' Pearl offered, feeling sorry for the younger woman.

'Thank you,' Penny told her, her eyes wide with concern. 'Though I swear I won't be able to sleep a wink until I can be sure John and his family are safe.'

Pearl washed up in the communal bathroom before bed, and came out to find Freddy leaning against the wall outside the door, his ankles crossed, eyes shut, a deep frown on his face as though struggling against some inner unhappiness. That surprised her, for the doctor usually presented such an upbeat, cheerful front. But she'd seen how affected he'd been by the air raid not to realise he had many different layers beneath that professional smile.

'I'm sorry,' she muttered, 'I didn't mean to take ages.'

His eyes opened and he straightened up. 'I wasn't waiting for the bathroom,' he assured her. 'I wanted to make sure you were fully recovered. You seemed unwell down in the shelter.' His gaze scoured her face. 'It wasn't just the bombs, was it?'

Wordlessly, she shook her head.

'Do you want to talk about it?' When she again shook her head, he nodded with a wry look of understanding. 'Another time, then. And you're right, it's very late for a chat. Or too early, depending on your perspective.' He paused. 'But if you ever need anything, Pearl . . . a shoulder to cry on, or something for your nerves, don't forget there's a doctor in the house. Even if he doesn't like the sound of that damn siren or the planes overhead any more than you do,' he ended, his mouth twisting.

Her response was the usual bright performer's smile that kept people at bay and concealed a thousand wounds. 'Thank you,' she whispered, and hurried into her bedroom, closing the door and standing there in silence until she'd heard him retire into the room he shared with his children.

Don't forget there's a doctor in the house.

How could she forget, when Dr Tyson was all she ever thought about these days? Him, and the loneliness and fear that kept threatening to swallow her whole.

When she and Penny walked out early the next morning, they found John Pascoe's row of cottages by the bridge intact, but a still-smoking building a little further on. 'The Americans used it for storing ammunition,' John confided, one of a small crowd of onlookers gathered to watch the fire service volunteers as they worked to make the area safe. He kissed his fiancée on the cheek. 'Good morning, Pen,' he said, grinning at her relieved expression. 'Fancied I'd been blown to kingdom come, did you?'

'It's not funny – I was worried,' Penny complained, though she hugged him thankfully. 'Nobody hurt, then? Your mother and father? They're both all right too?'

'Ma and Pop are both whole and hale,' he insisted, 'and there was nobody about when the bomb fell, so there's no need to fret yourself. Only Mr Holm isn't too happy, for he owned the land and buildings. Now it will all need to be rebuilt.' Belatedly, he turned to shake hands with Pearl. 'How are you, Miss Diamond? Nice to see you again.'

'Just dandy, thank you,' she said.

He gave her a speculative look. 'A little bird told me you're to give a concert at the hospital in Stratton. Is that true?'

'I wouldn't call it a concert, but yes, I'm going to give a performance for the wounded they're bringing in.'

His interested gaze shot to Penny's face. 'Any soldiers arrived yet?'

His fiancée nodded, instantly solemn. 'I've had my hands full, sorting out beds for them all. The wards are already packed.' She scratched her brow, looked worried. 'We're all doing our best, of course. But if they send many more, I'm not sure where we'll put them.'

'And how are the doctors and nurses coping?' Pearl asked her friend, thinking of Dr Tyson and his strained look last night, escorting his kids back home after the air raid.

'Brilliantly as always,' Penny said, brightening. 'Though none of the patients need major surgery, thank goodness. We're only being allocated the less serious cases. Long-term care or non-life-threatening injuries, you know.'

'Sounds like hard work to me, love,' John said, putting his arm about her waist. The young fisherman's smile was sympathetic, though he added with a mischievous wink, 'Still, at least now you know I won't be up there too, all blown up.'

'Oh, you!' Penny let him kiss her but shook her head at Pearl. 'Men, eh? They think they're so funny.'

'Only because some of us are,' John protested.

Pearl hid her smile.

After a little more chat about the smoking remains of the bombed-out building, Penny kissed John goodbye. 'I'd better get to work,' she said. 'It's getting late.'

'I'll walk with you to the hospital, if you don't mind,' Pearl said. 'I need to do some rehearsing. Get used to the space.'

'I'd love the company.' Penny looked troubled though as they waved goodbye to John. 'Thank goodness that bomb didn't hit somebody's home. Only think if it had!'

'I know, it's too horrible.' Pearl understood that fear only too well. She had been with the troops on the outskirts of London briefly after first arriving from the States, and had seen first-hand the dreadful toll these nightly bombings could take. Homes and businesses flattened, people killed, others left homeless and destitute, having lost everything . . . 'But they say this big push on France is working.'

'Yes, but at what cost?' Penny turned a bleak face towards her, eyes filled with tears. 'These wounded men at the hospital . . . I played it down to John, because I don't want him to worry for me. But it's been awful, trying to keep smiling as stretcher after stretcher is carried in. So many young men . . . Some will never walk again or have lost the use of an arm. And most will never *fully* recover. Oh, maybe their bodies, but their minds . . .' She shuddered. 'I'm told they cry out in their sleep. Poor devils. And there's me, telling them everything will be all right.'

'Honey, I'm so sorry.' Pearl gave her friend a quick hug. 'I guess all you can do is your best,' she added, though her heart was aching and she couldn't help wondering if some of the new arrivals might be men she knew from the US Rangers. 'That's all any of us can do, isn't it?'

She'd heard a rumour that Americans wounded in France might be shipped back to wherever they'd previously been stationed, once their conditions had been stabilised and they were well enough to travel. Would she be giving her show to any of those strong young men she'd laughed and flirted with when they were here in Bude, now bedridden and seriously injured?

It was a horrible thought.

But if those men had sacrificed themselves for freedom, she would have to be brave too and keep smiling, for their sakes.

CHAPTER SIXTEEN

Alice was feeling guilty. Hundreds of miles from the terrifying bombs and the bloody fighting in France, her summer in Porthcurno had been warm and unthreatening. Aunty Violet was over the moon about her baby daughter, Sarah Jane, always exclaiming how pretty or clever she was for blowing bubbles or wiggling her toes, between telling Joe off for calling her 'Sally' – a diminutive she apparently considered common – though Gran had recently fallen into using it too. The baby's crying still woke Alice some nights, but she just stuffed cotton wool in her ears and turned over. The farm was at its busiest at that season, Joe mobilising a small army of Land Girls and young lads hired as casual labour to bring in the harvest, but it was hardly warfare. For weeks there was barely a cloud in the sky, the weather fine and settled as another long, glorious summer drew to a close in their quiet corner of Cornwall.

All the same, tramping the fields in her spare time, Alice had not missed the first leaves turning a brownish yellow or orangey red and falling to the ground, or spiders spinning webs between shrubs along the damp verges. Soon autumn mists would be creeping through the meadows every morning and the nights would draw in, with the crackle of log fires to look forward to, and thick warming stews for dinner.

Some mornings, strolling down to Eastern House and listening to the murmur of waves breaking in the sandy cove, Alice would come up against the barbed-wire barricades with a shock, abruptly remembering there was a war on and she wasn't a character in one of the library novels she loved to read before putting the light out at night. Though the urgent buzz and bustle in the secret tunnels soon brought her back to reality, harassed personnel rushing to and fro with message slips and folders marked TOP SECRET, and Mr Hurst frowning at her whenever she failed to identify a pattern in a new German code protocol. In fact, the constant clatter and click of decoding machines and Morse perforators would follow her back up the hill at the end of each shift, until Alice could hear those infernal noises even in her sleep.

She listened to the wireless each morning and evening, and some Saturday mornings would travel the bumpy miles between Porthcurno and Penzance by bus with the Land Girls to watch a film at the picture house, though the Pathé newsreels were what really caught her imagination. Whenever they showed scenes of French towns being liberated, she would study the faces of citizens cheering or watching in silence as the Allied troops rolled past in trucks, and wonder how it must feel to live under enemy occupation.

She also found herself thinking about her dad more often, longing to explain to him what had happened with Jim in London. She wondered if anyone would tell them if he was exposed as an undercover agent and executed. There was a chance the government might not tell them for years, the whole thing shrouded in red tape. Those were her worst times, when she feared she might never see her dad again, never hug him and tell him how much she loved him.

Yet she was enjoying being at home again, back in the heart of the family, even with Aunty Vi's new baby girl wailing day and night.

Gran, who often got funny notions in her head, had decided recently that she ought to teach Alice how to cook. 'To stop you moping about with that long face,' she'd said, tying an apron firmly about her granddaughter's waist. 'Anyway, you'll need to know the basics for when you're married. So no moaning.'

Alice had stiffened at the mention of marriage, her brain flashing back to the night Jim had died – the dark alleyway, the loud shots, and his head in her lap afterwards – but she hadn't argued, merely accepted the mixing bowl that had been thrust into her hands.

She didn't want Gran or Aunty Vi to know how unhappy she still was over Jim's death, despite the months that had passed, her arm long since healed and out of its sling. Her family would never understand the sense of turmoil churning inside her. How could they? There had never been a formal engagement between the two of them, after all. To them, he had been a good friend and colleague, nothing more.

Now and then, she had found herself mentioning Jim to Patrick, usually during their breaks at Eastern House, over a meal or during one of their regular strolls down to the cove. Since Patrick had known her before she went back to London, it felt natural to discuss the changes she'd undergone since leaving the training unit at Bude, and Jim had been a part of that.

She'd had no idea how sheltered her life had been in Cornwall until she encountered the network of enemy sympathisers in and around London. It had opened her eyes to how ruthless some people could become when they believed their cause to be a righteous one, even to the extent of betraying their own country, something she could never imagine doing, whatever the reason.

While that horrifying knowledge had made her grow up fast, Alice felt as though she'd aged about ten years when Jim died. Her innocence had finally been stripped away that night. Watching her beloved die in her arms, she'd seen the world for the cold, cruel place it truly was, and nothing now could ever make her feel safe again. Not even these quiet rural fields and grassy lanes of Porthcurno . . .

That day, she and Patrick had been ordered to team

up to work on a particularly tricky string of code that had so far defeated their newest code-breaking machine.

After slaving over it for hours without success, until Alice was almost seeing double, they mutually decided to take a break, stretching their legs with a walk around the busy communications room.

Patrick turned to her. 'Hey, shall we take the . . . outside? Maybe a change of . . . will help . . . see the solution.' He saw her grimace, having missed part of what he'd said, and grinned, steering her towards the exit. 'We can grab a cup of tea from the canteen on our way,' he shouted over the racket.

Only too happy to escape that noisy environment, Alice accompanied him into the sunshine, blinking and yawning.

'Blimey, it's still daylight out here,' she exclaimed, only half joking as she held up a hand against the sun's glare. 'Hard to keep track of time in them tunnels, ain't it?'

'I do feel a bit like a mole coming up for air,' he agreed, and pretended to clean dirt off mock-whiskers while she chortled.

After they'd queued lengthily for the tea urn, Alice managed to charm the cook into parting with two thin slices of Victoria sponge, a high treat usually reserved for officers and key personnel. Together, they ambled out onto the lawn at the front of Eastern House, manila folders marked TOP SECRET tucked precariously under their arms while they each balanced a cup of tea and plate of cake in both hands.

'Let's hope Cotterill doesn't see us,' Patrick muttered, glancing over his shoulder. 'Or we'll be for the high jump, taking these Top Secret documents outside the tunnels.'

'Oh, George won't mind,' she said airily.

'Maybe not with you. He's got a soft spot for you, has old Cotterill. But I'd be in hot water.'

'I don't know what you mean,' Alice insisted, though with a smile, because it was true that George was more of a family friend than a boss. Though she wouldn't like to test that theory by being caught doing the wrong thing, she thought cautiously.

Once they'd decided on a shady spot to sit and work, Patrick took off his jacket and spread it gallantly on the grass for her. 'No, I insist,' he said when she tried to protest. 'The ground's a bit dank under this tree, and you deserve not to get a damp bottom.'

'How do you work that out?' she asked, laughing.

Patrick studied her seriously. 'Because you're better at code-breaking than me. And you don't need any of those machines in there to do it either. Just your brain.' He paused. 'You're the smartest person I know.'

'Oh.' Blushing and taken aback by this compliment, Alice sat down on his jacket and flicked her folder open to the line of code they'd been working on. 'Well, I hope my brain's feeling up to the task today. Because this one's a right bleedin' nuisance.'

'It's a tough nut to crack, all right,' he agreed, sitting opposite and taking a large bite of his cake. 'Delicious.'

Alice took another bite. 'The sponge isn't bad. But this jam . . . It's so gritty. It tastes like sand, don't it?'

'Well, we're not far from the beach.'

She deliberately ignored this mockery. 'Do you ever think back to the days before the war, when cakes tasted nice and there weren't no such thing as *powdered egg*?' She grimaced.

'Only every blessed time I sit down to eat a meal.'

They caught each other's eye and laughed. She was surprised what easy company Patrick had turned out to be, after fearing at first that they would soon be squabbling. After all, they had barely spoken a civil word in Bude. Yet now he was fast becoming a friend. If boys could ever simply be *friends*, that is.

'So, this code . . .' Alice muttered, hurriedly bending to her folder to study their work again. She didn't like the way her thoughts were moving.

'Yes, let's get stuck in.' Patrick rubbed his chin, also beginning to read back through the notes they'd made over the past few hours. He shook his head. 'It's a conundrum. But maybe the clue lies in what's *not* there.'

Something sparked inside her. 'Yes!' She sat up straight, staring at him. 'I was just thinking about how we substitute ingredients in recipes, because of rationing. I don't think that was a coincidence.'

He nodded slowly. 'That egghead of yours trying to nudge us in the right direction again?'

'More scrambled than hard-boiled at the moment. But I think we're on the right track. Looking for what they ain't put in, that is, or for them substitutions.' Picking up her pencil, she frowned, making rapid notes on the lines of code, circling and underlining certain markers, and hunting for patterns.

'I meant it, you know,' Patrick said softly, watching her.

'Hmm?'

'You're clever . . . Sharp as a tack. It's pretty impressive.'

'What? For a girl?'

'I wasn't being patronising.' He paused, scratching his head. 'Or maybe I was. I'm not sure. But I apologise. You're damn clever, that's all. And I'm glad you've come to join us here at Eastern House. I think we could change the course of the war with people like you on our side.'

Flattered but blushing, Alice cast him a forbidding glance from under her brows, like the one her aunty was so good at with the evacuee children when they were playing her up. 'Best concentrate on this bloomin' code, all right? Or the only thing we'll be winning is a boot up the behind from Mr Hurst.'

It was nearly an hour later by the time they felt they had cracked the conundrum enough to take it to Mr Hurst.

He was sitting in his office, reading through a stack of paperwork, his pipe in the ashtray, a cup of tea by his elbow. But he listened politely enough and then checked their working out. A smile spread over his face and he jumped up, knocking the table so the tea slopped in its saucer. 'By Jove, you two! I think you've hit on the solution. Let's take it to the others in the code room, see what everyone else thinks.' They followed as he hurried along the dimly lit corridors, saying over his shoulder, 'Well done, Patrick.'

'It was Alice who worked it out, sir,' Patrick blurted out. 'Most of the basics, at any rate. I just chipped in the odd idea.'

Alice felt her heart lift, so relieved that he hadn't claimed the victory entirely for himself. Some men would have done, she knew, and not thought twice about it.

'Well done then, Alice,' Mr Hurst corrected himself. 'Either way, you make a good team. I'll definitely be keeping you two together for future tasks.'

Patrick looked pleased, shooting her a grin.

At the threshold to the code room, Mr Hurst stopped to shake their hands, a solemn look on his face. 'Listen, I've got to tell you, we're up against the ropes in this fight. Our code-breaking machines can't cope with all the new codes being constantly thrown at them, so everything we do here at Eastern House helps. You two have done a smash-up job with this code.' He looked at them earnestly. 'And I need you both to keep doing it. Understood?'

Alice walked back to the farm with a light step that evening, thrilled to have been part of something important, and glad too that Patrick had turned out to be all right, in the end. She could hardly remember the awkward pimply youth he'd been back in Bude, even though it was only a matter of months since those days. The effect of the war, she supposed. It had made them all grow up incredibly fast.

A car horn tooted behind her on the narrow farm track, making her jump nearly out of her skin. Alice turned, staring, only to realise it was Joe behind the wheel of his old van. But beside him, squeezed up on the front bench seat, was her sister Lily, cradling her baby son in her arms, and Lily's husband Tristan.

As the van drew level, Tristan said through the open window, 'Hello, Alice! You can have a lift, Joe says, if you don't mind jumping in the back.'

'I'm fine walking, thanks.' But she was amazed. 'Lily, what on earth's going on? Why aren't you in St Ives?'

'My fault,' Tristan answered for his wife, grimacing as he held up his hands. To Alice's horror, they were both heavily bandaged, all the way past his wrists. 'Burnt myself again, didn't I?'

'Gawd blimey!'

'I can't seem to stay away from fire.'

Lily leant forward, her look disapproving, although it was clear from the strain in her voice that she was worried for him. 'He got himself trapped in a burning building, on duty with the fire service in St Ives. He was lucky to get out alive. They've given him a few weeks' leave while he recuperates, so we thought we'd spend it up here with Aunty Vi and Gran.'

'That's awful . . . But we'll look after you here, Tristan.' Alice gave him a sympathetic smile.

Joe put the van back into gear. 'I'd best get up the hill then, if you're walking. Else Vi will be wondering why we're taking so long. See you up at the farm, Alice,' he called out, and the old van shuddered away up the steep slope.

Alice followed on slowly through the quiet of the late afternoon sunshine. She was grinning at first, thrilled to have her big sister back at the farm, even if only for a few weeks. But her grin soon faded, the foolish pleasure she'd felt at her own success today disappearing along with it. As she thought back over what they'd said, her heart began to thump with alarm. If Tristan hadn't made it out of that burning building alive . . .

She felt sick at the realisation that they had so nearly lost a member of their tight-knit family.

Yet tragedies like that were happening every day to families just like them all around Britain, and further afield too. Loved ones being killed or seriously wounded in the line of duty. Dads and brothers and husbands going to war and never coming home.

Her work at Eastern House was important, and not just because she got to show off her decoding skills to Patrick or Mr Hurst. Every time they got it right, they saved lives, so that families like theirs didn't have to face a terrible loss. That was why she was doing this. Not for praise from her boss or to see that look of admiration in Patrick's face, but to protect people like Tris and Lily, and her aunt and gran, and especially that little bundle of joy in Lily's arms, so he could grow up knowing his dad.

Alice looked out to sea as she crested the hill, and wished she could see her own dad again, even if just for a few hours. Maybe one of the messages that came through Eastern House every day would be the one that saved his life, she thought. That told him to run or who not to trust when the enemy came knocking.

That was why she had to do the best job she possibly could at Eastern House. Study and train harder. Be smarter and think more quickly. Because one day it might be her own dad's life their work was saving.

CHAPTER SEVENTEEN

In church, Imogen sat a little nearer the front than usual, having decided the end pews were too far from the rest of the congregation. After all, she was there to watch Richard's interactions with his parishioners, not to wrestle with her immortal soul. Carefully, smiling her apologies, she squeezed past Mrs Tuttle and her three children to sit directly behind Mr Jolly and Mr Alsop, two of the men she'd been watching most closely, who were always hanging about the church and talking to Richard.

As she settled onto the hard wooden pew, picking up her hymnal, both men stopped whispering to each other and glanced around at her.

'Good morning,' she said breezily, giving them her most charming smile, the one that ordinarily could be relied upon to wrap even the trickiest male around her finger. 'Gorgeous weather for September, isn't it?' It seemed a safe enough topic.

Neither man smiled, though Mr Alsop replied testily, 'Hotter in France, I daresay.'

Richard had just emerged from the vestry and was shaking hands with people on his way to the pulpit. Both men looked his way with evident interest.

'Oh, quite,' she agreed, also with one eye on Richard. 'Where the worst of the fighting is, you mean? Yes, poor souls. Though better than having to cope with heavy rain, I guess.' She paused, adding experimentally, 'I do hope our lads can chase those invaders all the way back to Germany before winter sets in.'

Mr Alsop grunted something that was lost under the scrape of feet as the congregation rose for the first hymn. But she suspected from his shrug that his reply had not been full of rousing patriotism. Of course, that didn't mean anything. Many older people complained about the war, in general terms – how long it was dragging on, and the lack of anything in the shops – and that didn't make them Nazi sympathisers. But she had a hunch that Mr Alsop and his poorly named friend Mr Jolly were worth watching.

Richard was looking pale these days, she thought, studying him compassionately as he discussed the war in his usual earnest way, alluding to faith and the need for patience as though he himself had not lost a much-loved twin in this conflict. She noted how he choked at one point in his sermon, gripping the sides of the pulpit with a sudden whitening of the knuckles, and her own heart jolted with the same pain.

Simon, she thought, tears pricking at her eyes, and bent her head to keep that sorrow private. *Ah, dear wonderful Simon . . . Why did you have to be so brave?*

Though if she had been born a man, wouldn't she have gone to war herself? Not that she thought less of Richard for staying behind and ministering to his flock here in Bude. He had tried to enlist and they had rejected him. Twin brothers, but Simon's eyesight had always been perfect while Richard . . . She shook the memories aside, determined to keep herself from crying, and focused on what Richard was saying as he drew his sermon to a close.

His soothing words made a great deal of sense, she had to admit. 'Patience is a virtue, and we clearly need to be patient still. But it can be hard,' he admitted, a sheen of tears in his eyes. 'If you're struggling, turn to a neighbour or friend and help *them* instead. In helping others, we raise our spirits and help ourselves.'

After the service, she hung about in the cool of the church porch, pretending to read the noticeboard while secretly watching Richard outside.

It was not easy to spy on a friend, she was finding, let alone a vicar. It had been relatively easy to spot Doreen's shifty behaviour last year, having been taught what to look for. Nods, whispers, seemingly chance meetings that happened rather too frequently for it to be coincidence . . . These could all be done innocently, of course. Equally though, they could signal the existence of a ring of so-called sympathisers working against this country. So she noted who Richard spoke to, what seemed to be said, and checked for signs of covert activity, but unhappily.

'You always hope you'll be mistaken,' Mrs Elliott had told her early on in their association, 'but you need to keep an open mind too. And yourself safe. Report any suspicious activity to your control; never try to tackle a possible enemy agent on your own. Don't forget, these people are prepared to betray their friends and neighbours to the Germans, and would almost certainly hang if discovered. So they won't scruple at killing you to keep their secret safe.'

Could Richard be an 'enemy agent'? It was such a chilling thought. Because if she was to perform her duty to her country, she would have to pass on any suspicious activity she uncovered, and watch this friendly, popular vicar arrested for treason. And what if it turned out she was *wrong*? The damage that would do to Richard and this small church community did not bear thinking about.

But she had accepted this unpleasant task and must see it through.

By the time Imogen ventured out of the porch, most of the churchgoers had gone home, leaving only a few die-hards behind, eagerly chatting away. Among them were the men she had sat behind in church: Mr Alsop and Mr Jolly. These two men were deep in conversation with Richard, no doubt bending the vicar's ear on some weighty topic, she thought drily, like how slow the verger was with getting the grass cut in the churchyard. That was the usual complaint, for Mr Chandler had been laid up in bed for weeks with gout.

As she approached their little group, Mr Alsop straightened and cleared his throat, and the other two stopped talking. Richard looked sharply round at her. Mr Jolly, she noted, thrust something hastily into his jacket pocket. A sheet of paper?

She had been helping out at the children's church club during the summer weeks, organising daily activities to keep the younger ones occupied while their mothers were engaged in vital war work. But now that schools had restarted, her duties only extended to Saturday mornings, since the older and more experienced volunteers were in charge of Sunday school.

'Hello, Vicar. Mr Alsop, Mr Jolly . . . I must say, I'm missing the children's church club.' It was a safe enough opening gambit, she'd decided. 'I hadn't expected to enjoy working with children so much.' She laughed. 'Though I daresay those little mites are learning more at school than they did on our trips to the beach or fishing in the canal.'

Richard smiled with an effort, it seemed to her. But he remained as polite as ever, thanking her for volunteering and assuring her that the children would be missing her. 'It was our most popular summer club yet,' he admitted with a reluctant laugh. 'Your influence, I'm sure.'

Pretending to be flattered, though convinced he couldn't mean it, Imogen chatted about the church club for a few more minutes, and then said her goodbyes and set off home.

She didn't want to leave, frustrated and suspicious that she might be missing something important. But it would have drawn too much attention to stay longer without a good reason, and since that disturbing afternoon when they'd walked out together to the coastguard's tower at Compass Point, Richard had been avoiding her. Perhaps he had just been busy, or perhaps he was embarrassed by his grief for his brother's death, which had flared out so agonisingly that day. Certainly there had been no more lunch invitations for reminiscing about Simon over soup and salad.

However, it was also possible that she'd been too obvious and Richard had realised she was watching him. Which would be a disaster.

As she turned down Ocean View Road towards the boarding house, the blue-grey Atlantic was just visible across the rolling downs, the waist-high banks of marsh grass rustling in the breeze. Tasting salt on the air, she looked up to where the cool, cloudy skies stretched far away into haze above the ocean. She had begun to whistle softly to herself, thinking again of Richard and the odd way he'd glanced over his shoulder at her in the churchyard, when she caught sight of a figure ahead of her on the road. A man in an American military uniform.

The soldier was walking slowly, almost limping, an army pack slung over one shoulder.

Something about his gait was familiar.

Shielding her eyes, Imogen squinted into the hazy light,

not quite able to believe what her instincts were telling her. Then she gasped with sudden recognition, calling out, 'Miles?'

The man turned at her cry, and she saw with joy that it was indeed her brother-in-law, Staff Sergeant Miles Miller.

Miles had left with the Rangers shortly after his marriage to Florence, only allowed a few days for their honeymoon, and had been involved in the first assault at Pointe du Hoc in northern France, where so many Americans had sadly lost their lives. A brief letter from him had informed Florence that he'd survived, but conveyed very little else, perhaps due to security issues over writing about an ongoing mission. Yet here he was now, seemingly alive and well.

Her heart swelled, for she knew how much her sister had been worrying and praying for his safe return. But as she hurried to catch up to him, Imogen suddenly slowed, dismayed to see a vivid red scar across one cheek and a bandage over one ear, half hidden by the smart US Rangers cap.

'You're hurt,' she blurted out, staring. 'Oh, Miles . . . I'm so sorry.' She flung her arms about him, but felt him wince and drew back at once. 'I had no idea you'd been wounded. Is that why you've come home?'

'It's good to see you too, Miss Imogen,' he drawled in his smooth Texan accent, and touched a finger to the brim of his cap in a gesture of respect. His smile seemed crooked though, and she guessed he felt conflicted about this unexpected homecoming. 'Yes, that's why I'm home so soon. I didn't want to write and worry your sister further. But I've been in a French field hospital ever since the assault on Pointe du Hoc.'

'Oh no!' Imogen was confused. 'But you wrote to say it had gone well. Flo got your letter.'

'It did go well,' he pointed out mildly. 'Just not for me. Still, I count myself lucky to have survived. Unlike many of my fellow Rangers. We lost a huge number of men that day. Too many to comprehend. But at least I'm alive and still walking, though slowly. I got myself blown up. Nerve damage to my legs, scarring here and there, as you can see.' Miles gestured to the red-raw scouring of his face, where it looked as though some of the skin had been rubbed away. 'But there were many worse off than me in that field hospital, I can tell you.'

'Well, you're very welcome here.' She hugged him again, albeit more gently this time. Her gaze moved to the bandage over his left ear. 'What happened there?'

He tapped the bandage, an ironic gleam in his eye. 'You'll have to speak up now. I lost an ear.'

'Oh Lord! How awful for you. But let's get you inside...' She took his hand and together they walked the rest of the way to the boarding house, where she flung open the door and shouted excitedly, 'Florence! Come quick! You've got a very important visitor.'

In answer to her cries, Florence wandered into the hallway with Billy on her hip. There was a stunned expression on her face as she gazed at the two of them outlined on the threshold as though unable to believe her eyes.

'*Miles*?' Her voice trembled as she stuttered, 'Oh, my darling . . .' Putting her son down with a quick smile and a whispered 'Look who it is, Billy,' she darted forward to throw her arms about her husband and raise her mouth to his.

Miles kissed her with a great groan of happiness, lifting his wife off her feet. 'Florrie,' he was saying between kisses. 'My love, my beautiful woman . . . How I've missed you.'

Discreetly, Imogen scooped up Billy, who was staring at the American with a dazed look. 'Come on, little man,' she told him briskly. 'I think your mummy's got some catching up to do. Let's see if we can gather some more rosehips from the front garden, shall we? Maybe get another pot of jelly out of them if we're lucky.'

Outside, with the door pulled shut behind them to give the married couple some privacy, Imogen sat on the bench in autumnal sunshine while Billy hunted for rosehips among the bushes. She was feeling quite shaken herself. It was strange how a few moments could change the course of one's life, she thought, still reeling from Miles's reappearance in their lives and wondering what it was going to mean for them all.

She was not alone in wondering that.

'Aunty Migen, is . . . is that my new daddy?' Billy asked, bringing her a handful of rosehips, his eyes wide and troubled.

There was wonder in the little boy's voice but more

than a little trepidation too. Hardly surprising, of course. He'd barely had time to get to know Miles before the US Rangers left Bude, and Florence had been careful not to mention him in front of the boy too often, for fear he might become confused or upset. Billy had turned five now, and his own father, Percy, had died when he was too young to remember much about him.

But Florence had told Imogen privately that she didn't want Percy to be forgotten now that her son had a new father. 'It would be disrespectful to Percy's memory,' she had insisted, and Imogen had agreed.

Despite her fun outings with the children in the summer church club, she was not used to having difficult conversations with very young children. That was Florence's domain as an experienced mother. But her sister was otherwise occupied, so it was down to her. Somehow, she needed to make some sense of what was happening without reducing the boy to tears.

'Yes, that's Miles, your new father,' she told him solemnly. 'And it looks like he may be here to stay.'

Billy studied her face. 'Are we going to America?' His lower lip jutted precariously, his eyes brimming with tears. It was exactly the reaction Imogen had hoped to avoid. She felt ill equipped to deal with such naked emotion. But there was nobody else. He went on tremulously, 'I don't want to go to America. I don't want to leave Emily.' *I don't want* was one of the boy's favourite new phrases and he was putting it to good use here. 'Emily's my *friend*.'

It was true. He and his little friend Emily had been

thick as thieves since they were old enough to toddle about together, since Emily's mum Charlotte was one of Flo's closest friends in Bude. Small wonder he didn't fancy the idea of leaving these shores behind and never seeing her again. And it seemed little use to explain that he would find new friends in that unimaginably distant land. Emily was special to him.

Imogen bit her lip in quick sympathy. She might not be brilliant at talking to tiny tots, but she knew how it felt to lose someone special, at least. 'Oh, my dear . . . You poor thing.'

Imogen hugged him so tightly that Billy wriggled free, complaining loudly. But she found herself at a loss how to answer without lying. Because he had a point. Her sister had indeed discussed the possibility of selling the boarding house and moving to Texas to live with Miles's family there. Clearly, the boy had overheard some of this plan, despite her sister's best intentions, and had been fretting about it secretly ever since, poor soul. Now the man himself had returned to Bude, it must feel as though that threat of departure had become frighteningly real.

'I don't know, Billy. That's the truth. But it's too soon to be worrying about what will happen next. Your new daddy was wounded in the war. Did you see the bandage?' When Billy nodded, looking even more disturbed, she patted him on the shoulder and tried to sound reassuring. 'It's not serious. But he'll need to get better before anybody goes anywhere. Yes?'

Billy thought about this and then squinted at her thoughtfully. 'Daddy a war hero?'

'I think he must be, yes.'

'War hero, war hero,' he chanted, for this was a phrase he had heard them all using at the meal table in recent weeks, and even managed a shaky smile. 'More rosehips?' he asked, peering down at the meagre handful he had bought her before.

'If you can find more, yes, please.'

The little boy ran away, humming as he went about his task, his mind clearly relieved by the realisation that nothing was about to change in his life.

Imogen only wished she could feel the same. But she rather feared that her life was about to get even more horribly complicated than it already was.

If her sister did sell the boarding house and emigrate to America, she herself would have nowhere to live, and would either have to return to her parents or take war work that provided accommodation. She didn't mind those options so much. But she would miss Bude. Or more accurately, she would be sorry never to see *Richard* again.

Realising with a shock what that meant, she groaned under her breath and rolled her eyes heavenward. What on earth was wrong with her? Could she really be falling for a man suspected of being an enemy agent?

CHAPTER EIGHTEEN

Seated before the bedroom mirror, Pearl brushed her hair and set it into soft platinum rolls, before carefully applying her make-up, including a perfect Cupid's bow with her scarlet lipstick. Going to the wardrobe, she chose a flattering, feminine dress that would suit a family dinner, wriggled expertly into it, and then slipped on a pair of low heels. She had heard the children shouting and running about excitedly earlier, and peeked out of her door to see an American soldier coming upstairs with his arm about Florence. The landlady's husband, she'd realised, hurriedly retreating. She had met him, of course. Everybody had known Staff Sergeant Miller when the Rangers had been billeted on the town, for he had been the one in charge of organising everyone's billets. He'd also been popular with the men, for although he could be stern, he was always approachable . . .

Yes, Florence had made a good choice. And now her

husband was back in Bude. And wounded too, from the quick glimpse she'd had as Miles came upstairs.

She wished her own love life had not been so problematic and turbulent this past year. There was a niggle of doubt inside her too, for Staff Sergeant Miller would have known Terence – indeed she recalled Terry mentioning the man several times, usually with impressed awe – and she felt embarrassed about her own foolishness there.

Had the sergeant known that Terence was already married, for instance, while he was courting her? She knew men often kept quiet about things like that rather than cause trouble, especially among fellow soldiers. That would be upsetting. But it was hardly a question she could ask him, was it? She just hoped he wouldn't mention it.

At last, she heard feet on the stairs, and shortly afterwards the dinner bell rang. Once the doctor's children had also clumped noisily downstairs from their room, Pearl trod lightly after them, a determined smile on her face.

In the dining room, she found Staff Sergeant Miller, a broad-built, smiling man in the uniform of the US Rangers, seated at the head of the table where Imogen usually sat opposite her sister. His head was indeed bandaged, his hair razored back on that side, his face stained a deep, angry-looking red and heavily scored in places. He had suffered, that was clear. Yet he was laughing merrily with the doctor's children, partway through an anecdote about his field hospital stay where one of the younger officers had hidden under a bed and jumped out to make the nurses shriek.

As Pearl entered the dining room, his gaze turned to her and his smile broadened as he brought the anecdote to a swift end. 'Well now, you must be Miss Diamond.' He stood politely, holding out his hand. 'I'm Staff Sergeant Miller. But you can call me Miles . . . I'm Florence's husband.' He paused. 'I saw you perform on stage here in Bude. More than once, in fact.'

'It's good to meet you,' she said with a shy smile, shaking his hand. 'Florence told me you're from Texas, is that right?'

'The accent doesn't give it away?'

She laughed. 'Maybe a little,' she joked. The doctor was helping his son tie a napkin about his neck to avoid dropping dinner on his shirt. She glanced his way, adding, 'I'm going to be performing again soon, at the hospital, to entertain the wounded soldiers there. Dr Tyson has agreed to accompany me on the piano.'

'I see.' Miles grinned at the doctor. 'A man of many skills, it seems. And immense luck too. Freddy, you didn't tell me about this. I hope I'm going to get an invitation.' He indicated his bandaged ear. 'I am wounded, after all. I must be eligible.'

'I'll see what I can do,' Freddy agreed.

It was clear that the two men had already made friends, Pearl thought, and was pleased. She had noticed that Freddy had few male friends, even among the men he worked with at the hospital, tending to spend his spare time at the boarding house or with his children. Not that she disapproved of that. It showed what an excellent and conscientious father he was, in fact. But she did wonder whether he was a little too isolated in terms of adult company, for she had often seen him outside alone in the evenings after his kids had gone to bed, sipping one of the bottles of Cornish ale that the local farm shop delivered along with the vegetables once a week, and staring mournfully out at the ocean. Thinking of his late wife, no doubt, and how he had lost her . . .

Florence had come bustling in with a stack of deep bowls, and smiled when she saw Pearl already seated at the table, two chairs down from her American compatriot. 'Ah, Pearl, I was just about to call you down. Excellent timing.'

'Do you need a hand with bringing in the dishes, Florence?' Pearl asked, worried that she was not pulling her weight.

'No need, Imogen is helping me. Besides, it's a hearty warming stew for dinner tonight,' she explained, setting out the bowls in each place. 'Only one pot to bring out. Followed by apple pie and custard.'

'Apple pie and custard!' the children chorused with glee, even Billy joining in and banging his knife and fork on the table, which earned him a stern glare from his mother.

'Tonight is a special celebration, after all. To welcome Miles home to Bude. But don't go expecting fruit pies every day.'

To soften these words, Florence winked at the doctor's children before hurrying out again. Almost meeting her in the doorway, Imogen came in bearing a tea tray, with cups and saucers for everyone except the children, who were having barley water.

'Clear a space for the tray, would you, Pearl?' Imogen asked hurriedly, looking harassed, but beaming when Pearl jumped up to move things aside. 'You're a darling. It's very heavy tonight. But then we have Miles here – have you met Flo's husband, by the way? – and Flo allowed Billy to sit up for dinner with us tonight, even though it's long past his bedtime.'

'Not tired,' Billy announced, but then ruined this statement by yawning extravagantly.

Laughing, Imogen disappeared into the kitchen again, returning a moment later with the heavy stew pot, which she set centrally on a metal trivet. 'Watch out, it's hot,' she warned them, setting a large ladle in the unlidded pot.

'We've introduced ourselves,' Miles explained, 'though Miss Diamond is famous among the Rangers for her tap-dancing as well as her singing. Quite puts Ginger Rogers to shame, I can tell you.'

Pearl felt her cheeks heat up as everyone looked at her with interest.

'You can tap-dance?' Freddy asked, his eyebrows soaring.

'I know a few routines, yes.'

'Good grief.' Freddy laughed. 'I hope you'll be

incorporating some tap-dancing into your performance at Stratton.'

'If you insist,' she agreed, secretly flattered.

'I do,' he said, smiling back at her. 'To be honest, I can't wait to watch you rehearsing *that*.' His daughter glanced at him sideways, and his smile faltered. 'The patients will love it, I'm sure.'

It seemed like a good time to change the subject. 'I recognised you at once too,' Pearl told Miles, helping herself to the stew. 'I often saw you about town while the Rangers were here. And of course everybody was always talking about Staff Sergeant Miller, as the man to ask when anyone has a problem.'

'Me?' Miles looked astonished, and then chuckled. 'Is that so?' His Texan drawl was so pronounced, it made her smile, reminded of home. 'I hadn't realised I was so famous.'

'Infamous sounds more like it,' Freddy told him, his lips twitching with humour.

'But you must call me Pearl, not Miss Diamond,' she insisted, ladling stew into Miles's bowl, and then offering stew to the two children opposite as well. She knew that Florence would want to serve Billy herself, but enjoyed helping out at the dinner. It was strange how she had begun to consider the children part of her own family since moving here. Strange but rather lovely. She knew instinctively that she would miss them horribly if they ever moved on or she did. Not to mention their father. 'Stew, Freddy? It smells delicious.'

'Thank you,' he said, and pushed his bowl towards her.

'Don't want stew,' Billy insisted stoutly. 'Want apple pie and custard.'

Florence, coming back in at that moment and untying her apron, bent towards him with a whispered, 'Dinner first, Billy, before pudding. Sorry, but it's the law.'

'Wass . . . *law*?' Billy pondered, putting a finger to his lip.

'Whatever your mother tells you to do, that's the law,' Miles told him firmly, and the whole table erupted with laughter.

Pearl looked round at them all, her spirits lifting. She had been feeling lonely again recently. Apart from her rehearsal sessions at the hospital, most of which were undertaken alone because the doctor was too busy with his duties to join her, she hadn't left the house very often nor made any new friends. She had not even dared glance into the three wards at the hospital, fearing to see some charming young man she knew at death's door. But sitting around the table with this little group, who had become her family as well as her friends, she felt those burdens slip away. She had been feeling sad and alienated. But perhaps there was a place for her here in Bude.

After all, Miles was an American like herself. Yet he had found a place for himself in Florence's affections and was now one of the family. She too longed to be one of them, while also wishing she could visit her own family in America and make peace with them. It was too horrible to think of her folks back home, judging her for something she had never actually done, which was to marry Terence. She had not heard from them in so long, her heart felt as though it would crack in two. But it was all her own fault, after all. She could hardly blame them for being perfectly right about not throwing herself away on the first young man who came along. Because he had not loved her, had he? It had all been a wicked ruse to get her into bed, something she hated to recall, cringing at the memory of her naivety that night.

Later, as they joked and laughed together, Pearl told them about the routine she would be performing at the hospital near a Christmas. It was to include her old favourites and a few new tunes that Freddy had picked out specially.

'Give us a song, then,' Miles encouraged her, finishing his last few spoonfuls of stew with gusto. 'I miss those performances of yours.'

'Now?'

He shrugged. 'Why not?'

'Yes,' the children insisted, grinning at her. 'Sing for us, Miss Diamond.'

'No, not a song. I want to see you tap-dance,' Clara announced, her young face bright with curiosity. 'Please?'

Flustered and off guard, Pearl stammered, 'But I . . . I can't. Not in these ordinary heels. I'd need my tap shoes for that, and they're up in my room.'

'In that case, you'd better run up and get them. We'll wait.' When she sucked in a breath, frozen in place, Freddy gave her an encouraging smile. 'You don't want to disappoint your audience, surely? Now they know you can tap-dance, they're going to want to see first-hand evidence.'

'Oh, you!' Clasping both hands to her hot cheeks, Pearl reluctantly got up. 'Okay, I'll put the shoes on,' she told the children, 'but I'm awfully rusty, you know. I haven't gotten around to practising the routine yet.'

'Excuses already?' Miles laughed. 'Oh no, you don't get off that lightly. Time to sing for your supper, Miss Diamond.'

The expensive tap shoes were wrapped in crepe and stored in a box under her bed. By the time she'd slipped them on and come back down, Florence had brought out the fruit pie with a huge jug of custard. Freddy and Imogen were both already devouring their slices, in fact.

Pearl gazed on the delicious-smelling dessert in consternation. She was already feeling a bit stodgy after that generous bowl of mutton stew. If she were to add apple pie and custard to it . . .

'I won't be able to dance after eating all that,' she said dubiously.

'Dance now then,' Florence told her, and whisked away the last portion in the dish. 'I'll keep yours warm in the oven. And you greedy lot,' she added, addressing the children, 'no stealing all the custard while she's dancing, do you hear? Make sure you leave a good portion.'

Freddy finished his pie and came to help her clear a dancing space, moving furniture out of the way and rolling back the hearth rug.

'Entertainment while we eat our dinner,' Staff Sergeant Miller said, tucking into his apple pie with enthusiasm as he watched these preparations. 'Now this is what I call entertainment. I like how you Brits do things.'

'I'll have to dance without music,' Pearl muttered awkwardly to the doctor, 'unless there's something suitable on the wireless.'

Catching this, Florence leant over and turned on the wireless. As it slowly warmed up and came on, they heard a voice intoning lists of battles being fought along the front line. Miles frowned, his face tightening, and Freddy stiffened too, pausing in his work.

Hurriedly, Florence snapped the wireless off. 'Sorry, no music. Can you improvise?' she asked, one eye on her husband, who looked grim after that reminder of the war still raging hundreds of miles away on the front.

Pearl glanced for help at Freddy, who stuck his hands in his pockets, tilting his head to one side. 'How about I whistle a snappy tune while you dance? Would that work?'

'Depends how snappy,' Pearl told him frankly. 'Though even humming would be helpful, thank you. Just to get me going.'

After a moment's thought, the doctor began to whistle a recent dance tune. Nodding gratefully, she took up position in front of the fireplace and began to tap in time to the music. With the floorboards showing, her special tap shoes made a lovely clicking sound against the wood, capturing everybody's attention. After a few basic taps and shuffles, she got into a groove and began to really enjoy herself, kicking and flicking in a lively way, using her arms to keep balance and smiling throughout the routine as she had been taught.

When she flopped down into her chair afterwards, hot and exhausted, everybody burst into cheering and rapturous applause, especially Miles, who stood to clap louder than anyone else. He put two fingers in his mouth and whistled heartily. 'Bravo, that was marvellous, Miss Diamond,' he called above the noise. 'Thank you for the floor show.'

Freddy was smiling too. 'Truly magnificent, Pearl,' he said softly, and briefly touched her hand before heading back to sit opposite beside his children.

Her heart was already thumping from all that dancing about. But goodness, when Freddy's hand touched hers, her cheeks burst into glowing heat too. Embarrassed by that reaction, she covered it by patting her hair and smiling shyly at Florence. 'I'll take that apple pie and custard now, if you don't mind, Mrs Miller,' she said in her most demure tone, and everybody laughed.

After the meal was finished, the three children were taken upstairs by Imogen, who had volunteered to make sure they all had a wash and were tucked into bed with a story. 'Bless you, Immi,' her sister breathed, blowing out her cheeks with fatigue as she unfastened her apron, which had been straining over her prominent tummy. 'I'm bone-tired tonight.' She stole a secret smile at her husband, and he took her hand, drawing her to sit beside him in Clara's empty place.

'I wonder why,' he murmured, and Florence looked down, still smiling.

It wasn't surprising that she was exhausted, Pearl thought, watching them indulgently. Florence was expecting another baby and must be near her term. Though how marvellous it must be, she thought with a twinge of envy, to be about to give birth, knowing her husband was finally safe and close at hand.

In the peace that followed the children's departure for bed, they lingered at the table long into the evening, the men drinking and smoking, the women doing most of the talking. When Imogen returned from her duties, she talked about her work with the church club, which still seemed to be occupying her time even though the children were back at school now. But maybe, like many in these difficult times, she had turned to religious belief for solace.

Pearl couldn't be sure, but there was an extra sparkle in Imogen's eyes these days. She guessed from the younger woman's frequent mentions of Reverend Linden that he might be the real draw for her. A vicar seemed an odd choice of boyfriend, and from a few things Florence had said, their history was tangled. But Pearl said nothing. It was none of her business.

Besides, she was hardly qualified to be giving other women advice on men. Not with her dismal track record.

Miles talked briefly about what he'd seen in France, falling silent when the details became too unpleasant. Florence filled the gap, hurriedly discussing her plans for a new nursery once the baby had been born, her smile nervous. It was clear that Miles was still unhappy at having been forced to leave his unit and come home.

'Have you been formally discharged?' Pearl asked the sergeant, eyeing his bandaged head.

'I have, ma'am, yes,' he said solemnly, and put down his teacup. 'The army doesn't want me back. Too damaged, apparently. So that's my military career over. But I hope to teach when I get back to the States. At a military school, that is.' He took a deep breath. 'I don't want to sound self-pitying. But I'm not sure what else I'm good for, besides fighting. Though my fighting days aren't finished yet. I'd sure make an effort if any Jerries were to land on the beach here.'

'Hear! Hear!' Freddy agreed, a fierce look on his face. 'I feel the same. I'm not a fighter by profession, of course. But if there was an invasion, I'd pick up whatever was to hand and defend this town to my last breath. I may have lost a foot, or the use of it, at any rate. But I can still shoot a rifle and hit something.' He grinned. 'Though it would have to be quite a big something. I wouldn't call myself a crack shot!'

Everyone laughed, though there was a serious undercurrent to the talk. Pearl looked at Freddy sitting opposite and thought how immensely brave he must be. He'd been blown up and injured, and probably wouldn't stand a chance in a hand-to-hand fight against a trained enemy soldier. Yet he was plumb keen and willing to give it a try. The same went for Miles, who was clearly not fit to fight either. But she knew that wouldn't stop him. Neither of these men would have the slightest thought for their own safety if they had to protect this household and the women and children within it. And she couldn't be prouder of them for that bravery.

CHAPTER NINETEEN

'Gawd blimey, Alice, keep still in the back there, would you?' Gran turned once again to frown through the grille that looked into the back of Joe's battered old van. 'It's like when you was a little girl and got ants in your pants over summat. I know you're excited to be a bridesmaid again, but that's no excuse for all that argy-bargy. What on earth's going on in the back?'

Alice, squeezed into the back of the van alongside the three Land Girls – Caroline, Selina and even Joan, who had insisted on coming to Penny's wedding in Bude, though she didn't know the bride – struggled to be polite and stifle her indignation. But it was hard, given how uncomfortable she was. 'It ain't my bleedin' fault if we keep getting thrown this way and that every time Joe goes round a bend,' she complained. 'This old thing was never meant to take so many people.'

Huddled opposite, the three evacuee children – also crammed into the back – giggled at her expression.

'Besides, I don't know why so many of us needed to go to Penny's wedding,' she added.

'That's right.' In the front of the van, Arnold Newton turned around with his gravelly laugh and nodded his white head, saying slowly, 'It's like being in a can o' sardines, only on wheels. How you doing in the back there, kids?'

'We're 'aving a whale of a time, Arnie!' Timothy piped up. He was not only the youngest evacuee but Arnold's favourite, probably because he was also the cheekiest of the three. Of course, Janice was too old to be considered a child. But she'd chosen to stay and help out at Joe's farm when she could have taken war work in Penzance or further afield. And Eustace was becoming a strapping young lad himself, with an eye for the girls and some skill with a football, according to Joe.

The three children had insisted on coming to Penny's wedding, despite the glaring lack of room for them in the van. 'We miss Penny,' Janice had explained, glancing at the other Land Girls with a defiant expression. 'She always shared her weekly sweet ration with us.'

'That's right,' Eustace had agreed enthusiastically. 'Bullseyes, aniseed balls, the lot. A right good 'un was Penny.'

'And I want to see Alice all dolled up in her bridesmaid's togs,' Timothy had slipped in with a chuckle, and the two brothers had fallen about laughing and clutching their

262

sides, as though this was the best joke they'd ever heard, while Alice had sucked on her teeth, glowering.

Not being able to afford a second vehicle or the train fare all the way to Bude for so many people, a tough choice had been made.

Thankfully, Lily had volunteered to stay behind, and look after her own baby as well as Violet's, so that Aunty Vi and Joe could have a day away in Bude. 'Lord, bless you,' Violet had said with a cry of delight, hugging her niece when this scheme was first outlined. 'If you're sure? I mean, he's just old enough to be left. I only hope you won't have any trouble with him. He can be a right pain in the evenings.'

'Aunty Vi, I'm a trained midwife,' Lily had reminded her, laughing. 'I'll know what to do for him, don't you fret. You and Joe deserve a day in Bude. Have a wonderful time and a knees-up for me, won't you? Tristan and I will look after the farm, and feed the animals, and make sure the babies don't waste away. Trust me.'

Joe had heartily approved of this plan. Probably because he was sick of having his sleep interrupted with a crying baby. Though he was too nervous of Violet ever to say such a thing to her face. 'That's grand of you, Lily. I know you'll do a proper job of it too. Come on, Vi, it'll be a great day out. And I'd like to see Penny wed. Such a nice girl. Her beau sounds like a solid young man too. I'm pleased for her – that's what I am.'

So they'd got up at the crack of dawn, which was not an unusual time for Joe and the Land Girls to start work but had left Alice sleepy and yawning, and piled into his old van. They had already been on the road several hours, being jolted up and down over every bump on every lane between Porthcurno and Bude. But the rain had held off so far, and every now and then Joe would stop to let them get out and stretch their legs, and duck behind a bush if need be, and eat some of Violet's sandwiches, washed down with a swig of water or some of Arnie's strong bottled beer.

The Cornish landscape was gloriously lush at this time of year, deep into autumn now, the falling leaves yellow and red, grass growing thick and coarse on every hill and dale, and the sea a silver ribbon on their left as they headed north alongside the Atlantic.

Joe drove slowly through the tiny, remote villages, touching his cap to passers-by, and sometimes having to pull right into the hedge when they met a tractor or some other large vehicle on the narrow lanes. Arnie pointed out moorland pubs that he'd visited as a young man, and told a few colourful anecdotes that had Gran shrieking with laughter and Violet clapping her hands over her ears in mock horror.

Finally, they were winding through the valley that led to Bude, and Alice, who had traded places with her aunt in order to guide Joe on the approach, began to get excited, recognising familiar landmarks. She grinned at the thought of seeing her old friend Penny again, not to mention John, and Florence and Imogen, of course. This wedding was going to be a grand treat and she couldn't wait.

'Not far now,' she called into the back of the van, and a cheer went up, their voices rather ragged now after so many hours in the back.

By the time Joe pulled up in front of the boarding house, the sun was beginning to drop lower on the horizon. They jumped thankfully out into the last cool rays of autumnal sunshine, Gran complaining about her old bones while the two boys ran wildly about her and Arnie like animals released from a cage.

Alice also stretched wearily, shielding her eyes against the sunset as she stood in the middle of the quiet road and stared oceanward, remembering so many good times here in Bude. Though she'd had bad days too, like when she and Patrick had been 'taken captive' by the Americans they'd been sent to tail. It had turned out to be yet another test of their abilities but at the time it had seemed horribly real and frightening. Patrick hadn't exactly covered himself in glory that day, but she had long since forgiven him for that. Almost forgotten all about it, in fact. It was as though working with him every day at Porthcurno, seeing a different side to the young man – a sharper, funnier side – had eventually softened her opinion of him . . .

Barely before they were through the garden gate, the door to Ocean View Boarding House flew open, and Florence was there, heavily pregnant, with her American Ranger by her side. 'Welcome back to Bude again,' she said, holding her hands out to Alice. 'It's lovely to see you. And you've brought so many of your family with you . . .' Her smile faltered as she began silently counting heads, no doubt wondering where they would all sleep. 'How, erm, wonderful.'

Penny had written to say Miles had come back wounded from the front, though Alice was still shocked to see the bandage about his head. He had always seemed so strong and dependable during her time in Bude. But his arm was about his wife's shoulders and he seemed relaxed and happy as they greeted each other, not suffering too much.

She shook hands with him and hugged Florence, exclaiming frankly at how huge she looked, and grinned when Imogen came out to say hello too.

'We've been fairly battered about in that van,' she told her friends. 'So I hope you've been putting the kettle on, Imogen. Because I'm fair parched and I bet my gran is too.'

Behind her, Arnie gave a bark of laughter, and even Gran chuckled. 'You're not wrong there,' her grandmother admitted, coming to shake hands with everyone as well. 'My tongue's hanging out for a nice hot cuppa. Now listen, I've brought some cake, love,' she added, turning to Florence. 'Never visit anyone empty-handed, that's what my old mum taught me. I hope you like walnut cake and vanilla.' She paused. 'There ain't too many walnuts in it, and not much vanilla or sugar neither, but it is *cake*. That is, it's made with real eggs. From our Joe's best layers, up the farm.' She glanced at Violet, who dug deep into her wicket basket and produced a bundle wrapped in cloth. 'And we brought you a dozen fresh eggs too.'

'You brought us *eggs*?' Florence's eyes were wide with

wonder as she took the well-wrapped bundle. 'Thank you, how absolutely marvellous. And cake too. My little boy Billy will be over the moon. Please, come in, all of you.' Her gaze fell on the three evacuee children, and her smile broadened. 'Oh dear, you all look a bit crumpled. Have you been crammed in the back of that van all the way from Porthcurno? Come in and meet the other children living here. I'm sure you'll all soon be playing together. Clara's a bit younger than you,' she told Janice with an understanding smile, 'but she's a sensible girl and I expect you'll get along well. And you boys should like Toby,' she told Eustace and Timothy, who beamed.

The children ran into the house, shouting excitedly. Miles laughed and hurriedly followed them inside. 'Hey, hang on there, kids,' he called after them in his amused drawl. 'Wait for me.'

Alice asked Florence, 'Where's Penny?'

'Upstairs in her room, with her mum and dad.' Florence nodded her inside. 'She's expecting you. Go on up while I get the tea made.' She hesitated. 'She's been a bit nervous about the big day tomorrow. But now you've arrived, her nerves are sure to be settled. I'm glad you agreed to be her bridesmaid, Alice. You always did have a steadying influence on her.'

'Blimey, did I?' Alice wasn't sure about that, suspecting it had been the other way around, but headed upstairs anyway.

'Aw, poor little lamb, I know 'ow she feels. I was married first time around when I was about her age,' Gran could be heard saying as she trundled after Florence and the others to the guests' lounge. 'Me nerves were so bad, I was sick as a parrot. Nearly ran away rather than go through with it.'

'Not your wedding day stories again, Mum,' Violet groaned.

Gran ignored her daughter. 'Thank goodness I didn't, eh? Or Vi wouldn't be here today. No, nor Lily and Alice. They're my Betsy's girls, you know, Mrs Miller. We lost our poor Betsy to the Blitz, rest her soul.' She gave a muffled sob. 'Gawd, them was 'orrible times. We love Cornwall – it's bloomin' Paradise on Earth, I swear it.'

Upstairs, Alice knocked on Penny's door, grinning. Everyone in the family had heard all her old anecdotes before, and every time Gran retold her favourite stories, she added new flourishes.

'Alice!' Penny dragged her inside as soon as she saw who it was. The two hugged each other tightly. 'Lord, I'm so glad you made it. I was getting worried. You've taken ages.'

'You remember Joe's old van? Somehow, he managed to nurse it all the way here with a football team's worth onboard. Though from the racket it's been making, I think it left its bleedin' exhaust somewhere north of Polzeath. And gawd knows how we'll get 'ome. We used up all the petrol we'd saved just reaching Bude.' Alice laughed at her friend's horrified expression. 'But I wouldn't have missed your big day for the world. Even if I have to push the van all the way back myself, I'm still glad we came.'

She turned hurriedly to shake hands with Penny's parents, whom she'd already met briefly. 'Good to see you again, Mr and Mrs Brown. 'Ow d'you do?'

After everyone had established they were well and thriving, Penny's parents took themselves downstairs for a cup of tea and a slice of Gran's cake with the others, leaving Alice to admire Penny's wedding dress. Her friend had chosen to be married in a lavishly embroidered white lace and satin dress that John's mum had worn for her own wedding, according to Penny's last letter. Alice was no expert on wedding dresses, but she knew only too well that *bridesmaids'* dresses tended to be flouncy, embarrassing affairs. So she was relieved when Penny brought out a plain cream dress with red piping that her mother had made and asked if she would wear it tomorrow at the ceremony. When she'd got her wedding invitation through the post, Alice had been taken aback, having almost forgotten her promise. But she was determined not to let her friend down.

She beamed and tried on the dress, which fitted perfectly. 'Just as well I haven't been stuffing my face with food like I used to,' she told Penny frankly, 'else this might've been a bit tight.'

'You did say in your last letter that you'd lost a little weight. Irregular mealtimes and all that,' Penny reminded her. 'I suppose they've been keeping you busy up at Porthcurno. How's the code-cracking going?' When Alice hesitated, she added swiftly, 'Sorry, *loose lips sink ships*, I know. I shouldn't have asked. No need to say a word.'

'The work is pretty much hush-hush,' Alice agreed, wriggling out of the dress. 'What I can tell you though is that I'm enjoying it. Far more than what I was doing in London. Maybe not as exciting.' She pulled a face. 'But I've had enough excitement for a lifetime. Workin' at a desk suits me just fine, thanks.'

'You're happier now, and that's what's important,' Penny said wisely.

Alice wasn't sure she was happier. But it was true that she was finally beginning to put the horrors of Jim's death behind her, so she didn't argue.

'And you?' Alice studied her closely, for Penny never gave much away in her letters. 'John's a good sort. But you and he haven't known each other much above a year. You're sure about this marriage?'

'Goodness, what a question!' Penny laughed, blushing. 'Of course I'm sure. I hope John is too. A bit late if he isn't. We tie the knot tomorrow.' Then she must have caught the twinkle in Alice's eye, for she gave a gasp of exasperated laughter, planting both fists on her hips. 'You're pulling my leg, aren't you?'

'Maybe a bit.' Alice took Penny's hands and looked at her seriously. 'I envy you though. Not about getting married. I'm sure nobody in their right mind would want to marry me, I'm such an odd bod. But having someone else to talk to, to keep you company, tell your secrets to . . . That's special. I envy you *that*.'

'You'll find someone like that one day, Alice. You may be odd at times but you've got a heart of gold. Somewhere out there is a man who'll be perfect for you.' Penny gave her a quick hug, then drew back, her face solemn too. 'But when you find him, you have to promise me one thing.'

'What?'

'That you'll ask me to be your matron of honour.'

'For gawd's sake, you're my only friend, who else would I bloomin' ask?' Alice demanded, and they both stared at each other, and then gripped their sides, giggling fit to bust.

CHAPTER TWENTY

The day of Penny's wedding to John Pascoe dawned bright and clear, though with clouds approaching Bude from the west, suggesting there might be rain later. Imogen got up early to help Florence, who had agreed to lay on the wedding breakfast at the boarding house after the ceremony. They had already made the wedding cake some months previously, with the help of John's mother, a dour little woman but an excellent cook. There were sandwiches to make too, and a rum punch using a recipe sent by Penny's godmother, who was sadly too unwell to travel down from Exeter.

Both families had chipped in with extra ration coupons so the happy couple could have a proper send-off. They would be taking a few days for their honeymoon further down the coast, in an ancient fisherman's cottage near St Ives that belonged to John's family. Apparently, it was in dire need of renovation. 'Falling down around our ears, more like it,' was what John had said, laughing, when his father fondly described the place as 'a little ramshackle'. 'But it'll do me and Pen nicely for a few days away. Then it'll be back to Bude and the *Mary Jane*.' That was the boat he and his family kept moored in Bude Harbour. Imogen thought him very brave for taking the boat out on lengthy fishing trips, knowing that German U-boats could be right beneath them and they wouldn't know until it was all over. Many boats – both fishing vessels and non-military supply convoys – had been lost to attacks by enemy submarines since the war began. But people needed to eat, and fish were plentiful, so these Cornish fishermen kept sailing courageously out.

Once all the wedding food had been prepared and covered with cloths to keep it fresh, Imogen ran upstairs to brush her hair and change into her best frock for the wedding. She applied her make-up with a hand that was not quite steady, checked her nylons for ladders – thankfully there were none – and slipped on her heels. She ought to have been thrilled for Penny. And she was, of course. But she knew the day ahead must hold some challenges too, at least for her.

Richard would be officiating over the wedding ceremony. So she was killing two birds with one stone today. She could attend Penny's wedding and keep an eye on the vicar and his parishioners at the same time. Not a terribly comfortable thought. And she still found it hard to believe that Richard could be involved in anything shady. But it was her duty to find out for sure. And there had been that piece of paper she'd seen him discussing with Mr Jolly and Mr Alsop after church one time.

Had she imagined the furtive look on Mr Jolly's face as he stuffed it into his pocket at her approach?

But what with the preparations for Penny's wedding, having to strip so many beds and lay on extra food for the wedding guests, she'd barely had a moment to herself recently. She felt guilty, aware that she was neglecting her mission. But Florence was far too alarmingly pregnant to be expected to do much more than swan about the kitchen occasionally, and although they had a local girl helping out with household chores, she was only there for a few hours a day, which meant the majority of jobs fell on Imogen's shoulders instead.

Only yesterday she'd received a letter from Mrs Elliott, a reminder that she had not yet filed an official report. Imogen had read the letter several times, fretting over how to reply. Any report she sent now would feel like a betrayal of Richard, who was fast becoming a friend and who was, besides, still mourning his lost brother.

In her bleaker moments, she allowed herself to wonder how Simon's widow Rosie and her child were faring. But that was none of her business. The sad truth was, Simon might have amused himself by flirting for a while, but he had never been seriously interested in her. The sooner she got used to that idea and stopped refiguring ancient history to better suit her fantasies, the better for everyone. She had a task to do and this lingering confusion in her mind over Simon's death was getting in the way of her doing it. So she had resolved to move on and put Simon back into the past where he belonged.

First though, she had Penny's wedding to get through, and that unnerving report to write for Mrs Elliott. Given how little she'd discovered, she wasn't sure it would be more than a few meagre sentences. But she couldn't simply ignore the request.

The clouds were thickening above Bude by the time everyone was ready to leave for the church. But nobody paid any heed to the weather, except Miles, who brought a handful of umbrellas, 'For the return journey, just in case.'

The wedding party walked to church in a long, straggling procession. Florence and Miles led the way with Billy between them, holding both their hands and chattering ceaselessly in his high-pitched voice. Imogen walked behind with Alice, who was Penny's bridesmaid and looked smarter than Imogen had ever seen her, carrying a pretty floral bouquet. Behind them, the five evacuee children hopped and skipped excitedly, with Janice in charge as the eldest, though Clara was an excellent deputy. Their little crew, all hailing from the London area, had quickly bonded and were now inseparable. After the children came Penny herself, arm in arm with her parents. The bride had chosen to walk to church since it was such a short distance from the boarding house – so long as the rain held off, which so far it seemed to be doing.

Imogen thought Penny looked splendid in her white lace wedding dress, with her brown hair curled softly and dressed with greenery for the occasion. And radiantly happy too.

Imogen envied her such uncomplicated happiness. To her, being happy had always seemed the hardest thing in the world. Unattainable, in fact. She had often pretended to others that she was happy. But it had only been a front, never the truth. Deep down inside, Imogen wasn't even sure she knew what true happiness felt like.

Behind Penny came more members of Alice's eccentric family – her aunt Violet and uncle Joe, her grandmother with her husband Arnold, the old couple walking slowly and pointing out landmarks the whole way as though on a sightseeing tour. Finally, bringing up the rear, came Pearl with Dr Tyson, whose head was bent, listening intently to the American woman without saying a word. Another complicated relationship, Imogen thought, throwing them a backwards glance. But after the way Pearl had been treated by that nasty young man Terence, she deserved a little romance in her life. Though it wasn't clear to Imogen if romance was even on the cards between those two . . .

''Ere, what you looking at?' Alice demanded in her usual blunt fashion, also glancing back over her shoulder.

'I was just making sure everyone is accounted for,' Imogen fibbed shamelessly. 'We wouldn't want anyone left behind. Not on Penny's big day.'

'Impossible,' Alice said, sniffing her bouquet. 'Smashing bridesmaid's dress, ain't it?' She smoothed down the cream linen with awed pride. 'Though I daren't eat more than a few sarnies at the do after. Just in case I split the seams. Or drop food on meself.'

'Nonsense, you'll be fine. You should enjoy yourself.' The church was in sight. Imogen swallowed, wishing she could take her own advice. But her heart was pounding. Richard would already be there, talking to the organist about the hymns to be played and waiting for the wedding party to arrive. She was partly looking forward to seeing him again and partly dreading it too.

'John should be at the church by now,' Penny could be heard saying nervously to her parents. 'I only hope he isn't late. It would be just like him to oversleep.'

'Now, don't fret,' her father told her firmly. 'John is a conscientious young man. He'll be on time.'

'His mum will have had John up and dressed at dawn,' Alice muttered to Imogen. 'She's a right dragon.'

'I wish we could have had the bells ringing,' Penny's mother said, and sighed. 'It's not a proper wedding without bells.'

'Agreed,' shouted out Alice's grandmother from the back of the procession.

'Now, love, you know why we can't ring the church bells,' Arnold told his wife. 'That's the signal that an invasion's started. Can't have Penny and John at the altar and the army swooping in to shoot us all dead, because they think we're Jerries.'

'Bloomin' Hitler again,' his wife replied sharply. 'He's the cause of all our problems.'

The children took this as a cue to start singing a rude little song about Hitler that had Penny's parents rolling their eyes and Alice giggling.

The parish church was packed, both outside and in. It was clear that the Pascoes were a popular local family. Fishermen and their wives lined the gravelled path to the church door, caps in hand, cheering Penny on her way. Imogen spotted both Mr Alsop and Mr Jolly in the crowd of well-wishers, noticeably neither of them smiling. At the church door Richard was waiting to greet the bride and her father, while everyone else filed into the cool interior to find a pew.

He looked so strikingly handsome in his vicar's collar and surplice, it took her breath away. But she forced her gaze to Alice instead and even managed a smile. 'See you afterwards,' she said, turning to go inside. 'Good luck.'

'Immi, are you all right?'

Surprised, she glanced back at Alice. 'Of course.' Had her face given her away? 'Weddings, you know. I've never been comfortable with, erm, crowds.' It had been intended as a fib to cover her reaction. Yet it was true at the same time, she realised. She did hate crowds.

'Or vicars?' Alice murmured astutely.

Imogen stared. Goodness, the girl was observant.

'Shall we?' Richard said, not looking at her.

Inside, the organist had begun to play with pomp and gravitas, signalling the start of proceedings. A thready cheer went up around the uninvited crowd gathered outside, curious neighbours and townsfolk there to wish her well, the fishermen's wives looking with frank admiration at the young bride waiting at the church door on her father's arm. Penny's dress flapped in a sudden gust from the sea, her father catching at his hat to prevent it being whirled away, but the bride seemed oblivious to the change in the weather, whispering something to Alice and beaming with joyful anticipation.

Imogen hurried inside, avoiding Richard's eye, her cheeks warm. If even Alice, who'd only been here five minutes, could see there was something between her and the vicar, what had everyone else noticed?

Worse, what did Richard think of her constantly hanging about as though besotted with him?

After the ceremony, Richard's key message of 'fresh hope in a time of great personal sacrifice' still echoing in her ears, Imogen hurried back to the boarding house ahead of the wedding guests. With Florence unable to walk quickly, it was up to her to lay out the food on the buffet table and make sure there were enough glasses for everyone to raise a toast to the bride and groom. Although the wedding party were posing for photographs at the church door, she knew others would already be making their way down Ocean View Road. In these times of tight rationing, a promise of free food and drink was enough to draw even the uninvited to attend a celebratory party.

In her haste, Imogen took a shortcut behind the houses, the track shady and overgrown. A few hundred feet ahead was a figure stooping under a gnarled old tree, its trunk bent almost in two by the prevailing ocean winds. She stopped, frowning, and shrank close to the undergrowth as he looked back. It was Mr Jolly, she realised.

The man didn't appear to have spotted her, for he lit a cigarette in a leisurely fashion before continuing to walk on towards the coast.

But she'd seen what he'd done . . . Left something under a large rock at the base of that old tree.

Her heart thumping, she stayed out of view for a count of ten, making sure he was well out of sight, and then carried on. Stopping beside the rock, she first checked nobody else was coming, and then bent to lift the heavy rock.

Beneath was a brown envelope.

Imogen stiffened, her chest tight, breath halting.

What on earth was this?

She had been taught about 'dead-letter drops', where targets sometimes left messages in secret, pre-arranged locations for other targets or even enemy agents to collect, thus avoiding any need for them to meet in public and potentially blow their cover.

Was this a dead-letter drop?

Gingerly, she picked the slender envelope up and turned it over. No name or address. Nothing to signify what it contained within.

It was all so unexpected, she was struggling to think clearly. It was sealed, and if she broke the seal, anyone coming to collect it later would know it had been intercepted. She could take it and read the contents, which felt like a single folded sheet of paper. But then Mr Jolly might eventually learn that it had not been collected by the intended person, and be scared off. Or she could leave it, keep watch on the spot in the hope of seeing who his contact was, and trust that no major secrets were being passed to the enemy in this message.

On impulse, she took the envelope and hurried home. There were already guests gathered in the front garden, complaining at the long wait. She apologised, letting them in and hurriedly setting out the buffet food before urging Janice to put a record on the gramophone. 'Something lively, but not too loud,' she told the girl, who grinned and began arguing with Clara over which record to choose.

Thankfully, Florence and Miles were soon back, with Pearl and Dr Tyson in tow, and Imogen made an excuse to slip away briefly to her room before the bride and groom themselves arrived.

There, she tore open the envelope.

The sheet of paper was written in code. Tiny squiggles, like shorthand, but utterly incomprehensible, greeted her.

She had no time to think.

Hurriedly, she took a sheet and wrote, 'Urgent. We need to meet. Church porch, noon, Wednesday.' Then she slipped this sheet into a similar-looking brown envelope from those in her correspondence drawer, and dashed downstairs in time to see Penny and John walking up the road, hand in hand, looking joyous, with Alice behind her, and a crowd of guests following behind . . .

As petals rained down on the happy couple at the gate, Imogen slipped past them and threaded her way through the guests. At the corner, she dashed down the shady track and hid the envelope under the rock again. Then walked back to join the wedding party, breathless and agitated.

She would pass the coded letter to Mrs Elliott, of course, and tell her everything. But it might not reach her handler for several days. She was on her own until she received a reply.

What if she went to the church on Wednesday to see if anyone turned out and found *Richard* there?

Horror churned inside her. She would have to report him to Mrs Elliott. Though he was the vicar, so he might be there legitimately. Perhaps she ought to have chosen another location. But in her hurry, she hadn't been thinking straight and the church had seemed a logical place. Few people about in the middle of a weekday, plenty of places around the churchyard to hide and watch the porch from a safe distance.

If Richard was a traitor to their country, he would be arrested and put on trial. If found guilty, he would go to prison, and might even hang for his crime.

Oh, what had she done?

CHAPTER TWENTY-ONE

Late on Wednesday morning, a light drizzle was falling on Bude when Imogen put her head around the door to the guests' lounge and reminded Pearl that they were due to go out soon.

'Darn, I'd forgotten about that.' Pearl sighed, closing the American fashion magazine she'd been reading. An old friend in Chicago had mailed it to her and she'd read it cover to cover, though it made her homesick.

'You promised you'd come with me.' Imogen's eyes were pleading. 'You can't let me down now.'

'Honey, it's raining out there. Surely nobody will expect you to turn up in this weather. What are you doing again?'

'Flower arranging. At the church. It's my first time, and if I don't go, I'll never hear the end of it. They arrange the altar flowers in pairs, you see, and I've been paired with Mrs Crabtree.'

'Mrs Crabtree, huh? She doesn't sound too friendly.'

'She's an absolute tyrant. And she hates me because . . . Well, I'm not sure why she hates me. But she does.' There was passion in Imogen's face, her eyes alight with it. 'Please, Pearl. If you're with me, she'll be nice. But if I turn up alone,' she went on fearfully, 'or not at all—'

'She'll gobble you up and spit you out.' Pearl got up, glancing ruefully out at the weather. She didn't want to go out. But she owed Imogen a favour for letting her stay at the boarding house at a reduced rate. So she could hardly say no, could she? 'Okay, I'll come with you. Give me five minutes to change.'

'You're a lifesaver, Pearl. Thank you.'

They arrived at the church around noon, both sheltering from the rain under an umbrella. There was nobody in the graveyard, which was hardly surprising given the weather, but the church was empty too. Imogen had brought some greenery in a wicker basket and she set this on one of the front pews, stripping off her gloves as she glanced about the deserted church.

'I wonder where Mrs Crabtree can be?' She asked, seeming a little agitated. Her voice bounced eerily about the stone walls. Pearl had never been religious, and although she found quaint old English churches interesting, she didn't feel completely comfortable there. She half expected a ghost to float out from behind one of the pillars or the ornate wooden screen.

'Maybe Mrs Crabtree decided not to come because of the rain,' she suggested, hanging back. 'In which case, she was smarter than us.'

'I'm sure she'll be along any minute.' But it was clear that Imogen didn't believe that, for she stood in silence after the echoes of their voices had died away, a look on her face that could almost have been fright.

'You okay, honey?' Pearl had a tingly sensation up her spine.

'I'm getting a headache – that's all.' Imogen spun, her eyes widening, at the sound of a male voice outside the church. The colour seemed to desert her cheeks and a hand crept to her mouth. 'Goodness, who . . . who could that be?'

'Well, if it's Mrs Crabtree, she has a very deep voice.' Seeing how Imogen stood stricken to the spot, Pearl walked to the heavy church door and pulled it open. Imogen came dashing up behind her but stopped dead on the threshold, staring at the two people in the church porch. It was the vicar and an elderly lady in a mauve hat and matching coat.

'Richard!' Imogen gasped, and then blinked, looking confused. 'I mean, Reverend Linden . . . I didn't expect to see you here today.'

'Nor I you,' he said slowly, looking from her to Pearl in obvious surprise. Then he indicated the old lady at his side. 'I was just speaking to Miss Jacobs here about the verger. Poor Mr Chandler. He's not been well, so hasn't been able to attend to his duties recently. I'm sorry if I interrupted whatever you were doing.'

'Oh no, we were just . . .' Imogen paused, biting her lip, her eyes huge.

'Flower arranging,' Pearl supplied helpfully.

At exactly the same time, Imogen blurted out, 'Praying.' She locked gazes with Pearl and gave a tiny warning shake of her head. 'We were praying together. For the end of the war. For the Allies to win. We both feel very strongly about it,' she finished earnestly.

'No doubt.' The vicar hesitated. 'Please don't let me intrude on your prayer time. I only brought Miss Jacobs into the church porch because of the rain. I'm sorry if we were too loud.'

Miss Jacobs, who had listened to all this with pursed lips and narrowed eyes, shook hands with the vicar. 'Give Mr Chandler my best regards. I hope his gout improves soon,' she said curtly, and hurried away without another word.

The vicar watched her go, frowning. 'Oh dear, I do hope I haven't upset her. The Jacobs sisters – there are three of them, you know, all spinsters – are very generous when the collection plate comes around.' Turning to them, he added awkwardly, 'Would either of you like to speak to me about your concerns, perhaps? Or pray with you, perhaps?'

'No thank you,' Pearl said politely.

'That's very, um, kind of you,' Imogen said, her voice trembling.

Pearl glanced at her friend and was amazed to see tears swimming in her eyes. There was something strange going on here. Why on earth had Imogen told him they were 'praying'? Presumably because there was no flower arranging today. Either she'd made a mistake and didn't want to admit it, or she had simply made up that story in order to engineer this meeting with the vicar. Both of which struck her as very odd.

'I'm heading home now,' she decided out loud, and edged out of the church porch, opening her umbrella. 'Are you coming, Imogen? Or would you prefer to stay here and . . . *pray* for a bit longer?'

Imogen barely seemed to be listening to her. 'I'll see you later,' she muttered, her gaze still fixed on the vicar's face. Her face was so pale, she looked almost ashen.

After a moment's hesitation, Pearl gave up and set off back towards the boarding house, worried by how distressed Imogen had become after finding the vicar in the church porch with that old lady. She didn't know why that should be or what was going on between those two. But she hoped Imogen could start being honest with Reverend Linden, especially if romance was in the air, which she suspected it must be from her friend's emotional response.

She knew better than most what it was like to discover someone's secrets too late.

Pearl was on her way to the hospital, determined to finalise her routine with several hours of solid rehearsal. But when she arrived, shaking out her umbrella as she walked through the hospital entrance, she found a scene of chaos that stopped her on the threshold. There were new patients everywhere, most leaning against walls or on crutches, a few sunk into chairs, other men lying on stretchers in the middle of the lobby as though abandoned there.

Shocked, she turned towards the reception desk. Penny, back from her honeymoon, was deep in a heated conversation with a stocky man in uniform. 'We don't have any more beds, I've told you. I'm really sorry but you'll need to find somewhere else for these men to go.'

'There ain't nowhere else. Orders is orders. We've brought 'em here and you'll have to deal with them.'

Penny's colour was high. 'Says who?' she demanded.

'Says the Ministry,' the man insisted in his gravelly voice, and slammed a clipboard down in front of her, jabbing it with a stubby finger. From what Pearl could make out, peering over his shoulder, the form on the top had been given an official government stamp.

'See there? That's the order for these boys to come here. I've done my bit. Now you do yours.' He touched his cap, pushed the clipboard towards her, and walked out of the hospital. His gaze moved up and down Pearl as he passed, and he gave her a cheeky grin. 'Good morning, Miss.' And with that, he was gone.

Pearl stared at her friend. 'How awful,' she said, keeping her voice low so the wounded soldiers round them wouldn't overhear. It wasn't their fault the hospital had no room for them, after all. 'I heard what that man said. What are you going to do?'

'I've no idea,' Penny said, clearly exasperated, and shook her head. 'I feel like weeping, to be honest. But that won't do any good, will it? These men will still be lying on the floor and there still won't be any beds available for them. I'm going out of my mind, Pearl, I don't mind telling you. They started arriving an hour ago, in a whole fleet of trucks.'

'Where's Dr Tyson?'

'He's been in surgery for hours. I dare not disturb him. He's performing a very tricky operation. And our nurses are at full stretch. I can't ask them to deal with this lot as well.' She groaned. 'The worst thing is, this is our second consignment of new patients this week. We ran out of beds days ago. And I've got men queued up outside theatre, waiting their turn for an op, some of them in dreadful pain. It's beyond unacceptable.'

Seeing how close she was to tears, Pearl gave Penny a quick hug. 'I had come to rehearse,' she said, trying to tackle the situation in the most practical way, 'but there's no point in that now. Especially if Dr Tyson is needed in theatre and can't accompany me on the piano as I'd hoped. Besides you'll need our rehearsal space for beds, so that's that.' She took off her jacket and unpinned her hat, placing both carefully behind Penny's reception desk. Then she rolled up the sleeves of her blouse. 'Tell me where to find an apron, and I'll get started.'

Penny stared at her, blinking. 'Get started doing what?'

'Helping with this lot, of course. Honey, you can't do this alone and you shouldn't have to do. I may not be a nurse, but what training do you need to find spaces for wounded soldiers in a hospital? Put me to work. I've got nothing better to go, except maybe dance.' She glanced around at the bored and uncomfortable young men who had been abandoned in the hospital lobby. 'I mean, I'm sure they could do with a pick-me-up. A song and a dance. But right now, I think they'd be happier with a bed and a hot drink, don't you?'

'Oh, Pearl, you're a star!' Penny took her to a storage cupboard where she found her a hair net, and kitted her out in a starched white apron and cap, before giving her brief instructions on how to deal with the men and wash her hands at regular intervals. 'If you could take the names of the men who can stand and walk, and take them over to C Ward, that would be marvellous. I've no orderlies left who aren't already occupied, and although there's not much room in C Ward, at least they have chairs there, so some of these poor blighters can sit down while they wait.'

Armed with an official-looking clipboard and pen, Pearl went around the wounded, taking their names and ranks, and making quick notes on their physical condition. Then she gathered a dozen men who were able to walk, either unaided or on crutches, and guided them through to C Ward, which was not too far from the little rehearsal space she and Dr Tyson had been using. The men seemed bemused by Pearl, perhaps because of her American accent, or perhaps because her platinum hair and scarlet lipstick were more suited to an entertainer than a hospital orderly. But they followed her meekly enough and soon she had the satisfaction of seeing them installed in chairs or sitting on windowsills in C Ward.

On her way back to reception, she bumped into Freddy hurrying in the opposite direction, his dark hair spikier than ever, as though he'd been tearing at it in frustration. He stared at her, taking in her apron and nurse's cap with incredulity. 'What on earth . . . ?' he demanded.

Embarrassed by his expression, she explained the situation, adding awkwardly, 'I was just going back to deal with the others. Though I don't have a clue where we'll find room for them, given the hospital's already chockful of wounded servicemen.'

'I've just come from there. You're right – it's a mess. But I have found a solution, of sorts. Short of discharging the ones we've fixed up in a hurry, we're finding beds for the worst cases by moving those already on the road to recovery into a side building.' He grimaced, thrusting his hands into the deep pockets of his white coat. 'It used to be a storage hut. Not the most sanitary of places. But I've got some orderlies sweeping it out and dusting down the windows, such as they are. Once we've got some mattresses down on the floor, the longer-term patients can consider the place their own until they're ready to leave. Meanwhile, the sicker ones can take their places on the wards.'

'That's a swell idea,' she agreed. 'Well done, Freddy.' She said his name shyly, for she probably ought to call him Dr Tyson, considering they were 'at work' in the hospital now. Yet somehow that felt wrong. They had become friends in recent months. Perhaps more than friends. But she didn't dare think of that now, especially in this emergency situation.

With a hurried goodbye, she made her way back to reception, glad he didn't know what she was thinking. The doctor was clearly still pining for his wife, for she had frequently caught a faraway look on his face when mentioning her to his children. It would be dreadfully cruel of her to expect any attention from him.

Besides, he had probably never thought of her like that anyway.

It was some hours before the side building was tidied out and ready to be occupied. With the help of the hospital orderlies, they moved the sicker patients into the wards, some of them clearly in terrible pain.

Once the men were safely tucked up in bed, Pearl went around the ward, holding their hands and asking where they were from, those who were able to answer anyway. Here and there, she caught an American accent, and even recognised one or two faces from among the Rangers who'd been stationed here before the big push on France.

By the time Penny came to find her and say they should both go home, having been there long into the evening, Pearl was feeling weepy and disoriented. It was not the day she had planned. But she'd discovered a great inner joy in helping those who were hurt and unable to help themselves.

'I can walk with you as far as the cottage,' Penny said, also looking exhausted. She had moved in with John and his parents after they were married, and seemed happy enough there. But John and his father had gone out on the *Mary Jane* for one last fishing trip before winter storms set in, and it was clear she was missing his company. 'I'll wait while you clean up.'

In the nurses' washroom, Pearl dropped her soiled apron into the laundry basket, unpinned her cap and hairnet, and washed her hands, staring at herself in the mirror. Her face looked different, as though she was somebody new. Drained, fatigued, yet somehow at peace. She wondered whether a career in nursing would suit her better than being on the stage. But another part of her wished she could lie down and close her eyes for a spell. No performance had ever left her feeling this weary, her legs like lead.

As she stumbled back to reception, the air-raid siren went off, its wail distant but unmistakable. It had to be a false alarm, she thought, perplexed. They hadn't been targeted by bombers in months.

Before she'd gone even a few paces, a hand gripped her arm, tugging her in the opposite direction from reception. It was Dr Tyson, a grim look on his face. He said hoarsely, 'This way, quick!'

'It's a false alarm,' she told him as he led her insistently down a side corridor. 'It must be.'

Too late, she saw how pale and unsteady he was, clutching at his chest as though struggling to breathe. He flung open a door and stumbled out into the chilly dark with her. It was spitting with rain.

The siren had already stopped.

'See?' she told him. 'Someone must have set it off by accident. Or for a lark.'

Closing the door, the doctor leant against it and shut his eyes. 'I'm sorry,' he gasped, torment in his face. 'Whatever must you think of me? That bloody siren . . . Ordinarily I can handle it. When the kids are there and need me to be strong . . .' His chest was heaving. 'But I suddenly couldn't bear to stay trapped inside a moment longer. Not after what happened in London.'

With a stab of pity, she understood then. She looked up but could see nothing. There was no sign of enemy planes. Even the stars were hidden behind a mass of dark clouds.

They were in the rose garden, Pearl realised. 'Come on,' she whispered and drew him towards one of the benches, sitting down with him there. It was damp but she didn't mind that. 'I won't make you go back inside,' she promised, patting his hand. 'We'll sit out here together until you feel better. How's that, honey?'

'Thank you.' Freddy gave a gulp and met her eyes in the gloom. 'Oh God, I'm such a coward,' he groaned, and bent his head. 'A filthy, rotten coward.'

'No, don't say that. Anyone who isn't afraid when that awful siren goes off is either a liar or a fool.'

He ran a hand across his forehead, looking away. 'That's kind of you, Pearl Diamond. You're a good woman.'

Pearl said nothing but her heart leapt inside her. Nobody had ever called her a good woman before.

CHAPTER TWENTY-TWO

The lush Cornish hedgerows at Porthcurno were draped in spiders' webs sparkling with dew and Alice stopped to admire one on her way to work, drawing in lungfuls of the fresh country air, so different from the lung-clogging smog in Dagenham where she'd grown up. She was meant to be at Eastern House soon, but her attention had been caught by the fat-bodied cobweb spider, spinning at the centre of its fragile net. She was impressed by its industrious attitude.

'Busy little fella, isn't he?'

Startled, she spun around, surprised to see her brother-in-law Tristan coming up behind her.

Tris and Lily had decided to stay on at the farm until after Christmas, at the earliest, not least because they had nowhere else to go. With Lily still nursing her young baby, another midwife was caring for the pregnant ladies of St Ives, and since their tiny cottage had come with the job, Lily had been asked to give it up to the new midwife. So it was a good job she would always have a roof over her head with Aunty Vi and Uncle Joe at the farm. And since Tristan was still recuperating from his accident with the Fire Service, there had been no point him trying to find work and new digs for them in St Ives. Not until he was back to full health, anyway.

In return for their bed and board, Lily was mucking in with cooking and household chores, while Tristan was helping Joe and the Land Girls about the farm. Joe had been delighted by this arrangement, for his false leg made it hard for him to get up and down from the top fields, and another man about the place was always welcome. Besides, Tristan had grown up on a farm, and was not only handy with the livestock but an expert in farm management too.

'The spider, you mean? He's doing a crackin' job with that web,' she agreed, grinning. 'Where are you off to so early then, Tris? Off for a walk into the village?'

'Off to work, actually. Arnie's not feeling well this morning,' he explained, falling into step beside her as they continued down the hill. 'So I've offered to mind the village shop for him until he's better.'

She was instantly alarmed, for she had never known Arnold Newton to take a sick day off work. She could already imagine how Gran must be fussing around him. 'I didn't hear a peep about that. Nothing serious, I hope?'

'A touch of flu, your gran says.' He gave a shrug. 'I wouldn't worry too much. Arnie's as strong as an ox. And could probably eat an ox for breakfast, sick or not.'

Alice laughed. 'I might drop into the shop later, just to see you serving up sweets and baccy to the villagers. And how are your hands?'

Tristan no longer had to wear bandages and his burns seemed much improved. But she knew he was still careful with his work around the farm, often wearing gloves to prevent injury to the tender new skin.

'Damn itchy.' He laughed. 'But on the mend and that's what matters.' Her brother-in-law studied her sideways, his expression curious. 'How about you, Alice? We're all dying to know about your work but you're awfully close-mouthed about it.'

'You can blame the Official Secrets Act for that.'

'Lord, I wasn't prying. Mum's the word. We just want to be sure you're happy and thriving at Eastern House. Your aunt Violet had a hard time when she was housekeeper there, remember, and as for Lily . . . Well, you know how your sister worries.' He hesitated, glancing at her. 'Have you made any friends, for instance? Lily reckons they'll be too posh for you down there. All public schoolboys and Oxbridge types in tweed jackets.'

She bit back a laugh, hearing that; it was an almost perfect description of the men she worked with day in, day out. With the exception of Patrick, who had told her he was an orphan, his past darker and less privileged than the others.

'But I'm sure you can hold your own, even with a room of eggheads.'

'They're all right once you get used to them,' she

admitted, kicking a loose stone ahead of them down the steep track. 'A few plummy accents, maybe. But we're all doing the same job and for the same reason, ain't we?'

'Fair enough.' He picked a long feathery stem of grass and chewed on the end, looking down into the valley towards the heavily camouflaged edifice of Eastern House. 'Anyone special among them?'

Something in his casual tone made Alice suspicious. She narrowed her eyes at him. 'Lily put you up to this, didn't she? Grilling me on my new mates down in the village?'

Tristan pulled on his ear, looking embarrassed. 'Your sister's worried about you – that's all. You were in a state when you came back from London. I'm not judging you,' he added, seeing her expression, 'this war has messed us all about. But we look out for each other. We're family, aren't we?'

She couldn't argue with that. 'There is someone . . .' Alice looked away under his quick scrutiny. 'A boy I used to know in Bude. But we're just friends.'

'What's his name, then? Is he a good sort of chap?'

'Patrick,' she admitted, and felt herself blush just saying his name out loud. To cover her reaction, she added swiftly, 'Yes, he's a good 'un. I like him, at any rate.'

As she made her way past the guard post with its rolls of barbed wire and sharp-eyed sentry, and into the secret tunnels beyond, awkwardly balancing a cup of tea in one hand and her briefcase in the other, she was met by Patrick coming out.

'Alice! At last!' he exclaimed, stopping on the threshold.

She smiled shyly, remembering the conversation she'd just had about him with Tristan. But one glance at his face told her something was badly wrong.

'What's up?' Worry coiled inside her when he hesitated. 'Spit it out, for gawd's sake. My gran says nothing ever got better by keeping schtum about it.'

Frowning, he took her cup of tea. 'You won't be needing that. I'll drink it for you.'

''Ere, give me that back!' She laughed at his cheekiness, but stopped when he didn't smile in return. Dread crept through her. 'Patrick, you're scaring me. Why have you nabbed my cuppa? What's going on?'

'No idea.' Patrick was still barring her way inside. 'But Mr Cotterill has been tearing the place apart, trying to hunt you down.' His brow quirked. 'Typical of you to roll in late on a day when everyone's scouring heaven and earth for you.'

'*Hunt me down?* Gawd, what've I done now?' She racked her brains to work out how she could have messed up again.

'I told you, I don't know. But I've never seen old Cotterill look so serious. He insisted I send you to his office as soon as you walked in that door. So you'd better hurry.'

'All right, keep your hair on; I'm on my way.' But after a few steps, she turned with sudden suspicion, quick as a rattlesnake. 'You ain't pulling my leg? Because if you are, I swear—'

'Honestly, it's no joke. Cotterill wants to see you urgently.' With a look that sent a thrill through her, Patrick put a hand on her arm. 'Go and see him, Alice,' he said huskily. 'Trust me.'

At his touch, Alice sucked in her breath and headed for the door. Because Patrick was no longer the unreliable, slipshod boy she'd known back in Bude and she did trust him now. She'd trust him with her life, in fact.

It was a strange realisation.

Alice half walked, half ran past the sentry guarding the tunnels and across the yard into Eastern House itself. George Cotterill had his office on the upper floor. The building was busy that morning, with new trainees for the communications department arriving from London. She wove her way up the stairs through groups of raw recruits with bags slung over their shoulders and lost expressions on their faces, saying as she sidestepped abandoned luggage on the stairs, 'Excuse me . . . Best move that, love, unless you want me to tread on it.'

She halted outside George's office to smooth down her hair and take a deep calming breath before knocking, and she heard George bark from inside, 'Unless you're Alice Fisher, go away!'

That astonished her. Alice creaked open the door and peered around it, seeing George at his desk. 'Funnily enough,' she said, 'I am bloomin' Alice Fisher, so I guess I'd better come in.'

Realising her boss was not alone, she stared in surprise

at the man outlined against the window, standing with his back to them. For an instant, he looked achingly familiar, and her heart jolted in her chest. But it couldn't be, could it? She must be dreaming . . .

'Come in quickly and shut the door,' George instructed her, a brusque note in his voice. 'Where on earth have you been? I've been waiting for ages.'

She closed the door behind her. 'Sorry I'm late, I got waylaid.' Her gaze was still on the fair-haired man at the window. He was dressed in civvies, so he wasn't military. Yet surely she knew that rugged figure and the tilt of his head? 'Old Arnie's not been well, you see, and . . .'

The man at the window turned around, looking straight at her from under level brows. 'I'm sorry to hear that.'

Alice gave a squeal of ecstatic delight, dropped her briefcase, and ran across the room to be caught up in his arms like a little girl again. 'Daddy?' she cried breathlessly. 'Is it really you? You've come home at last?' There were tears in her eyes and her voice choked. 'Oh, Dad!'

'Careful,' he said, laughing at her enthusiastic welcome. As she drew back, not wanting to hurt him, he added, 'I'm not in perfect shape.'

Shock stabbed through her. 'You're *hurt*? How bad? What . . . What happened?'

He patted his middle gingerly. 'I'm bandaged all the way around under this shirt. Trussed up like a Christmas turkey. Someone in Germany realised I was working for the British and tried to slice me open. She made a good job of it too.'

'*She*?'

'I'm afraid so, yes. Thankfully, I had a revolver in my pocket that Helga didn't know about. Or I'd be dead for real now.'

Her father gave her a crooked smile, for that was the original cover story everyone had put about to keep him safe while he was working behind enemy lines, that he was 'missing in action, presumed dead'. Nobody would think to go looking for a corpse, after all. For a long time, she had believed it herself and mourned him. Now here her father was, back in her world again, large as life.

She felt angry that anyone could have tried to kill him, but queasy too at the idea of him shooting a woman, even though she knew that was foolish. Women could be just as dangerous as men. But she couldn't help recalling that night in London, when those men had fired at her, and she shuddered.

'This Helga . . . Did she die?'

He hesitated. 'Yes,' he said, his tone sombre.

'Blimey.' She swallowed, trying not to let him see what she was thinking. He might be her dad, but he was also rather scary, and this was the first time she'd realised it. But she was glad his attacker had died rather than him, she thought fiercely. 'So is this another flying visit or are you back for good?' When he hesitated, she glanced around at George Cotterill, her heart pounding. 'Do you know? Will my dad be staying this time?'

George Cotterill got to his feet, smiling indulgently at them both. 'There's no question of him going back. But he'll need to lie low for a while. To avoid awkward questions about why he's not dead, for instance.'

Alice was confused. 'But what does it matter? We've got Jerry on the run in Europe. I don't understand.'

Her dad took her gently by the shoulders, looking down into her face. 'Alice, my dear, it's not just about me. There are people back in Germany who still need protecting from the Gestapo. People I worked with, people who sheltered me and kept my secret. Their lives will be in danger if it gets out that I'm still alive and was working undercover with their knowledge. The tide may be turning in our favour but this war isn't won yet. We need to stay cautious.' He paused. 'George has been telling me about your work here. And your training too.' A shadow crossed his face. 'I was sorry to hear about your friend Jim. I'll be forever in that young man's debt. It sounds to me like he saved your life that night in London.'

'Oh, Dad . . .' A single tear spilled down her cheek as she struggled against a wave of misery and guilt she'd been holding back for too long. 'It was 'orrible . . . I'll never forget it. Jim was so brave. I wish you'd known him.' She dashed a hand across her eyes. 'The worst thing is, him getting shot . . . It was all *my* fault.'

Ernest Fisher held her in his arms for a few minutes while she sobbed her heart out, then said slowly, 'I know how it feels to lose someone like that. Someone who gave up their life for you. But your friend made that choice of his own free will. It certainly wasn't your fault that those men were traitors or that they shot at you that night. I'm sure Jim wouldn't have wanted you to be unhappy, would he?'

'No, he wouldn't.' Alice realised the good sense in what he was saying and took out a hanky, blowing her nose. 'I'm so glad you're back, Dad. And Aunty Violet will be amazed to see you. She and Joe had a little girl called Sally this summer, and she's got the cutest dimples. Though you'd best call her Sarah Jane in Aunty Vi's hearing – she don't like to hear her called Sally, though everybody does.' She stepped back, tidying her hair and rubbing damp cheeks with the backs of her hands. 'Lily and Tristan have come back to live with us at the farm. Oh, and Lily had a baby too. A little boy called Morris. So you're a grandfather!' she told him, beaming.

He was nodding, grinning from ear to ear. 'I'm afraid George stole your thunder, darling. He's been filling me in on everything that's happened since I went away. I can't wait to walk up there with you, see the family again and meet my new grandson.' His voice had thickened with emotion, but he cleared his throat, adding huskily, 'I suppose this means nobody gets any sleep up at the farm these days, with two babies under the same roof. It must be Bedlam.'

'I sleep through most of it,' she admitted, and turned round to say to George, 'You'll know how it feels, since Hazel had her little one.' Only George wasn't there. He'd slipped out of the room unnoticed while she was crying, she realised. Typical George. The soul of discretion.

Her dad chuckled. 'I guess he decided we needed to

be alone. Or maybe he was embarrassed by the sight of you blubbing.'

'Dad!' She gave him a playful punch on the arm. 'To be honest, I don't know how we'll squeeze you in. We did some rearranging when Lily moved back to the farm. Now I share the attic rooms with the Land Girls, then there's Lily, Tristan and little Morris, plus Aunty Vi and Uncle Joe and their baby in the master bedroom, of course. Gran and Arnie took the last spare room.' She grinned. 'Gran said there was no way she was living above the village shop, so Arnie moved up to the farm to keep her sweet. He wasn't happy though. Now he has to walk down to open the shop every morning.'

'I must pop in to the shop.' He smiled. 'I can't wait to shake his hand. A brave man, this Arnie, taking on your grandmother.'

'He ain't well today. Tris is minding the shop for him.'

'Well, you can tell me about him instead. And their wedding day. I was sorry to have missed it.' He stroked her head, his look wistful. 'I've missed so much of your lives.'

'You were doing your duty, Dad,' she reminded him. 'You ain't got *nothing* to apologise for.'

Sitting side by side, they chatted about the family and the war for over an hour, while George came and went, not seeming to mind that they had taken over his office. But no doubt he had other duties on his mind, such as the daily briefing, which happened in the communications room just before lunch most mornings.

'I should probably go and get some work done,' Alice said at last, getting up with a sigh. 'Can't have George docking me a day's pay for skiving.' She glanced out of the window. It had started to rain softly. 'Are you planning to walk up to the farm right away?'

Her father shook his head. 'Actually, I believe George intends giving me a tour of the tunnels before lunch.'

'The tunnels?' Alice was genuinely surprised. 'I'll be blowed. He don't do that for many people.'

Her father looked at her with a gleam in his eye. 'He's giving me the grand tour because he's offered me a position here . . . and I've accepted.'

She stared. 'I beg your pardon?'

'Hurst has been recalled to London, so I'll be taking over here as team leader, effective immediately.' He shrugged. 'I may not be fit to go back to Germany undercover, or even to take up a job in London. But I can't sit around twiddling my thumbs up at the farm either. I can still be of use to this country.'

'What happened to keeping a low profile?'

'I'll be using an alias here,' he explained. 'Mr Townsend. We'll tell people I'm a distant relative of Joe's, to explain why I'm staying up at the farm. Nobody is to know that I'm your father. Not until the war's over, at least.' He searched her face. 'Understood?'

'Blimey. But what if I slip up and call you Dad in front of everyone?' She clapped her hands to her cheeks, horrified.

'Alice, from what I've heard, you're an excellent

operative and a fast learner. You're also my daughter and I know you won't let me down.'

'Oh.' She gulped at this praise, her eyes filling with tears again. 'I . . . I'll do me best, I swear it.'

'That's my girl,' he said approvingly, and dropped a kiss on her forehead. 'It's wonderful to see you again, Alice. But we have work to do.'

'Yes, Mr Townsend,' she said meekly, and led him from the room in search of George Cotterill.

CHAPTER TWENTY-THREE

On a grey, rainy day in October, Imogen kept a rendezvous with Mrs Elliott at the same Bude teashop where they had met before. They ordered tea and cake and exchanged a few pleasantries about the weather until they were sure nobody was paying any attention to them.

Mrs Elliott poured a cup of tea for them both and pushed Imogen's towards her. 'Your report was excessively interesting. Well done, my dear. It was just as I suspected all along. The vicar *was* involved . . . Only now we have proof and can arrest him.'

Imogen looked miserably down at her uneaten slice of cake. Ever since she'd heard that familiar voice and followed Pearl outside to find Richard in the church porch, the same, dismal little sentences had been running through her head. *I don't want it to be him. It can't be him.* With her logical mind, she knew there was no other explanation. Even if he had been there purely by coincidence, that wouldn't explain why noon had come and gone with nobody else in sight. Except the old spinster, of course, come to complain about the verger not performing his duties.

One of their neighbours on Ocean View Road, Doreen had been proved an enemy sympathiser. But she had been found to have family connections to Germany. But this was different. It seemed unlikely that one of three elderly sisters, apparently famous in the parish for their charitable works, always first to donate to any fundraising for the war effort, could possibly be in league with the enemy. It was simply ludicrous and she knew it. But more ludicrous than Richard?

Perhaps there were things she didn't know about the vicar though. They'd never discussed politics, after all. Perhaps his leanings were towards authoritarianism, though she couldn't imagine that. Also, she had seen him often in company with Mr Jolly, a Londoner who had come here to escape the Blitz, a well-known intellectual and writer whose letters to the newspapers about the war often scandalised the local Cornish.

Jolly was the one who'd left the coded message in the dead-letter drop. She had seen that with her own eyes. And Richard was the one who had responded to her fake summons, left in place of the original letter. The inference was inescapable. The coded letter had been left for him to collect, which meant he was a traitor.

She knew these facts to be true and indisputable. Yet it still ripped her heart out to betray him.

'Do you have the message?' Mrs Elliott asked softly, her pudgy hands drumming on the white tablecloth. 'You were wise not to entrust such a vital piece of evidence to the postal service. It would have been a nightmare had it gone astray. Besides, these things are always better dealt with in person.'

Her heart thumping painfully, Imogen reached into her handbag and drew out the brown envelope. This she passed cautiously to Mrs Elliott. 'I've no idea what it says,' she admitted drearily, feeling like the worst kind of traitor, even though she was doing this for her country. 'They look like Egyptian hieroglyphics. I hope your people will be able to decode it.'

Mrs Elliott secreted the envelope away in her own capacious handbag, giving her a brisk nod. 'I have every confidence in them.' She took a bite of cake and raised her eyebrows approvingly. 'Excellent sponge. It's a pity I won't need to come back. Not now we've caught our villain.'

'But there may be others,' Imogen pointed out. 'That man who left the message . . . Mr Jolly,' she went on, her voice dropping to a discreet whisper. 'You'll be investigating him too, I presume?'

'He'll be picked up too, don't worry. You've been helpful in exposing another key member of their ring. Perhaps even the leader. A vicar too.' She tutted, her gaze roving around the teashop. 'Yes, a great shame I won't be returning to Bude. We've heard there may be something fishy in Holsworthy. So I'll be concentrating my efforts there instead.'

Imogen nibbled at the sponge cake. It tasted dry to her. 'I'll keep my eyes open anyway. Just in case.'

Mrs Elliott regarded her severely. 'You won't be staying here, Imogen. We need you back in Exeter. Your work here is complete.'

With a cold feeling of dread, she stared at the woman. The cake wasn't just dry; it tasted of ashes. 'I'm sorry? I don't understand. You want me to go back to Exeter? Back to my parents?'

'This place is tiny. But Exeter is a city and has an entire rogues' gallery of sympathisers for you to uncover. We'll be sending you train tickets and further instructions as soon as we've made the necessary arrangements.' Mrs Elliott added another dash of milk to her tea and stirred it in. 'You can work with your old team there. I'm sure they'll be glad to have you back.'

Imogen, who had spent nearly a year working with a close-knit team in Exeter, uncovering enemy sympathisers and watching out for odd behaviour, felt it unlikely they would want her back. There had been clashes with other members of the group, and she had eventually left for Bude with relief, glad of an opportunity to work solo for a while.

'But I don't want to go back. I've got friends here now. And my sister is expecting her baby any day now. In fact, it's overdue and we're all rather worried. I can't possibly leave Bude now.'

Mrs Elliott's eyes bulged with indignation. 'My dear girl, you'll do exactly as you're told. This is war work. You are required by the government to obey your handler.'

Imogen felt heat creep into her cheeks as she glared back at the older woman. 'I thought this was a voluntary position?'

'We work with volunteers, yes. But those volunteers are still expected to follow orders.'

'In that case, I quit.'

'You can't *quit.*' Mrs Elliott had grown almost puce. Her hands clenched into fists on the tabletop, her cheeks quivering. 'Soldiers can't simply put down their weapons and walk away. Those who do are shot as deserters.' Her gaze locked fiercely with Imogen's. 'What you are suggesting is no better than desertion.'

'What are you saying? Are you going to have me shot, Mrs Elliott?' Imogen demanded, rather too loudly, and several heads turned in their direction.

Aware of this scrutiny, Mrs Elliott made a conscious effort to relax her fists. She sat back, a false smile on her lips. 'Now you're being ridiculous, dear. Please, have some more cake. It's really quite delicious.'

'I'm not going back to Exeter,' Imogen insisted.

'Yes, you are.'

'Then you'll have to drag me there yourself. And I won't go quietly.'

'You really are the most stubborn, ungrateful, pig-headed—'

Imogen stood abruptly, collecting her gloves and handbag. Shakily, she dropped a few coins on the table to cover her refreshments. 'I did what you asked and completed my mission,' she hissed under her breath, struggling against the temptation to scream at the woman. 'But I've had enough of being ordered about. I delivered you a traitor. Now leave me in peace.'

'If you insist on abandoning your post like this, you must expect a letter from the Ministry, drafting you for war work.'

Imogen drew on her gloves. 'I look forward to it.'

'I'll make sure it's a factory up north. Somewhere cold and unpleasant. You'll be forced to wear clogs and overalls.'

'I'd rather wear clogs than do your beastly work any longer.' And with that, Imogen strode from the teashop, turning more heads as she went.

Imogen stormed back up towards the boarding house, ignoring the rain that had begun to fall, but at some point stopped to stare blindly into a shop window, her vision obscured by tears.

In her mind's eye, she saw Richard standing in the pulpit, preaching one of his wildly over-optimistic sermons about peace and hope for the future. She had betrayed him. He would be arrested now and stand trial for treason. And it would be her fault. Hers alone. Because she was the beastly spy who had given his name to the authorities.

She would have to cover every mirror in the house, for she would surely never be able to look herself in the face again. Worse still, at some point during the trial, he would probably discover who had betrayed him. And he would hate her for it.

She had thought this a marvellous adventure at first, especially when her long investigation had exposed Doreen as a traitor and the woman had been arrested. It had felt like a triumph. But this felt like the worst kind of betrayal, for it was the betrayal of someone she loved.

It was Saturday, and Miles had taken Billy for a walk along the clifftops, to give Florence a breathing space from his antics. It was a windy day, perfect for laundry, so Imogen had washed the linen in a tub outside in the yard and was beginning to feed it through the mangle before it was pegged out. She had told Florence to go and lie down several times, but her heavily pregnant sister was ignoring her, pacing about the backyard like a caged animal.

'I'm sick of lying down,' Florence complained, rubbing her lower back. Her restless gaze fell on the basket of wet washing. 'Let me help you with that . . . Please?'

Reluctantly, Imogen agreed, but moments later turned to see Florence bent nearly double, her hands resting on her knees. 'Florrie? Are you in pain?'

'My waters . . .' Her sister jabbed a finger towards the glistening flagstones beneath her, and Imogen belatedly realised that dripping sheets alone could not have made the yard so wet. 'The baby. It's coming. Now!'

'I'll fetch Miles. He can run for the midwife.'

'He took Billy for a walk, remember? You'll have to go yourself. Take his bicycle. It'll be quicker.'

'I'm not sure I should leave you,' Imogen said, eyeing her dubiously.

'I'll be fine. Just help me up to bed first.'

In the master bedroom, the curtains closed, Florence knelt beside the bed and rocked back and forth, moaning under her breath.

'I'll go for the midwife,' Imogen muttered, not liking the pasty look of her face. 'I'll be as quick as I can.'

But on her way down the road, she met Dr Tyson with Pearl and his children walking home, and explained what had happened.

Dr Tyson took charge, asking Pearl to telephone the hospital from the exchange at the top of Belle Vue. 'I believe the midwife is at the hospital today. Tell her about Florence and ask her to come as soon as she's free.'

Pearl cycled away while Imogen shepherded the two children, who were looking confused but excited, inside the boarding house. Dr Tyson had already gone upstairs and she heard him talking soothingly to her sister. She gave the children some barley water and biscuits to keep them quiet, and asked them to stay out of the way.

'Is Mrs Miller really having her baby today?' Clara asked, wide-eyed.

'It does looks like it, yes. I'm sure she'll be fine,' Imogen assured the girl, though she was horribly worried herself. Birth was a dangerous time for both mother and child; she knew that much. And Florence had not looked well when she left her.

She went upstairs to sit with her sister. To her relief,

Dr Tyson didn't seem concerned. 'I've examined your sister,' he told Imogen, 'and everything seems to be fine. She's already well dilated.'

'I have no idea what that means,' Imogen stammered.

The doctor smiled and even Florence gave a half-hearted laugh. 'It means things are progressing nicely,' he explained, and turned to her sister. 'How are you coping with the contractions, Florence?'

'Is there any gin in the house?'

'Try to focus on staying calm. Breathe slowly, in and out.' He met Imogen's frightened gaze. 'Don't worry, she's doing marvellously. I'm going to see if Pearl has returned yet. No food or drink for the patient, I'm afraid, except the odd sip of water. But I shall bring *you* a cup of tea.'

When he'd left, Imogen helped Florence get comfortable by putting one cushion under her knees and another on the bed for her to rest her forehead on as she leant forward. 'Is it very bad?'

'Only when I breathe,' Florence said indistinctly, face buried in the pillow.

Imogen wasn't sure if that was a joke or not.

'Oh!' Florence jerked upright, a stricken look on her face. 'Oh no!'

'What's the matter? Flo, you're scaring me.'

'The washing.' Her sister turned a horrified face in her direction. 'We've left it sitting in the backyard. Mangle and all.'

'You're worried about the washing?' Imogen gave a hysterical crack of laughter. 'I promise, when the doctor comes back, I'll go down and peg it out.' She shook her head, amazed. 'You're having a baby, Florence. Stop fretting about the housework.'

When Miles returned from his walk with Billy on his shoulders, he was greeted at the door by the doctor's children, shrieking with excitement. He handed Billy to Pearl, who had long since come back from the telephone exchange with the depressing news that the midwife couldn't leave because of complications with a labour she was supervising, and ran upstairs to see his wife.

Imogen hurried after him, having finished pegging out the washing while Dr Tyson sat with Florence.

'How is she, Doc?' Miles was asking the doctor. 'Is she all right?'

'She's fine,' Dr Tyson began, but was interrupted.

'Where have you been? Why were you away so long?' Florence glared at her husband accusingly.

'I'm sorry, sweetheart. After our walk, I took Billy into town for an ice cream. We met little Emily and her mom and stopped for a chat.' Miles sat on the bed and lifted his wife's hand to his lips. 'But I'm back now, and I'm not gonna move an inch from your side.'

'Sorry?' Florence frowned.

'My pops was at my birth, and attended all my siblings' births, and he made me swear I would do the same when my turn came to be a father.'

Florence stared at him, scandalised. 'You . . . You want to stay? For the *birth*?'

'With your permission.' Miles removed his jacket and rolled up his shirtsleeves, as though about to assault a beachhead. 'I'm all yours, ma'am. Just tell me what to do.'

'Goodness me.' Dr Tyson chuckled but didn't object, merely adding that by his estimate, the baby should arrive before midnight.

'*Midnight*?' Florence repeated weakly, glancing at the bedside clock. 'But that's over ten hours away.'

'I'm here for you, honey.' Sticking out his chin, Miles loosened his tie, his expression determined. 'You and me, we're going to do this together.'

'I'm not sure about the fair division of labour,' Florence muttered under her breath, but managed a smile for her husband. 'Thank you, darling. I do love you, Miles Miller.'

'I love you too, my beautiful Florence,' her husband replied, his adoring gaze on his wife's face.

'I'm not leaving either,' Imogen insisted stoutly.

Dr Tyson raised his eyebrows and went to the door. 'In that case, I'll leave you in their tender care. But I'll be downstairs if you need me.'

The two of them sat with Florence long into the evening, slipping out now and then for something to eat and drink, and to give updates to the rest of the household, all waiting anxiously for news below.

Dr Tyson checked on Florence every hour, and only once seemed concerned, saying her pulse was 'thready' and noting that she was in a great deal of pain. But the midwife, Karen, arrived soon after this, and pronounced the baby ready to arrive. For the next tumultuous hour,

Imogen squeezed one hand while Miles held the other and grimly averted his eyes, until there was a squalling baby being checked and wrapped up for an exhausted Florence to hold.

'It's a little girl,' the midwife announced, smiling. 'Perfectly healthy and an excellent weight too. Congratulations.' She had clearly found it distracting to have the father in the room during labour, but since it was obvious she couldn't shift Miles, and Florence had seemed happy to have him there, encouraging her and holding her hand throughout the long labour, there had been no further argument about it.

Weary but elated, Imogen peered across at the wrinkly, red-faced baby in Florence's arms. 'Oh my, what a . . . what a beauty,' she said gallantly. 'What will you call her?'

Florence glanced at Miles, who said, 'I believe we decided on Hope, didn't we? It's a family name. Unless you have any objection, sweetheart?'

Florence shook her head, smiling proudly down at her newborn. 'Hope . . . What a perfect name.'

CHAPTER TWENTY-FOUR

Pearl had left her special dress and dancing shoes hanging up at the hospital ready for the Christmas Eve performance, so all she needed to do was her make-up and hair before leaving the boarding house that evening. As she came downstairs, she found Freddy and his two children waiting for her in the hall. The door to the guest lounge was open and she put her head round the door to tell Miles and Florence they were leaving. Miles was decorating the Christmas tree – which was a vast, lavish affair – strewn with tinsel and glittering baubles. Apparently, his folks back in Texas were keen on elaborate festive displays and he was keen to keep up the family tradition. Seated in a deep armchair, Florence was nursing her baby and humming along merrily to the Christmas tune playing on the gramophone. They both looked around as Pearl came in.

Miles came to shake her hand. 'Break a leg, Pearl,' he said warmly.

'Yes, all the best for tonight's performance,' Florence agreed, smiling. 'I would get up but as you can see, I'm rather occupied at the moment.'

'Such a cute little baby.' Pearl admired Hope's pretty profile. 'How is she?'

'Growing bigger every day,' Miles joked.

'I'm still sorry you two won't be watching me tonight. You won't reconsider?' Pearl asked, for she had offered them tickets for the show, but they had both politely declined, saying others needed them more. Besides, Florence had insisted that Hope was too young to be left with a sitter, even for a few hours, and Miles had flatly refused to go out without his wife.

'Perhaps you could give us another of your private performances one night next week?' Miles suggested, looking past her at the doctor. 'What do you say, Freddy? I think they have a piano a few doors down.'

'Maybe, but we need to be moving,' Freddy said, helping his children on with their coats and hats. 'Or we'll be late.' He looked up in relief as Imogen hurried downstairs. She was coming with them and had offered to sit with the children while Freddy and Pearl were performing. 'Nice frock, Imogen,' he told her, grinning. 'Looking to catch somebody's eye tonight?'

Pearl had to admit that Imogen was looking particularly fine, in a blue woollen dress pulled in with a belt at the waist, her hair styled in smooth waves that fell to her shoulders. But she looked pale and strained as she pulled on a beret and swung a matching blue jacket about her shoulders.

'Sorry I'm late,' Imogen muttered, ignoring his cheeky question. 'I quite forgot the time.'

They walked briskly down to the hospital together, Pearl chatting to Imogen while the doctor walked with his children. She was curious to know why her usually lively friend had seemed so withdrawn in recent weeks. She asked a few probing questions, but Imogen was still disinclined to talk. In the end, Pearl despaired of getting her to open up, and merely said, 'I hope tonight will cheer you up.'

Imogen seemed ruffled by that. 'I'm perfectly cheerful,' she insisted.

It was hopeless, Pearl decided, and gave up the struggle. Whatever was upsetting Imogen, she was determined to keep it a secret.

Almost as soon as they had arrived at the hospital, somebody whisked the doctor away to look at one of his patients, even though it was not his shift. He apologised to Pearl and assured her he would be back shortly. But as time passed, she began to get butterflies in her tummy, afraid he might not return in time to accompany her on the piano.

Imogen had found front-row seats for herself and the two children, who sat kicking their feet and chattering with excitement. Clara was in a pink dress with a bow in her hair, and young Toby had washed his face for once and had been wrestled into a clean shirt.

The room began to fill up with patients and staff. Some of the patients couldn't walk and had to be wheeled in.

Thankfully, the space they had chosen was large enough to accommodate most people, though they left the door ajar so that others could gather in the corridor to listen or catch a glimpse through the open door. The room was soon buzzing with conversation and laughter. Christmas decorations had been strung along the walls to make the space seem less spartan, and a few of the older patients began singing Christmas carols while they waited for the show to start, which soon others took up, the air ringing with deep male voices.

As so often when she'd been entertaining the Rangers, the majority of her audience tonight would be male. But there were nurses too, and a few local women standing at the back, no doubt curious to see what all the fuss was about. She'd already caught sight of Penny in a smart frock, with her husband John on her arm, finding a seat near the piano.

She was used to entertaining raucous young men, and usually wearing something far more revealing than her dance dress tonight. Yet still those butterflies persisted.

Her heart beating erratically, she had just turned to adjust the microphone stand to her lower height and check everything was working, when a young man tried to catch her attention.

'Hey, Miss Diamond,' he called out, and she recognised him as one of the US Rangers who used to hang about the Donut Dollies' stand near the officers' hotel, hoping for a kiss or more from the girls handing out doughnuts and candy to the troops. 'I remember you.'

She smiled politely, struggling to recall his name.

'You were Terry's girl, am I right?' The young man nudged the patient beside him, adding, 'Terry loved to mess about with the ladies, even though he was already hitched to a girl back home.' He chuckled, sneering at her. 'Bet he kept that quiet, didn't he?'

Sucking in a breath, she stared at the young man and groped for something to say. A sharp or witty comeback to make it seem as though she didn't care about Terence and his deception. Instead, she stood speechless and immobile, the old agony seeping back through her like ice water . . .

Imogen hurried over. 'Shouldn't you go and change into your dancing togs?' she whispered.

'I was waiting for . . . for Dr Tyson to return.' Pearl caught her pitying look and had to get out of there. 'But you're right – I'd better get dressed.'

She collected her special dress and shoes from the store cupboard and changed in the nurses' washroom. It was cramped, and nurses kept coming and going, staring at her in her silver spangled gown and polished tap shoes. Once she was ready, Pearl reapplied her lipstick and stood staring at herself in the mirror, trying to slow her erratic breathing. Her voice would never carry throughout the whole room if she couldn't get her breathing under control. But at the back of her mind, she kept seeing that sneering young man, and hearing him call out, 'You're Terry's girl.'

'Oh,' she whimpered, and hid her face in her hands.

A nurse stopped to peer at her. 'Are you all right, Miss?'

Pearl felt cold and unwell. She put a hand to her heaving chest. 'I . . . I'm just feeling a little faint.'

'I think they're waiting for you out there. I'm sure you'll feel better once you get started. Come on, let me help you.' The nurse led her out of the washroom and down the corridor. Her legs felt wobbly and her mouth was dry. She couldn't sing in this condition, she thought in desperation. She could barely talk.

To her relief, Freddy was waiting at the door, looking up and down the corridor anxiously. When he saw her, he hurried forward. 'Thank you, Nurse,' he said to the woman, who smiled and slipped into the room. He frowned, looking into Pearl's face. 'Blimey, you look awful. What's wrong?'

'I don't think I can go on,' she admitted. 'I must've eaten something bad. I feel dreadful.'

'Is that so?' Freddy studied her for a moment, and then took her by the hand. 'Let's take a quick walk, shall we? They're ready to tear the place apart in there. But they can hang on another few minutes. Right now, you need fresh air.'

He took her outside into the rose garden, though it was a clear and chilly December night and the ground was laced with frost. The rose bushes were bare stalks at this season, the benches too damp to sit on, and far above them the stars glittered in a black sky.

Freddy stroked back her hair, smiling down at her in the glimmering half-light. 'Tell me if I'm out of line, Pearl, but this looks more like a case of stage fright than food poisoning.'

'I'm never nervous before performing. That can't be it.' But she knew he was right. There was nothing physically wrong with her. She was simply suffering from stage fright. She met his gaze and groaned. 'Oh Lord, what am I going to do? All those men in there are waiting for me. I can't let them down.'

'You won't,' he said simply and bent to kiss her on the lips.

The world spun as Pearl stood within the circle of his arms, lost in a trance. At last, she saw the stars again and his handsome face smiling down at her.

'Why did you do that?'

'You looked like you needed to be kissed. And since you haven't slapped my face and stormed off yet, I'm assuming you weren't offended.'

She didn't know what to say. But her nerves had been forgotten, all that churning anxiety replaced with a steadily growing sense of joy. 'Oh, Freddy . . .' She stared at him, craving answers to questions she barely knew how to ask.

Did this mean he liked her? Or had he just been trying to shock her out of her trance with that kiss? It had certainly worked . . .

'Let's not talk about it now,' Freddy urged her. 'Let's go back inside and entertain those young soldiers the best way we know how. They're wounded and hurting and away from their families at Christmas, some of them for the first time in their young lives, and they're desperate for something – for *someone* – to take their minds off the horrors of war. And that someone is you, Pearl.'

The doctor was smiling, but she knew he was partly serious. 'Besides which,' he added, 'that frock looks smashing on you, but there's not much of it and you'll freeze to death if you stay out here much longer. Ready now?'

She nodded and took his arm.

As they walked back into the room, a huge round of applause greeted them, hordes of bandaged men in pyjamas and wheelchairs whistling and stamping their slippered feet. The long wait had indeed left them ready to riot, Pearl thought, but she no longer felt nervous at the prospect of dancing and singing for these men. How silly she had been. Yes, she had never performed solo before. She had always performed in a group with other people. But that didn't mean she was unable to dance or sing on her own. She had just needed to believe in herself . . .

'Right, let's put on a show,' Freddy said in his gravelly voice, and strode across to take his place at the piano.

With a tremulous smile, Pearl turned to the microphone and addressed the room, calling out, 'Sorry to have kept you waiting so long. But I believe it's a lady's prerogative to be late.' She dropped her voice, teasingly husky as she asked, 'How are y'all doing tonight, gentlemen?'

The room went wild, with even louder whistling and stamping and cheering, the floor shaking under her feet with the vibrations. She laughed at how easily she could control them, confidence flowing through her like a warm tide.

Glancing her way, Freddy played the opening chords of their arrangement, which was their signal to start.

'I think you'll like this one,' she told them. 'So join in if you know the words, boys,' and she opened her mouth and began to sing.

Back in her ordinary frock and heels, and walking back to town with everyone after the performance, Pearl felt as though she were still dancing. 'They loved us,' she breathed, her heart swelling with pride.

'They loved *you*,' Freddy corrected her. The road was slippery and he took her arm, pulling her close for safety. 'You're such a marvellous singer,' he whispered into her ear. 'I still can't believe I had the honour of accompanying such a wonderful voice.'

'Careful, Freddy, the children . . .' She glanced back at Clara and Toby, who were walking a few feet behind with Imogen, giggling and whispering.

'I don't need to hide our friendship from the kids. Though I hope it may become more than a friendship in time.'

Pearl could not decide if he was serious or not. Everything between them had changed tonight, and yet everything still felt undecided.

His kiss in the rose garden had opened her eyes to the truth. These past few months, she had been steadily falling in love with Dr Freddy Tyson, without even realising. She had been lying to herself about it and only now realised why. She had trusted Terence and he had lied to her, made a fool out of her. That young man in the audience had sneered at her because of him. When she'd met Freddy, she had resisted her feelings, secretly afraid that he too would somehow betray her. But she saw now what kind of man he was. A man of integrity and honesty, a family man. He was not the type to pretend something he didn't feel just to grab some alone time with her.

His kiss tonight had steadied her nerves and allowed her to go on stage with new confidence. But had it been more than that for him? She needed to be sure before things went any further. She hated the idea that Freddy might have grown close to her out of pity, wishing he could make things better for her after Terence.

But doctors were like that, weren't they? Doctors needed to make sick people better. Only she didn't want that kind of relationship.

'What do you see when you look at me, Freddy?' she asked in a low voice, not wanting his children to overhear. 'Do you see a woman who's broken? Who needs to be fixed? Because that ain't me. I like spending time with you, don't get me wrong. But I need a man who'll love me for who I am, not a *doctor* looking to fix someone to make himself feel good.'

He digested that impassioned little speech in silence, looking down at the icy ground, then said slowly, 'Yes, I'm a doctor and I fix people for a living. But that's not who I am as a man.' He paused, frowning. 'When war broke out and my wife volunteered as a nurse, I was overjoyed to be working alongside her. I knew how much she loved the work, how much it fulfilled her. And if she was happy, then I was happy. I've never understood why women are automatically expected to give up their work when they marry. Because what a woman does is as important to me as who a woman is. In fact, the two are inseparable.' His voice thickened with emotion, and she was shocked to see tears in his eyes as he turned to her. 'What I saw tonight was a woman at the height of her talents, having a tremendous time and giving joy to so many others. You lit up the room with your smile tonight. With your songs and dancing. You made those men *feel* again. And I love you for it.'

'What?' Her eyes widened, fixing on his face. 'I'm sorry, did you say that you love . . . ?' She couldn't finish, her voice faltering.

'If we were alone,' he said softly, 'I'd show you how I feel, not just talk about it. As it stands, I can only say, you've found a place in this tough old heart of mine, Pearl Diamond, and I would be beyond honoured if you would consider me more than just a friend.'

Pearl struggled for the words inside her. She could sing a song that somebody else had written, but she couldn't find her own words to express what she felt when he looked at her like that . . .

'I'd like that,' she said huskily, and felt his arm tighten on hers.

330

But before he could reply, a shout brought them all to a halt. Penny was hurrying up the icy street behind them with John on her arm. She reached them, her cheeks flushed, out of breath. 'I say, Pearl, you were absolutely splendid tonight. We loved it, didn't we, John?'

John grunted his assent, nodding enthusiastically. 'Proper job,' he added.

'But you'll never guess what's happened,' Penny went on hurriedly, her glance shooting to Imogen as she asked, 'Unless you've heard? It's all over town.'

'What is?' Freddy asked, frowning.

'The vicar . . . He's been arrested. And nobody seems to know why.'

'Oh no . . .' Imogen turned pale, a hand darting to her mouth as she staggered.

Freddy hurried to her side. 'Imogen? Are you all right? Here, let me help you home.' His look to Pearl was apologetic, but she didn't mind. She was too concerned for her friend. Their conversation had left her heart singing but it would wait until later.

It was obvious that Imogen had suffered a terrible shock. She and the vicar had seemed very close at times over the past few months. And now he had been arrested?

'It has to be a mistake,' Clara said, wide-eyed, looking at them all in astonishment. 'I mean . . . why would anyone want to arrest a vicar?'

But nobody was able to answer that.

CHAPTER TWENTY-FIVE

It was Christmas Eve in Porthcurno and Alice should never have felt happier, surrounded by all her family, with even her long-absent father here this year. Though he was in fact absent again that evening, having gone out into the icy fields with Joe in the pitch-black, carrying a storm lantern and some rope, to deal with a pregnant ewe that had strayed from the flock and might be giving birth. Tristan had offered to accompany them, used to dealing with such emergencies on his father's sheep farm near Penzance. But Joe had insisted that Tristan should stay behind, since he'd spent most of the day digging out foundations for a new chicken coop and looked too tired to go tramping over the fields at night.

Naturally, Violet had put Tristan to work as soon as the door had closed behind her husband, asking him to wash up the dinner plates and then make the tea while the women rested, having cooked a slap-up meal for

Christmas Eve and contemplating another feast for tomorrow's lunch. Tristan had set to these tasks without complaint, only a grin at his wife.

'Let's see that letter again, Alice,' Aunty Vi said, reaching across the kitchen table. 'What did she say Florence and Miles are calling their new baby?'

'Hope,' Alice told her, handing across the letter from Penny. Since it contained nothing too personal, she had read the letter aloud to everyone after supper, as she often did when she received news from Bude, knowing how her aunt and gran enjoyed a good gossip.

'Bit old-fashioned, ain't it?' Gran asked, knitting away furiously at a scarf she wanted to give Arnie in the morning for his Christmas present.

'I like it,' Lily said decisively, reading the letter over their aunt's shoulder. 'When I was working as a midwife, you should have heard some of the baby names . . . I don't approve of names that are too modern. You never know if it's going to be a fad. Then the poor child's stuck with it for life.'

'Here you go, ladies,' Tristan said cheerfully, bringing the teapot to the table and popping a crocheted cosy over it to keep the tea hot for longer. 'Tea's up. Then it's bedtime for you two whipper-snappers,' he told young Eustace and Timothy, who were playing cards with Janice at the other end of the long pine table.

'That's not fair,' Eustace exclaimed, throwing his cards down in disgust. 'What about Janice?'

'I ain't a kid anymore, am I?' Janice pointed out loftily,

then spoiled the effect by sticking her tongue out at her brothers. 'I get to stay up late while you brats have to be in bed for midnight. Else Santa won't come.'

'There ain't no such person as Santa,' Eustace told her with cool disdain.

Timothy glanced at him uncertainly. 'Eh?'

Lily smiled at the young boy. 'Pay no attention to him, Timothy. He's just pulling your leg. Of course Santa exists. But if you don't go to bed in good time, he may not leave you a present. And that would be a shame, wouldn't it?'

'Huh. It's only ever some miserable orange or a piece of coal wrapped in brown paper anyway,' Eustace muttered.

''Ere, don't you go complaining about presents you ain't even had yet.' Aunty Violet shook her head, tutting at the three of them. 'When I was your age, I was happy whatever I got for Christmas. Not all of us were lucky enough to get a present, you know.'

'Some of us still don't,' Gran grumbled. It was obvious she was in a difficult mood this Christmas, Alice thought, but couldn't blame her. Not with her bad hip playing up and Arnie still spending most of his days in bed.

'Oh, Mum, you old fibber,' Aunty Vi told her, her eyes wide. 'Joe and I gave you that nice box of ginger snaps last year. And a bag of chestnuts for roastin'.'

'Hmm.' Gran pursed her lips but didn't deny this. 'Well, I still say we should all have gone to Midnight Mass together, just like in the old days. Especially now Ernest is home at last.' She rolled her eyes. 'Assumin' we're allowed to call him Ernest, that is. Not Mr Touchstone, or whatever we're supposed to say.'

'Townsend,' Alice and Lily chanted in unison.

'Such nonsense. I don't know why we have to call him by a different name and make up some story about him being related to Joe.'

'The Land Girls,' Violet hissed across the table, shaking her head in warning, though the three girls had long since scraped their plates and gone up to their attic rooms.

'Gawd's sake, who are they goin' to tell? Besides, it's years since Ernest was declared dead. Them Jerries won't know who he is, not unless their spies are outside the back door right now, listening to every bloomin' word we say. And if they are, rather them than me, in this nasty cold weather.' Gran finished the scarf and started tying up the loose ends with expert fingers. 'Anyway, it ain't right, not holding Midnight Mass on Christmas Eve. This country's turned heathen since this war started.'

'The vicar couldn't manage to black out all the church windows,' Alice reminded her patiently, 'so they had to cancel the midnight service. It wouldn't have been safe. Not when Eastern House is such a big target. You know their bombers are always looking for the place.'

'Well, you'd think Mr Hitler would have given his boys a day off at Christmas, wouldn't you? He's lucky they don't go on strike.' Gran held up the scarf to admire her handiwork, allowing herself a smile at last. 'There now, that's grand. Arnie will be pleased. Blue and yellow. His favourite colours.'

'How is Arnold?' Tristan asked, pouring tea for everyone. 'He's been in bed a lot recently.'

Gran's smile faded, emotion clouding her eyes. 'Not so good. Doctor says it's his chest. He can't seem to stop coughing, you see. Well, you've all heard him, hackin' away like he's on fifty Woodbines a day, when he barely smokes anymore.' Her voice had grown unsteady, her lip trembling. 'I said, he needs Joe to drive him to the hospital in Penzance. Get himself looked at proper. Only he won't listen to me, stubborn old fool . . . He don't trust hospitals. Says they're full of quacks and charlatans, and anyway, he'll be right as rain in a few weeks.'

'It's just this cold weather, Mum,' Violet told her soothingly, getting up to fetch the sugar bowl, though it was only Gran who still took a spoonful in her tea these days, what with rations being so tight. 'It's gone to his chest, that's all. Once this frost is over, he'll be out of bed in no time.' She hesitated. 'I'm nipping upstairs to check on Sarah Jane and Morris. Shall I take him up another cuppa on my way?'

'No, love, he'll be out for the count by now.' Gran had taken up a supper tray to him earlier. She accepted a mug of tea from Tristan with a muttered word of thanks. 'Let sleeping Arnies lie, eh?'

Feeling unaccountably depressed, Alice took back Penny's letter and reread it herself before folding it back into the envelope. Then she wandered outside into the icy farmyard to listen for Joe and her dad coming back. She missed Bude and her friends there. Yet when she'd been living there, she'd missed Porthcurno and the farm. Same in London.

Home is where the heart is, she told herself firmly. And her heart was right here, coming down from the high fields with a swaying lantern and a rumble of male voices.

'Put that light out!' she shouted, putting on a gruff voice, and heard their laughter.

'You not in bed yet, Alice, love?' her father called back.

'I was waiting for you to come back first. Tris just made a fresh pot of tea, if you fancy a cuppa.' As they reached her, she took the lantern from Joe and extinguished it, just in case of danger, though there was no sound of plane engines, only the distant whisper of the sea and a dog fox barking in the valley. 'It's almost midnight.'

Her dad put his arm about her shoulders. 'Merry Christmas, Alice.'

'Merry Christmas, Dad.'

And Joe smiled, holding the farmhouse door open for them to get inside out of the cold.

Patrick turned up for Christmas lunch the next day. Once Violet had learned that he was an orphan and would be staying at Eastern House over Christmas, she had insisted on Alice inviting him up to join them for lunch. 'No, he's a mate of yours,' her aunt had said firmly when Alice looked uncertain, 'and you can't leave him down there with all them strangers over Christmas. Not when he could trot up the hill to us for a proper family lunch. Besides, he'll be a good role model for them tearaway boys.' Eustace and Timothy had been driving her round the bend during the school break, dashing about the old farmhouse with whoops and screams. 'Gawd knows they need a lad nearer their own age to show 'em how to behave.'

'Patrick's not that young . . . He's about my age, Aunty Vi,' Alice had protested.

But to her surprise – and with a burst of happiness Alice had struggled to conceal – Patrick had accepted his invitation up to the farm, even seeming pleased by it. She didn't quite dare wonder if that meant he liked her as much as she liked him. Besides, few days went by when she didn't find herself remembering Jim, all those things they'd said and done together, and missing him like crazy. In comparison to that unforgettable whirlwind romance, Patrick was just a friend. Wasn't he?

Patrick came through the back door just as everyone was rushing about with hot pots and pans, wiping his boots and taking off his cap, staring about in astonishment.

'Alice,' Gran yelled huskily, 'your little friend's on the doorstep. Leave that and look after 'im, would you?'

Alice, who had been helping Joan baste the turkey, left the job to her and grabbed Patrick by the arm, hurriedly propelling him out of the busy kitchen.

'Best not get underfoot if you value your life,' Alice explained when he frowned. 'It can be downright dangerous when my aunt and gran are cooking a big lunch.' She grinned, noting the shiny ironed crease on his trousers and that he was wearing his best shirt and tie. 'I say, you've made an effort.'

'It's Christmas,' he said defensively.

'You look very smart.' There was an awkward silence, then she added, thrown off balance by seeing him so well-turned-out, with a fresh shave too and his hair smoothed down, 'So, this is my uncle Joe's farm. Want the guided tour?'

'Rather,' he agreed.

Alice showed him around the farm for the next half hour. It was good fun, and rather nice to escape the steamy atmosphere of the kitchen. They peered up the track to the top fields, lit up in chilly sunshine, and stopped by the pigsty, though there was only one pig in residence, the others having been sold in the run-up to Christmas, along with several plump chickens. But there were still hens to see, scratching in the dirt for seed and clucking comically.

'That's Betty, our best layer at the moment,' she said, pointing at a fat hen, settled broodily in the doorway to the old coop, which was leaning precariously. 'We're buildin' a new run over there. See? In fact, Da—' She snatched back the word 'Dad,' but he was already staring at her. Heat flooded her cheeks as she tried to cover her stupid mistake, saying quickly, '*Don't* go too close. It's quite a deep hole.'

He followed her towards the barn, hands in his pockets. 'Sounds like hard work, running a farm. Especially with the country at war.'

'Yes, but Joe has the Land Girls to help. And Tris pitches in too, now he and Lily are living with us.'

'And you?'

'Oh, I lend a hand when I can,' she agreed airily. 'In fact, one of me duties is getting them bloomin' hens into the coop at night, to save 'em getting ate by some wicked fox,' she added, and saw his eyes widen.

'I didn't know you could still surprise me,' Patrick said slowly, his gaze fixed on her face. 'You're not only smarter than most anyone I know but braver too. I haven't forgotten how you resisted those interrogators back in Bude, even though you didn't know it was only a test. You showed far more courage than I did that day. And now this . . . Hens!' He gave a short laugh. 'You even help out on the farm after a long day's work.'

'I don't mind doing my bit. I eat the eggs, don't I?' She began to laugh but stopped, aware of his sudden stillness. 'Patrick? What is it?'

'Nothing.'

'Don't give me that.'

'All right . . .' He looked away, running a hand through his hair. 'When we first met in Bude and you told me you were an orphan, I suppose I imagined your life must be like mine. You know, the feeling that you're all alone in the world, so you need to make your own way, follow your own rules.'

She nodded, not sure what to say.

'But you've got your aunt and uncle here,' he went on, 'and your gran and her husband. Even your sister and brother-in-law too. You may have lost your mum and dad like I did, but you've still got this whole tribe at your back. So I guess it's not the same. What you've got here at the farm . . . You're lucky. Having this big family looking out for you.'

She felt awful then, not least because her father was still alive and she couldn't explain that to him, for the sake of her dad's safety. This massive lie was a wedge between them, a lie that might not have mattered to anyone else, but with him being an orphan, it was almost heartbreaking.

'I'm sorry,' she stammered.

'Hey, it's not your fault. I wasn't trying to make you feel bad.' Patrick grinned reassuringly. 'I'm adjusting my view of you, that's all.'

He was so generous, she thought. But her heart was thumping. She liked Patrick and hated having to lie to him. Soon he would be sitting down to Christmas lunch with her family, including her dad, whom he knew only as their new team leader at Eastern House, Mr Townsend, a distant cousin of Joe's. She'd have to hope nobody slipped up. Though they were used to guarding their tongues around the Land Girls and the evacuee kids, so she wasn't too worried.

But this would be their first Christmas since the war began with her dad back in England, and she longed to spend it with him as his daughter, not having to pretend they weren't related. And Patrick was eagle-eyed and trained to spot inconsistencies in stories and people's actions . . .

She almost wished Violet hadn't invited him to lunch

or that he had declined the invitation. And yet she was glad he was there. It had given her a secret joy to see him walk through the door earlier, taking off his cap and smiling at her. Even though she saw him down at Eastern House most days, there was something different about having Patrick here, in the bosom of her family, joining in with their Christmas festivities.

She dragged open the barn door, deciding she was addled in the brain. 'Well, this is the barn,' she said unevenly, nodding toward the hayloft. 'I like to sit up there with a book where nobody can find me. There's an amazin' view from the hayloft window too, right over the valley.'

'Show me?'

Alice checked her watch. 'It's close to one o'clock. We should probably get back.'

'They'll shout for you when lunch is served, won't they?'

'I suppose.' She began to climb the ladder into the hayloft, wishing she was wearing trousers instead of a skirt. But Patrick was a gentleman and looked away until she was up before following her. She clambered across the loft, navigating the remaining hay bales with difficulty, to show him the narrow, cobwebbed window that looked down into Porthcurno. 'All right . . . There's the view.'

'Beautiful,' he murmured, standing behind her.

She turned, warned by something in his voice, and was stunned when she found Patrick looking directly at her, not the view. He lifted a hand to brush her cheek with the lightest touch, and she froze, staring at him bolt-eyed.

'Sorry,' he said jerkily, his brows tugging together at her expression. His hand dropped to his side. 'Did I read the signals wrong? I thought that maybe you . . . you liked me.'

'I do like you,' she whispered.

He smiled then, his brow clearing. 'Good, because I like you too, Alice Fisher.' And he bent his head and kissed her.

She didn't know how long they stood there, locked together in a satisfying silence, arms about each other, but she suddenly became aware of scratchy straw prickling at her neck and realised he had leant her back against a hay bale, his kiss deepening . . .

'Alice?'

The shout broke them apart, Patrick breathing hard, a flush along his cheeks. He straightened his tie and stepped back.

'I know that voice,' he muttered, his gaze locked with hers. 'Mr Townsend. I'd forgotten he was staying here.'

'Oh.' She pulled straw from her hair, tidying her clothes. 'Erm, yes . . . Lunch must be ready. We'd better go.'

They climbed down from the hayloft, not looking at each other, to find her dad waiting below for them. He studied both their faces, and then said coolly, 'Lunch is on the table. Mrs Postbridge sent me to find you.' He shook Patrick's hand. 'Good to have you joining us for lunch.'

'Thank you, sir.'

When he'd gone, Patrick turned to Alice, an odd look

on his face. 'Mr Townsend . . . He's related to your family, is that right?'

'Erm, that's right.' As they walked back to the farmhouse, she told him the official story and he listened without saying anything. 'Back there,' she added softly, 'what we did—'

'Is he your father, Alice?'

She stopped dead, staring at him in dismay, her mouth open. She wanted to laugh and say *no, of course not, what are you talking about*? But there wasn't a single word in her head.

She didn't want to lie to him.

How on earth had he guessed? Had someone at work let slip who 'Mr Townsend' really was? But only George Cotterill knew the truth at Eastern House, and nobody in the village could possibly know his identity. And he'd barely spoken to anyone in the family yet.

Unless it was her stupid slip earlier, almost referring to him as 'Dad,' that had aroused his suspicions?

'You look just like him,' Patrick said simply, sinking his hands in his pockets again. 'As soon as I saw you together at Eastern House, I was curious. But now seeing him here, with all your family . . .' He looked at her intently, and she felt herself blush. 'He is your dad, isn't he? The one you said was missing in action, presumed dead.' When she still didn't reply, he pressed on, refusing to give up. 'That was what you were going to say before, wasn't it? *Dad.*'

'Yes,' she whispered.

It would be ludicrous to deny it. He'd guessed most of it, anyway. All she could hope was that Patrick could somehow be persuaded to keep his mouth shut and pretend he didn't know.

He drew a long breath at her admission. 'Good God.'

'But it's hush-hush,' she told him urgently. 'You mustn't tell anyone. We're all sworn to secrecy. Please promise me you won't say a word.'

He looked taken aback. 'Of course I won't say anything. I'm not a blabbermouth. Besides, he works at Eastern House and I've signed the Official Secrets Act, meaning I couldn't discuss it without committing treason, even if I wanted to. Which I don't,' he added firmly.

'Oh.'

'Plus, he's your dad. So I'd never do or say anything that might endanger him.' He took her hand, squeezing it gently. 'Please say you believe me, Alice.'

Her smile was crooked as she fought to hold back tears, amazed at the strength of her reaction. She was usually so calm and in control, even when everyone else was falling apart. In fact, the only other time she'd come close to losing control had been the night Jim had died.

After his death, she'd been sure she would never feel the same again, never look at another man the way she'd looked at Jim, never kiss anyone else . . . But she knew Jim wouldn't have wanted her to pine for ever. He hadn't been that sort of person.

'I . . . I do believe you.' Alice squeezed his fingers in return. 'I've just got so used to keeping his secret, that's all. It was a shock to know you'd realised the truth.' A dreadful thought struck her. 'Blimey, you don't think the others know, do you? At Eastern House, I mean.'

'I doubt it.' Patrick frowned. 'You're both tall and fair-haired, similar bone structure, but it was only when I saw him here at the farm that I put two and two together and made the connection.'

They both heard a shout from the farmhouse. Violet was yelling her name and shouting that their Christmas lunch was getting cold.

'We should go in,' she said hurriedly, 'before Aunty Vi hunts us down with a rollin' pin. But please don't let on that you've guessed he's my dad. Not everyone in there knows who he is.'

Christmas lunch was a rowdy affair. Arnold had been helped down from his bed, despite his constant coughing, and sat in pride of place at the head of the table, with Gran at his side, while Joe sat at the other end, Violet to his right. For everyone else, it was a free-for-all. Alice ended up squeezed in beside Eustace on one side and Joan on the other, both of whom had taken most of the veg at their end of the table, and had to suffer the indignity of a scrap with little Timothy over the last roasties, yet she still managed to eat a lunch so enormous it left her groaning and holding her sides.

'Delicious,' Joe announced, pushing aside his plate with half a roast parsnip still uneaten, which Tristan swiftly leant across to snatch before Caroline could snaffle it. 'You've outdone yourself, Vi, love.'

'Ahem,' Gran said loudly.

'You and your mum, I mean, and everyone else who helped,' Joe hurriedly corrected himself, and grabbed up his glass of homemade wine. 'A toast to the cooks! Thank you all and I wish you a very merry Christmas!'

'The cooks!' they all said, raising their own glasses.

Apart from the kids, they'd all been served a generous glass of Gran's homemade elderberry wine, which had been bottled around the same time as her infamous sloe gin. Alice coughed after one cautious sip and, taking another, felt her cheeks begin to burn.

'Blimey, Gran, that's strong stuff,' she managed to gasp, her eyes watering, only to snort with laughter at the sight of Patrick opposite her, also red-cheeked and winded, staring into his glass in disbelief. 'Maybe we should have warned the newcomers about your elderberry concoction.'

'What . . . What is this you've given us, Gran?' Lily breathed. 'Paint stripper? I swear my lips have gone numb.'

'Paint stripper? Tastes fine to me,' her dad said, enjoying another good swallow of wine with no change of complexion. 'An excellent vintage, Mrs Newton.'

'Why, thank you, Mr, erm, Townsend.' Haughtily, Gran took a sip of her own creation and sat back at once, blowing out her cheeks in shock. 'All right, Arnie . . . None of my elderberry wine for you, d'you hear? It's bloomin' lethal.'

And everybody laughed.

CHAPTER TWENTY-SIX

Imogen had tried her hardest to smile and behave normally during Christmas festivities at the boarding house. But inside she was in terrible anguish. As soon as Penny had told her about Richard's arrest, she had been imagining the worst and blaming herself for it. There had been no further news and nobody seemed to know what had happened, except that police had come to the vicarage and taken him away on Christmas Eve, of all days, in front of his housekeeper.

The mass on Christmas Day had been held by another vicar, while everyone in the town was agog with curiosity and speculation. What had the Reverend Linden done to merit being arrested? Where had he been taken? Would he ever return?

For Christmas lunch, they had eaten as traditional a meal as they could manage with rationing tighter than ever, crowded about the table like one big happy family.

She had helped Florence prepare it, while Pearl had prepared the vegetables and laid the table. Miles had entertained the children, as the doctor was at the hospital all morning, working as he did most days. 'I know it's Christmas Day,' he had told them all as he set out that morning, kissing his son and daughter goodbye and warning them to behave themselves while the others were busy preparing lunch. 'But those men still need medical attention.'

They had eaten lunch quite late, waiting for Dr Tyson to return, which he had done at last and sat down with the rest of them to enjoy an excellent meal. It wasn't like the Christmases she remembered from her childhood. Many ingredients had to be substituted and although 'mock turkey' – which was really just mutton – smothered in gravy and served with boiled greens might be filling, it wasn't as tasty as the real thing. But Miles knew a man who'd managed to procure several bottles of fizzy wine for them, which were almost impossible to get in the ordinary way of things, and after two glasses of this contraband, Imogen no longer cared what the food tasted like and was simply enjoying herself.

Eventually, Imogen went to lie down upstairs, the room spinning, and fell into a fitful doze to the sound of Billy and the other children running about outside in the cold, shrieking with laughter and playing with their new toys.

On Boxing Day morning, she woke with a headache and decided to blow away the cobwebs with a brisk walk along Maer Cliff. But as she was pulling on her hat and gloves, someone knocked at the door, and when she opened it, her heart almost stopped to see Richard standing there, a free man.

Seeing her shocked expression, he gave a faint smile. 'Surprise!'

'They said you'd been arrested,' she stammered. So many questions were running through her head, she didn't know which to start with. If he had been arrested, why had they let him go? Was it because he was innocent? And if he was innocent, did he know who had supplied the information that had incriminated him to the authorities?

Had he come here to accuse her? But if so, why was he still smiling?

'Rumours of my arrest were not entirely unfounded,' he admitted, 'but if you let me explain, I hope you won't think too badly of me. Merry Christmas, by the way. I know it's a day late but I was rather busy yesterday. That is, I'm usually busy on Christmas Day, being a vicar and all, but yesterday I was helping the police with their enquiries. So I wasn't able to give you this.'

He was holding something out to her, which she barely looked at.

Imogen stepped outside, hurriedly closing the front door behind her. She had been planning to go for a walk anyway, but she didn't want to risk Florence coming out to discover who she was talking to, worried what he might say in front of her sister. Uncertainly, she took the package from him. It was small and wrapped in brown paper but with a pink ribbon around it, tied in a fancy bow.

'What's this?'

'Open it and find out.'

Her gaze darted to his face and her cheeks burnt; she felt so horribly guilty, she could barely focus on what he was saying. Fumbling at the bow, she tore the package open to find a lidded box.

Inside, nestling on black velvet, was a silver ring. She stared down at it, uncomprehending. 'I don't understand.'

'Perhaps you would do me the honour of going for a walk with me. There are things I have to tell you, and something I need to ask. Afterwards, the significance of my gift may become clearer.'

'I wish you wouldn't talk in riddles!'

'I'm sorry,' he said gently. 'I was awake all night, thinking of this moment. Please forgive me if I'm not making much sense. I probably ought to have left it a little while before coming over. But I couldn't rest until I'd spoken to you.'

Saying nothing, she slipped his gift into her pocket, still consumed with guilt at having betrayed him, unable to think of much else.

They walked in silence along Ocean View Road towards the Atlantic. There was a cold wind blowing off the ocean but it was bright, the rain holding off for now. Sunlight glittered on the wind-flecked water and her coat flapped, letting in the chill. There was an air of unreality to this situation, she thought, glancing at him sideways. When she'd got up that morning, it had been with the sure knowledge that Richard was probably in jail by now, awaiting his trial for treason. After which, she had shuddered to think what his sentence might be.

'You're not on the run, are you?' she demanded.

Richard threw back his head and laughed. 'You have a rich imagination.'

'Tell me what's going on, then.'

There were others out for a Boxing Day walk. An elderly man with a dog was ambling along a short distance away, and a lady with three young children was not far behind him.

'Let's walk a little further first.' He waited until they were climbing the steep cliff-path, turning to help her up the rocky slope, before saying quietly, 'The thing is, Imogen, there are some rather beastly people in this world. And if we let them go unchallenged, it could spell the end of everything we hold dear.'

Reaching the top, she let go of his hand, staring at him. Was he about to confess to being an enemy sympathiser? 'What are you talking about?'

'If I tell you,' he added, 'you must promise never to tell anyone else. Can you do that?'

'I won't know until I hear what it is,' she said honestly.

'Fair enough.' He began to walk along the cliff top and she fell into step beside him. 'Very well, then. Back when I first came to Bude, I was lonely, so I decided to make some friends locally. As you know, I enjoy playing chess and there's quite a lively chess club here. One or two of them are brilliant players, in fact,' he added with a burst of enthusiasm. 'Only we didn't just play chess.

We discussed books and politics, and the war.' He rubbed a hand across his forehead, frowning. 'Then one of the fellows from the chess club asked me to tea, and we got talking about the war, as usual. Only this time he made it clear how much he disliked our government for not appeasing Hitler. I didn't agree, of course. But he was good company and I kept meeting up with him.' He paused. 'After Simon was killed, this chap suggested his death could have been avoided if we'd chosen not to go to war with Germany.'

'Good God.'

'Yes, that was my reaction too.' Richard drew a deep breath. 'But as I told you, when Simon died, a part of me died with him. I was lost and floundering. For a while, to be honest, I wasn't thinking straight.'

'I remember.' She thought of that day up at Compass Point when she'd feared he might be considering suicide. 'Go on,' she whispered, choked up by the emotion in his voice.

'Well, one day he asked if I'd like to "get my revenge", as he put it.'

'By doing what?'

'Spying for Hitler, essentially.' He saw her instinctive recoil and added quickly, 'Oh, he didn't put it like that. He described it as giving the Germans a "helpful nudge" every now and then. Watch a few people for them. Pass on a little information.' He looked out to sea, distaste on his face. 'I wasn't interested. Losing Simon had cut me in half, it's true. But it hadn't addled my brains. My brother was proud to die for his country. Helping the Nazis would have been like spitting on his grave.'

'So what did you tell him?'

'I wanted to kick the slippery fellow around the room, frankly. But I hung fire . . . Told him I'd think about it.' He gave her a grim smile. 'I was worried if I went straight to the police, he might deny it all and try to incriminate *me* instead. So I started to watch him. I took notes on what he said, where he went, who he spoke to. I soon realised from his behaviour that he must have recruited a few others here in Bude. Only they never seemed to meet in public, and when he did speak to people in passing after church, it was impossible to overhear what was being said. So I wrote to an old school chum who works for the MoD and sent him my notes. He thought it would be a good idea to rattle this chap's cage, in the hope he'd panic and lead us to the others involved.' He looked at her grimly. 'I agreed to make it look as though I'd been arrested, so he could be watched.'

'So you weren't arrested? It was all a ruse?' When he nodded, the knot of pain in her chest loosened. 'Oh, Richard, I'm so glad you're not a traitor,' she cried.

His brows rose. 'You thought I could be?'

'Only because I was expecting to see a traitor in the church porch that day . . . And you were the only one there. Apart from that old lady.' Briefly, without giving away any operational information, she explained about her mission and how she had been tasked with watching him. 'Now I see why they suspected you in the first place.

Because you were in regular contact with this other chap.' She bit her lip. 'Was it . . . Mr Jolly, the writer?'

'That's the man, yes.' His gaze bored into hers intently. 'I have to say, I did wonder for a while what *you* were up to. The two of you sat near each other in church a few times and seemed rather chummy. I almost suspected you might be tangled up with their lot too. But I didn't want to believe it.'

'I was sure you couldn't be a traitor either. I'm sorry I even doubted you.' She felt dreadful. 'You must know I gave the authorities your name as a potential ringleader.'

'I know.'

She buried her face in her hands, too ashamed to look him in the eye. 'What an idiot I was. I should have realised you were innocent.'

'What, with all the evidence stacked against me?' He shook his head. 'I don't blame you, Imogen. And now I know you were engaged in the same business as me, it all makes sense. Look, I came here today to tell you something important, not accuse you of anything.'

Her hands dropped to her sides and she stared at him. 'What do you mean?'

'I went to enlist again last week, and they've accepted me. I'll be going over to France soon as an army chaplain.'

'No!' Imogen was horrified.

'That ring in your pocket,' he went on, the wind almost snatching his words away. 'I love you, Imogen. Say the word and I'll consider us engaged to be married. Then, once the war is over, we can tie the knot.' He stopped, grimacing. 'Not the finest marriage proposal of all time, was it?'

'Oh, Richard . . . I don't know where to start.' She was trying to get her disordered thoughts under control, her heart thumping. 'First though, yes, I will marry you.'

Joy was followed by blank shock in his face. 'You will?'

'But not if you go to France.'

'What?' Richard took a step back, looking as though she'd slapped his face. 'But it's too late. I've already put my signature to it. Besides, you can't make *cowardice* a condition of our marriage.' He looked affronted.

'If you really loved me, you'd stay.'

'It's because I love you that I have to go,' he insisted, very much on his dignity. 'Every man is needed in this conflict . . . Yes, even those of us who can't see well enough to shoot straight.' He shook his head when she began to protest. 'I've *always* loved you, Imogen. Since long before you fancied yourself head over heels with my brother. Though you had eyes only for him, so I kept quiet about it. But I didn't stop loving you. In fact, I only came to Bude to be closer to you.'

She was shocked. 'What?'

'I went to visit your parents in Exeter, meaning to ask you on a date, and they told me where you'd gone. So I got myself sent out here as soon as there was a vacancy. You could have knocked me down with a feather when you turned up at church that day.' He took her hand. 'I'd been watching you secretly for weeks, trying to drum up the courage to approach you. I knew you'd never been interested in me, only Simon. But I thought perhaps if we spent more time together . . . Then you kept hanging about the church, and I was sure you must have feelings for me after all.'

'I do have feelings for you,' she told him shyly. 'I would hardly have accepted your marriage proposal otherwise.'

'And Simon?'

'I was in love with your brother once, yes.' Her cheeks were hot but she held his gaze steadily. 'But he didn't want me and it was over a long time ago. I didn't understand you at first, it's true. But I've grown to love you.' Her vision swam with tears as she finally admitted the truth. 'You're brave and noble, Richard, and you feel everything so deeply, I can't help loving you.'

'But you won't marry me if I go off to war?' The question had been put savagely. He was holding both her hands now, drawing her closer.

'Only because I couldn't bear to lose you the way we lost Simon. Don't you see that? It would break me.' Tears were running down her cheeks. 'I need you. Here. With me.'

'My darling.' Richard enfolded her in his arms and they stood together a while, the ocean winds snatching at them. 'I'm sorry if I'm hurting you. But you have to let me go,' he said at last. 'It would mark me for ever, knowing I had the chance to serve my country and didn't take it. Please try to understand.'

She found a hanky to dry her tears. 'I'm afraid you'll never come back.'

'I'm a little afraid of that too. But if I do come back, I promise we'll be married. Assuming you haven't changed your mind by then. It could be weeks, months, even years before we see each other again. But however long it takes, I'll still be yours once this war is over, Imogen.' He studied her face. 'The real question is, will you be mine?'

He kissed her and she clung to him for a while, standing on tiptoe, her eyes shut tight. There didn't seem to be anything for it but to let him go. Because she did want to marry him, and not simply because he was Simon's twin. She had fallen in love with this man, slowly and steadily, without even noticing, and now couldn't imagine a future without him.

'Yes, I'll be yours,' she whispered as he pulled back, and could only hope he would come back safe to her.

CHAPTER TWENTY-SEVEN

Bude, North Cornwall, April 1945

It was a warm spring day in 1945 and Pearl was on her way to the hospital, where she now worked several days a week, helping patients with their letters home or to sit outside in the rose garden for a spell, or whatever they needed that the doctors couldn't provide. She didn't need to be there for another hour though, so she was taking her time, gazing into the shop window displays in Bude and imagining what it might feel like for the war to be over and rationing to come to an end. Especially clothes rationing, which had become increasingly restrictive this past year, as Freddy had discovered to his dismay when he'd tried to furnish himself and the kids with a new spring wardrobe.

She had her very own ration book now, thank goodness, thanks to a lovely man at the American

Embassy in London to whom she'd written, explaining her predicament. So she could afford to feed and clothe herself at last without constantly dipping into her savings. But the haute couture fashions she'd always worn before the war weren't really catered for in its humdrum pages, nor did the shops in Bude carry much beyond rather utilitarian-looking skirts and dresses. And although she could try to make her own, borrowing Florence's sewing machine, she was admittedly not much of a seamstress. The wardrobe department for the entertainers' troupe had always handled dressmaking and repairs, so she'd never needed to learn such skills. Now she dreamt of all the luxury hats and dresses she would be able to buy when supply ships could once more reach these shores, not to mention nylons . . .

With battle after battle going their way, everyone seemed optimistic that the tide had finally turned in the Allies' favour. But she would only believe it once she'd heard on the wireless that Germany had surrendered. And there were no guarantees that such a fine day would ever come.

Although America had entered the fray late, it still felt as though she'd been away from home for ever. Homesick, she had written a letter to her parents early in the new year, explaining that she had met someone new, a doctor, and they were dating. So far, there had been no reply.

The absence of news from home fretted at her, like a deep ache in her heart. Were her parents unwell? Had something happened to prevent them from replying to her letters? Or was she still unforgiven for having made such a fool of herself over Terence?

On her way down Belle Vue, she passed the newsstand and stopped dead, her heart in her mouth. She had overslept that morning and missed the BBC news bulletin on the wireless. By the time she'd gotten out of bed, the house had been empty. She had heard Florence and Miles taking Billy to school with their new baby in the vast, old-fashioned pram they'd been given by a generous neighbour. Imogen would probably be at the church, where she was so often these days, helping out with repairs to the building, which was being renovated. The doctor had also walked his children to school, of course, and so she had seen no one as she ate a solitary breakfast and got dressed for work.

Now, she grabbed the newspaper off the stand and paid for it, stricken with horror at the headlines. She dived into the nearest teashop to read it before work.

As she sipped her coffee and devoured the dreadful news, a shadow fell across her table.

'I see you know what's happened.' It was Dr Tyson, looking grave. He took the chair beside her, reaching for her hand. 'How are you feeling, love?'

'Awful, to be honest. I can't believe it.' Her gaze dropped to the photograph that accompanied the newspaper report. 'President Roosevelt dead . . . I can't take it in. It's such a shock. And with everything else going on too. I suppose the strain of the war must've been too much for him.'

'That's possible. And now Truman will become president?'

'I expect so. He's the vice president.' But she couldn't help feeling anxious as she met his gaze. 'Do you think it will help us, having someone new in charge? Everything seems to be hanging in the balance at the moment. I won't pretend. This scares me.'

'Yes,' he agreed. 'It's a dangerous moment for a major change. But I think the Allies may have the upper hand. That's what people are saying, at any rate. So try not to worry, sweetheart.' He looked at his watch. 'I'm on shift soon.'

Leaving the teashop, they walked to the hospital together in the bright April sunshine. She was finding her work satisfying, helping Penny with hospital administration and doing the rounds of the wards every other day, chatting to the soldiers being cared for there and trying to cheer them up with a smile or by reading to them at the bedside.

Some of the boys had injuries that would likely never heal, and she would listen to their troubles and struggle not to weep. But she knew tears wouldn't help them as much as smiles and laughter, so she kept that sorrow for her private moments, when she could escape to her room at the boarding house and cry about it in private.

Thankfully, Freddy would often find her at such dark moments and sit with her, talking about the patients or his life back in London, until she felt able to smile again.

She knew he missed living in London, even though he

loved Cornwall too. They had often talked about what they might do after the war, whether he would eventually move back to London with his children. If he did, he had asked if she would go with him and be his wife. She missed America. She missed her bustling home city of Chicago and all her friends and family there. But the war had changed everything. Now she saw the world with different eyes. Perhaps it would not be so very hard to live in a different country if she could be with the man she loved. And she did love Freddy. He was the best man she had ever known.

'How was Clara this morning?' she asked.

His daughter had been in a rare taking the night before, stamping her foot, pink-cheeked with fury over her brother sneaking a look at her journal. The boy had apologised and they'd all tried to calm her down but with little success. Pearl had noticed how upset Freddy had been by this unfortunate episode and wished she could do something practical to help.

'A little better, thanks, though still sniping at Toby on their way to school. I had a stern word with him about never reading his sister's journal again.' Freddy sighed. 'I just wish I could figure out why Clara's being so moody. She never used to fly off the handle so quick.'

'Well, she's becoming a young lady,' Pearl said. 'It can be a difficult time.' She frowned, remembering herself at that age, how many times she too had flown into a temper over the slightest thing . . .

Freddy looked at her now, slowing his steps. 'What's

wrong, love? You still worried about the change in the presidency?'

She shook her head, returning to the problem that was still nagging at her. 'It's my mother. She still hasn't written back to me. It's been months now. They must've gotten my letter. Unless it went astray.'

'So write to her again.'

'I said I'd wait to hear from her before sending more news. Besides, if she hasn't replied, it suggests she doesn't wanna know me anymore.' A tear ran down Pearl's cheek despite her determination to stay cheerful and she rubbed it away. 'I guess I don't belong there anymore. That they're no longer my folks.' She raised her chin bravely. 'You're my new family. You and the kids.'

He smiled, taking her hand. 'I can't wait for you to be a part of our family, Pearl. In fact, if you want to get married straightaway, I'd be happy to do it. To make you Mrs Tyson.'

Pearl managed a smile at that, for the words lit up her soul. 'You're such a wonderful man, Freddy. And I do want to marry you. But only after the war's over, when life finally starts again. It feels like we've been holding our breath for years, don't you think?' When he nodded, she went on slowly, 'Please don't think I don't want to be your wife. Because I do. I want it more than anything. And to be a mother to your children, if they'll have me.' She paused. 'But I want to breathe freely on our wedding day. For the world to start turning again.'

'I understand.' They'd reached the hospital. Freddy

paused before going inside. 'I feel the same, in a way. I'm sick of everything being hard and brutal. Let's hope for a better future, all right? And when that day comes, we'll set a date for our wedding.'

Penny raised her head from the reception desk as they came in, Freddy heading off to the surgical unit to check his patients' list for that afternoon and Pearl unpinning her hat and collecting her apron ready for another shift.

'Hello, Pearl,' she said, looking concerned. 'Did you hear the news about Roosevelt?'

Pearl showed her the newspaper. 'I did, indeed. America owes him a great debt.'

'So does Britain,' Penny said earnestly. 'If he hadn't agreed to enter the war . . . Oh, it doesn't bear thinking about. I hope the new man will keep up the good work.'

'Truman? I don't know much about him. But let's hope.' Pearl looked more closely at Penny, noting her heightened colour and the loose-fitting smock dress she was wearing. 'That's not your usual style. Suits you, though.'

'Thank you.' Penny bit her lip, blushing deeper. 'I couldn't squeeze into my work skirt any longer. The truth is, John and I . . . We're expecting a baby.'

'How marvellous!' Pearl hugged her, ecstatic for her friend, for she knew Penny had been hopeful of starting a family. 'Is he pleased?'

'Bit late if he isn't,' Penny said frankly, but she was beaming. 'I'm just pulling your leg. He's over the moon, of course. His mum and dad too.' She showed Pearl the letter she'd been writing. 'I'm just sending the news to my parents. Though I know they'll want to jump straight in the car and dash across the country to see me, petrol rationing or not, as soon as they read my letter. And my mother will start knitting for Britain.'

'What are you hoping for? A boy or a girl?'

'I'd like a little boy,' Penny admitted shyly, 'but John says he hopes it's a girl. Though we'll be happy with either, just so long as the baby's healthy.'

Pearl went about her work in high spirits after that good news, and told Freddy the first chance she got. He grinned and suggested again that they get married as soon as possible, but she merely laughed and hurried away. Not only did she want a wedding day free of the long shadow of the war, but she was partly nervous about what his kids would say to her being their new mother, in particular Clara.

Her worries weren't just about Clara's recent tantrum. Freddy's daughter had clearly guessed there was more than mere friendship between Pearl and her father, and more than once had shot Pearl a warning look, as though to say, 'Hands off my dad'. No doubt Clara was unhappy at the thought of another woman taking the place of her late mother, and that was perfectly natural. Her glowering looks made Pearl a little uncomfortable about spending too much time with him when the kids were around. But if Clara was genuinely unhappy about his choice of new bride, her objections would need to be sorted out before they could be married.

*   *   *

The next day, she took Freddy's advice and wrote again to her parents. Two weeks later, Florence came to her at the breakfast table with a letter postmarked from the States. 'The postie just called. Is this what you've been waiting for? I hope it's good news.' Then she discreetly scooped up Billy, who had just finished eating, and left Pearl alone to open the envelope.

Freddy came back in at that moment, having just seen the kids off to school, who were walking in with Miles that morning. He stopped short at the sight of the postmarked envelope. 'From your parents?'

She nodded, sick with nerves, and began to read aloud while he poured them both a fresh cup of tea from the pot.

Dear Pearl

We were so thankful to receive your letter. You mentioned a previous letter sent in January, but we never got that. I suppose the mail boat must have been blown up crossing the Atlantic or maybe the letter was simply lost in transit. But please know, we would have replied at once if we had received it. I'm only sorry you did not write again sooner.

Poppa and I are both overjoyed by news of your engagement to Dr Tyson and wish you both very happy. We miss you so bad here. I was unhappy when I replied to you

last year and I'm sorry for what I wrote.
Poppa wants you to know, we're not good
with words, but whatever happens, you
will always be our little Pearl, our
shining star. And we hope you will keep
in contact with us, even if you choose to
stay in England.

You may be married to your handsome
doctor by now. But if you're not, please let
us know the date, so we can send a
telegram of congratulations. And I hope and
pray you will come to visit us someday
soon, maybe when the war is over. Which
God willing could be any day now.

Momma x

Her voice broke on the last words and she bowed her head, weeping uncontrollably.

'There there, my darlin'.' Freddy took the letter and put an arm about her shoulders as he read through it again silently. 'That's a very generous letter,' he said at last.

She nodded. 'I . . . I must write back to my folks at once,' she said, as soon as she could speak again. 'How stupid of me. You were perfectly right. That last letter did go astray. But I thought . . . I just assumed they didn't want to know me anymore, after what Momma wrote last time.'

'All's well that ends well, eh?' He kissed her on the forehead. '*Handsome?*' he queried, a twinkle in his eye.

'I may have exaggerated your looks a little, honey,' Pearl

admitted, and laughed when one of his brows quirked. 'Though only a *very* little.'

She felt so happy and relieved now that she knew her parents weren't cross with her anymore. But she knew there was still a trial to come when Freddy finally told Clara he was planning to remarry.

One problem at a time, she told herself, and gave him a brave smile.

CHAPTER TWENTY-EIGHT

Porthcurno, South Cornwall, May 1945

One evening in early May, almost dusk, Alice nipped out into the farmyard after supper to bully the hens into their coop for the night. Making clucking noises, she stretched out both her arms to herd them towards their run. As she was closing the latch against foxes, she heard an engine chugging up the hill.

Frowning, she walked to the top of the track that led to Porthcurno and looked down.

A battered old vehicle was dragging itself up the last few hundred yards to the farm entrance. Its headlights were on full, for few people in recent weeks were bothering with the blackout anymore. Everyone knew the war was almost over. Hitler was dead, Germany on her knees, and the Allies were days, maybe even hours, away from accepting her surrender.

It had taken Alice quite a while to believe what everyone had been saying lately, that they were nearly out of the long dark tunnel of the war. But now that even George Cotterill was whistling in the corridors, she had tentatively allowed herself to hope at last . . . and to look forward to a future without rationing and the fear of invasion.

The vehicle drew closer, and she saw with a shock that it was an old ambulance, heavily dented and with grass stuck to the front grille.

As it pulled up, the passenger door creaked open and a bulky figure came lumbering towards her. 'Alice?' It was a woman's voice, thick Cornish accent, and familiar. 'My God, you've grown.'

She found herself seized in a bear hug. Meanwhile, the driver's door had opened and another large figure emerged, reaching her in three strides and also seizing her in a bear hug.

''Ere, watch out . . . You'll crack me ribs!' As they released her, she took a few steps back, blinking. 'Demelza? Robert? Well, blow me. They let you out of Germany, then?'

Demelza was Tristan's sister, who had married Robert, an ambulance driver who had refused to fight in the war, being a Quaker and conscientious objector, and the two of them had insisted on going abroad as ambulance drivers.

'I didn't want to leave,' Demelza told her, glancing at her husband. 'But Robert said we had to come home.'

'Well, my dear,' Robert said calmly, 'it was getting

increasingly obvious that you could no longer work as an ambulance driver.'

Alice looked Demelza up and down. 'Blimey, you don't mean . . . You're having a baby? Congratulations!' She watched as Robert turned off the headlights and brought out their bags. 'Don't tell me you brought that dreadful old banger all the way from Germany to Cornwall?'

'He wouldn't leave her behind. I think he loves that ambulance almost as much as me.' But Demelza was smiling. 'We've got so much to tell you. The things we've done, the places we've seen . . . It was the most marvellous adventure of my life and I'll never forget it. But I'm glad to be home. Where's Tristan? I can't wait to see him.'

Alice led her into the kitchen where the family was still gathered about the table after supper. Tristan was washing up a pot in the sink and turned around blankly at the sound of his name. He stared as his sister stepped into the light. 'Dem? Thank God.' And he rushed across the kitchen to hold her tight.

Robert came in, stamping mud off his boots on the threshold, and was instantly seized by Lily and Aunty Violet, while his hand was pumped up and down by Joe, who then hurried off to fetch Alice's dad and some home brew.

Gran didn't recognise the couple at first, so Alice quickly reminded her who the newcomers were, since she'd barely met them before. Besides which, Gran had not been sleeping well lately, sitting up late into the night with Arnie, whose chest had worsened over the winter months. A fortnight ago, at the hospital in Penzance, they'd explained he had a tumour in his lungs and there was nothing to be done. He had only weeks, at most a few months, to live. Gran had wept bitterly for days, but Arnie had taken it stoically enough. 'My own fault, for not looking after my health better. Well, I've had a good life, and loved two women, and that's more than enough for any man.'

Demelza sat down wearily at the table, but not before Aunty Violet had spotted her prominent bump and exclaimed, 'Is that what I think it is? Oh gawd . . . Another baby on the way?'

'Pay no attention to her, love.' Gran tipped a wink at Demelza. 'Congratulations. We've bloomin' dozens of outfits for newborns here. Take whatever you need.'

'Thank you,' Demelza said happily, already cooing over Lily's baby boy. 'We were so thrilled to hear about Morris. May I hold him?'

'Please, no more baby talk,' Robert muttered, sinking into a chair. 'I've had nothing but baby talk since leaving Germany.'

At that moment, Joe came limping into the kitchen with a few bottles of home brew for him and Robert, and Alice's dad behind him, catching that remark, looked at their visitors with interest.

'Germany? You've come from Germany?'

Robert nodded. 'We were working as volunteer ambulance drivers there. But it was getting dangerous, and we had a few near misses, so I decided to bring Demelza home.'

'Whereabouts were you stationed in Germany?' Ernest

took a seat next to Robert, shaking his hand. 'I'm Alice's father, by the way.' As soon as he'd heard that Hitler had committed suicide, he'd stopped calling himself Townsend and had admitted his true identity, though still asked people not to make it known too widely until Germany's surrender had been formally agreed.

'Please to meet you, sir. I'm Tristan's brother-in-law, Robert.'

Robert began to talk about the places they had been in Germany, driving the ambulance and working closely with the army medical units. Alice sat listening, happy to see her father's rapt expression. Being half German himself, born in Germany and having spent the past few years undercover there, she knew he still sometimes missed his homeland. But he had served this country from the very start of the war, and had been dreadfully disillusioned by what had happened in Germany, the rise of the Nazis and fascism. Now, for a few minutes at least, he was indulging in a little nostalgia.

On her other side, Tristan was talking to his sister, exchanging news and smiling as she played with baby Morris.

'Goodness, he looks just like you.' Demelza handed him back to Lily with a broody expression. Thoughtfully, she rubbed her tummy. 'I've heard all about the sleepless nights. How bad is it?'

'You get used to it,' Lily said cheerfully.

'It's like being tortured,' Tristan muttered, and was rewarded with a glare from his wife.

'You're staying here tonight, I hope,' Violet asked the couple. She glanced at Joe, biting her lip. 'Where can we put them up? In the snug? We could push two chairs together to make another bed. They won't both fit on the sofa – that's for certain.'

'I can sleep in the old ambulance,' Robert said calmly. 'We've slept in the back all the way from Germany. It's no trouble.'

Gran looked horrified. 'We'll have no guest under this roof sleeping in a van. Them armchairs are big enough for a cosy night's sleep.'

'I'm sorry we don't have enough room here for you to stay long, Dem. Will you go to your dad in Penzance?' Lily asked tentatively.

'I'm not sure.' Demelza turned to her brother. 'Have you been home much, Tris?'

They had both clashed with their cantankerous father, a sheep farmer and widower who disapproved of both Robert and Lily as spouses for his two children.

'No, but I'm sure he'd be happy to see you, Dem. Especially given *that*.' Tristan nodded towards her tummy. 'I'll go with you, if you like. Break the ice.'

Alice turned to Robert. 'You must have had some interesting times, driving that ambulance,' she said, keen to hear more about his work on the front line.

'Robert is too modest to talk about himself,' Demelza said proudly, 'but he's being awarded the George Cross.'

Joe looked fascinated. 'What did he do to get that, then?'

'We were near the front line and being shelled so heavily, it was a miracle anyone could get out of there alive. Robert sent me back to the field hospital to do stretcher work, but he kept going. Managed another four journeys to and from the field hospital under heavy bombardment. He saved so many people that day, carrying the wounded off the battlefield . . . He was a hero. My hero.' And she looked at her husband with glowing eyes. 'That's why they're giving him a medal.'

'You're a brave man,' Alice's dad said, and shook Robert's hand again.

'Anyone would have done the same,' Robert insisted, looking embarrassed, but everyone got up to shake his hand, assuring him that his actions had indeed been heroic.

'Well, my stars! A hero at our kitchen table.' Gran raised her glass of home brew to him, but her gaze slid past to Ernest, and she smiled. 'To all our heroes,' she said, and they echoed her, drinking deep.

At that moment, a squeal came from the snug, and the door burst open. The Land Girls and Janice had been sitting in there, listening to the wireless, as they often did in the evenings.

Selina looked white with excitement, but Caroline was flushed and Joan was clinging to her, all of them breathless and speaking at once.

'Blimey!' Violet had been feeding Sally a little apple sauce to help the baby settle for the night, but now stared around at them in astonishment, spoon poised in mid-air. 'One at a time, girls . . . What's up?'

'Oh, Mrs Postbridge, they just interrupted the programme on the wireless to say, *we've won*. Germany has surrendered and tomorrow will be Victory in Europe Day.' Selina collapsed, weeping with joy, and Caroline helped her friend to a chair. 'I'll be able to go home and see Johnny again. We can get married at last.'

'It's true.' Joan was nodding, her eyes alight. 'They announced it on the special bulletin just now . . . We've won the war in Europe.'

Gran put a shaking hand to her mouth. 'Oh gawd.'

'I can't believe it,' Joe said slowly.

'Thank God,' Alice's dad said, and dropped his head into his hands.

'I'm goin' to tell the boys,' Janice said, wide-eyed, and dashed out, thudding upstairs to the cramped room she shared with her brothers.

'Oh, Tris,' Lily breathed, looking at her husband over their infant's head.

'My darling.' Tristan put his arm around her and little Morris, but was looking across at his sister Demelza, a wry smile on his face. 'You and Rob turn up, and Germany promptly surrenders . . . Was this your doing, sis?'

'Of course,' Demelza said, grinning.

Robert was silent, looking down at his hands. Then he said heavily, 'It's marvellous news. But so many lives lost to get here. So much sacrifice.'

'We'll never forget them,' Joe muttered.

Alice, who had stood silent all this time as she listened to the confusion and excitement around her, burst into tears. Her dad got up and drew her close.

'Everything's going to be all right, Alice,' he said, and smiled into her eyes. 'It's finally over.'

CHAPTER TWENTY-NINE

Imogen trod delicately around the children playing jacks on the garden path and marched out into the street, holding aloft an apple pie that smelled delicious. Like many others in Bude, they were holding a 'Victory in Europe' street party on Downs View Road and, despite the extra work this entailed, she couldn't wait for the festivities to start in earnest. Everything had been grim and hard for so long, and her task of sniffing out hidden enemies in her own town had almost broken her spirit. She'd all but forgotten what it felt like to be genuinely cheerful, rather than just putting on a brave face.

Now at last they could start living again and looking to the future.

Florence and Miles had been up since daybreak, dragging out and arranging a series of rectangular tables in a long row straight down the middle of the road.

'Woe betide any vehicles that might wish to pass,' Imogen had said, eyeing this structure.

But Miles had simply shrugged. 'You heard them on the wireless. It's a public holiday – nobody's going anywhere today. Victory in Europe Day. So you can stop worrying. The fighting's over.'

'Japan hasn't surrendered.' Florence resumed this conversation now, unfolding spare tablecloths in the kitchen and measuring them with her eye. 'It was just on the war bulletin.'

'They can't be far behind, honey, not now Germany has fallen. What would be the point of hanging on?' Miles picked up a large tray of cutlery. 'I'll take this out, shall I?'

'Yes, please. Give me a hand with these tablecloths, Immi?' After the tables had all been draped in cloths, carefully pinned to prevent the breeze whipping them off, they returned for the assorted sandwiches that Imogen and Pearl had been preparing for the past hour.

'Nearly ready.' Florence was beaming with pleasure, even though baby Hope could be heard wailing from her pram in the front garden. 'Immi, could you bring out the pie from the pantry? The big apple pie.' Then she'd disappeared again, bearing a wicker basket of sandwiches.

Now, Imogen placed a golden-brown apple pie decorated with intricate pastry leaves in the middle of the table, alongside all the other fruit pies that the other ladies in the street had baked.

'Looks like the whole street will be at this party.' Imogen

grinned down at Clara, who had left the game of jacks to follow her. The girl was wearing her best dress and frilly white socks but she didn't look particularly happy. 'Today is a very special day, Clara. You're going to remember this day for the rest of your life.'

'Because the war is over?' Clara chewed on her lip. 'But is it really over though, Imogen? Really and truly?'

'Cross my heart and swear to die, the war is over.' Imogen watched the girl skip back to her game and hoped that she had managed to reassure her. It would indeed be a wonderful day and one for the history books.

Despite her excitement, she couldn't help feeling a few niggles of doubt herself. She hadn't heard from Richard since he enlisted as an army chaplain and had no idea where he was or how he was doing. She had told Florence they were engaged, and her sister had shrieked and hugged her, while Miles had shaken her hand. But she'd pointed out, as coolly as possible, that he might not come back, since the war had still been waging at that time.

Now though, everything had changed. Hitler and his horrid cronies had killed themselves in some underground bunker, Germany had offered their surrender, and VE Day had been announced at last – Victory in Europe, people were calling it, because there was still fighting in some parts of the Far East. Despite all this, Richard had not been in touch. Not so much as a brief note to say when he might be coming back or that he was thinking of her. She knew some soldiers were being kept on overseas, even though fighting had theoretically stopped. There were still pockets of danger across Europe, word of the ceasefire not having reached everybody at the same time.

Besides, as Miles had pointed out, there would be a great deal of work to do, helping the people of Europe get back on their feet, to rebuild shattered towns and cities, and care for civilians left homeless and destitute by the war. The army would be needed for that too, he'd said, not merely for keeping the peace.

She imagined many of those men must be weary and desperate to get home. Yet here in Britain, people were celebrating the end of the war. It was the end of a conflict that had dragged on so long, Imogen struggled to remember what life had been like before war broke out. It felt as though they been crawling on hands and knees through a dark tunnel for years, and finally the light was just ahead . . . Only they weren't quite there yet.

'I've brought out all the tinned fruit and tins of condensed cream,' Pearl said behind her, depositing her treasures on the table. 'And the tin opener. Florence said we mustn't open the tins until the last minute though, or the cream may go off.'

'Good idea.' Imogen took a deep breath and began putting a plate on each place setting along their half of the table. She might not have heard from Richard, but she could still enjoy today.

The next two houses along were responsible for laying the other side of the table, though the whole street had mucked in to provide the feast itself. And old Mr Bottomley, who some claimed was as rich as Croesus but never let on about his wealth, had brought out from his cellar two cases of French bubbly that he'd been keeping back until the end of the war.

The local bobby, turning up with a Bude-Stratton councillor to check their placement of tables for the street party, stood eyeing this undoubted contraband with disapproval, until Mr Bottomley hobbled out and offered them a bottle each, murmuring, 'For yourself and the missus.' Politely, the bobby had thanked him, touched his policeman's hat, and promptly disappeared. The councillor, after some hesitation, had done likewise, catching Miles's stern eye and no doubt deciding it wasn't worth complaining about bribery and corruption.

'I like the way things are done in your country,' Miles had remarked to his wife, watching this transaction.

The neighbours began to assemble, kids running about noisily, men proudly wearing their uniforms if they had any, women bustling about in pinnies and carrying yet more food and drink for the already groaning tables. Miles set up the gramophone at the open window at Ocean View and kept hurrying back and forth to change the records, though the music was soon lost in the hubbub and buzz of conversation and laughter.

Pearl sat with Clara and Toby, eagerly watching for Dr Tyson, who was due home from a quick visit to the hospital to check on his patients. The doctor came trudging up the road at last just as Miles and Florence sat down at the table with Billy, having settled Hope in her pram within easy reach.

'Well done, this all looks splendid,' he told them, grabbing a dainty triangle of cucumber sandwich as he bent to kiss his son and daughter on the forehead before sitting beside Pearl. The two seemed to have fallen in love, though nothing had been said officially and Imogen wasn't even sure the doctor's children knew how serious it was between them. She wondered what Clara would say once she knew.

'Immi, do stop hovering and sit down,' Florence told her, patting the empty seat to her left. Nearly everyone else had taken their seats at the long table that now ran almost a third of the street. 'What are you waiting for?'

Imogen didn't know. She sank down beside her sister, feeling unaccountably restless, and allowed the doctor to pour her a glass of bubbly.

'There are street parties everywhere in Bude,' Dr Tyson was telling everyone within earshot, his deep voice audible above the chatter. 'As I walked back through town, I saw street after street celebrating, with dancing and music, and people enjoying party food together like this. Someone clever's managed to string half of Belle Vue with bunting too. We can take a walk down there later, if you like,' he told his children, though Imogen noted how his smile was for Pearl alone.

'I'd love to walk down with you too,' Pearl said, then glanced uncertainly at Clara. 'If that's all right with you.'

Clara said nothing, but her lower lip was jutting as she reached for a second slice of fruit cake.

'I want dance,' Billy muttered through a mouthful of

paste sandwich. The music playing on the gramophone was a catchy tune, one of a stack of records left behind by the Rangers, and her nephew's pudgy fingers thumped the table emphatically in time to its beat. 'Do do dah! Do do dah!'

Miles chuckled. 'He'll make an excellent drummer one day,' he told Florence, his arm about his wife's shoulder.

Jeanette from Number Six had jumped up and was dancing with her grandfather while the whole family clapped along. Mr Bottomley was waving his glass about and fondly urging everyone to drink more of his black-market bubbly. Some slick-haired young soldiers, presumably on leave from Cleave Camp, had crashed the street party and were chatting in a lively fashion to the Edmonton sisters, blonde twins who were pink in the face and giggling, no doubt having drunk *too much* bubbly. And the town clerk, whose mother lived near the end of the row, was leaning his elbows on the table and talking earnestly to some of the older gentlemen about Winston Churchill's tactics and what the prime minister ought to do next.

Everyone was enjoying themselves, Imogen thought, nibbling on a thin slice of cheese and broccoli flan. Except her.

'Immi,' Florence whispered, nudging her urgently. 'Look!'

She stopped mid-chew, for on lifting her head she saw Richard coming steadily towards her. Steadily but not quickly, for although he was in his army uniform, he was seated in an old bath chair, like something out of the last century, that was being pushed by one of the church wardens. He also had a blanket over his knees and a huge plaster cast on his right leg, which was sticking out at an odd angle.

People stopped talking, staring round at the vicar in astonishment. But they were all too polite to say anything.

'Thanks, Samuel,' Richard told the man as they reached Imogen's seat, shaking hands with him. 'I'll be all right from here. You go and enjoy the festivities.'

Florence greeted Richard with a smile and then discreetly occupied herself with cutting up Billy's food. On their other side, Pearl and the doctor were deep in conversation. Thankfully, the hum of conversation soon rose again, covering the awkwardness of the moment.

Her heart thumping, Imogen turned to face Richard, not sure what to think. 'You're home . . . I had no idea. When did you get back? But you're hurt?' She stared at the plaster cast on his leg. 'Was it the enemy? Were you shot?'

'Nothing so heroic, I'm afraid. I fell off a ladder, trying to rescue a cat from a bombed-out house,' he admitted, shamefaced. 'Broke my leg and a couple of ribs. Two weeks in a field hospital, then they shipped me back home to England. I only got back yesterday.' He hesitated, not looking at her directly. 'An ignominious end to my military career . . . I'll understand if you don't want to marry me, after I made such a shambles of it.'

'Oh, Richard, you idiot,' she choked, partly with

laughter, partly with a rush of love so strong it left her breathless.

Jumping up, she hugged him – though gently, bearing in mind his broken ribs – did not quite dare kiss the vicar in full view of the residents of Ocean View Road, most of whom had no idea they had even been courting. For weeks, she had been on tenterhooks, fearing he might never come home, steeling herself to face the worst possible news . . . Now here he was, back in Bude with nothing more dangerous than a broken leg, and the war was finally over.

At last, she could stop looking over her shoulder constantly, forget about hidden enemies and impossible choices, and start living her life. Everything was still in a hopeless jumble, it was true . . . But the one thing she knew for sure that she wanted in her life was Richard.

'I'm a blithering idiot, yes. My entire regiment would no doubt heartily agree with you.' He was blinking, his smile uncertain. 'Though just to be clear, and I apologise for being so dense, but was that a . . . a *yes*, you're still willing to marry me? Or were you just letting me down kindly?'

'It's a yes,' she whispered, tears in her eyes. 'Yes . . . Yes, I'll marry you.'

Beside her, Florence, who had clearly only been pretending to listen to one of their neighbours holding forth about his adventures during the Great War, gave a muffled shriek and turned to shake Imogen's hand, and then Richard's, saying joyfully, 'Congratulations, you two . . . Such wonderful news!'

People were staring at them in earnest now. Pearl got up to hug Imogen and shake Richard's hand, congratulating them both, as did Dr Tyson, and then their neighbours, one by one, as the news spread rapidly along the party table. 'Eh, Vicar,' one old gentleman said, 'wishing you and your lovely lady all the best. But how did you do that?' And he jerked his head towards Richard's broken leg.

Embarrassed, aware of everyone listening, Richard began to tell his story again, about the cat stuck on the top floor of a bombed-out shell of a house, and soon the crowd were in stitches, laughing uproariously. But what Imogen noticed most was how happy everyone seemed, faces beaming everywhere she looked, relaxed and smiling as they celebrated the end of the war. Union Jacks fluttered in the sea breeze from every gate and lamp-post, with colourful bunting hurriedly strung up to jollify the street, and people wearing their best clothes for the occasion.

It was true, she thought, feeling dazed. The fighting was over and they could all begin to rebuild their lives . . .

Yet there was still a strange air of unreality to her own life. Richard was back from the war and she had said yes to wearing his ring. But did she really want to marry a vicar?

A vicar's wife was the last thing she'd expected to be, growing up. People back home in Exeter would be astonished, especially her parents . . . Imogen had been the flighty, rebellious one, always the first to make eyes at the boys at parties. Yet soon she might soon be arranging cream teas on the vicarage lawn or hosting the local women's lunch group. It all seemed impossible.

Devouring a slice of sponge cake while juggling a cup of hot tea, Richard met her eyes. 'Immi?'

Catching the uncertainty in his face, she guessed what he was afraid of. That she had indeed changed her mind. She had never felt protective towards anyone before, except perhaps her sister. But she realised in that moment that she couldn't bear to see him hurt.

'Look out, you're about to spill your tea.' She took away his cup and saucer, placing them on the table within his reach. 'Goodness, that's a dreadful old bath chair they've given you. It's positively Victorian. Where on earth did you get it?'

'Yes, bit of an eyesore, isn't it?' Hurriedly, Richard twitched the blanket off his knees and sat up straight, trying to look masterful and commanding despite his injury. 'They'd run out of wheelchairs at the hospital, but someone found me this. Ancient old contraption, but good for long distances until I'm better on my crutches.'

'Perhaps I could help you back to the vicarage after the party. That would give us a chance to talk.' She saw him frown, and added with gentle reassurance, 'About our wedding, I mean.'

'Our . . . wedding?' He still appeared worried.

'You'll need to be back on your feet first, so you can walk me down the aisle afterwards. And I'll need to invite my parents and relatives, and your family too. Plus all our friends here in Bude. Could be quite a gathering of the clans. And I was thinking, now the war's over, we should redecorate the church hall for our wedding reception, as it's been looking a bit dingy lately.' She pursed her lips. 'Hmm, it's not going to be easy.'

'No,' he agreed heavily.

'Thankfully, I'm excellent at organising things. So you can leave it all to me and concentrate on getting better.' Imogen handed him back his tea, seeing that he'd finished his cake. 'By the way, did you manage to rescue that poor cat before you fell off the ladder and broke your leg?'

Richard grinned at last, giving her a sketchy salute. 'I certainly did. Cat saved. Mission accomplished.'

'Well,' she said, 'thank goodness for that.'

CHAPTER THIRTY

Pearl had woken that morning with the most tremendous feeling of happiness. At first, she hadn't known why. Perhaps it was because of the spring sunshine pouring through the gap in the curtains. In Bude, they had stopped using blackout curtains ages back, and now she seemed to be waking at dawn most days, unaccustomed to brightness at such an early hour. So she had stretched and yawned, staring up at the ceiling of her bedroom in puzzlement, and then smiled, for the reason had finally come to her . . .

She was happy because the war was over.

It had been confirmed on the wireless yesterday, though rumours had been flying around since Hitler's death. Then the man on the bulletin had announced that Germany had surrendered and the next day would be a public holiday, so the whole country could celebrate the end of fighting, at least in Europe.

She knew her folks would be partying too, back in the States, and ached to see them again, to join in the festivities. People would soon be free to travel again, she reckoned. Though heavens knows when she'd be able to take Freddy across the Atlantic to meet her parents.

Hearing that announcement, she had wanted to run about screaming for joy. But that would have been childish. Instead, she'd hugged the pleasure to herself and closed her eyes. 'We're free,' she'd whispered.

After getting up, she tried to find a minute alone with Freddy, to discuss what the end of the war might signify for them. But she'd quickly been roped into preparations for the street party. They had still not said anything publicly about their friendship having blossomed into romance, though she imagined a few people had probably guessed, given how much time they'd been spending together lately.

The obvious thing would be to announce their engagement. But it was not so simple.

Clara was already suspicious that she and Freddy had grown close. And it was clear that the doctor's daughter was furious about it. That problem would need to be sorted out before anything could be announced.

How to reassure a smart girl like Clara that her father remarrying would make no difference to her life? Because it would change everything and Pearl knew it.

The street party had been a revelation. She couldn't remember ever having a street party where she lived in Chicago. And the flags and colourful bunting had given

Downs View Road such a cheery look, she'd found herself smiling as she hurried back and forth, carrying dishes and plates of party food, and saw others doing the same.

She had sat next to Freddy for the meal, exchanging shy smiles with him occasionally, though they were both careful not to make things too obvious in front of his children. When the vicar had arrived with his leg in a cast, Freddy had pointed him out to her. 'Did you know the reverend had gone off to war? As an army chaplain, I mean. Brave fellow, but he came back yesterday with a broken leg. I spoke to him myself at the hospital.'

A few minutes later, unable to avoid overhearing the vicar's conversation with Imogen, it had become obvious that the two were engaged to be married.

'I'm so thrilled for you, honey,' she'd whispered in Imogen's ear as they hugged, and then turned to shake the vicar's hand. 'Congratulations!'

Pearl was deliriously happy, knowing that her friend Imogen, who'd been such a help when she'd first found herself alone in Bude, had found a soulmate at last. Imogen was a lively girl, but didn't seem to make friends easily. Which made it more surprising that she'd hooked herself a vicar, of all people.

'I think she had a crush on his twin brother, back when they were kids,' she whispered to Freddy, 'only the young man was killed in France last year. Not that they were ever more than *friends*. But it shook poor Imogen up dreadfully when he died.' She finished her glass of fizzy wine and watched as he refilled it. 'I'm so thankful she's finally found someone. She's a great gal and a tremendous help to her sister, but she's always struck me as being a loner.'

'I know what you mean.' Freddy touched her hand. 'You and Imogen have something in common there.'

'You think I'm a loner?' She was taken aback.

'Quite the opposite. You're the life and soul of the party, Miss Pearl Diamond. But there's a part of you that's untouched by all that. Whenever I look at you, I think of that fairy story . . . Sleeping Beauty, trapped in a castle surrounded by thorns.' His mouth worked in a crooked smile. 'I'm not saying I'm a prince come to kiss you awake, or any old guff like that. But I would like to be a part of your life, Pearl.' He had lowered his voice, both of them aware of his children within earshot. 'Now the war's over, surely we don't need to wait anymore?'

'I guess not,' Pearl said quietly, sipping at her glass of fizzy wine. Perhaps the bubbles had gone to her head. For she felt quite dizzy, struggling to meet his gaze. 'Though it's odd . . . Getting hitched seemed like a far-off dream while we were still at war with Germany. I can't help wondering if you still feel the same.'

Freddy, one eye on his daughter, who had stopped playing games with her brother and appeared to be listening to them, whispered back, 'Of course I still feel the same. Why on earth would I change my mind just because we've won the war? Is this because we haven't said anything to anyone?'

'I don't want you to feel trapped, that's all,' she began to say, and saw his brows snap together.

'*Trapped*? Pearl, you are the light of my life,' he said intensely. 'After my wife died, I never thought I could love another woman again. But I was wrong. Because I love you and I want us to be together, even if there may be a few difficulties ahead.' He meant explaining to his children and perhaps also having to tell her folks, she guessed. Freddy stood, holding out his hand to her. 'Would you care to dance, Miss Diamond?'

Glenn Miller was on the gramophone, the snappy music making everyone tap their feet and nod their heads. Pearl loved this tune too. But she blushed. 'In front of all these people?'

'As soon as we start dancing, others will join in. Trust me, I'm a doctor.'

'But your foot . . .'

'I'll manage,' he insisted, a glint in his eye.

Unsteadily, she took his hand and was whirled into his arms. They danced together in the middle of the street, just beyond the tables, with everybody watching. It was like a fairy story, after all, she thought happily. Her head was spinning and she was laughing, and she had eyes for nobody but Freddy Tyson, the doctor who had captured her heart.

Sure enough, seeing them dancing in the street, other couples soon joined them. People began clapping along to the music. Even when the music changed to a slower tune, they carried on dancing, with his arm about her waist, until she felt quite light-headed . . .

'I should sit down,' she gasped, clinging to him.

'Your wish is my command.' Heading back to the table, Freddy stopped, his face concerned. 'Toby, where's your sister gone?' he asked his son.

Toby looked at the empty seat beside him and shrugged. 'Sorry, Dad, I was playing I-Spy with Roger,' he said, nodding to the boy sitting next to him. 'I didn't see her go.'

'She must have gone back into the house for something,' Pearl said, but she was worried too. Suddenly, she felt uneasy at having agreed to dance with Freddy before having told his children they planned to get married.

'I'm going to find her,' Freddy said.

'I'll come with you, if I may.' Pearl followed him back to the boarding house.

'You think I'm being overprotective?'

'Not at all,' she assured him. 'Clara's a sensitive young lady and you're right to keep a close eye on her. But this might be a good time for us to have a chat with her about you and me. She's not been happy lately, has she? And I guess that's partly because of us.'

Freddy turned to her, looking perplexed. 'Unhappy because of us? I don't understand.'

'Oh, honey, haven't you noticed? Clara doesn't like it. You and me getting close, I mean.'

He looked thunderstruck. 'Why should she get upset about that? She likes you – I'm sure of it. The two of you have always got along famously.'

'Clara liked me at first, yes,' she agreed gently, and put a hand on his arm, trying to make him understand. 'Try to look at it from her point of view, Freddy. She lost her mother in the Blitz. Now she must be worried sick that she'll be expected to forget her if you and I get married.'

'Good grief, I never realised. But you're right, of course.' Freddy rubbed a hand across his forehead. 'In that case, we do need to talk to her, try to explain. Perhaps she's gone to her room.' Upstairs, they found Clara in her bedroom, sobbing her heart out, face down on the bed. Freddy took one look and gathered his daughter in his arms, rocking her back and forth. 'There, there, my darling. What on earth's the matter? The war's over, life can finally get back to normal. Why are you crying?'

With red-rimmed eyes, Clara stared bitterly past him at Pearl. 'Because of her,' she said thickly, pointing an accusing finger in Pearl's direction. 'I've seen you two together. Not just dancing, but kissing.' Her voice dropped to a hiss. 'I know what's going on. You're going to *marry* her.'

Mortified but not surprised, Pearl thought it better not to comment.

Freddy released her, grimacing as he said awkwardly, 'You're right, sweetheart, we are getting married. But I don't understand. I thought you liked Pearl. What's made you change your mind?'

'I liked Pearl when she was just your friend. But now . . .' His daughter glared up at him. 'Have you forgotten Mum so soon?' When he protested, she went on, 'I don't want a new mother. We were happy together, you and me and Toby. We don't want her around!' And she burst into noisy sobs again.

Freddy looked helplessly at Pearl.

'Could I have a moment alone with Clara?' she asked quietly. 'You don't need to go far. Just give us some privacy. There's something I need to ask her.'

Freddy hesitated and then left the room, telling his daughter, 'I'll be right outside if you need me.'

Perched on the edge of the bed, Pearl began, 'Honey, please believe me, I don't want to take the place of your mother. Nobody could ever do that. But your dad and I are in love. When two people are in love, they naturally want to be together. I'm never going to replace your mom though – that would be impossible.' Gingerly, she drew a hanky from her sleeve and offered it to the weeping girl. 'But I'd like us to be friends instead.'

'Oh, get . . . get knotted!'

Pearl suppressed a smile at this. She studied Clara closely, noting her pallor and frenzied expression. 'Honey, be honest with me. Are you in pain?'

'*What*?' Clara's eyes flew wide open. Now she looked horrified. 'No.'

But Pearl knew the signs. 'Is it your monthlies?'

Now the girl was blushing fierily. 'Shut up,' she insisted, but her voice lacked conviction.

'I started quite young too. I didn't know who to tell when it first happened. I was so shocked to see blood . . . My mom helped me the second time, after I plucked up the courage to tell her.' Pearl had dropped her voice to a whisper. This was something she didn't want Freddy to overhear. 'I know your dad's a doctor. But it's not the same, is it? When it's something private like this, you need a woman to talk to.' She touched Clara's hand and, to her relief, the girl didn't shake her off. 'I can help you, if you'd like that?'

Shyly, Clara nodded.

'I know this won't fix things between us, honey,' Pearl added with a smile, getting up off the bed. 'We still need to talk about me marrying your dad and how that makes you feel. And we will, I promise. But I'd be thrilled if you could think of me as a friend, not an enemy, and to feel you can come to me with problems like this.' She paused. 'Truce?'

Clara raised her tear-stained face. 'Truce,' she whispered.

'Was this why you were so mad when Toby sneaked a look in your journal?' Pearl asked astutely, and saw the girl blush.

'I didn't want him to know.'

'Of course not. Though next time, you tell us when Toby's acting out of line; don't just scream at him. Because he's still young and doesn't understand. Okay?'

After a loving hug and a few more womanly words of advice about coping with her monthlies, Pearl left Clara to dry her eyes and tidy herself up before rejoining the street party.

She found Freddy outside the room, restlessly pacing the landing.

'I think it's going to be okay,' she told him, smiling. Briefly, she explained the situation, and saw Freddy's face clear.

'How stupid of me not to realise,' he said though, slapping his forehead in exasperation. 'Given her age, I should have guessed what was up.'

'I've promised her we'll all sit down together soon and have a proper chat about us getting married. So Clara can let us know how she feels and get it all off her chest. She may still never accept me as part of the family but it's worth a try.'

'Agreed.'

'I'll never take the place of her mom,' Pearl said firmly, 'but I want to be a friend to her. And to young Toby too.' His son needed a mother figure for sure, she thought, though he was less open about his feelings. But she would take things cautiously there. It would take a while for both children to warm to the idea of their father remarrying.

'Besides, if this *is* a fairy story,' she added, smiling as he took her in his arms, 'I don't want to end up cast as the evil stepmother.'

'If anyone can pull this off,' Freddy said softly, 'it's you, love. I'm constantly in awe of who you are, Pearl. Not just as a talented performer, though you're a marvel at that, but as a woman and a friend, someone who truly *cares* about other folk. And I don't just mean your work at the hospital, though it takes my breath away to see you chattin' with the wounded, cheering 'em up with your smile.' He gazed down at her fondly. 'I mean the woman who cares for my son and daughter like they were her own. I hope I don't need to tell you how much that means to me, Miss Pearl Diamond. Because you *are* a diamond to me.'

She blushed at the look in his eyes, pulling away. 'Oh my, that awful stage name! Will I never live it down?'

He laughed. 'No, but you can change it,' he pointed out. 'To Mrs Tyson.'

'Pearl Tyson . . .' she tried aloud, wonderingly, and let him draw her close again for a kiss. 'Yes, why not?'

When Clara came out of her room, they rejoined the street party, where someone had put on a swing tune. Everybody was either dancing the 'Jitterbug' or banging their spoons to the fast music, while Miles and Florence were energetically gyrating and swinging about, showing the younger ones how it was done.

'Where on earth have you three been?' Imogen demanded, flushed and with tears of laughter in her eyes. 'You missed me dancing with Richard in his bath chair!'

'Well, I can't be outdone by a reverend, gammy foot or not.' With a grin, Freddy took Pearl's hand. 'Time you taught me how to do the Lindy Hop,' he told her, and she did.

EPILOGUE

Porthcurno, South Cornwall, September 1945

Alice stood waiting outside the farmhouse above Porthcurno, blinking up at a too-bright Cornish sky. Too bright because it was September 1945, and autumn ought to be on the way, instead of what felt like endless summer down here on the sandy coast of south Cornwall. And too bright because her eyes stung just being open. She'd sat up half the night with her family, sharing anecdotes over bottles of home brew or cups of tea, none of them wanting to be the first to go to bed. Sometimes they'd laughed, and sometimes tears had come, so blinding she hadn't been able to speak for weeping. And her mouth ached from the false smile she'd been wearing for days, as they all sought to keep Gran's spirits up and the household from crumbling under its weight of grief.

Demelza and Robert emerged behind her, talking quietly. They were living with Demelza's dad on the farm in Penzance – apparently Farmer Minear was no longer such a bully since his children had all grown up and left home, almost a changed man, Robert had told her – and were hoping that Lily and Tristan might move there too in time, so they could make a go of the farm together. But they had made the trip back here to be with the family today.

Lily came out in their wake, pushing young Morris in his pram, followed by Joe and Tristan, and finally Aunty Violet, who stooped lovingly to place baby Sally alongside him. 'There, my darlings, you and Mo can get some lovely shut-eye while we walk to the church,' she cooed, straightening abruptly as she registered what Joe was wearing. 'Where's your black tie?'

Joe shuffled awkwardly. 'Couldn't find it, love. This one will do.'

'No, it won't. It's *brown*.' Scandalised, Violet bustled him back inside, adding, 'Hurry up and take it off. I know where your black tie is.'

The Land Girls had started down the hill ahead of them, respectfully dressed in muted colours and dark hats. Foolishly, Selina had expected to be sent home once the Japanese had finally surrendered and the war was over for good. But as Caroline had pointed out, in her usual practical way, 'They won't be sending most soldiers home for yonks, Selly. And those crops won't pick themselves.' Selina had cried a little, hugging her cache of letters from her fiancé, Johnny, whom she'd been hoping to marry when he came home from the front. But he'd written to say he was unlikely to be back for at least six months, maybe longer, and it had taken all their cajoling to get her smiling again. Meanwhile, Joan, who never said much anyway, had grown even quieter and spent more time these days painting watercolours of the Cornish landscape, which was her hobby.

Lily, wheeling the pram up and down to help settle the babies, glanced at her. 'Well, at least we don't have the boys and Janice to worry about.'

The evacuee kids had finally been driven to Penzance station back in July and put on a train for London. Gran had wept, as had Aunty Violet, though both of them had seemed strangely cheerful on the way home afterwards. Alice had waved her hanky until the train was out of sight, enveloped in clouds of steam, and had even felt a little tearful herself, which was odd, given how much of a bloomin' nuisance those two boys had been.

Janice had pressed her address into Alice's hand as they hugged on the platform, making her promise to write soon. 'I want to know everything that happens,' she'd insisted. Alice had started a letter to her two days ago but hadn't been able to finish it yet, bursting into tears every time she put pen to paper.

Tristan said nothing, looking glum. 'I can see the hearse,' he said.

Alice stiffened, turning to view the large black vehicle

creeping slowly up the farm track. She reached for her hanky, tears pricking at her eyes again.

It was almost time to go.

At last, Violet and Joe re-emerged, and this time they were followed by Gran, leaning heavily on Ernest's arm as though she couldn't walk without his support. She was wearing a black pill-box hat with a thick veil drawn down, for her face was ravaged by tears – as Alice knew – and a long, old-fashioned black dress she'd first worn to her father's funeral, Alice's great-grandfather.

The hearse arrived outside the farmhouse, the pallbearers walking behind in sombre black. After a moment's discussion, they went into the house with some of the men, and came out soon afterwards, the coffin borne on their shoulders, which they slid into the back of the waiting vehicle. Alice and Aunty Violet stood on either side of Gran, supporting her as she wept bitterly, and then they all followed behind the hearse in slow, silent procession as it set off down into the village.

As they passed through the village, people came out of their houses, removing caps and bowing their heads in respect for one of their own, and then most fell in behind them, accompanying the hearse to the church. The village shop was closed, with a wreath and black crepe on the door. Gran let out a piteous cry as they passed it and buried her face in her handkerchief. 'Arnie,' she kept whispering, 'oh, my dear ol' Arnie . . .'

Porthcurno shone like a jewel, bathed in warm

sunshine. Alice saw the glint of the sea through a gap in the rocks and thought longingly of the beach there, for the mines and most of the anti-tank and landing-craft defences had been removed, leaving soft gold-white sands that she had crossed barefoot in wonder only a few weeks back, hand in hand with Patrick. Now that the soldiers' encampment had gone, based there to protect the secret tunnels behind Eastern House that were helping the Allies win the war, the valley itself was gradually returning to a tangled green expanse leading out onto dunes.

Patrick met her at the church door, having stayed on specially for the funeral, even though Eastern House had let most of the cypher staff go. 'How are you?' he asked quietly as she watched her father, Tristan, Robert and the other pallbearers carry the coffin into the church. Joe had wanted to share the weight with them, but his false leg had made that impractical, so he stood with Gran and Aunty Violet instead, head bowed. 'You bearing up all right, Alice?'

'More or less,' Alice said, dabbing at her eyes.

George Cotterill was there too, holding their little girl by the hand, with his wife Hazel and her grown-up son. Charlie was looking almost smart these days, having got himself through basic training and earned a scholarship for university. Alice still remembered him as a tearaway youth who'd shared his mum's home with them after they were left homeless. His dad had been killed in active service, leaving young Charlie devastated, and for a while he'd gone off the rails, even trying to falsify his age so he could enlist. But when George and Hazel had finally married, that seemed to settle him down.

They all shook hands, and everyone murmured their apologies and commiserations to Gran, who gave a husky 'Thank you' to each one, her voice choked with tears.

The villagers and others who had come for the funeral shuffled inside to find seats, while the close family waited outside in the breezy sunshine. Alice's black dress flapped in the wind, but her hat was pinned on so tight, it wasn't going anywhere. 'I'll see you inside,' Patrick murmured, but she gripped his hand, shaking her head wordlessly. She needed him with her today.

The Reverend Clewson had come out, talking lengthily to Gran and Dad. Then he signalled for the coffin to be carried into the church, the family following slowly down the aisle, though Lily parked the pram at the back before slipping into an end pew so she could keep an eye on the little ones. Demelza, always a kind-hearted girl, sat with her for company.

Inside, the church was bright with pools of sunlight filtered through stained-glass windows. Someone had brought in sprays of white flowers and decorated the ends of pews and the altar with them, the whole place awash with their sweet, heady fragrance. Every pew was packed, the place hushed, everyone on their feet, watching respectfully as the coffin passed.

Reverend Clewson asked them to join him in a moment of silent prayer before beginning his funeral address with: 'Today, we say goodbye to Arnold Newton, not only a wonderful shopkeeper who we all knew and loved here in Porthcurno, but also a kind and loving husband to Sheila. He was also stepfather to Violet, a proud step-grandfather to Lily and Alice, and a step-great-grandfather too!' He turned a sympathetic smile on Gran, who had dissolved into tears again, Alice's dad putting a supportive arm about her as she wept. 'You and Arnold were married here in this very church, Sheila, not so long ago. I know you were not together for as long as you had both hoped. But from what you and your family have told me, the brief time you had together was blessed with happiness and joy, and so we give thanks for that, and for Arnold's long and productive life.'

As the vicar went on, Alice stared at the stone floor, squeezed Patrick's hand tightly, and tried to control her sobbing. Though she realised, taken aback by the force of her sorrow, that she wasn't only crying for Arnie, or even for her gran, widowed for the second time. She was crying for her dead mother, and for Jim, and for all those lost in the war, and for the dark days they'd suffered, and the hard times, and the innocence they would never get back . . .

It was early October, and Alice was sitting with Patrick on the bench beside the kitchen door, enjoying the soft autumn sunshine, when a familiar car came chugging up the farm track.

'It's George,' Alice said in surprise, getting to her feet.

'Mr Cotterill? What's he doing up here?' Patrick

came to stand beside her as the car pulled into the farmyard.

'Probably bringing his wife Hazel to see Aunty Violet. They've been good friends for years, you know. Ever since we came to Cornwall, in fact.'

But George was alone in the car. He got out and came loping towards them with his easy stride. 'Hullo,' he said, shaking both their hands. 'I hoped I'd catch you both together. Two birds with one stone, as it were.'

Alice sucked in a breath. Down at Eastern House, they had both put in requests for a transfer to the Communications Headquarters in London. The war might be over, but they still needed skilled operatives on the communications network, and both she and Patrick had decided to apply for positions at the same time. Their dream was for both of them to find work in London, since getting married would be a bit of a flop otherwise. Alice didn't want to end up a housewife, bored out of her skull at home. Besides, they would need two incomes to be able to afford somewhere half-decent to live in London, with so many homes destroyed in the Blitz.

Her heart was thumping. 'It's about London, ain't it?' she asked their boss.

George nodded, smiling. He held out envelopes to both of them. 'You've both been accepted. So congratulations. You'll be starting work next month. The details are all in there.' He looked keenly at Alice. 'Have you told your aunt yet?'

'Not likely,' Alice said, feeling guilty. She dreaded her

aunt's reaction once she discovered that Alice was planning to move back to London. As for the marriage part of their plan . . .

'Thanks ever so much for your reference, Mr Cotterill,' Patrick said feelingly, having torn open his envelope and devoured the contents in one quick glance. 'I'm sure it's all down to you that I got offered the job.'

'Yes, thank you,' Alice agreed.

George laughed. 'Not at all – your own skills got you these jobs. I hope you'll both be very happy in London. I believe they're starting to rebuild everywhere. Though the Germans haven't left much unbombed, so it'll take quite a few years to get the capital back to its former glory.'

'All the same, thank you, George.' Alice hugged him, which felt like an odd thing to do. Though she was getting far more used to hugging these days. But she saw the surprise on his face as she drew back, and hurriedly added, 'Sorry.'

He laughed again, shaking his head. 'Well, I'd better get home to Hazel. I'm on baby duty tonight while she goes out to her knitting circle. I'll never hear the end of it if I'm late back. Again, congratulations. Don't forget about us here in Cornwall, will you?'

'No fear,' Alice assured him, grinning.

When he'd gone, she looked at Patrick and smiled. 'Phase one of our grand plan is complete. Now what?'

'We tell your family.' Patrick grimaced. 'First, I have to speak to your father alone.'

Alice blinked, unsure what he meant. 'Speak to him about what?'

'What do you think? I need to ask his permission to marry you.'

She stared. 'Blimey!'

'Well, you didn't think we were simply going to run away together, did you? Where will he be, do you think?'

'This time of day? In the snug, reading.'

'Right.' He smoothed down his hair, and then put on his cap. She thought he had never looked more handsome than in that moment, about to go and brave her dad in his den. Not a trace left of that pimply youth she'd mocked so often in their Bude days. 'Maybe it's a bit old-fashioned to ask *permission*. And it would be dashed awkward if he refused. But I'll ask for his blessing, at least.'

With a smile, Alice let him go. She was sure her dad wouldn't refuse permission, though he might raise his eyebrows at the idea of his daughter marrying so young. She was not quite twenty-one, after all. Dad was still working part-time at Eastern House, dealing with the mass of communications that still came through the underwater cables every day from all over the world. Somebody had to sort those messages out and deal with them.

But although George had offered to find permanent work for her too at Eastern House, and perhaps even Patrick, she couldn't imagine herself settling down to spend the rest of her life in this quiet Cornish village. Yes, it was breathtakingly beautiful here. But there was a big world out there and she wanted to explore it before getting too comfortable.

With a last appreciative glance over her shoulder at the sun lighting up lush green fields, the glint of sea in the distance, she went inside just in time to see Patrick and her father coming out of the snug together. To her relief, her father was smiling and had an arm about Patrick's shoulder.

Gran was kneading dough at the table, keeping herself busy so she wouldn't fall into grieving for Arnie, and Aunty Violet was chopping carrots, while Lily chatted about a cardigan pattern she'd seen in a crochet magazine that would be perfect for little Morris, who was asleep on her lap. Joe and Tristan were still out somewhere on the farm with the tractor and the Land Girls. It was just family here, and somehow that felt perfect.

'All right, you two boys, what's going on?' Gran asked in her rasping voice. Her keen ears had overheard Ernest and Patrick discussing the availability of housing in London. 'Are you planning on moving on, young man? I thought you and our Alice were an item.' Her eyes narrowed suspiciously. 'Don't tell me you're leaving 'er in the lurch?'

'No, Mrs Newton,' Patrick stammered, and looked to Alice for help.

'We're getting hitched, Gran,' Alice said bluntly, 'and moving to London. Patrick's just been asking Dad's permission, and I'm guessing he said yes.'

'You *what*? You're getting married?' Gran looked astounded.

'Blessing,' Patrick muttered. 'Not permission.'

'London?' Aunty Vi echoed faintly.

'I did indeed say yes,' her dad said calmly, and came to kiss Alice on the forehead. 'But say the word, and I'll kick him back down the hill to Porthcurno.'

'Dad!' Lily squealed.

But Alice knew he was only joking. Or she hoped so, at least. 'We've been planning it for ages,' she admitted sheepishly, seeing her aunt's mouth agape. 'I'm sorry we kept schtum about it. But we were waiting to hear if we had jobs to go to in London. And we do. Communications work. George Cotterill just brought us the news.'

'I told them I heard a car,' Lily complained.

'Well, I never.' Gran wiped floury hands on her apron, her eyes suddenly swimming with tears. 'Oh, Vi . . . Our little Alice is getting married. I can't believe it. I still remember when she was just a wee nipper. Always swiping the last sarnie and blaming it on her sister.'

'Gran, please . . .' Alice rolled her eyes, blushing.

Her aunt and grandmother both descended on her at the same time, and she found herself enveloped in two warm, floury hugs at once. Then Lily handed Morris to Patrick, who stood stiff and aghast peering down at the sleeping child, and came to kiss Alice, her eyes twinkling.

'I hope you've got me lined up as matron of honour,'

413

Lily said with a grin, 'or I'll help you with the wedding dress and deliberately make it two sizes too small.'

'Duly noted,' Alice said.

She felt a moment of indecision, looking around at her loving family, their faces wreathed in smiles, and wondered if it might not be easier to stay put, get married in Porthcurno, and simply try to be happy with a child and a house to run. But she wasn't ready for that life yet. First, there were exciting new adventures and opportunities waiting for her in London. And this time, she would have Patrick to share them with.

ACKNOWLEDGEMENTS:

My grateful thanks as ever to my wonderful agent Alison Bonomi for her continuing support and advice, and to everyone at LBA for their hard work on my behalf.

Heartfelt thanks also to my fab editors Rachel Hart and Amy Baxter, and indeed to the whole team at Avon Books over the past four years since *Wartime With the Cornish Girls* was first acquired. It's been fantastic working with you all on these six lively adventures of the Cornish Girls, the dedicated crew at Avon always so attentive, hard-working and professional, despite there having been a global pandemic in there somewhere!

Also, a shout-out to my ever-patient husband Steve, and to my youngest three kids, Dylan, Morris and Indigo, who keep coming home from university to find me working on a novel or three and don't seem to mind having to do their own washing these days . . .

A special thank you to Clair Roberts from The Kitchen

Front in Bude, my lovely hometown, for her fascinating anecdotes about American Rangers stationed here during World War Two. A big thank you and well-done also to everyone else involved in organising the annual 'Bude At War' re-enactment weekend, a major event which draws visitors from all over the world. Your amazing true-life stories and exhibitions have been an inspiration!

Lastly, a huge THANK YOU once more to all my readers, both old and new. A book is nothing without a reader, so I've dedicated this sixth book in the series to you, my friends. I hope you enjoy reading my Cornish Girls stories as much as I enjoy writing them. Thank you, thank you, thank you!

Betty x

Go back to where it all began – don't miss the first book in the glorious Cornish Girls series…

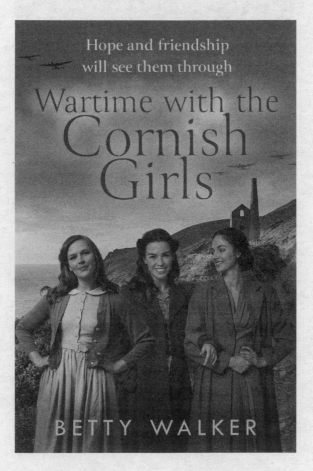

Hope and friendship will see them through

Wartime with the Cornish Girls

BETTY WALKER

Available now in paperback, eBook and audiobook.

Follow up with some festive fun for
the Cornish Girls…

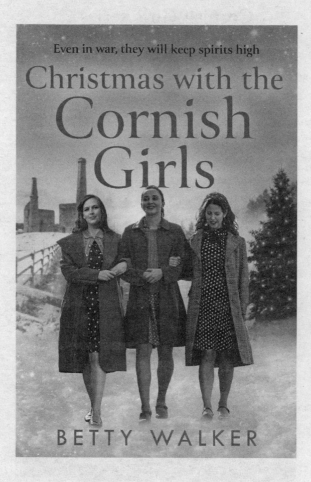

Available now in paperback,
eBook and audiobook.

Enemy gunfire on Penzance
beach brings the Cornish Girls
rushing to the rescue...

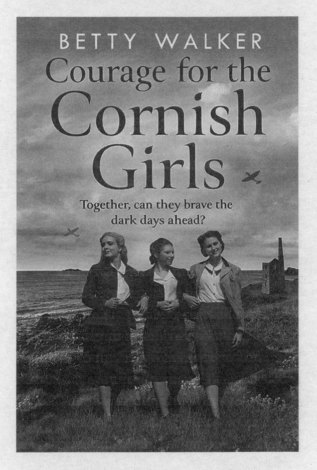

Can the bonds of motherhood
give them the strength they'll need
to get through the war?…

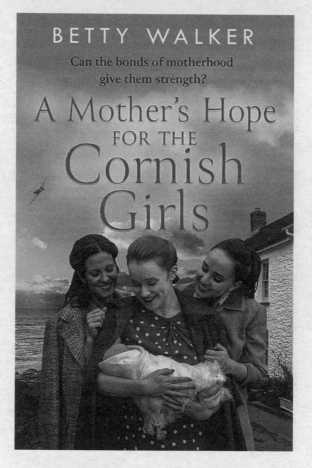

Available now in paperback,
eBook and audiobook.

Can love still thrive in the
uncertainty of war?

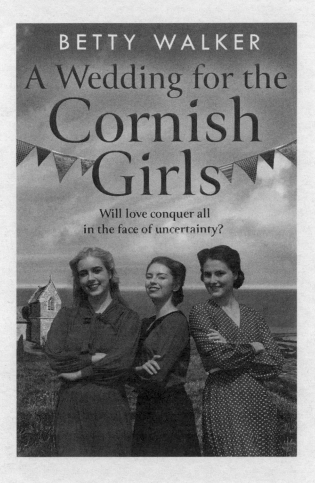

Available now in paperback,
eBook and audiobook.